Praise for Step

'Possessing a more complex and nuanced worldview than its predecessor, *Our Child of Two Worlds* is modern, emotionally sophisticated science fiction. Stephen Cox's tale of the charming but lost alien child Cory shows us that humanity, for all its flaws, is worth saving, and that the power of the human heart stretches from this world to the next'
Dan Jones, author of *Man O'War* and host of *Chronscast*
on *Our Child of Two Worlds*

'*Our Child of Two Worlds* is a stirring novel about family and home. Rich with humanity, it explores our species' tendency to damage ourselves, our relationships and Planet Earth. A powerful, sad but satisfying sequel'
Sue Hampton, climate and peace activist and author of *Intact* and *The Waterhouse Girl* on *Our Child of Two Worlds*

'Another beautiful book that is so much more than a defining genre'
Kathryn Dawson, *Tea Leaves & Reads* on *Our Child of Two Worlds*

'Part *ET*, part *Wonder*, part *Snow Child*, *Our Child of the Stars* has the same combination of science fiction and heart-tugging tenderness that Stephen King does so well'
Grazia* on *Our Child of the Stars

'This strong and generous first novel wears its heart on its sleeve and embeds all the thrills and chills in credible human, and non-human, emotions'
Daily Mail* on *Our Child of the Stars

'An out-of-this-world winner'
Weekend Sport* on *Our Child of the Stars

'A pleasing, big-hearted read, its late-1960s setting well evoked'
Financial Times* on *Our Child of the Stars

'Sympathetic characterisation and fine storytelling . . . This is an optimistic take on the *ET* theme, done without the schmaltz of the film'
The Guardian* on *Our Child of the Stars

To Sarah, of course

CHAPTER I

Amber County,
the first week of November 1971

Cory ran through the woods, kicking dry leaves, wanting everything. He wanted so-much to laugh with the joy of it, but he needed all his breath to run. At his heels bounded Meteor, grey shaggy curls and cheerful barks, in case any living thing could not guess they were coming. Dogs were such good friends. Close behind, Chuck and Bonnie ran too, his truest human friends, and behind them, the whoops and calls and crashing noises of the rest of the gang. Counting to two hundred might not have been enough . . . The teenagers had longer legs, and this race would not last much longer.

Run Cory run. His tentacles tasted the air, to enjoy the damp kicked up under the leaves, the faint trace of a male fox, the dog scent that was not Meteor. Among friends he ran tail out, signalling enthusiasm. Cory felt the touch of cold in the air and enjoyed how November light was lower; he saw the trees that day by day were shedding their leaves, their glory of

1

gold and flame. Cory felt the solemn presence of each tree, he felt as well as heard the startled birds rising and the little lives scuttering to hide.

Cory-wants-it-all-all-all. How good to have older children to play with, and a dry day of running and talking and kind games. Soon Thanksgiving and rain and snow and dark, Dad's birthday and Christmas . . . Cory loved First Harbour, his home-world of eternal gentle summer, but Earth seasons were glorious.

The narrow way twisted and turned through oak, maple, and ash. Cory knew it well now, but still felt ahead with his mind. A big shame that the woods behind his house, the woods beyond the Fence, had been spoiled. There were too often people watching for him – people who called for him, or chanted strange songs, or lit fires where they shouldn't. All the fuss scared away the animals.

In those woods, people left tripwires to set off cameras, thinking Cory was silly enough not to feel the tripwire – or pools of stuff so he would leave footprints. People pinned envelopes in clear plastic bags to trees; the letters begged, and threatened, and asked, and sometimes had money. Cory never opened them; the grown-ups took them and dealt with them. People knowing about Cory spoiled having fun. The rough scrubland below was spoiled too, with its tents and trailers and wandering snoopers, the smell of latrines and coarse smoke. If he was spotted, people would come running. Crowds would soon gather, even if he hid straight away. Groups of humans could seem friendly but be wild in their enthusiasm, unpredictable, dangerous . . .

Better the grown-ups drive him here, a short way northwest, to be free in the woods where he was not known to go.

Chuck's hand on Cory's shoulder, a sign to stop. Cory and Chuck and Bonnie panted, just a little, and heard the racket move closer. Meteor barked three times from the sheer joy of the splendid game, telling everyone where they were. No more kicking up a trail. It was time to make the teenagers work for their victory.

Cory ruffled Meteor's head with a four-fingered hand. 'Quiet.' His splendid striped ears sought to find the exact approach of the chasers. Cory's friends knew to grab him, and Cory hid all four of them. No living thing would notice them. Step by careful step, Cory led them off the trail, weaving through bushes and trunks. The teenage friends would overshoot. But they were smart – Zach and Simon would be grown-ups soon – and they had played this game before.

Hiding was almost cheating, but a minute or two did not count. The plan was to find an unmarked way down to Butler's Folly, the long-closed mill that was now a riot of creepers through empty windows. Emblazoned with old signs and new that warned children not to enter and not to play, it was a castle of secrets by an overgrown creek. They had watched lizards warm themselves on summer days and fireflies dance brilliant green messages on summer nights. Dancing all-together to the radio, teenagers and kids as friends. Zach had fallen off the wall and gained a most exciting scar.

The wind changed and Cory smelled smoke, heard the whining roar of some machine, a double note. Something about that noise tugged at his stomach, brought a touch of fear. But up above were the Ship's machines, its flying hands and eyes; somewhere nearby would be the Ship itself, resolute to protect him.

As they walked, he felt his friends grow solemn. The noise grew, and the smell. Animals hid in fear, birds flew . . .

'A dozen or more humans ahead, Little Frog,' said the Ship, through the silver communicator on Cory's wrist. 'Gene and Molly have not arrived yet. Be careful.'

Earth was a planet of many dangers. Cory was always careful. A little further and they would see . . .

Cory stopped, his friends too, and stared. Their castle of brick and stone was changed, there was a fence, and a giant pile of long drainpipe. Great stupid machines were grubbing up the bushes, destroying the picnic places hidden from the road. Places where Cory had watched frogs spawning and wild bees bumble in the flowers. Where they had harvested berries and wormy apples from abandoned trees, where they had photographed the eerie beauty of fungi. A tree crashed somewhere near. And there were fires, men were feeding them with damp branches, throwing up smoke.

There stood Zach and Simon Robertson, and VJ, Bonnie's cousin, watching. Distracted, Cory realised the teenagers had cheated – divided their number and sent one party by the other, shorter track. Admiration for their boldness outstripped his outrage, but the whine of chainsaws, the rumble of a truck, filled his head.

Humans found it hard to talk hidden. Cory pulled his friends down and unhid them.

'What are they doing?' Cory said.

'Dad said the Mill was sold again,' Chuck said, his face still summer brown with freckles.

Bonnie had that frown, that chewed lip, that meant someone

4

was going to get told off. 'We should go and find out.' Even in dungarees to run in the woods, she tied a bright red cloth in her hair. 'They're going to reopen the State Park. Where the Meteor fell. I bet it's something to do with that.'

'We're not supposed to play here anyway,' said Chuck.

Bonnie clicked her tongue. 'You're *scared*, Charles Henderson.'

And so Chuck and Bonnie walked towards the nearest men, waving the teens to come too. Cory and Meteor would go crouching, hidden, to listen. Cory must be careful. Already too many people knew about his clever hiding with his mind; it had been an accident that the Robertsons had found out, and that day of emergencies when VJ had. But everything Cory did or could do was news. It brought reporters and Trouble, and Mom said things were best with a Quiet Life.

The man in charge wore a hard hat, in case a tree fell on him. He was not the kind of bossy human that made him angry at kids.

'You kids need to stay away.' He gestured at the teenagers, now ambling towards them too. 'Tell your friends.'

'What's happening, sir?' asked Chuck.

'Twenty-four vacation apartments, four houses and a fancy restaurant – so all this has to be cleared.' He waved, to left, to right, as if he could wave away the old mill, old trees, the foxes and raccoons, the birds. Wave away the crisp leaves and the smell of fall. 'Our boss's after the rest of the land too.'

'What about the trees?' Bonnie asked.

The man looked puzzled, then laughed. 'Plenty of trees left. Even if he logs right up to the ridge. We have to move real quick, the weather won't hold off long.'

The smoke stung Cory's eyes, bringing tears. Bringing memories too, of those first days on Earth. Amber Grove had burned, and Molly, his Earth-mother, had shed tears from emotion; one of a hundred strange things. He remembered the humans' dreams of that time, of fire and smoke and destruction.

'Now, you need to stay away. We're going to be spraying, to make it easier to clear.'

'What kind of spray?' Bonnie asked.

The man shrugged. 'Army stuff, does all the work for us. Kills every plant it touches, works like a charm. As good as burning it off and works in the damp. We're putting in drains too.'

That was the ponds with their frogs and dragonflies gone too.

Bonnie steamed, getting herself boiling hot, ready to argue. Chuck grabbed Bonnie's arm, and the whole gang walked two hundred yards to the edge of the woods. Cory was trying to see in his mind, the trees gone, the land poisoned. It brought up other images, bad ones. Memories of lessons on his homeworld.

'I guess if he owns the land, we can't stop him.' *How can you own land? It's like owning sunlight.*

The humans argued. 'There's plenty of other places. Millions of trees.'

'We should start a protest.' That was Bonnie.

'Who'd care? If it was nearer town maybe . . .'

'Everyone's always protesting. My dad says we need more jobs in the town. New buildings are good.'

Cory was silent. Birds nested in the cracks in the walls. Cory remembered the drum of woodpeckers, the curious work of the ants. There would be living things ready for the sleep of winter, who would have to find new places. The squirrels' caches of food would be lost.

Cory gave the *tock-tock-tock* of frustration. 'Humans must do something. Yes-they-must.' They all fell silent.

'Burning trees and seabirds all covered in oil.' He had seen it on TV, thick tarry oil choking the birds and killing the fish. 'Rivers so poisoned even water burns. What Army spray do to the animals? To people?'

Talk properly, Cory. The teens teased him if he did not, like they made jokes about his birth name meaning Little Glowing Blue Frog. He was angry enough not to care.

'It's kind of sad,' Chuck agreed.

Humans were so stupid. Soon, Zach and Simon could be ordered to be soldiers, sent to kill or be killed in a land far away, a vast murdering that had been happening since they were babies. They each promised Cory they would not go to the stupid war; they would hide or go to Canada.

The humans, the rest of Cory's gang, were silent. They must feel his alarm, his fear, his anger pouring out of him. They were his friends, good people.

'Your folks are here,' Simon said. And yes, up the road came the baby-blue camper van. Dad and Mom and Baby Fleur, his sweet human sister.

'We could go further down, by the creek,' Zach suggested. Zach and VJ liked each other but there was some big horrible human thing. VJ was dark like Bonnie and Zach was paler like Chuck. Because of that and only that, some people didn't like them hanging out. Cory felt cross enough to pull his ears off sometimes, humans were so weird.

'If you don't protest, I will,' Bonnie said, and everyone knew she meant it.

Supper was tuna with macaroni and cheese. Mom put a little hot spice in, which Cory liked. The radio played 'Have You Ever Seen the Rain?'

Mom and Dad were not agreeing with him, and he suddenly had no appetite. Meteor gnawed at her rubber bone.

Mom held Fleur sleeping and ate one handed with a fork. Under her eyes was dark; Fleur woke often in the night. 'Cory, if you write to the paper, it will create a massive row. You know we've got to keep a low profile.'

Cory had written one letter, to the *Hermes*, about the poor fish dying in the lakes to the north. The *Hermes* now sold a hundred thousand copies each week round the world, because Cory had made Amber Grove famous. The Great Lakes had been there for millions of years and then humans came and used them to dump poison. Cory's letter about pollution had brought all the TV crews to the bottom of the road where the barrier was. Two trucks of workers had come from the power-plants in the north, and Mom and Dad had four of them to drink coffee while Cory hid on the stairs.

'Do you want the plant closed? How will we feed our families?'

So many people had come to town, to protest or to support him. Senators had come from Washington to ask Cory to endorse their ideas for new laws. Grown-ups said that the tall one, Muskie from Maine, might be the next President.

'One little letter . . .'

'Remember the beef letter?' Dad said.

Those schoolchildren in Houston had asked why Cory didn't eat meat. All he did was just explain. Ranchers came all the way from Texas with a TV crew to offer everyone in Amber Grove free steaks from poor, gentle, murdered cows. Founders Green was a barbecue for two days, stinking of burned flesh. It was called a 'stunt' and it made the town cross for weeks.

'What is the point of being famous?' Cory moaned.

'Maybe it would be better if we weren't,' said Dad, trying not to yawn. 'But you know why it happened, and we can't get the milk back in the bottle. I'm sorry Cory, you know there are people who want us to go. You want to stay near your friends, don't you?'

'Yes of course yes.'

Cory guessed what his Earth-father was about to say.

Grown-ups were so predictable. Dad said, 'Cory, maybe someone else should lead the fight.'

Cory gave a massive fed up noise. Cory kept telling humans his Excellent Plan, but they weren't listening. His people survived the Times of Hunger, had healed the Poisoned Land. His people must come now and get the humans to listen.

'Cory, don't sulk,' said Mom.

'Not sulking.' He ate tuna from duty, his mind elsewhere.

Cory's people must come right now. 927 days since he had landed on Earth. The colony starship *Dancer on the Waves* had been destroyed by the vicious snake machines. Yet it sent messenger ships forward and back, many months to have reached old home, and the colony-world which was to be his home. Many-many months for more starships to be prepared and to come and rescue him.

They had not come. As ever his terrible fear, colder than any ice, that they were not coming. That the messengers had been destroyed, and his people did not know he was here. Or that his whole people had been attacked by the predator snakes, and they were too busy fighting to send a starship for one little boy. This nightmare idea was a big hole that could swallow him up.

Dad put his big human hand on Cory's. They must feel his sadness. He loved his human family and his friends, but he wanted the smell of his own people, the oneness of the lodge, the dreaming-together. He touched his communicator. How he missed his mother who died saving him . . . The device held her dying words left in love. How sweet and painful they were. Everyone on the ship but him had died.

Cory saw his sorrow on Gene and Molly's faces. Dad took Fleur, and Molly held out her arms. His human parents held him in love.

That evening, in Cory's bedroom, Dad yawned and played a new song, a silly one about Cory with a chorus about his scrapbook in four volumes: 'All The Places I Want to See'. Then he sang old favourites, slow songs for sleep. Cory did not ask for more; he was impatient to sleep, to dream, to recharge for the next day. In the dark, sleep came, his swift and reliable friend.

Cory went swimming in his dreams, down through the top layer where humans dreamed, down through memories and stories and music, down down down to the cool dark layer where his people should be dreaming with him. Of course, it was empty and lifeless, as it had been every night on Earth. Even if he had been a solo, sailing the Northern Ocean of his home-world, he would have known others dreamed far from him.

He had loving family and friends and yet how alone he was.

Then: a spark. Something astonishing in the emptiness. He swam towards it, a tiny bright fleck like a lightning bug. It flickered and moved. This was new; he had to chase it with all his dream muscles not to lose it.

Somehow – he just knew – it was a dreaming-together . . . yet one he could not join. It was so fragile, so far and yet he knew it was of his people.

It took so much effort to focus. Yet he was closer to it now. It was like looking at a dream through a pinhole. Yes, it *was* a dreaming-together, sixteens of his people in an *open dream* he could join. To be on the edge of it and, for moments, touching it, was a moment of yearning so strong it was pain. He could not tell what was him, and what was them. A few moments of joining, then it was gone.

He called out, here I am, here I am. In vain.

There were healthy dreams and unhealthy. They did not follow day logic, and every child knew that sometimes dreams showed you things you wanted rather than things as they were.

Yet his birth-mother told him the old saying: what comes in the dreaming-together is true.

Cory swam on in darkness, looking and listening, feeling and smelling for the others. He swam longer than was wise or restful, chasing hope until the dawn, until he could dream no more.

For when his people came, all would be well.

CHAPTER 2

An unexpected caller

Far too early, Molly sat in the big chair by the bedroom window. Fleur, blue-eyed and born with a little fuzz of Gene's black hair, snoozed innocent and well fed on the breast. Fleur was perfect, she was beautiful, and she was as persistent as a jackhammer ripping up the road.

Fleur had woken twice in the night, that Molly remembered. Dimly she thought Gene had gone to the baby too, then retreated to the spare room.

There was a relentlessness to it; how shallow sleep was when you had an ear open for the hungry cry. Molly wondered if she could catch another hour before Cory bounced in for a talk. Or stay in the chair, rather than risk waking Fleur when she tried to put her in the crib.

A call of nature decided it. With care, Molly moved Fleur to a shoulder and stood. She walked to the sunshine yellow crib and, heart melting, put Fleur into it. John had made that stout wooden crib for his son Gene; it had come to them when

Molly was first pregnant, beautifully restored. After the miscarriage, Molly had kept it as a sign of hope amid despair. Gene had made the mobile of yellow birds and pink clouds, and Eva knitted the blanket.

Books talked about making a routine, but Molly kept telling everyone, 'Fleur hasn't read the books.' It wasn't helpful that everyone was so ready to give unwanted, contradictory advice, particularly once she said she was breastfeeding.

Molly went to the bathroom and, as she left, tuned in to a noise downstairs: a raised voice, hooting and trilling. Two voices in fact: Cory and the Ship. She went down the stairs, feeling cranky and straining not to take it out on her son.

In the kitchen, Cory was cross, *tock-tock-tocking* in frustration and interrupting the Ship. He strode up and down, talking into the silver bracelet. His tentacles emphasised the swoops and trills of his voice, his ears twitched and his tail lashed. A bowl of oatmeal steamed; he'd fixed his own breakfast, and Meteor was slavering at her toy. Both alien voices fell silent.

'Cory, look at the time. You might wake Fleur.'

'Morning Mom. Ship is being oh-so-very-annoying.'

'Well, argue outside or not at all.'

It was a school day, and Cory would be happy and off her hands in a while. How often she pushed him away because of Fleur. Going to Amber Middle School was impossible – the school would be deluged with gawking tourists outside, maybe a lunatic with a gun – but the School Board supported an ad-hoc school sometimes as big as twelve students. World-famous academics begged to teach there.

'Well, I'd like to go back to bed, sweetie-pie,' she said. 'But if it won't wait . . .'

'Should wait for Dad, tell both of you. Don't want to wait.' He sat and grabbed a spoon of raisins. 'My people are coming.' Said with all the certainty he might declare a sunset beautiful or point to magnetic north.

Cory said that often, but as hope, not this blunt certainty. And Molly felt many things. Heaven knows the world needed the purples, as a wake-up call to humanity. Humans needed allies against the snakes. Cory needed his people too – she knew that – and yet what she felt prickled at her eyes and turned down her mouth. A feeling of loss swept in, swamping the things she should feel. *What if his people take him back?*

She filled the kettle, trying to hide it. No time for tears. 'Well, that's wonderful, Cory. When will they be here?'

Cory didn't answer. She looked, and he was eating, staring into the bowl as if it could give an answer.

'Ship says no messages. Network always listening out for them. There are beacons.'

Barely awake, she couldn't understand. 'So how do you know?'

'I dreamed it. A splendid dreaming-together, sixteens of my people . . .'

Gene had taken pages of notes on Cory's extraordinary dreaming, how the purples shared their dreams and guided them. It seemed to knit their whole society together. Cory took her silence as invitation to give a longwinded description, but for all his superlatives, it sounded like moonshine: something and nothing.

He was waiting for her response. She sipped coffee,

remembered a discussion of a month ago and said, 'So how close are your people? How soon before we'll meet them?'

His ears dipped; a bit defensive. 'Don't know.'

'I can't remember, did you dream with your dads on your moon?'

Ears down a little more. 'Much too far, everyone knows that.'

Be gentle. 'So, Cory, if your moon was too far, that means your people would have to be really close. They'd have to be here on Earth . . .'

'*Tock-tock-tock* Ship says I am wrong.' Cory gave that odd shiver of the head which served as his eye-rolling protest. 'Even little child of my people knows what is made up in a dream. First-graders. A proper dreaming-together. I wish-dream all the time. I know the difference.'

'Who knows? Let's hope they come soon. Let's hope they can tell us how long they will be.' She felt the insincerity behind her words.

Cory trilled an emphatic statement, then said, 'Whatever comes in the dreaming-together is true. It would be nice to be believed.' He leaped up. 'I will take Meteor for her run. Meteor is always interested.'

How painful when you disappoint your child. Two and a half years since Cory arrived. Molly had named him and saved him. But where were his people?

What if his people take him away? What if they don't come, and the snakes destroy us all?

When Gene came down, holding Fleur freshly diapered, he found Molly sobbing.

★

Evening, and Molly sat at peace in the big chair by the bedroom window. She had the drapes a few inches apart, so she could watch the sky. The Ship could be anywhere, but she liked to think it hung over the town, guarding them directly. Molly had always enjoyed watching the sky, but since Cory came, she had new reasons. New hopes and new fears. But right now, all that was far away. A nap, then a wonderful coffee with her soulmates Janice and Diane, a chance every day to talk about other things. Mrs Robinson had dropped off supper. Molly felt safe and well . . .

The guitar next door had stopped. Gene sneaked his head through the door.

'Need anything, Molly-Moo?'

'Just you.' The six huge blue correspondence folders on the other chair almost glared at her. But she didn't have to be the mother of the most famous boy in the world every minute of the day. Publishers had sent Gene another crate of space stories too.

'He's still cross with us about the dream,' Gene said, coming in. 'He's going to try to have it again.' He put down a brown square parcel on the table, proofs of the new guidebook for Amber County.

'The Ship is sure it couldn't be true.'

'Sure,' Gene said.

Molly stood, pulled the drapes together and embraced him. How sweet his kiss, tasting of mint, and how her body remembered. He knew how to hold her. That hand stroked where her back ached sometimes. In other times that could have been a pass . . .

17

'I'd like to,' she said, meaning it.

'But not tonight? That's okay.'

They sat on the bed, his arm round her shoulders, cherishing their time alone.

'The book is there,' Gene said. 'Bit more on the last film, then that's done.'

Gene could no longer work at the library; he'd be mobbed by tourists and reporters. Nowadays, he was finishing films for the new Visitor Centre. But the eternal question hung in the air: what then?

Molly knew where he was headed, and she didn't want the conversation. 'Can we not talk about this now?'

He shrugged. 'Just, I can write songs anywhere. We may not have long before his people turn up. Cory sure wants to see more of Earth. We could make a plan.'

Molly had joked that Gene would have kept the family travelling until she went into labour, on a boat, or up some glacier in Alaska. He frowned, but it was not much of an exaggeration; it was Molly who had insisted they come home, to have their baby with Dr Jarman and Rosa Pearce, to be surrounded by her friends – people she liked and trusted. For her, two months on the road had been more than enough. Too many false alarms and the odd real danger, too many demands for their time, too many hasty departures and unfamiliar beds. Day by day, great or good, the travelling had palled. For her but not for him.

She used her discouraging sigh, but Gene was picking up strength.

'Cory wants everything. Our time on the road just fed his appetite. We're not locked up, let's show him a bit more. Take a month or two. The Grand Canyon, Yellowstone, the Rockies. The West Coast, right up into Canada.'

This tired her. 'We can decide later.'

'We were going to travel, when we got together. We talked all the time. You were keen, we were going to cross the country . . .' Gene was in his stride. 'People travel with babies. People say they can be easier to handle when younger. We don't have to worry about trains and planes, the Ship will fly us. It could bring us home in an hour or two if we needed.'

She didn't want to discuss this. Was that so hard to understand? 'I get airsick.' The Ship had never let them inside. The three times it had flown them, their vehicle had been gripped to its hull with metal tentacles.

'It would give us something to look forward to. Say, skip the West. We could go to Europe.' He clearly thought this was a winning card. 'All those galleries and museums, old castles and so on. Great hiking.'

'Of course, that would be great.' She could fake enthusiasm but didn't. 'A motor tour, like an ordinary family. Two adults, two kids, a dog . . . followed by half the world's press and a spaceship as big as the White House. Let's talk after Christmas,'

He was frowning now. 'Don't you feel cooped up? You can't even go for a walk without having Cory along to hide you. Being everyone's business?'

They both hated it, all of it, the trucks of mail and not daring to open a newspaper. Hiding behind the alien Fence to have some privacy, stopping everyone telling them what latest nonsense was in the press. The threats, the adoration, the endless attempts to use them for this or that. These were twisted, troubled times. To Molly, it was such a gamble they would be safer anywhere else.

Gene fell silent, looking at Fleur for long minutes. For all his fretting, he was a good father.

'After Christmas,' she said, reaching for her book. If he wouldn't take a hint.

'You promise we'll go?'

'I'll promise we'll discuss it, after Christmas.'

'I think if we moved, for the summer, we'd have a month or two before anyone figured it out. Wouldn't it be great to feel free? Maybe one of the other families would come too. The kids would entertain themselves and we'd have babysitting on tap. We'd feel freer than we are now.'

He wouldn't give it a rest. He'd ruined the mood. She snapped, 'You're kidding. You know what it was like.'

'We're young,' he pleaded.

'I'm tired, Gene. I'm going to the other room. If Fleur wakes, feed her yourself.'

She stood, and after a moment, he stood up. 'Fine,' he snapped and walked out.

It took an hour for her to feel she might have handled it better. Then forty-five minutes when pride prevented her making the first move. She was getting ready for bed when he reappeared, looking rueful.

'Of course, it can wait,' Gene said.

'Write it in your diary,' she said, kissing him. 'We'll talk after Christmas.'

'When you want to.'

'Let's go to bed,' she said.

The conversation was gentle, about shared joys, shared frustrations. To their surprise, desire came, and they made the old moves, slow and gentle. Physically it was still awkward for her, but still, it was a blessing, a healing, a renewal of vows.

Molly woke with a start from the deepest of sleeps. For a few moments she did not know where she was. An Army cell? That place they'd stayed in Vermont? No, she was home in her own bed, Gene still snoring, her sidelight still on. It was the phone ringing.

She made her way down the stairs, in the half light from the landing. The clock said half past eleven, and the latest ex-directory number was top secret, only for people they trusted. Lifting the handset, she said through a mouth thick with sleep, 'Molly Myers.'

'It's Selena.'

Molly wasn't expecting her sister. There was something odd in the voice, some note of strain.

'Hi, are you okay?'

'Yes, I'm fine.' No, Molly decided, she wasn't. 'Look, M, this is short notice, but could we drop by? Would you mind?'

Drop by? The way Molly liked to drive, Indianapolis was two days away. 'Uh . . . yes, I guess. When were you thinking?' She grabbed at the calendar. 'Next week might be—'

'Well, we're in this motel. Not very clean, to be honest, and the lock on the door's broken. And the man at the desk is a creepy brute. I've had to put the bed against the door. So we could be at yours by suppertime? I have the boys with me.'

'Right. Sel, it's almost midnight.'

A long silence. 'Oh, okay. Sorry. We're in some creepy two-bit place in Ohio, like one of those awful slasher stories. I know it's short notice. I'll find somewhere to stay.'

'We'll put you up,' Molly said, then regretted it. How many to cook for? How many beds? Perhaps Mrs Hardesty could help. 'Is Mason with you?'

'No, he's busy.'

Molly paused, trying to hear under the words, wondering if Selena would say more. Once the sisters had been so close.

'I have to go. Suppertime at yours.'

'Call me when you're at Bradleyburg. It's complicated, getting here without a fuss.'

'Speak soon, Sis.'

And she was gone.

Molly hung up. They still sent diligent Christmas cards, and Molly sent athletic Connor and bookish Rory money for birthdays – but, for years now, the sisters had been so distant. Each happily pretended that they meant vague promises that 'next year, you really must come for Thanksgiving', but somehow it never happened.

Through childhood, Selena had been younger Molly's best friend, role model, confidante. By her teens, however, for her own survival, Selena had become their mother's enforcer, the good girl, the example. Selena had conformed, Molly had rebelled, and they had grown apart. And yet when Selena married Mason, the dullest man in Indianapolis, a tearful Selena had whispered in Molly's ear, 'You soon, Molly. You'll be away from them too, and free.'

Molly, half asleep, was still holding the calendar. She hung it back on the wall.

She had tried to like Mason for her sister's sake. Old-fashioned Catholic, and that hearty patriotic Rotarian Elk can-do attitude, she could live with. But he was a defence contractor in an Army town – when Cory came, they had to keep him secret. She could not have risked Mason learning about Cory.

Then Cory had become the most famous boy in the world. Selena and Mason had been interrogated by the FBI, so Molly had called Selena, dreading it, feeling the need to apologise. Her sister had been shocked, confused, and to Molly's astonishment, hurt. 'You should have told us,' she'd said. 'I would have understood. Of course, I would have helped you hide him.'

Molly fumbled and said, 'Oh, I knew you would. But Mason . . .'

'Mason would have kept his mouth shut, if he knew what was good for him,' Selena said, with a sharpness that had surprised her.

And now her sister was coming.

It was not quite a meteor, but Selena's call was the order of things turned upside down.

CHAPTER 3

A sister arrives

In the kitchen, Gene rolled his eyes at the news that Selena was coming and poured coffee in silence, without even a gruff, 'Fine!' Cory was ebullient, delighted with the announcement of new children. He rattled off questions about Rory and Connor but, as the distant aunt, Molly mostly didn't know the answers.

'Why didn't you take me to see them?'

'That's grown-ups making things complicated,' she said. There was no point her fretting over what might be wrong; in a few hours, she'd meet her sister and find out.

When the story of Cory had broken, the press had swamped Selena too. There'd been photos of the O'Regans taken in the street and a lot of unpleasant speculation. The Myers were safe in Crooked Street, but when they left it, the world felt like a goldfish bowl.

Molly did not want the press nosing into her family business.

Six months on, the Myers and their friends realised most of the press were just doing their job, and the majority could

25

be pleasant about it. There was a quiet compromise. Mostly, the big newspapers and TV people kept away from Crooked Street. The deal was, Mayor Rourke or Dr Jarman dropped by Francine's diner every so often, to chat to the press who hogged the upstairs room. Once a month, the Myers would agree to some brief photo-call, to keep the beast at bay. Those photographers were polite and respectful. Yet there were dozens of stringers and freelancers in town, and dozens of townsfolk who would sell the Myers out for a cheque. And all the ways the Myers could drive out were watched by freelance photographers on motorbikes.

Of course, Cory could hide, but that brought its own problems. There was far too much gossip in town about strange occurrences and the woods being haunted. Roy heard people talking in bars. 'But he'd gone!' they'd say. 'Disappeared! Do you think he can turn into a squirrel?'

'Nah, it's like that TV show, you know, the space transporter.'

Hints about Cory's power crept into those wilder magazines that printed anything they were told about the Myers. They got it wrong, of course. Cory did not become invisible, he became *ignored*, *overlooked* – but a camera had no mind to be confused. It was inevitable that, sooner or later, someone would get a photograph or film of him and work out his hiding and they would all be less safe.

The Ship could send drones to knock a photographer off their bike, or cloud their film with a careful dose of X-rays, or blow out the tyres on a TV truck – but it would only create a new story, and editorials raging about attacks on the press.

The Ship had shown restraint but, if something worried it – 'an assassin might pretend to be a photographer, Mrs Myers' – it would act without discussion.

Evening promised rain. Selena called from a phone box in Bradleyburg, childish voices squabbling nearby.

'Venneman's Diner, a mile out of town towards Amber Grove,' Molly said. 'You can't miss it.' The place had doubled in size since the Meteor fell.

Selena snapped, 'Shut it, kids!' at her children, then whispered, 'I think he's following me.'

Molly's world skipped a beat. 'Who?' There was clearly something wrong.

'You know who.'

Mason? 'Tell Mrs Venneman a nurse sent you. She'll let you park out back.'

'Not you? A nurse?'

'Sel, who knows who'll be listening? A nurse.' It was a standard procedure and Mrs Venneman's discretion could be relied on.

There was a new urgency now, and Molly set up their best double-bluff game, with two cars. At the junction was a metal, human-made gate and two National Guardsmen waited day or night in their little wooden hut. A phone call and she knew exactly who was waiting, two motorbikes, Mr and Mrs Repent-Ye!, the man in the Stetson and the three hippie jugglers. The TV van had gone at sunset.

Gene had sighed, and now took Cory and Fleur for a random drive in the old Ford. With Cory visible in the window, giving a cheeky wave before ducking down, the photographers would assume that was their best story. Meanwhile, Molly would be in the back of Mrs Robertson's car, following ten minutes later. Mrs Robertson was a new friend by necessity, an eager conspirator among the neighbours. Molly lay in the back, while Mrs Robertson drove and gave a running commentary.

'It worked; they've all gone after Cory.'

Molly fingered the communicator. She hated it – the Ship used it to listen in on conversations – but she might need its help.

As Mrs Robertson drove Molly to the rendezvous, rain speckled the car windows. The diner was busy, bright light spilling across the parking lot, and Molly steeled herself for people recognising her, even under a headscarf and wearing her ugly disguise glasses.

She saw Selena at once. Far from parking discreetly out back, she was right under the light in the front parking lot. She sat on the front of her car, smoking, in one of those modern transparent raincoats. Anyone driving in would see her.

Molly got out of the car and trotted over. Selena dropped the butt and stubbed it out. She held out her arms for an awkward embrace, trying to smile. Selena was adept at make-up, but her face was in the light. There was a dark bruise around her left eye, and Molly could not shield her shock.

Selena embraced her anyway, holding her for a long time.

'What in the name of heaven—?'

'Mommy had an *accident*, falling down the stairs, and we don't have to talk about it,' Selena said.

Molly felt an old, protective anger bubbling up. 'Mommy's sister doesn't believe a damn word of it. Was it Mason? Who's following you?'

Selena shrugged, breaking the embrace. Molly studied her face. The last time they'd met, Selena had looked the younger. Now, there was strain and sorrow, and not enough sleep.

'You're going to get wet here,' Molly said.

'The air's fresh, and the boys are dozing at last. They couldn't sleep last night in that horrible place, such nightmares . . . It's been hell. Mason talked such garbage about you and your boy. It's good to see you, Sis.' Selena swallowed, holding something back. 'Look, this might be more than a day or two. If you can't—'

'Stay as long as you need. Mrs Hardesty lets the house next door. I checked and it's free for the next few days. Or Dr Jarman could put you up . . . His place is huge, a mansion out of town with a wall round the grounds. Cory loves it. You have to tell me what happened.'

Selena put her hand over her eyes and began to cry.

'Safe sounds good. M, it's such a mess. You were right all along.'

Molly held her, and knew the interrogation had to wait. Practical things – showers, food, beds. And Molly wanted to look at that bruise.

By Crooked Street, the rain was drumming on the car roof. Molly bustled Selena and the sleepy boys into her house. Gene was waiting, and his special polite expression vanished when he saw Selena's face. He looked at Molly and she frowned back.

'Grab the bags, Gene.'

'We're eating in the big room, just for space,' Gene said.

Cory had a cloth over his arm like a waiter, ears perked up

with anticipation. The boys stopped, so suddenly that Molly bumped them. Every child on Earth knew what he looked like.

Selena went straight up to Cory, saying, 'Well, I'm your special auntie. It's such a pleasure to meet you.' Cory accepted the embrace, his tentacles tapping Selena's right unbruised cheek.

'Sorry you are hurt,' Cory said, and she said, 'That's kind. It's fine.'

People often said that there was something about meeting Cory for real that went beyond what you expected. Just how much his tentacles moved, the mobility of his strange striped ears, the faint *otherness* of his smell.

'Say hello to Cory,' said Selena to her boys, with a little edge to her voice. 'We talked about this.'

Many kids loved Cory at first sight, but a fair number were wary, like the brothers. Connor and Rory were quiet, anxious and exhausted. They stared at Cory as he tried to engage them in cheery conversation about his toys and games.

Gene produced his near approximation to Molly's fish cakes. It turned out the boys hated fish. He suggested yesterday's lentil bake, which produced raised eyebrows from Selena, as if he had suggested moonshine.

'We've got beans, cheese and bread.' Grilled cheese got a cautious nod.

Selena took fish cakes from politeness and tried hard not to stare at Cory eating. Just sometimes, he forgot and used his tentacles to taste a sauce or pick up a carrot stick. On autopilot Selena took out a cigarette, a lighter, then carefully put them down, remembering. Mostly she ate the fancy salad, made to

Janice's famous recipe, and bread. Amber Grove had its own honest-to-goodness bakery again.

Cory tried to keep up the conversation, rattling off a long list of exciting things to do, questions about Indianapolis, and a plan for Connor and Rory to meet his friends. All this produced sullen silence from the boys, ferocious looks and *tuts* at them from Selena. Cory's dismay was obvious. The adults, meanwhile, made conversation, avoiding the discussion they wanted to have. Selena had no interest in music; current affairs and religion were out, so Molly ended up telling light stories about the changes to Amber Grove.

As soon as he could, Gene told the boys, 'We should get ice-cream and go to where you're staying next door. Why don't we make up a den there, for sleeping?' That produced polite nods.

The moment Gene had all three boys out of the house, Molly said, 'How often has Mason hit you?'

'He'll come after me,' Selena said, gazing into the distance. 'He says I'm too ill to look after the boys, that I'm an unfit mother.' Her voice broke a little. 'He knows the judge . . .'

Molly touched her hand. 'Nonsense.' The way Selena was staring into nothing, she guessed she was on some medication. 'How often, Sel?'

'Three times. He hit me three times, the kids a couple. This time, I'd warned him, if he hit the kids again . . . He was so angry . . . He said I'd never see them again.'

'No one knows you are here; if he does come, he won't find you. Sheriff Olsen won't take any nonsense. We know a great lawyer, we'll protect you.' There was a nasty story about Olsen, and what he thought about wife-beaters. The vengeful half of Molly almost approved.

Selena's grip tightened. 'I haven't got anyone else. We were at a party, and I realised – all my friends were the wives of his friends, his colleagues. Our lawyer, our doctor, our neighbours are all friends of his. It's like they all came out of a box. These Hoosiers all stick together. Not like *your* friends, Molly. Real friends.' A sob, and Selena blurted out, 'He betrayed me with other women. I want a divorce.'

Molly blinked, because Selena's Catholicism ran very deep. Selena saw the Church as a harbour against life's storms, not an arm of their mother's power. Florida had not mellowed that poisonous icy woman, whose lies about Molly had gone around the world. Their mother would turn on Selena too.

'Well, let's keep you and the boys safe . . .'

'Oh, the boys. Mason's such a brute, the things he said to them. *I was going to leave them. I was lying.* Sorry M, I'm in pieces. I have to smoke.'

A disgusting habit, but they threw on coats and went out to the porch. The rain wanted to remind her, it was November and real cold was coming.

Selena pointed at the Fence – elegant, silver, alien – and the gate in it that let you out, to go down Crooked Street. The Ship had made the homes at the top of the hill safe, but visibly different. Somehow, the Fence could watch, deter or repel attack.

'It's like something from one of those films.'

'Well, people are far too nosy.'

'I'm not surprised. Little Cory doesn't really have a nose, though, does he?' There was an odd note to her laughter.

Molly quelled her anger. By now, she should be immune to the tactless things people said.

Selena went on, 'He was a real charmer at supper. Really trying to make friends. Such an amazing thing you did, Molly. You're so brave. And Gene, I'm sorry he doesn't like me. He's a real gentleman.'

'Of course he likes you,' Molly lied.

'Mason knows the judge. He says he going to take my boys away. That crew of his, they always back him up. And the priest.'

Molly couldn't claim to be a lawyer, but nurses did see the seedier side of life. 'He's trying to scare you,' she said. 'Even in Indiana, they're not going to take kids from their mother and give them to a violent man.'

'He'll say I'm sick in the head – that I don't know what's true or false.'

'Well, we'll prove he's lying. I should examine you, the bruises and so on.'

'No.' She stubbed the cigarette out under the porch rail, out of sight. 'Thank you.'

Molly suppressed her irritation; she would always know the burn was there. 'For court, I meant.'

'I'll think about it tomorrow. At least the judge is a human being.'

Where did that come from?

'I mean, what happens when Cory's people come?' Selena waved at the sky. 'I've thought about this a lot. It must worry you. His kind will want him back.'

Molly's tears prickled, out of nowhere. Suppose tonight was

the night. The Ship would chime through the bracelet when the purple starships were here – and everything would change. She'd fought these thoughts off many times.

Selena carried on, not looking at Molly, 'An American kid, stranded on some savage island, in the middle of the ocean. We'd take them back, wouldn't we? Well, they'll see us as painted savages, with bones in their noses. You won't have any choice.'

Gene would say, 'We don't know that.' Gene wouldn't talk about what it meant for their family. 'Two civilisations meet. It'll be as big as the day we tamed fire. It's bigger than one family. It won't be up to us what happens.' Gene loved and needed Cory as much as she did – but he was also sure the purples would need an Embassy, probably in space.

Molly trotted out the ready answer. 'We'll cross that bridge when they come. If the adults have half Cory's compassion, they'll figure something out.'

Selena frowned a little, then silence fell between them.

Pulling out another cigarette, Selena said, 'I mean, we'll just be brutes to them, won't we? Animals. And people are best with their own. Boys grow up, and he can't date a human.'

Molly always changed the subject. She hated to think how alone Cory might be when he was older. And some people had dirty minds. She hated the sordid, unnecessary speculation and sneers.

Cory had made Molly a mother. Cory had changed her life, and Gene's, beyond imagining. She had fought and lied and run, risked everything for him, and Gene too. Everything Cory taught her about his people, everything he said about his world where no one was left behind, told her that the purples would want him back.

Yet Molly's heart burned with a mother's heresy. What better claim did the purples have?

'Will you pray with me?' Selena asked, putting the cigarette unlit in her pocket. Molly tried not to sigh.

A thought kept coming, something she had not said aloud. Yes, his people would come. Yes, they would change everything and humanity would have to adapt. But Cory was her son, and she would keep him. She would not let strangers take Fleur, so why should her son be any different? She believed in Gene's steadfast courage and love. He would stand by her side.

Molly closed her eyes, shutting out Selena's words and the complex feelings they threw up. She made Cory a silent promise.

Let your people come, with all their power and wisdom. Whatever they think, I am your mother and I will keep you. My cause is just. Cory, I swear I will not give you up without a fight.

The wind roared in the trees and the rain rattled on the roof of their home. Applause.

CHAPTER 4

The next few days

The first night, Molly heard movement around the house and found Selena had let herself in. Wrapped up in a blanket, her sister smoked in her kitchen and stared into the trees. It had taken Molly nearly an hour to convince Selena there were often people in the woods. The Fence kept them well back from the house; it was best just to ignore them.

The next morning, Molly got the boys fed and washed with no sign of Selena. Connor and Rory were polite to Molly, talked to each other, but were wary of Cory, as though he was a growling dog. Cory was quiet, talking to Meteor in alien.

Gene leaned his head to Molly's. 'He tried to be friendly in their dreams and it freaked them out.'

It was like the Eversons at number 7, all over again. Or that family further down the road, who'd asked them to leave. She'd told Cory not to do it, but it was hard for him to accept it.

Selena floated in with an eerie chemical calm, fully dressed and made up. She had always chased fashion more than Molly ever

37

did. Their guest embraced her sons, gave Cory a pat, cooed at the baby, and took black, sweet coffee. Molly got straight to it, there were decisions to be made, but her sister waved them away. Selena must speak to a lawyer, and Molly would call the Sheriff if she wouldn't. Selena was vague. Then, as if it was a minor thing, she said, 'I'll need to borrow some money. I spent every cent on gas.'

Molly was shocked. 'Don't you have money of your own?'

'Mason didn't want me to work. I've got my jewellery though. We could pawn it.'

There wasn't a pawnshop in town, not officially, though Molly knew who to ask. Gene said, without hesitation, 'No, let us help you out.'

After a long pause, Selena said, 'We don't need charity.'

'Helping family isn't charity,' Gene said, frowning, jaw clenched.

'It could be a loan,' Molly said.

The night before, Selena had refused to be examined by Molly, or Dr Jarman. Now Molly launched into extolling Rosa Jarman – once her boss and now her friend – her long nursing experience, her absolute discretion, and as an aside, her unbendable Catholic faith. That did produce a reaction.

'I'm fine,' Selena said, fumbling in her purse. 'But if you want me to, I don't mind. She must look at the boys too. I'm going for a cigarette.'

Molly called Rosa at once. Then she had to take Cory in her arms and reassure him again he hadn't done anything wrong.

'*Why-yyy* they don't like me? So many bad feelings.'

'Well, it happens with children on Earth too. And it's all difficult for them . . .'

'I will try harder, share dreams with them tonight.'

'No, Cory!' She was sharper than she intended, and he cringed. 'Cory, that's not working.'

'Most excellent way to know people better.'

'Yes, it's wonderful, sometimes. But they don't like it.' She spoke from bitter experience. It was so natural to him; he still couldn't accept he'd done the wrong thing.

Eventually, Rosa came, examined the boys and spent an hour with Selena. Then she slipped away, leaving Molly a note to come around tomorrow. An annoying little mystery.

The next day, 'Meteor Day' played on the radio, sad and eerie. Simon and Garfunkel had not been there, none of those who sang about it had been.

At breakfast, Molly brightly suggested going to the Jarmans'. 'Lots of running around room. The hot tub . . .'

Molly made the call to the National Guard, pleasant men who the street kept friendly with an endless succession of lunches, baked goods and coffee. To a man, they adored Cory and, from kindness, hid their guns from him.

'Car just turned up, Mrs Myers. Not one of the regulars. A blue Oldsmobile.'

Her stomach turned. 'Indiana plates?'

'I'll just wander over, friendly-like, and explain the ordinance.' Mayor Rourke and the Sheriff made sure there was no parking anywhere near the junction. The TV people had to pay one of the neighbours a fortune to park.

Ten minutes later, the National Guard said, 'He drove off. One of the photographers asked who he was, pushy, of course, and the guy in the car didn't like it.'

'Let's go,' Molly said.

The Jarman place always had its press too, a little campsite of tents and trailers and TV trucks. There was little point in playing games. Molly squeezed everyone into the camper and drove, followed by the relentless motorbikes. At least there was no Oldsmobile.

Molly saw the familiar turning.

'Wasn't there some trouble here?' Selena said.

Molly shuddered. The Chicago Mob had tried to seize Cory, one evening in spring, just about here. Four cars of armed gangsters and a waiting helicopter. Cory had hidden the Myers, slipping them through the attack. Then the Ship had arrived at inhuman speed, full of fury and vengeance . . .

'Tell you later,' Molly said.

By agreement, Dr Jarman offered the tour to the O'Regans, while Rosa admired Fleur and took Molly to a warmed greenhouse, full of fresh herbs, just one of the many homely touches she had added to the house.

Molly's first question sounded foolish as she said it. 'Did Sel say why she didn't let me examine her?'

Rosa looked grim. 'She's ashamed that you were right about Mason and she doesn't want to discuss it with you. But the good Lord help me, if I see that man, I will take a scourge of thorns to him.'

'Mason might be here.' Molly explained about the blue Oldsmobile, then said, 'How bad was it?'

Rosa said, 'Face, arms. A punch in the stomach. I think two or three times in the last few weeks. Worse than the kids.

Nothing broken.' Then she went quiet. Rosa was not one for more words than was needed.

'I didn't take to the man, but I never thought he would be violent,' Molly prompted.

'Men are barely above the beasts.'

'Well, doesn't she need to report it, or . . . something?'

'She'll talk when she wants to.' Rosa touched the modest crucifix round her neck. 'And she's not well. She promised to talk to Edgar about her medication. I'll hold her to it.'

Molly was about to form the next question, but Rosa wasn't done.

'He told the boys that Cory's people worship the devil – what a wicked liar.'

'*What?*'

'Selena let slip that she might come here, and he started throwing all sorts of abuse around. She's worried the boys heard that. Maybe I should ask Father Dolan over.'

'He still after baptising Cory?'

'Oh, the bishop is even keener. The moment the Holy Father gives the word.' Their eyes met and Rosa smiled. 'I said you were a hard case, but I'd work on you.'

'Thanks.'

Rosa picked up her gardening gloves. 'Let me know how we can help.'

'I need a walk.' Molly checked Fleur and took her outside in the stroller, if only to clear her head. Somewhere, children were whooping and a dog barking – but Selena was sitting on the long porch, sobbing, while Dr Jarman kept a paternal hand on her shoulder.

'M, I saw someone, in the bushes.' She waved towards the tangled trees. 'He had a camera.'

Dr Jarman caught Molly's worried gaze and gave a slight shake of the head. People were always trying to get over the wall, whether after Cory or Dr Jarman's priceless knowledge of him, so the place was now a fortress. There was vicious barbed wire on top of the wall, and alarms. The Ship stationed spies to keep a watch out, keen to protect the human doctor it most trusted if Cory was sick or injured.

Jarman took other precautions too. 'I'll get Reuben to let the dogs out.' Reuben was a veteran of Korea and a man of few words – groundskeeper, security and driver in one. There were six black German Shepherds that you could not mistake for pets. 'They'll find if anyone is there, two minutes flat.'

'I did see something, I did,' Selena said.

Molly nodded – but, half an hour later, neither the unsmiling Reuben nor his eager canine crew had found even a twig out of place.

Back in Crooked Street, the kids and Gene were upstairs playing a chess tournament and Connor had discovered a use for Cory, who was a fair player.

In the big room, Molly tried to get Selena interested in the endless correspondence files, if only to distract her, but Selena was too tearful today. It didn't help that there had been people crashing around in the woods last night, drunks calling for Cory to fly out and talk to them.

'Those men – Mason paid them,' she repeated.

'Oh, Sel, they come all the time. Bachelor parties last time, can you imagine?' Molly picked up the letter, fretting about Roy Disney, who had said he would close the theme park for the day if Cory came, and promised no press.

'Sel, your doctor. Have you said that sometimes . . . ?' *You see things*.

'Oh, *doctors*.' She gave a dismissive wave. 'He was a friend of Mason's. These Hoosiers all stick together.'

The phone was ringing. Molly welcomed the interruption, but when she lifted the receiver, the Guardsman told her, 'Mrs Myers, Johan at the end of the road. That blue Oldsmobile is back. I walked over and warned him about the parking and the guy in it gave me his card. He's a lawyer. Indiana licence plate. I wrote it down.'

An Indianapolis address. The scribbled phone number of a hotel in Bradleyburg. Molly wrote them down on autopilot.

'Thank you,' she said. 'What did he look like?'

Fair, so not Mason. About his age, though. A bit nervous, but having press hovering nearby while an armed man asked you your business might do that.

'Thank you, Johan. Call Sheriff Olsen please and tell him the guy has been hanging around. I'll call our lawyer.'

Selena was in the hall, listening. 'He's come, hasn't he?'

'His lawyer. I'll call him – deny you're even here.'

'Get the Ship to scare him.'

Molly was tempted, but said, 'We can't do that. Look, I'm going to call this guy. It might get unpleasant.' She wanted Gene there and Selena not listening in, but if she went into the upstairs bedroom, Selena might listen on the extension.

★

43

'This is Molly Myers.' Gene stood by the phone, while Selena was in the Hardesty house with the kids.

'Thank you so much for calling.' He had a pleasant, professional manner.

'I don't know why an Indiana lawyer wants me to call him.'

'Your sister, Selena. Has she been in touch?' Molly strained to hear; you could sometimes tell if someone else was by the phone. A slight intake of breath, perhaps; some microscopic sign.

'We spoke in September; I had a card in October. Is she all right?'

'She's not with you? The children?'

'Heavens, no. What gave you that idea?'

'Well, she's disappeared, with her children. I'm a friend of her husband. Mr O'Regan noticed that she took a detailed road map of New York State and two containers of gasoline from the garage. And you have been much more in touch in recent months.'

How subtle the change to a gentle interrogation. But Molly had been grilled by the FBI and the Army. 'That's odd. I can't account for that. I haven't seen her for years. We spoke on the phone, I guess two or three times – you know, after it all came out. We're not close.'

'Mr O'Regan wants to know that Selena and the children are safe. Mrs O'Regan has been unwell. She talked a lot about you, recently.'

Gene was scowling, but Molly touched his lips with a finger. *Stay out of it.*

'Well, I hope she's okay.' Molly wanted them to show their hand.

44

'So, I guess Mrs Venneman was mistaken? You know Venneman's Diner on the Amber Grove Road? She says there was a woman, with two children in the car, waiting outside for a while. We had a bit of luck – young Henry Venneman is one of those harmless oddballs: he collects and remembers licence plate numbers. Astonishing.' A careful pause. 'So it *was* Mrs O'Regan's car.'

Molly was shocked. She'd failed. She should have spoken to Mrs Venneman. *Don't be distracted*, she told herself. Deny it. Say they helped Selena go to Canada. And yes, she thought, straining to hear again, there *was* someone else on the lawyer's phone.

'It's not the only sighting,' the lawyer said, while Molly firmed up a Canada story.

Another voice came on the line. Mason said urgently, 'Molly, I just need to know the kids are okay.'

Brute.

'You're getting no help from me,' she said, icy and certain.

'Molly, I swear, I just need to talk.' He sounded hurt, desperate.

You told lies about my son.

'Mason, keep out of this,' the lawyer said.

Molly used her voice of steel. 'We've spoken, Mason. She's safe, she is well away from here, and I want her to talk to the cops. She's getting a lawyer. Men like you should be in prison.'

'We can fix this,' Mason said.

But his friend took back control of the conversation. 'Mrs O'Regan will not be talking to the cops. We're concerned for her and the children. We don't want this in the press. Can you imagine?'

If it's a threat, thought Molly, *it's very skilfully done.*

'We know lots of journalists,' she said. 'Anything with my name on it will be on the front pages. Maybe Sel should get a court order, give an interview to the Indiana papers, see if your church and colleagues like the wife-beating marriage-breaker.' Molly would rather make her sister drink battery acid than risk telling the press her personal life, but Mason didn't need to know that.

'What has Selena told you? About the cheques? About the . . . accident. Is she listening in?'

Gene was miming cutting his throat, hanging up the phone.

'You daren't go to the press, or the cops either,' Molly said.

The lawyer paused and she imagined a hand over the phone, some hasty conversation.

'Mrs Myers, Selena stabbed my client with a carving knife. Fortunately, it was only the arm; she was aiming for his body, but he defended himself. Mr O'Regan wants to keep the family together. He won't press charges. She took the children from his mother's house under false pretences and disappeared. Mr O'Regan then discovered she'd stolen cheques from the business chequebook and forged his signature to cash two of them. That's his company's money, Mrs Myers. He'll cover every cent, but the company might take a less lenient view.'

Gene rolled his eyes and Molly felt the world shift under her feet. If Selena had just done as Molly told her, Mrs Venneman would have said nothing.

Selena lied to you about the money. The gas.

'She's not herself,' Mason said. 'I know we've had problems, but I'm worried about her. About the kids. If she loses her temper again . . .'

Molly knew she should not engage anymore, but . . . 'You slept with other women,' she said.

The lawyer said something. Mason said, 'I haven't been a perfect husband. I need to make things right.'

He was pleading; he even sounded ashamed. Certainly, it was no denial.

Gene took the receiver from Molly's hand and hung up. 'Holy cow,' he said.

'It might not be true,' she said, not even convincing herself. Of course a woman might grab something to defend herself. And stealing money to keep her kids safe . . .

'Do you think she did stab him?'

'He hit her, Gene. We can see the bruises. The kids say so too.'

'Whatever happened was at night,' said Gene. 'She has the family temper; she's always struck me as that calm mountain that's really a seething volcano. Remember the prom story you told me a dozen times?'

'Yes.' Maybe Selena did have money and gas to get to the Myers place. Or maybe it really was bank fraud. Molly herself had lied, robbed and broken the law for Cory. What would she have done without friends, or family, or Gene? Suddenly, all of Selena's fears made perfect sense.

Gene looked at her, concerned, and Molly felt gratitude and warmth. Thank goodness Team Myers was so strong.

They needed Selena to tell the full story.

'What are our options?' she asked.

CHAPTER 5

New York City, that week

In the TV studio's waiting room, Dr Pfeiffer pretended to read the newspaper, so he had an excuse not to talk to the other guest. The tweed-jacketed academic espoused the sour slops of left-liberal thought and Pfeiffer had clashed with him before. The third guest, Augustus Mablethorpe, was an English author, unfamiliar, and late.

Pfeiffer once had his pick of the best TV programmes, the best channels. Back then, he would have laughed at a call from *Debate with Dempsey*. People clamoured for Pfeiffer's fiery opinions and his willingness to take on his opponents. He had all but spoken for the Administration. But now that he was the 'controversial, disgraced' former advisor to the President, he took what opportunities he could get, even this second-rate mud-wrestling match.

They had the *Vigilant* among the papers. He made a point never to read it.

The President had appointed his secret enquiry, to blame

Pfeiffer for the imprisonment and mistreatment of the Myers, but Pfeiffer had fought it. A great enthusiast of the Xerox machine, he had kept files on the scientific scandals of two Presidents, worse things than even the most paranoid potraddled hippy could imagine. The nastiest, juiciest story of all had shocked Pfeiffer to the core as a citizen, a doctor and a scientist. Even now, he shuddered to think of it. His blackmail worked, but it had been a poor victory. The vague report exonerating Pfeiffer had been universally derided. He had walked free, but his reputation was stained and diminished.

When would this programme get going? He had an important appointment this evening, and the producer had promised them they would be done in time.

He flicked through another paper. Governor Wallace had made another speech, whipping up his followers against Cory. Or more precisely, against some great danger talking to the purples might pose. Wallace was a demagogue, and a smart one. He might run for the Democratic nomination, to poison the water, to strengthen the racist, segregationist powers in the party. Behind him marched shadowy forces who had bombed churches and synagogues. Liberals forgot that in the Fifties, Pfeiffer had poured scorn on the so-called science behind racism, so Wallace's people saw Pfeiffer as part of a sinister leftist world conspiracy. But at least being smeared as a Jewish Communist made a change from being hated by liberals as a fascist warmonger.

Here was Mablethorpe, the third guest, one of those very long, angular Englishmen, arrogant enough to patronise a Boston blueblood, and whose voice conveyed mediaeval courtyards and bad drains.

'Dr Pfeiffer.' He held out a long bony hand. 'As our civilisation *gasps its last*, we men of learning are reduced to entertaining the mob like trained monkeys.'

Pfeiffer shook his hand and wondered what the man could possibly have to say that was so interesting. Pfeiffer felt a stirring in his stomach, a tightness in the throat: symptoms of 'fight or flight'. Just as the boxer or the airline pilot feels those nerves and uses them, he expected them before a debate.

They were hurried under the brilliant lights of the studio. Their host, Dempsey, a famous war reporter brought low by alimony and drink, shunned a first name. It was the four easy chairs format, so difficult to know exactly how to sit. Mablethorpe opted for folding himself into his seat; it looked both peculiar and uncomfortable.

The programme was live but transmitted with a small delay in case someone used bad language. They were introduced, and the host went straight into the discussion. 'Dr Pfeiffer – I don't see how the purples coming will make ten cents' difference to Joe Public.'

Ah, an easy shot. 'This is one of the most profound moments in our history. What we already know today should change us. Another intelligent species exists. Like us, they are social, they write and use mathematics, and they base their civilisation on science. If this tiny corner of the galaxy has at least two such species, we know there must be many more. The purples show us what we might be. They have made astonishing advances – thinking machines like the Ship, faster-than-light travel that takes us far beyond Einstein; they have medicine, communications and technologies we can only dream of. But we are not

51

a simple people who can only gape at magical wonders. We need not be natives on the shore willing to sell our land for a fist of beads.'

The leftist was already twitching to leap in. Pfeiffer disapproved of long hair on men in principle, but on anyone over twenty-five it looked ridiculous.

His next example might be misunderstood, but it was important. 'In the middle of the nineteenth century, Japan was backwards, feudal, using swords and horses. However, they opened themselves to the world and made the crucial decision to learn. In two generations, they were an industrial society. They beat Russia, a major power, in a modern war. In another generation, they posed a serious threat to the United States.'

The leftist was sitting up, but Pfeiffer just raised his voice and sped up. 'Now, that was very different. But America should be the smartest and hardest-working country in the world. Let's commit ourselves to partnership with the purples and Western freedom – Western science – will solve many of the world's deepest problems. The greatest days of America lie ahead of us. We can stand proudly beside them as leaders of humanity, a great civilisation.'

Dempsey made a gesture and the leftist broke in, 'Emmanuel, you miss the point. It's telling that you talk about winning wars. Cory's people have no war, no poverty, no famine, no violent crime, no racial prejudice. You claim we're the most advanced civilisation on this planet? A few stops from here on the subway, children go to bed hungry and suffer diseases the rich have not suffered for fifty years. Innocent people are daily shot in the street. Yet we have the wealth to fight endless wars and to topple elected leaders in other countries. Cory sees this and he calls us out. He shows the horror we should feel. That's the real challenge to America today. A moral challenge . . .'

He was in the pulpit and away. It was a decaffein- ated Communism, without the brutal discipline that made Communism dangerous. But these were new times and America might require difficult alliances. The sinister snakes would slaughter free and enslaved nations together.

The Englishman coughed. 'Oh, dear, oh dear,' he said, pulling faces as his hands writhed together. 'Of course, I am no *expert* on the wonders of science like Dr Pfeiffer. But isn't it far more likely that this child is a *hoax*? We are being *gulled*, gentlemen, dear viewers at home, for some *nefarious* purpose. *Non sunt multiplicanda entia sine necessitate*, after all.' Mablethorpe looked smug.

For a moment, Pfeiffer was without words, furious that his time was being so wasted. But his blood was up, and he was ready to fight. 'Occam's razor is a prejudice, not a principle,' he said, jabbing his finger at the man. 'Samples of Cory's blood and cells were examined by twelve scientists from six different countries. No serious scientist disputes that Cory Myers is from a different species. No other Earthly species has his form of DNA, no Earthly creature absorbs oxygen in the same way . . .'

The leftist looked bewildered. 'The family gave a televised press conference,' he said to the Englishman. 'There were two hundred journalists there. The Ship flew over Washington. Use your eyes, man.'

Pfeiffer nodded vigorously, welcoming any ally against this nonsense.

Their host sat back, gloating.

Mablethorpe waved a hand, brushing away these points like someone dismissing a bad smell. 'A hoax.'

Pfeiffer said, 'Three more proofs. His immune system—'

'Oh Dr Pfeiffer, I would never *dream* of suggesting this was a *poorly constructed* hoax. It's clearly required a vast amount of time and money, and no doubt the best brains in America colluding. It's a *magnificent* achievement, the very Manhattan Project of fraud. But let's tug at the green curtain, shall we?'

Pfeiffer reined in his temper. There was a jug of water beside him and he imagined the man getting it in the face . . .

Mablethorpe continued, 'The child is seen, sometimes, but mostly *hidden away*, appearing and vanishing like dear Saint Anthony. So convenient. The *Ship* has not been examined by all these independent experts, has it? Dear viewers at home, our civilisation is rotting from within. You can smell the gangrene, the barbarians are at the gates and cruel tyrannies across the world wait to finish us off. And the President of the United States of America appears on TV with a *carnival sideshow* — a children's comic-book character. Who benefits?'

Pfeiffer felt his temper building again. This man was calling him a liar. 'I've studied Cory — I've talked to the Ship, many times. Scientists I know and trust have worked with me to examine alien artefacts—'

'And it is all *magnificent*, Dr Pfeiffer. I don't know if he is a puppet or something you grew in the laboratory. But why, Dr Pfeiffer, why? Who pays you? Surely there are *limits* even to your greed and ambition?'

Cory stirred up many things. There were those who used

his childish hopes to back up their own political views, those terrified and gullible over contact with another species, those who longed to give up their freedom. Those who believed this was just the latest wonder and TV would find something better in a month. Pfeiffer had a special loathing for educated people who chose not to believe hard facts. Even worse were those who denied objective truth just for the joy of argument.

'We are faced with a new threat to our civilisation, our entire species. The Russians were attacked by another hostile force . . .'

Mablethorpe twisted his body and made more idiotic grimaces. 'Oh, now we trust the barbarian hordes of Muscovy and the Great Helmsman of Peking?'

Pfeiffer was treading a careful path. He loathed the Soviet Union, and the man who ruled China was probably worse, certainly less rational. Yet faced with an attack from space, the USA, the USSR and China might have no choice but to work together.

Did the smirking Englishman believe any of what he said? He was a brilliant, slippery eel in an argument and apparently quite willing to fuel paranoia.

'If these purples really exist, we should ask the Cherokee and the Sioux what the friendship of a great civilisation is like. Ask the first Tasmanians. Our future may be in alien museums, our cities the ruins their tourists may visit. Beggars for scraps at their table, "*all as one with Nineveh and Tyre*".'

The long, sorry argument was over. As the cameras stopped rolling, the Englishman smiled at Pfeiffer and said, 'Well, Dr Pfeiffer, I do feel we gave the soap companies their money's worth. Let us plot a rematch, shall we? I know a bar with genuine Scotch not a block from here.'

Pfeiffer brushed away the bony hand, ignored the leftist, and nodded at the host because he wanted his fee.

In the lobby of the TV studio, some bright-eyed young man said, 'A car, Dr Pfeiffer?'

'No. I have other plans.' He did not want to keep the Six waiting.

'Your friend is here.'

Abe Kaplan of the *Vigilant* had appeared in the lobby. The worst journalist on the most hostile of the big newspapers, he had been out of the country when Cory was unveiled to the world. He had been chasing the story ever since. The Myers hated him as much as Pfeiffer did.

'He's a journalist. Call security.' Pfeiffer knew he'd squeaked it. At all costs, Kaplan must not know where he was going.

The studio man looked a little flustered. Kaplan, piggy-eyed, took the opportunity to get close, exuding a great wave of peppermint mouthwash and carbolic soap. The coat was foreign-cut, expensive, and in need of a clean.

'Dr Pfeiffer, I only need a few minutes.' That grating voice.

'Go to hell,' Pfeiffer said. 'I have nothing to say to you.'

'I'm close, Dr Pfeiffer, so close. And how I write it, how you come out of it, will matter.'

'Call security!'

The studio man held up his hands. 'It's only the lobby.'

Kaplan was taller and ten years younger. Pfeiffer could not outrun him, but neither did he want to talk. He considered going back into the building. But he needed to get to his appointment. It would be a disaster if this journalist found out about the Six, even though those great men never met without an innocent explanation.

'Three minutes.'

'Five.'

Pfeiffer dragged Kaplan over to the window – outside, November rain was bouncing ankle-high – and said, 'I've told you before, I have nothing to say to you.'

'Cory Myers can do things with his mind, extraordinary things. You were by the lake when the Myers were arrested. Soldiers were seriously harmed, picking up two peace campaigners and a little boy. Perhaps they have some alien weapon, but I think it is Cory himself.'

Pfeiffer had indeed been there, had experienced the attack, and he tried not to show his shudder. *Cory spun nightmares, monsters from his mind, a great fear gripping armed men and rendering them helpless . . . three soldiers screaming, unable to breathe . . .*

'Huh!'

'Those soldiers have been moved like pieces on a board. The Army brought down a wall of silence. I've been digging for six months and I think the rumours are true. I'm so close. What was the plan? To use the country's favourite child as a weapon? To hide what his people can do? It is all realpolitik now, isn't it? I heard you just now. Our enemies' enemies are our friends.'

'That's all nonsense.'

'Dr Pfeiffer, will you stake your professional reputation, and tell me on the record, that what is claimed of Cory is impossible?'

It was a trap. Because the rumours *were* true, because the

Government had used everything within its power to suppress it. Because, if Pfeiffer confirmed that story, he might end up in jail.

'I have nothing to say to you.' He put on his hat and undid the snap on his umbrella. He was going to get wet. And he was never sure if the FBI were following him.

'I know it's his mind. This time a year ago, three thugs tried to kidnap him. They were arrested and disappeared. The government drops a hint it's witness protection. I have highly placed sources in the Five Families, the New York Mob. They're scared, Dr Pfeiffer. Our local capos have ordered "hands off" the Myers, on pain of ending up buried under a freeway. They're fighting a turf war with those Chicago goons to protect him. It's the kid that frightens them, not that lunatic spaceship.'

'Our time is up.'

'You'll come out of it badly. Everyone will rake over the other allegations. The first story sets the tone.'

'No one who reads your paper matters. It's yellow journalism with a bigger dictionary.'

Kaplan snarled his smile. 'And how can he hide, Dr Pfeiffer? How do the family keep disappearing?'

'Our time is up.' Pfeiffer turned and trotted back towards the elevators. The studio flunky was there, watching the confrontation.

'I want a car.'

'I have one waiting. It will be here in two minutes.'

The flunky helped Pfeiffer into the sleek car. Pfeiffer gave a downtown address, but a block later told the driver, 'I'm going to get out at the next corner.'

Pfeiffer went through the smoky bar, not his kind of place, but it was easy to walk past the restroom with his hat on. The jukebox played that sentimental dross you heard everywhere that month, 'Will You Still Love Me When the Purples Come?' There was a man with a cheroot at the rear fire-door. He said nothing, just stepped aside to let Pfeiffer through and slammed the door behind him.

At the end of the alley was a taxi. The driver said, 'I'm waiting for someone, Mac.'

Pfeiffer gave the password – 'Valley Forge, please' – and the man leaped into action, gunning the engine and shooting off the moment Pfeiffer shut the door. A second car appeared behind them, with no job but to block the way to anyone following. Whizzing through dark streets, Pfeiffer tried to steady his breathing, and pushed Kaplan from his mind. He would soon be in the presence of the Six.

Pfeiffer mulled the great question. When the purples came, who would they negotiate with? Would they share their true wealth, their scientific knowledge? Faced with all the countries of the world, the tyrannies, the chaotic and backward former colonies, the faded glories of Europe – surely, logic dictated they should side with the States. In truth, they would probably be guided by the boy. But that was why it was so important the family listened to a realist: someone who understood the balance of power.

Let the purples come before the snakes. He saw in his mind's eye New York, Boston, Washington in flames, and shuddered. The decisions that would have to be made.

The boy was the key. It had taken months, but despite the

mishaps of the past, Mrs Myers had finally met with Pfeiffer, so he still had an opening of sorts to the family. Precious Cory, the key to the power of the Ship and the trump card for when his people came.

Kaplan might turn the public against the boy, but he had not published his story in all these months so he clearly couldn't prove anything.

The Six met in houses and clubs that smelled of money and power. Round the table sat moguls dealing with aircraft and cars and shipping, oil and mines. Markham, self-appointed chairman, the brash industrialist whose empire helped build the defence of America's interests on Earth and in space. There were two rival banking empires, newspaper tycoons who gave Pfeiffer a column, a voice – and Overton, the pharmaceutical king who funded Pfeiffer's research. They were the resources and power he needed, now the government was closed to him: odd allies but needs must. He waited in the car, finishing his line of thought.

Pfeiffer had exaggerated his power and influence when he'd been courting Mrs Myers, and likewise exaggerated his rapport with Mrs Myers to the Six, all part of the necessary game. When the purple aliens came, he needed to be in those first conversations, to ensure the aliens had a sound, rational guide, not be led astray by the childish filth of the anti-war demonstrators, the simple slogans of the Communists, or even the profitable nonsense of Madison Avenue.

The Six liked to think they could buy anything they wanted, including him. But he had things they could not buy, and he would not be used.

Pfeiffer would play a clever game. He would be there when history was made; he would make the mocking papers eat their words. He would have his revenge on that unprincipled crook in the White House. He would mediate between the two worlds, and his would be the name people remembered: not ambassador to a mere country.

Pfeiffer would be ambassador to a whole civilisation – Ambassador to the Stars.

CHAPTER 6

Stick out your thumb

In the Hardesty place, Gene was playing the guitar to the boys, in the big room with the door shut against the shouting. Cory's ears were right down and his body shaking. Rory and Connor were silent, pale and shut down. Selena and Molly were arguing. It started in the kitchen, but it was getting louder. They were in the hall outside.

At least the boys were a little more used to Cory now; Rosa's pet priest had spoken to them and Gene was starting to get to know them.

'Okay, we'll *pack and go*.'

Gene gave the boys a smile he didn't feel and said, 'I'll be back in a moment.'

He opened the door to look. Molly stood blocking the way out of the house, Selena held her suitcase. Each sister glanced at him but didn't stop.

'Get out of my way,' Selena ordered.

Molly was in full flow. You sure could see the family

63

resemblance: the mouth, the eyes, the shape of the chin. The temper.

'Selena, it's a simple question. It's not about the money, it's about lying to us.'

'You believe *him*, not me. I don't have *anyone else*. I don't have *anywhere to go*. Keep your stinking money.'

'I believe you,' Molly was saying, 'I believe he's a violent man. We're glad we can help. Can't you see you were wrong, though? We deserved to know—'

'Have you ever been scared for your life? Really scared?'

Yes, we have. We've been chased by the Army. Gene slipped into the hall, between them, closing the door. 'Molly, Selena, can we keep it down? The neighbours . . .'

Molly glared at him. 'I can handle it.'

'I guess Gene thinks adultery is just dandy,' Selena said. 'Fine, I'll take the boys and go.'

'Don't be ridiculous,' said Molly.

'Get out of the way,' Selena said to Gene.

'If everyone calmed down . . .' he said, hands up.

'I can handle it, Gene.'

'I want my boys. Out of the way.'

'They're playing with Cory. Let's just all calm down and . . .'

Selena swung the suitcase at him, the metal corner catching his knee in a jab of pain.

He cussed – wow, it hurt – and Molly snapped, 'Put it down.'

Selena came right up to him, in his face. She smelled of forbidden smoke. 'Get them out of there. We're going.'

'Put the case down,' he said, 'and everyone take a few deep breaths . . .'

Selena roared, stepped back, and swung the case back for a second, two-handed blow. Her keys clattered to the floor.

Molly huffed, like he'd done something wrong. 'Gene!' She stepped in, to ruin Selena's swing, and the suitcase fell too.

Selena's face fell into sadness. The fight went out of her.

'Let me see my kids.' It was more of a wail than a roar. Molly put her hand to Selena's shoulder; she shook it off, but no one was shouting anymore.

'You're not helping, I've got this,' Molly said, and seething, Gene walked away.

Rosa wouldn't put up with these tantrums. Go stay with her.

That night, in his own house, Gene finished changing Fleur, Little Boo, in the trance of the midnight parent. Molly had gone into urgent labour at the Jarmans' wedding: a frightening couple of hours. Gene had stared into Fleur's face and fallen in love . . . but love can mean heavy lifting.

At last, glorious sleep beckoned. Then Gene heard a clink, someone or something downstairs.

He grabbed his communicator, in case help was needed. Then he went to the dark top of the stairs one careful step at a time, ready to shout, or call the Ship.

Someone was crying, whimpering. He turned on the light.

Selena was in nightgown and bathrobe, in a huddle by the front door. She was trying to cry quietly. *Give some people a key and you're never rid of them.*

Gene came down the stairs, moving steadily, so as not to spook her. The knee ached at each step.

'He's out there,' she whispered.

'Who?' Gene realised that was a stupid question.

'Mason. And I left the boys next door. Suppose he takes the boys?' She put a frozen hand to his.

She wasn't well. 'Sel, the Ship will tell us if there's anything out there bigger than a squirrel.'

'He's out there.' She scrambled to her feet, sobbing, distraught. 'I'm sorry . . . I'm sorry about everything. He's come for me. He'll be armed.'

'You're okay. He can't be—'

'I did stab him, Gene. I just grabbed the knife . . .'

'Okay.'

She was barefoot, crazy in this weather. 'Let's look together, and check your boys are okay.' He raised his communicator to his mouth.

'Any trouble, Ship?'

'There's nothing, Mr Myers,' the Ship replied.

Gene threw his thickest coat round her shoulders – the cold was bitter now – and grabbed the summer coat for himself. She pulled on Molly's gardening boots. He walked Selena back, she took his arm, playing with the big flashlight's beam here and there. Two of the drones whirred overhead, hard to see against the night sky.

'I don't like them,' she said, looking up.

Gene only grunted. It was the price they paid.

The door was shut, and she fumbled for the key. 'I can't believe I left the boys,' she said.

'They're fine kids.'

She gave him a grateful smile. 'You have such a way with them. Fleur is so lucky.'

Wary of flattery, Gene said nothing. He got his key and let them in. 'No harm done. Shall I just look round?'

'Both of you are right. I think I'm seeing things,' Selena said, her face full of fear and grief. 'Isn't that terrible? How can anyone trust me?'

'You're safe with us.'

'Thank you.' She got out a cigarette, offered him one. He felt a need so strong he could taste it. Maybe smoke just one, to build rapport.

But before he could give in to the urge, she had pulled it away. 'Oh, sorry. Molly would kill me, seducing you into wicked ways.'

They both smiled.

Those long, difficult years for the Myers; the death, depression, the alcohol-soaked rift in their marriage – and where had Selena been? What help had she offered her sister? Gene could think of nothing. But she was family, and the right thing to do was the right thing to do.

'I'd like to travel when I'm well,' she said. 'See the West. M and I thought Hawaii was so exotic, we used to cut out pictures and hide them.'

He blinked, had Molly been venting about him to Selena? Her eyes were soft, there was no malice there. She said, 'It's hard, the first year with a baby. Molly . . . she'll come around.'

Gene thought about California; it was just his opening bid. He was worried his deepest dreams would scare Molly off completely . . . but he couldn't let go of them.

★

Two days later, they closed the library early. Gene was back to give his feedback on the last film for the Visitor Centre. The film people, Mayor Rourke, and some other worthies watched in the library basement. Cory wanted a little time alone, and after Selena's latest drama, her latest weeping three ring circus of an apology, Gene knew how he felt. Gene had given Cory the keys and let him go explore.

Rourke worked the projector himself. The latest film: the fauna and flora, the sights and the hikes of the area. Gene hated seeing himself on screen, and thought his presentation was wooden. But Rourke clapped, and the film people looked very pleased with themselves.

They looked at him.

'It's okay,' he said, wanting rid of it.

The Mayor beamed. 'Gene, you're a natural teacher. You're no Hollywood actor, but you know your stuff. It really made me want to go hiking, with a bird book in hand.'

'Well, if it does the job,' Gene said. There was another film, of course, about Meteor Day, the relevant sights, how the town had rebuilt; the way the Army had fenced off Two Mile Lake and footage of the Ship. Gene had refused to be in that one. And, finally, one careful film about Cory, mostly clips from newsreels and interviews with their friends. A famous scientist took down the sceptics using simple words and a kind tone.

The town had changed more since the Meteor than it had since the railroad came. Now, you might hear that the Prime Minister of India had turned up in a motorcade, wanting to meet the Myers. Like most VIPs, all she got was her photo in front of the Meteor fragment on Founders Green.

Gene gave his thank-yous and disappeared upstairs to the long room where the archives brooded, and where Cory would be waiting. There was a stack of new books and Cory's telescope, but no friendly greeting. Then Gene looked behind the shelves and found Cory wrapped in a blanket, asleep.

There was something beautiful in seeing a child in healthy sleep. Gene put on the old-fashioned Sam Spade hat Molly had bought him and sat looking out at the town. The lights were going on and the sky was darkening, and he felt Amber Grove close round him like a trap. That scene in *Pinocchio* where the whale swallows the ship.

His best friend Roy had warned him that the new baby would suck up time and sleep. It wasn't unusual that Molly wanted a padded fortress, a hand-picked world of people she trusted. It was not surprising that she wanted no more adventures, no part of his daydreams. But he was beating his wings against the bars.

He'd talked often about travel with Molly, those first years they were together. Then, the spring the Meteor came, she'd said yes to a trip to the West Coast. He knew it was her peace offering but she'd managed to smile about it. He'd hoped it would heal them. Then the Meteor came and there was no trip. And now she had rewritten history, forgetting that she'd meant it.

Those months on the road had smelled of sweat and dope and incense and too long in a car. Gene had talked to real artists, rolling stones, free spirits, doers and thinkers from all over the country, people who'd encouraged his music, talked of new chances and new sights. He had seen the possibilities – he could see them right now.

Their name could open extraordinary doors.

Cory muttered something and stretched extravagantly, like a cat. Then his eyes opened, and he did his curious yawn.

'Good dreams?' Gene said.

'Looking for my people,' Cory said. 'I want them to come and fix everything.'

Gene wanted them to come too. He feared they wouldn't – but, whatever happened, he would keep Cory safe and well as long as he could.

The snakes were implacable enemies of life itself. The chaos of Meteor Day would be as nothing if they returned.

One of Roy's men ran Gene and Cory home. At the bottom of Crooked Street there were floodlights, two TV trucks parked illegally, perhaps a dozen photographers: the whole circus. One of the Olsen cousins, in uniform, was arguing with a TV presenter next to someone on a motorbike.

Almost by instinct, Gene pulled Cory down. The communicator trilled and Cory began talking to the Ship. The National Guard swung open the barrier and the truck went up and through the Fence. Who knew what had brought the media this night?

Molly met them at the door. 'There've been some explosions in Australia,' she said as they went in.

The fact the press had come to the Myers was ominous. Gene saw that the phone receiver was droning, off the hook.

'Ship says go inside,' Cory said.

They sat round the kitchen table, Fleur asleep in her basket, Cory playing with Meteor and listening. Gene was astonished at how dry his mouth felt. 'What's going on?' he asked the Ship.

'The Australian authorities have announced a nuclear accident in a remote part of their country,' the Ship said, 'an accident involving an experimental bomb. They are trying to explain away fallout reaching deep into the desert interior. There was a snake landing – a small one – and they began assembling some form of structure. The Australian authorities sent three planes to observe what looked like some unexplained phenomena. The snakes destroyed all three – but not before a clear description was radioed back.'

Gene gripped Molly's hands. Her eyes closed, she swallowed, and Cory sent out his own cold fragments of frightened dreams. Fear rose again, familiar and heart-breaking.

'The authorities wanted it dealt with, so I obliged. The threat is removed.'

'Is that all of them?' The Ship and its Network were for ever searching the skies and the surface of the planet for intruders.

'There has been nothing since the deep Atlantic episode in July. Two weeks ago, a single snake vessel landed in a remote part of the Himalayas. I watched it closely, but it was largely inert: I suspect a monitoring station. The political situation there – the war between India and Pakistan, tensions with China – is complex even by human standards. I have taken advice from Professor Zarin in Moscow and others. I find the Chinese government opaque to deal with.'

Gene asked, 'How much does the world know?'

'Australia? There was a French documentary crew filming wildlife in the region. French television is reporting "extraordinary revelations", so I think the crew has evaded the authorities.'

'How could they land on Earth?' Molly pleaded. 'You said the Network was fool-proof.'

'They did not fool me for long and I will increase my vigilance. Mrs Myers, these are small-scale intrusions. The Himalaya outpost will be no more within the hour.'

Gene thought the Ship sounded sure of itself – but it was not all-powerful, nor was it infallible.

'The fallout,' Gene said, thinking of invisible poison on a desert wind; the clean snows of the mountains turned to a dangerous rain.

Molly gripped his hand tighter. They had marched to ban the bomb, had won an end to the tests that poisoned children. But the snakes brought closer a time when the weapons might be used in large numbers.

'The authorities are moving swiftly. They understand what they need to do to protect human health.'

'My people need to come,' Cory moaned.

The adults' eyes met, and they exchanged worried smiles.

'Of course, they'll come,' Molly said. 'The Ship will keep us all safe until they do.'

The next day, Olsen and his deputies were busy clearing yet more members of the press from the bottom of Crooked Street. Cory went over to his friends, and Gene phoned his father. They assumed any phones in Crooked Street would be tapped, so anything really secret they did in code, or from phone boxes or friends of friends' houses. Of course, people with two alien communicators could talk to each other without human snooping – but then the Ship listened in.

The phone rang and rang; perhaps John had forgotten the arrangement and was out doing stuff on the farm. *Over*doing it.

Then a breathless voice answered, 'John Myers.'

'Hiding any symptoms?' Gene opened. John's 'indigestion' had been getting worse for months, until Molly had searched his bathroom cabinet and found his angina medication.

John had been brazen: *Nothing for you to fuss about.*

'Hah.' Today, John's breathing was heavy. Had he jogged back to the house? 'Red needed a second opinion on something. Your mother is with the church ladies. How's your new houseguest?'

'She'd try the patience of a mountain.'

John laughed. 'That was one of your grandpa's,' he said. 'Molly told Eva, you're wanting to up sticks and go wandering.'

'Yeah. It's not like Molly should be surprised. We talked about travelling at our engagement party.'

'Remember that summer when Grandpa and I took you out to see shooting stars?' Gene did; there had been many such summer nights. Grandpa had said, if Gene got straight As in his tests, he'd get a telescope. His grandpa had showed him the moons of Jupiter and the rings of Saturn and told him with love and care about life.

John's breathing was better now. 'You and he were chatting away, and that night, he told me, "That boy won't stay on the farm." Your mother and I knew that too. We figured it would be college and then away. Picking apples would never be enough, not for you.'

'I loved the farm. You didn't want me to go, but you wanted me to know I could.'

'You were a loud-mouthed know-it-all at eighteen. You still are.'

Gene laughed. Some kids knew their future was set in stone, following their parents, perhaps going to fight for Uncle Sam in some mysterious war or other. Some marched to a different drum. Gene had always thought the future would be astounding. He read about computers and space flight and revolutions in clean power, agriculture, and medicine, and how the world could be changed, for good or for ill.

John said, 'Bill Burrowes and I have been talking for a long time. Someone will have to manage the old place when I'm gone and we all know it's going to be Red Burrowes, not you. I called to say, don't worry about us. You and Molly do what you need to do.'

'Molly and I don't agree what we need to do.'

'You know she's a keeper. A man would be a sheer fool to throw a woman like that away.'

As if he would. Yet, Gene thought, his father would not be here for ever to say annoying things.

'I don't plan to.'

After the call, Gene wanted to be on the farm, to talk to his father face to face. All those dreams he used to have – and here he was, a librarian without a real job, in a pleasant backwater, not so far away from his parents. He had many blessings to count – but, in his heart, he knew he had far further to go.

Molly thought his dream was California, or Europe, even. His need was bigger and brighter than that; California was just what he could ask for.

The Ship wouldn't let humans inside it, but when the purples came, there would be other choices. Maybe they would take him to visit Mars and Jupiter and Saturn. Once those planets would have satisfied him, but now . . . that was just Earth's back yard. Gene imagined even bigger.

Gene wanted to see so much more than the wonders of Earth. The future had hit them like an avalanche. Who else deserved to return with Cory to the purple home-world? Gene knew the purple home-world night and day – from Cory's dreams and from Cory's long enthusiastic descriptions. He wanted to be the first human to breathe those strange, perfumed winds; explore the myriad islands and the vast artificial lagoons where the purples farmed the sea; those teeming green cities, full of music and dancing. He wanted to see silver boats and towns in space, a moon even more magnificent than Earth's, and meet a people wise and humane, a people who had found a kinder path, who would teach and inspire him.

How he wanted to hear a new music, new stories, and help bring humans and purples together. Of course, he'd be bringing the best of Earth to show them – and of course, with Molly by his side.

If he could only enchant Molly with the idea, all her worries about what might happen would melt away. He needed to share the adventure with her. No dream without her was worth having. The purples would save Earth, Crooked Street – and Amber Grove would always be there. But they were young, and this was a chance that four billion people could only dream of.

Now, when Gene looked at the sky, in his mind he stuck out his thumb. With guitar and a few bags, the Myers family would hitch a lift to the stars.

CHAPTER 7

A stand-off

Two days later, the news was full of the snakes in Australia. Molly had seen the snakes in Cory's dreams, with mouths of fire soaring through the skies like jet planes, turning at sickening, inhuman speed. The French wildlife researchers' film showed enough to be eerie, but not enough to convince the sceptics.

Selena was a little like those sceptics – thinking only of her own dilemmas, she waved away the snakes, politics, the war.

Together in Selena's bedroom, Molly held her hands. 'He can't come here. He won't come here. But we ought to make decisions . . .'

'Not now.'

'We could file the divorce papers.'

'Not now, M. Can't you just make him go away? Get the Ship to blow his car up, or something?'

Molly imagined the great silver machine hanging over Bradleyburg. That was the last thing they needed, even though she was so angry with Mason, with the abuse, and the lies he had told his boys about Cory.

'I don't feel well. I don't feel like *me*,' Selena cried.

Mason's lawyer had sent a long careful letter, urging a meeting. Selena had used the Myers' lawyer to send an undiplomatic reply. Mason could file criminal charges, she explained, but so could she. Gene thought Mason would have to go home eventually – surely his employer wouldn't give him weeks off just to chase his family?

It stuck in Molly's craw, but she decided that the best thing might be if both sides kept quiet about the assault. A sort of nuclear stand-off. Mason could admit adultery; Selena and the kids could stay in New York. They could compromise with a legal separation . . .

Yet a thought always persisted, nagging at Molly: would *she* walk away from her kids? *Ever? No*, she thought, *not even faced with a whole civilisation who wanted him back*. Mason might be just as resolute.

'Maybe I should talk to him,' Molly said.

'You take good care of me,' Selena said. Molly took that as a yes.

Molly was not surprised that Mason refused to come to Amber Grove, where Sheriff Olsen walked the streets. A controversial figure, the press had talked a lot about the Sheriff and the tales that surrounded him. It had been Olsen, of all people, who had found Cory and his dying mother, who had helped Dr Jarman and the Myers keep him a secret.

If the meeting had to be in Bradleyburg, Molly wanted to meet somewhere that was safe and private, but that could become public if they needed. She traded a favour. Bradley's Stores agreed to close the coffee shop an hour early, and make sure the window blind was down. It would be private enough, but if she screamed, there would be people around. The Myers knew the unknown way out of that building, so even if they ended up surrounded by press, they had options.

The temptation was always to take Cory into any tricky situation, her much-loved *Get out of jail free* card, but it just would not be fair to have him listen to what would be a disturbing adult conversation. Cory would be with Reuben in the getaway car and they would all be wearing those irritating, invaluable, communicators.

November fell on Bradleyburg's familiar streets like a dark blanket. The town didn't accept being overshadowed by its smaller neighbour and fought hard for its share of visitors' dollars. Molly wore a wig, tinted glasses and headscarf, and did what she could for Gene with a scarf, a borrowed coat and a logger's hat.

They slipped into the building through the staff entrance, where they were met by the manager, who took them through. They were there first. Molly sat where she had once drunk a painful coffee while deceiving Dr Pfeiffer, while the manager applied himself to a big ledger. She took slow sips, thinking the coffee at Francine's was better and half the price.

A few minutes later, Mason and the lawyer appeared. Mason wore his coat awkwardly, for his right arm was in a sling. The lawyer carried an attaché case.

'Molly, Gene,' Mason said. He had one of those bland, square, handsome faces. Molly felt a tremor of revulsion at the feeling that a man who'd hurt a woman was walking the streets free and respectable. She wanted him punished.

As they'd agreed, the Sheriff of Bradleyburg was there, a big, grey-haired barrel of a man.

'There's going to be no unpleasantness,' he said. 'I'm going to have a cup of coffee in that corner.'

Gene shrugged. 'No wife-beaters this side of the table,' he said.

Mason sat, wincing, and the lawyer frowned.

Molly folded her arms and wondered how bad the knife wound really was. With any luck it had got infected.

'How is she?' Mason asked. 'And the kids?'

'Fine,' Molly said. 'But let's skip the chat.'

The lawyer produced a document. 'Mr O'Regan still wants to try for a reconciliation. If there is a temporary period of separation . . .'

'Mason has been violent to Selena and the kids. There will be no reconciliation,' Molly said, although she had no specific instructions from Selena, except to get Mason to go away. 'We have a very detailed affidavit.'

'Well, Mr O'Regan could make the same claim.'

'Self-defence, a desperate act against a violent man.'

'The children need their father.'

'He'll need to move state, then. They're not going back. It will take a great deal before Selena even considers letting him near them.'

'Dragging this into the courts will hurt everyone. "He said, she said" . . .'

'Let justice be done, though the heavens fall,' quoted Gene.

Mason shifted and winced. His body language said he wouldn't let his lawyer speak for him much longer.

'Mr O'Regan's employers might insist on pressing charges.'

'Mr O'Regan's employers might never find her.'

Mason leaped in. 'Look, Molly – of course, you take her side. But, you do understand, I can't give up my kids? I must know they're safe – that she's safe too.'

'You should have thought of that,' Molly snapped.

'She's not well – the way she went for me. She just goes off into these dazes. She lets pots boil over. She might hurt the kids . . . not meaning to, but a fire or something . . .'

Molly had been wondering how well Selena would manage on her own. But that was irrelevant. Her sister wasn't on her own. The lawyer was staring at her, as though he could read her mind.

'We can mend this. The marriage vows . . .'

'She shouldn't be shackled to a dangerous man,' Gene said. He'd never liked Selena, but he was on her side.

'How's the Church with the adultery, the beating her up?' said Molly, wanting to make him squirm, to realise what a public struggle would be like.

She was surprised to see shame, guilt, on his face.

Mason said, 'Our priest told me to find her and make it right. He wants an update.'

The lawyer looked uncomfortable, and Gene was about to weigh into Mason, which was deserved but wouldn't get them anywhere.

'Go home,' Molly said. 'Take the pressure off Selena. The kids can be in school, they're making friends . . .'

Mason frowned, leaned a little forward. The eerie restraint was slipping. Something was burning in him. 'I need to see them now. I'm their father—'

The kitchen door opened, and everyone looked around.

Sheriff Olsen, bare-headed, nodded and walked over to the table. 'Bodge,' he called, 'we must surely owe you dinner.'

'Lars.' The big man was rising from his. 'You should come to ours. Well, I have an errand.'

The manager of the shop had speedily closed his ledger and was heading out. A play was unfolding which Molly didn't understand.

Bodge was speaking as if in court. 'Nothing is going to happen here to disturb the peace of the county. I am right outside the door.'

'Of course not,' Olsen said.

Bodge headed to the door.

'You have no jurisdiction here,' the lawyer told Olsen, a little too fast and high to be commanding.

Olsen slapped his chest. 'I'm not wearing a badge. Bodge and I know the boundary to the inch. He's said it: no disturbing the peace here. I've just come to see my friends the Myers.'

'You're no stranger to either side of the law,' the lawyer said.

Mason was glaring at Olsen, weighing him up.

Gene had a reassuring hand on Molly's thigh. Had he expected the Sheriff?

'This is a friendly discussion.' Keeping his voice level and calm, Olsen said, 'Mrs O'Regan doesn't want you around and I think that's a good place to start.'

'You can't keep me from my kids,' Mason said.

'Well, courts, that sort of thing – I mean, I haven't seen any evidence. I'm keeping an open mind on who started this fight, a big man who played football at college, or a housewife. Maybe we should ask my old friend the judge.'

'I'm not scared of you.'

Olsen's face did not change. 'Maybe you should be – afraid of the law, anyway. Mind you, the law doesn't always find the culprit. This guy I knew, a big drunk old farmer, he used to knock his wife around. She was a slip of a thing, half his weight. He hurt the kids too. Honey, the woman, was too frightened to testify – well, she was almost a kid herself. My wife spent an evening trying. There was nothing I could do.'

'This is hardly relevant,' said the lawyer.

That awful story. They said Olsen and three of his deputies had jumped the man – and, at that point, imagination took over, with lurid versions about what had been said and done. Olsen never denied the story; he'd just smile and refuse to discuss it at all.

'Anyway – strangest thing – the man fell off the barn roof one day, broke his leg and changed his mind in hospital. You could hardly believe it. Never climb on a roof drunk, Mr O'Regan.'

'Don't you threaten me,' said Mason, and there it was: the pretence was off. Mason was dangerous, and angry.

The lawyer looked at Olsen like he was a seventeen-foot-long crocodile.

'Lay a finger on my client, and you'll rot in jail,' the lawyer said.

'I'm not having a brute like you harassing a scared woman, O'Regan. Go to the press, go to the courts, and things will get nasty. There'll be a lot of mud your kids will hear. One step into Amber County, and I swear on the Good Book, the law will protect her.'

Almost on cue, almost as though he had been listening, the other Sheriff swept in.

'Lars,' said Bodge.

'I'm finished here,' Olsen said. Olsen: the man who had saved Cory twice. He was part of their circle, this flawed, dangerous man.

'Your threats don't frighten me,' Mason said.

Olsen grinned. 'I haven't made any threats, Mr O'Regan. Just offered neighbourly advice. You'd sure know if I'd used a threat.'

That evening, while Molly was reading to Cory in bed, he asked, 'Will Bad Man Mason stay away?'

'We hope so. And we can hide Selena and the boys if not.'

'Good.' Cory sighed, his copy of a human sigh. 'My people need to come very soon. I cannot find them again in dreams. Cory is despondent.'

'They'll come,' Molly said. Finding-in-dreams had come to nothing, as the Ship had warned. How much he must want his people, heart and body and soul. She understood how he must be feeling, because that was how she badly she wanted him.

'And they will sort this world out and then we can go to my home-world. Dad says all the Myers can go together.'

Odd, she thought. She wondered just what Gene had said. 'Well, sweetie-pie, I don't know that's going to happen.'

'Dad says we must go and see home-world. He promised. Big

adventure, chance-of-a-lifetime. You must come too, Mom.'
Cory looked anxious. 'All the excitement, all the people. First
humans coming to First Harbour . . .'

It made her crazy, Gene promising things he could not
deliver.

'Well, we can talk about everything when they come, can't
we.'

It wasn't the answer Cory wanted. He grew sadder. 'Mom
does not want to go,' he said.

'Cory, Grandpa and Grandma might not be well enough . . .'

'Huh. My people have much better medicine than humans.
Can bring everyone. I so love Earth, but I want to go home.'
Then, wailing, 'So fed up with being solo – being castaway
orphan. Being the only one.'

What could she say? What could she do? She kissed him and
said, 'We'll work something out. It would be such an adventure.
And Cory, you are not alone.'

'Don't leave me, Mom. Everyone left me. Everyone died.'

She sang to him, knowing she had disappointed him. He
closed both sets of eyelids, and turned on his side to sleep –
and, all the while, she told herself, Gene would not have
promised . . .

Molly slipped into the big room, where Gene was staring at
music sheets like they could bite. 'He's asleep,' she said.

'Great,' Gene said. 'I can't pretend this garbage is going anywhere.' He got up to embrace her.

'He was talking,' Molly ventured, 'about when his people
come.'

'They'd better come,' Gene said. 'Snakes landing – we need

their help. This is such small stuff, much smaller than Pevek. I wonder if they're testing us?'

Maybe, but she had to settle this first. 'It sounded . . .' Now it felt petty. 'He was saying, we ought to go with him, go home with him.'

Gene looked at her — and she realised that she had been a fool. The man who still read those stupid books wanted to go into space. Of course he did.

'It might be an idea,' he said.

She felt hot. *Keep calm, Molly.* 'You want to go — you promised Cory we'd go. Was that smart?'

'Molly-moo, just think: who else is going to have the chance? They're not going to be flying tourist trips on Pan Am, not for a while.' He was trying to persuade her, as if this were a fortnight vacation.

'I mean, it's dangerous,' she countered. 'Space — the snakes — alien diseases. And years of our lives? And why would they want us? We'd be alone.' The purples were not human, and humans would not fit into their world. Humans lacked the alien lodges, the communion of dreams. Humanity was more violent and savage than the purples had ever been.

'Not for ever,' Gene said, still trying to manage her. 'I mean, we'd really have to like the place to stay. But, you know, they'll sure set up an embassy here, so we'll need a human one there. Why shouldn't we go, for a while? We're family.'

'Yes, *family*. You'd leave your *parents*?'

Gene took her hands and she shrugged him off.

He looked wounded. 'Well, they might need persuading at first. But I'm sure the purple doctors will help them . . .'

Molly felt her anger rise. 'It would mean leaving our friends – bringing up Fleur without human doctors? Without other human children?'

'Maybe we'd take the whole gang. Crooked Street and all.'

She couldn't tell if that was a joke. An hour ago, she'd assumed talk of him going to the home-world was a pipe dream.

'Are you on drugs? The whole idea is *insane*.'

'So is adopting an alien. We made a success of that.' He was getting angry too, and louder.

'I'm telling Cory I won't go.' She went louder still.

'You're being ridiculous. He wants his mom, his sister. What are you going to do, refuse to let him go? Tell the purple civilisation to take a hike?'

It hung in the air for a moment. There was a moment where she could have dodged it, but the time was right. He needed to know.

'I'm not giving him up, Gene.' She stood up. 'We've suffered enough. His place is here, with us. Earth is his home now. The purples will have to live with it.'

He gasped. 'You are *out of your mind*.'

The tiredness, the strain of Selena and Mason, feeling surrounded, with so little safety. The trip west had been just a cover for this – this *betrayal*.

Molly lost her temper. 'I *won't* go,' she snapped. 'And you – you're going to abandon us? Leave Fleur? What kind of a man are you, breaking up the family?'

'Molly, that's not fair. You've just told me you want to pick a fight with a whole species – and I'm the one being crazy?'

'You're selfish. Reckless, thoughtless, dangerous! I won't do it, Gene, I won't. You're not going to run away from us. You're not going to leave the kids without a father. You're not one of those men.'

'It'll destroy him. What if he wants to go?'

'You'll wreck everything if you run away. I might lose both of you.'

'We'll sure lose him if we don't. You're being *impossible*.' He pushed past her and strode through the door, slamming it behind him like an Olympic sport.

You'll wake the baby.

Too late. Upstairs, Fleur wailed.

CHAPTER 8

The Jarman place

Molly sat in a bedroom at the rambling, half-empty Jarman place. Selena was standing by the window, where she could look out, hopefully without being seen. There was noise from the woods, a motorbike on one of the trails.

'It's not him,' Selena said. 'He checked out of the hotel – went back to Indiana.'

'He did. There are people out there – Press, Meteornauts, protestors. But he's gone.' That's what the two Sheriffs thought was more likely than not.

Selena sighed, turned away and walked to the bed. She sat.

'Thanksgiving together at last,' she said. 'This is what it took.'

Humour was good.

Molly said, 'That's right.' There was a lot to do that week. She was hoping all her family and friends could be together. Would John and Eva make it to the Jarmans'? Eva said John needed some more tests. Or would the Myers go to the farm?

Gene wanted to go and bring his parents back; it made her anxious, but it also made sense.

'I'm not one to put my nose in where not wanted,' Selena said, 'but I'm sorry if I've caused trouble between you and Gene.'

'No, not really.' And she found herself confiding in Selena.

But Selena was gentle in her criticism of Gene. 'I see why he's feeling wanderlust. Men feel so pinned down when the baby comes – pushed away. But he's too good a man to let you down . . . You'll figure it out.'

Well! Selena siding with Gene.

'How about *me*? I feel *pinned down* sometimes. I'm a good nurse – I'd like to go back to work. With Cory, now the baby . . .'

There was a muffled noise, a vibration. It took her some moments to realise that it was the communicator, tucked into a pocket. The Ship had turned it on remotely, which she hated. So rude, breaking into a personal conversation.

She talked into the machine. 'Ship, it's not a good time.'

'Mrs Myers, please find Mr Myers. It's urgent and I want to brief you two together. You and only you.'

Selena was staring.

'I won't be long.' Molly went into the corridor and hollered for Gene.

The two of them sat in an unused guest room, Fleur bright-eyed on Molly's lap, listening as the Ship brought them bad news. 'NASA has confirmed that it has lost contact with *Mariner 9*. The probe broke off transmission.'

The unmanned space mission to Mars.

Molly felt the earth lurch under her. She looked at Gene. From his face, he'd had the same thought. The tragedy of last year's Moon landing – the deaths of the two astronauts in *Eagle* – had been the first snake attack. She could think of other reasons why *Mariner 9* might have stopped transmitting – equipment failure, or a meteorite. After all, *Mariner 8* had failed on take-off. But perhaps it was something else.

'It is fruitless to speculate,' the Ship said. 'I will treat this investigation as a priority.'

Gene said, 'The Russians also have probes headed to Mars.'

'I'm aware.'

'Ship . . .' This sounded stupid, so she tried to make it less so. 'Ship, we do rely on you.'

'Of course, I have remotes I can use. However, I will still need to be in the vicinity of the planet.'

Molly rocked Fleur a little, singing to her, but it was not Fleur who needed reassuring. When she found Cory to tell him, his shiver filled the room. Her argument that *Mariner* might have been hit by a rock, or just suffered some malfunction, did not reassure him.

They heard nothing from the Ship until the following evening, when Cory was asleep. The Myers were preparing for bed when the Ship spoke from the communicator without warning, 'Set up the viewing disc and inform me when you are done.'

When they had unfolded the flat black disc about two feet across, on which the Ship could project images, the Ship said without preamble, 'The *Mariner 9* spacecraft was destroyed by snake action.'

Molly felt her stomach jump. Gene took her hand.

'It might have been an automatic reaction by a single snake machine, or it might have been a patrol. Therefore, I investigated Mars.'

The disc leaped into life. Moving pictures showed fast flight above a lifeless surface of rocks and desert, a few drifting patches of dust, and above a sky of murky pink, blue only around the low sun. No plants, no water, no glint of metal. Ahead reared a mountain, a vast cone, and from its flank rose a spume of smoke or dust. Perhaps it was a volcano – did they have those on Mars?

Answering their unspoken question, the Ship said, 'Olympus Mons, the largest mountain on the planet. That plume is a snake excavation.'

Molly felt her heart race as the perspective suddenly shifted. Three silver flames hurtled towards the camera with familiar speed. The unseen device carrying the camera speeded up, rose further from the surface and began a series of stomach-turning evasive manoeuvres. Then the Ship replaced that image with the planet Mars, half in shadow, against a field of stars.

Molly felt nothing but dread.

'They detected my remote. Every time they detect my presence, they attack it. The area was once volcanic, indicating rich mineral resources.'

'Get to the point,' Gene said.

'They are building a production complex like the one on Pevek, from which I deduce they will be building more machines, and more facilities. Even if humans learn of the activity, they are decades off sending a spacecraft, and it will take years to get there. And anything they do send will be swatted from existence: like pitting a child's kite against a military helicopter. However, this does appear to be the snakes' only active complex. They may have inactive facilities elsewhere. I continue my investigations.'

'So what do we do?' Molly wondered.

'Well, to be clear, if they send a scouting party to Earth, I will destroy it. The Russians have given me some of their ridiculous number of fission-fusion weapons, and I have my own resources. Maybe, deterred here, they have lost interest. But maybe they wish to come again, this time in force. The longer we wait, the more resources they will have.'

The Ship stopped a moment, a very human pause. 'The worst-case scenario is that they could build tens of thousands, then millions of machines, all capable of space flight, strategy and attack. They could set up a diffuse production system across the surface, which would be much more difficult to attack, and muster an army far beyond any response I could give, with or without assistance. Fission-fusion weapons are not ineffective, but the snakes will surely find ways to disable the primitive human missiles that deliver them. The war would spread to Earth itself. You can imagine the consequences.'

Gene said, 'Cory's people might come first.'

If they were coming at all . . .

'My analysis is speculative but gloomy. The builders rescue individuals at the most extreme cost. Also, the circumstances under which the colony ship was destroyed surely requires a mission. The builders have not come, which after all this time causes me a high level of concern. The two most probable solutions: they do not know where we are, or the builder civilisation is under too great a threat to come.'

A moment, then it said, 'My responsibility is to Cory, not the Earth. I wish to take Cory, put him in suspended animation and hide him.'

Molly bit her cheek, trying to hold herself together.

'No,' Gene said.

'Only Cory can make that decision. What will help him make it is this: humans are cellular beings. It would not be difficult to test the apparatus on humans; the builders have used it to transport a wide variety of animal specimens to other planets. Obviously with sentients, even minor brain damage must be avoided. I propose to make some urgent experiments, starting with low-sentience mammals, then moving onto humans. If the tests are successful, I might be able to place you, perhaps a dozen humans, all in suspended animation and hide them . . .'

'*Experiments?*' Gene's voice rose. 'We can't have you experimenting on humans—'

'Be logical. Cory will ask me if the machines are safe for you, and I cannot answer that question without experimentation. Assuming the system works, in two months I could place Cory and your immediate social group outside danger.'

Molly was speechless. The world would be left vulnerable to an implacable enemy. The snakes were metal bacteria, breeding and breeding until they could invade: sentient missiles which could make more missiles – and decide when to attack. And the Ship wanted to run away?

'So we nuke them,' said Gene, looking sick. 'Or you help humans build better rockets.' They had met marching for peace – how Molly had loved his passion for peace! – yet here they were, with the survival of Earth at stake and no good answers other than extreme violence.

'My pilot instructed me not to pass technology to humans. That order proves very unhelpful, but I must be clear: my priority is to save Cory, not the defence of the Earth. I regret this.' The machine managed to sound sorry.

Billions of lives.

Molly had never seen Gene grimmer. 'There must be another option.'

'We will need to discuss my plan with Cory, and I need your coöperation, since otherwise you will confuse him.'

'Suppose he refuses. What would you do then?'

'If I cannot hide Cory, then we must remove the threat while it is still contained. That will mean acting now to destroy the base.'

'How?' Gene said.

'Clearly it will be well defended. It is a complex problem. I rescued three major propulsion units from the main vessel. I have repaired them. They could approach the machine nest at very high speeds and be detonated. Other devices would follow them in to confuse and deflect the inevitable attack. One well-placed detonation of this scale could destroy the production facility and most of the robots, perhaps all. The probes and I would follow behind to carry out such further tidying up as necessary.'

Molly was feeling sick to her stomach, thinking of Dr King, all the petitions and letters she'd written, all the songs they'd sung. *Give peace a chance.* She fervently believed in peaceful ends and peaceful means because the human heart could be reached, human beings could be redeemed. There was no heart in a machine to change.

The Ship had learned persuasive intonation. 'They killed four thousand builders in an unprovoked attack. Many human casualties in Pevek. Mrs Myers, even this option poses its difficulties. I am risking mechanisms I cannot rebuild. I will have fewer resources after the attack.'

'But if the attack succeeds, that protects the Earth,' Gene said. 'Maybe. At least, it buys us time. And these things aren't people.' He looked at Molly. 'It's a sort of violent disarmament. Blowing up guns.' He'd used that argument before.

'I prefer evasion,' said the Ship. 'Advise me how to find volunteers, so that I can test suspended animation on humans.'

'We ought to call the President,' Gene said.

'I am not willing to have my freedom to act constrained,' the Ship said. 'Given these facts, the authorities' only logical move would be to force me to protect Earth. To do this, they have an even bigger incentive to capture Cory. That is unacceptable, and a distraction from what I need to do. Tell the government and I will have to fly Cory and you three somewhere beyond their reach.'

'Where?' Molly asked.

'An island, warm, with suitable dwellings and supplies. There are no other inhabitants.'

The humans digested that.

Gene said, 'We need to think about this – how we tell Cory . . . *what* we tell him.'

'Either option requires a quick decision. I am happy to answer further questions. I am making necessary preparations for either plan. The Soviets tell me they have lost contact with both their space probes. They are less easy to stall than the US government. They may go public. They see the Western powers as complacent about snake attack.'

The communicator fell silent.

How do you have that discussion with a child?

It was a restless night, filled with doom-laden dreams. Whenever Molly settled, Gene woke her, getting up to scribble thoughts on paper.

At breakfast, Cory was silent.

'Bad dreams,' he said at last.

'Okay,' Gene said, and set out the situation, as fairly as he could. Each revelation chilled the room until they were all shivering. Molly breastfed Fleur, stroking her cheek to stop her sleeping on the nipple. She said little. This was too much responsibility, even for someone as bright as Cory.

Cory sank his head in his hands. 'Mom, Dad, we can't run away, we just-can't leave and let everyone be attacked. Can't find my people in dreams. Maybe not coming soon. Maybe . . . maybe Cory wrong . . .'

Molly hugged him. She felt ill, thinking about an army which could grow faster than Earth could respond, a nuclear war fought not between people, but between humans and alien machines, machines which didn't need air or water or food, their soldiers without fear or morals, who couldn't be frightened or converted.

'So we tell the Ship to destroy the snakes,' Gene said. 'It's very clever, and if it doesn't get all of them, then we can discuss what we do.'

If the mission failed, then the world would have to work together; there'd be no other option.

It was Cory who spoke to the Ship. 'No running away, no hiding for us. Save Earth, keep yourself safe.'

The Ship didn't trust their friends either. They gathered at the Jarman place on the evening of the attack, listening to the wind outside while a fire blazed inside. Molly imagined death coming down from the sky, robot snakes landing on Founders Green, mushroom clouds rising on every horizon.

What do you do on the day which might be the end of the world? They'd settled for a vague message to their friends. 'You are packed and ready to go, aren't you? We haven't asked for months. Just in case you need to . . .'

Fleur slept, against her warm body. Gene's arm was around her, and Cory snuggled between them like a penguin chick. The dog gnawed at some old bone.

'There have always been predators.' Cory shivered. 'Things that ate us. We had to be better at hiding and scaring. We had to be smarter.'

Being a mother, Molly thought, *there is always something to fear, always something to hope for – and always some things you just don't know. Children think you are in control, and on your first day you learn you're not.*

Her amazing son kissed her hand and they gazed together into a dark sky and a hidden future.

'This is the Ship. I am moving into position at very high speed, following the other devices. It will take one direct hit to destroy the nest.'

The Ship chimed, bells and flutes, then added a few words in Cory's language.

'Hunting song,' Cory said. 'About . . . hunting sea beasts that kill.'

Molly had seen the monsters in Cory's dreams. The snakes were worse. She closed her eyes and breathed, in and out, in and out, asking the unfeeling universe for success.

'I am meeting defensive action and in force. I was wise to use remotes near Mars.'

'We don't need a commentary,' Molly said.

How foolish that sounded aloud.

The Ship ignored her and carried on, 'I have detonated the first missile, sacrificing it to clear the approach.'

Two left.

'My remotes are suffering significant losses – but so are they. I am making progress. The second missile is largely past their defences.'

A pause. 'A partial hit. The missile deviated off-course and exploded early. I cannot be sure I have done enough damage.'

'They've got some defence you don't know about?' Gene asked.

'The third missile is on track. Yes, some form of interference, but I am switching systems. On track.'

Gene was clutching Molly's hand so hard it hurt.

The machine made a deep ringing gong. 'I have made a direct hit. The facility is destroyed.'

The Ship began to chant.

'Hunting song,' Cory said.

> *'Harpoons hit home*
> *our aim was true*
> *have slain the demon*
> *killer of the people*
> *monster in the dark*
> *harpoon hit home*
> *big feasting tonight.'*

Odd, that Cory's people of old ate the clawed sea monsters, but practical, since they had killed them for self-defence.

Gene breathed out a little more. 'Ship, how many probes survived? Are you damaged?'

Cory's language trilled out of the communicator.

Cory's fear raised the hairs on Molly's skin and stopped the breath in her throat.

'Ship, are you there?'

'This is unfortunate,' the Ship said. 'The nest was destroyed, but I am under attack. There is a substantial craft approaching at very high speed, surrounded by smaller craft. An effective ambush. My detection systems are inadequate.'

'Ship,' Molly said, 'whatever happens, we need you. Don't take risks. Run away. We need you back here. You're our last hope, to help us defend, to explain . . .'

Cory spoke in his own language, and the machine answered in kind.

Then it spoke English. No emotion, just a little emphasis in the sentences. 'No time, Mrs Myers. This vessel is faster than I am. This has been a significant misjudgement. It has a faster-than-light capacity, and they are preparing to use it. If they wish, they can flee – and disappear from my reach. Maybe to alert others or build a fleet somewhere else, too big for me to defeat.'

'My people are coming!' Cory said.

'It would be better to have reliable evidence,' the Ship said.

Cory gave the Ship an order, shrill and angry.

Molly's skin crawled as she felt his fear.

'This is a threat to Earth, and to the builder home-world. I will act to fulfil the mission.'

Gene said, 'Ship, retreat. Regroup . . .'

It almost sounded gentle. 'Today, I may outgun them. In a month I won't. In six months, they could destroy the Earth with impunity. I must strike this formation and detonate my engines. It should be highly effective. If I am to be destroyed, at least I will take the danger to Cory with me.'

Cory fluted.

'I'm afraid I'm not going to do that, Cory. No time to debate, Mrs Myers. I leave you the mission. Keep Cory safe.'

Molly felt a great wash of horror from Cory. Meteor whined. The Ship was chanting again.

'Hoo-hoo,' Cory said. 'Song means . . .

> *I have mission*
> *to protect the lodge*
> *a sacred trust*
> *protect the young*
> *prepare my weapon*
> *protect the lodge . . .'*

Cory spoke to it, sharply, and the Ship answered in a few crisp syllables. Then there was silence.

'Disobeyed.' Cory moaned. 'Bad-brave-naughty Ship.'

A minute or so later, the communicator crackled static and fell silent.

The Myers were too stunned to act. Fear hung around the room like mourning clothes in an old photograph. Fleur woke up, grizzling, so Molly sat in the big chair and fed her. Gene sat on the bed, his face drawn, his arm around Cory. Every few minutes, intense coldness came off him, making Molly's skin crawl and her heart jump. Gene winced, and each time, Fleur stopped sucking and opened her mouth to wail. Molly couldn't tell where her son's sadness and confusion ended and hers began.

It can't be good to have Fleur near Cory in this state. It can't be good to leave Cory alone.

What were they going to do? Surely, as soon as the authorities knew, they would send soldiers to protect the Myers.

Her son wailed. 'Ship . . . Ship protected us in all ways and now Ship is gooone! *Hoo-hoo-hoo.* What if more snakes come?' Then he babbled in his own impenetrable language.

'Cory, it will be all right,' Gene said, the parent's hopeful lie.

Molly's communicator was dead. A sudden thought struck her: what would happen if the Ship's defences in Amber Grove went down with it? Gene's anxious eyes met hers. There was no book in any library for any of this. They needed information from Cory, but he was in no state to talk calmly.

Was the Network, the Ship's eyes and ears in space, still working?

'Everyone dead and now Ship gooone. *Hoo-hoo-hoo*. If anything breaks, I may not be able to repair it.'

Gene said, 'Perhaps we should hit the hay, Big Stuff. Your mutt will miss you.'

Cory had a hand to his head. 'What-are-we going-to-do?'

'Hot milk,' Gene ordered and led Cory from the room.

Molly looked at Fleur dozing on the breast and a weird fear gripped her, a dreadful idea that kept swimming up. She became paralysed with the choice facing them.

An hour later, Gene came back. He looked gaunt, like someone human had died, as he went over to the crib, and peeked in. Fleur was deeply asleep, a little bundle in pink. He touched her ear with a finger, as gentle as the thought of a kiss.

'He's going to chase up his people in his dreams. I just hope . . . I just hope they're coming.'

She rose and put her arm round his waist; instinctively, his arm went around her shoulder.

'We have to run,' she said. 'The Army. The Mob. The press. We have to tell our friends.' She looked down on her daughter and wondered what world she had brought her into. 'Do you think Cory . . . the sadness . . . do you think it will hurt her?'

'He's a great big brother. She's lucky. But it sure couldn't hurt just to . . . you know, avoid her being around his nightmares.'

Gene bent down to kiss her, but Molly was numb.

The Ship felt no need to respond to humans unless it wanted to. Its absence would not be noticed at once. But *Mariner 9* had gone. The Administration and the Russians would have suspicions within a day, at most. They had so little time.

Molly knew this would be a time of parting, a time of loss.

It was a bitter truth – their friends and family would seek the Governor's protection. Gene and Molly had their own plan, which was very different.

Molly made the decision. 'We've got to wake our friends.'

CHAPTER 9

Interstellar space

Thirty days into its mission, *Kites at Dusk* cruised through the brilliant sea of stars. It sang a duet with its sibling ship, *Repurpose Snakes as Dung Buckets*, the other half of the mission. Machine minds searched in every direction for the predators, the snakes, the enemies of life.

Thunder Over Mountains came into the feeding place, where he was hit by a symphony of smells, feelings and sound. He picked up the strong scent of four-spice, stirring his memories of beach feasts under the stars with a whole theme of briny sea mollusc notes. And, of course, he smelled the crew and felt traces of their emotions – the notes of anxiety and confinement. Barely thirty days from home, the mission just underway, and fear was growing. It muted his hunger. The first step of the mission was Waystation Jewel, and who knew if it would be there when they arrived? Out there among the stars were the metal predators, the destroyers of the colony-world . . .

The hymn of resistance was like a meditation.

We will make those predators our prey.

Crew were crammed sharing-elbows-and-tails in the feeding stations. Thunder took the food of the day and took the next free seat. He bent his face down to the plate of six-molluscs and land-kelp, savouring before tasting. An impromptu group was trying a joining song, and there was an orchestra of talk.

'Vat food,' said a crewmate he did not know well – a healer-leader. One of his fellow pattern-bridgers joined them.

'Few of us can tell the difference,' Thunder said. Planet-dwellers were always ready to complain about everything. Perhaps they used that to relieve the tension of things they could not change. The starship was less comfortable than he wanted, but what did they expect? The thing he missed to the point of pain was the children back home, those enjoyable, unpredictable hours on the children's roster. All-had-decided, it was now too dangerous to take children to the stars, or to risk conceiving in flight. It was one of a thousand costs of the Hardening.

The screens in the feeding place showed the stars as if to say, look, out there is real. A warning chime meant the ship would soon slip into other-space, to move faster than light. The pictures of stars would disappear and be replaced with reassuring clouds, forests and seas. The unease of being in other-space rather than true-space was almost entirely psychological yet Thunder still felt the difference.

The snake machines, the destroyers-of-life, could not attack in other-space as far as anyone knew. Therefore, it should be by far the more reassuring part of the journey. Some things are not governed by reason alone.

'Thunder wants to find *Dancer on the Waves*,' said his close-colleague.

Part of the mission was to seek out the lost starships, the unexplained losses since the coming of the destroyers. The lost colony ship was of course, the mystery of mysteries. Thunder would make the old discussion as short as he could.

'Is there hope?' the healer asked, a ritual.

'There is always hope,' Thunder said. Yes, the ship and its crew could survive out of contact for years. But there was not an atom of evidence where it was.

Some of the space to be searched for *Dancer* lay in space long conceded to the snakes. If it was there . . . many said there was no hope.

'Seeking the colony ship is little better than walking on the floor of the lagoon, hoping to tread on a particular thorn-fish,' Thunder said. How he wished that was not true.

'Choices must be made,' another said. 'Harder choices than we have known. Why devote any time to it?'

Thunder sent a glance at his lodge-mate: *be silent*.

But the healer gave her own answer. 'Dreaming-between-the-stars may find any of the lost vessels. If enough of the crew live and dream-together . . . if they are within the range . . .'

'. . . then we may yet find *Dancer* by chance, looking for the others.'

For Thunder, faint hope had been replaced with an obsession. He used it to mask his distress, his self-criticism. His unease at dreaming-between-the-stars, the dangerous and unreliable last chance.

The healer turned to Thunder. 'Are you on the search rosters?'

Thunder did not answer. He wasn't.

'Help us look,' the healer said, with enthusiasm. 'What is your lodge position?'

'Anchor, by choice.'

'We need strong anchors. And you are a patterner, a bridger-between by profession, which is a most excellent combination. The dreaming is hard, and not without risk. The more widely we share the burden—'

'The time may come but it is not now.'

He must be polite, so he lowered his mouth to the food and began tentacle feeding. The healer did the same to her last scraps. No offence taken.

Thunder would have his medicinal dose of privacy soon, a precious time to be alone. He almost envied the ship's handful of solos, whose cells were in odd corners of the great ship, allowing them respite from other people. A long and dangerous mission would send more solo. It might push one or two to the sickness-that-kills.

Thunder missed Spinning Disc, his wounded love. It had been the most unhappy of departures, almost a physical pain, as he headed to the stars. He was taking the hunt to the destroyers-of-life. And yet, he wanted others to take the risk of dreaming. Guilt nagged at him.

In the privacy cell, he called up the machine memory of Pilot, his old friend, the mother of his son Little Glowing Blue Frog. He watched scenes of them both, with the little one growing from a cub playing in water, to the splendid child doing the Pioneer dances with such joy for life. These visuals brought love and pain, just like the day the starship *Dancer on the Waves* had embarked for the stars. What a time of hope that had been, a new world for the people. No starship had been lost in twenty-seven years and only two in the sixty-four years before that. Thunder had been in the crowd, echoing the sounds and movements of those leaving. It was a moment of pride for the whole people. But, at that very moment, the snakes had been amassing around the colony-world. Unknown to all, they were only forty days from the home-world.

How Thunder missed Pilot and their son. All had sung their death-praises without the bodies, but how he resented not knowing the means of their death. From the faint fractions of chances, he conjured up the idea that *Dancer* might have survived. Or that Pilot and Little Frog were in suspended animation, hidden from the snakes. It was the most fanciful idea. He almost longed for this dreadful hope to finally die, just so that he could walk on.

He enjoyed the children of the space habitats. But Little Frog was different. Attentive fatherhood had never been the agreement. Sometimes he had skipped a chance to talk to Little Frog. He knew each occasion he had missed, and the boy, warned, was not unduly hurt. Now each time felt a wasted opportunity. He had a dangerous fantasy, that he would find Pilot and their son, and they would be in one lodge for ever.

The healer had sent him a message he did not want to hear. *We need strong anchors, holders-within. Share the burden.*

Mind amplification was respectable, in the hands of the cautious mind-healers. But the fringes of the field were full of risk-lovers, wild speculators and obsessives, making attempts to unite unnatural numbers in a dream, or to send dreams beyond their usual range. The tales of disaster were not exaggerated. Those in such experiments had been damaged in the nine senses, or driven to the sickness-that-kills. Worst of all, whole lodges had been dream-burned, frightening isolation from the-all. Before Thunder was born, all-had-decided on a strict prohibition.

Then the destroyers came, and the unthinkable had become thinkable, to save the people and their planet. Despite the-all-had-forbidden, it emerged that shocking experiments had continued, and now dreaming-between-the-stars was a tool, however flawed, to link the people across the vastness of space. Perhaps it could transmit a little knowledge faster than the snakes could – and any edge in the struggle to survive, no matter how desperate, could be considered.

That did not mean he wanted to take the risk. Even the training unnerved him. Dreaming-between-the-stars produced phantoms from children's tales, things that could not be explained.

Privacy time was over. He would search for lost ships using intellect instead, piecing together probability and clues.

Outside their private place was a crew-friend, hopping from one foot to another, eager to pass on every rumour and gossip.

'The dreamers—'

'Yes?'

'They found a person. A single dreamer, frightened and alone.'

'Impossible,' he said, and felt foolish. Dreaming-between-the-stars was new, but already the people knew that it could not always be relied on. What, less than sixteen days ago, there'd been the same claim of a finding a solo. Some in the dream had not been convinced; most now said it was a phantom.

'Do we have anything personal? Any idea of where?'

'Very little. A brief contact – terrified, calling for help, alone. Those in that other dream think it's the same person. The sceptics last time now think it is a true dreaming.'

Who dreams alone when they can dream together?

'They must try again,' he said, a torrent of feelings bubbling up. This was nothing. It was probably nothing.

It might be one of the crew of *Dancer on the Waves*. It might be Pilot, or Little Frog.

Terrified. Alone. Needing help.

'What did they sense of the dreamer?'

His friend knew what he was thinking and took his hand. 'They said, it might well be a child.'

He knew the odds against, yet the hope blazed up and burned until it hurt inside him.

Terrified. Alone. Needing help.

CHAPTER 10

Midnight

Gene and Molly were all but packed. Molly looked round the safe, familiar bedroom, a world she was about to lose for the second time. She wiped her eyes. 'I'm going to wake Selena.'

'Jeez.' Gene scowled and looked at his watch. 'Let's just go. We haven't got time.'

'She might want to come.'

'Tough. You saw the weather forecast.'

'Don't you think she deserves to decide?'

Gene slammed his case shut and snarled, 'How long will Big Sis take to get ready? Two hours? She likes the Jarmans, she sure needs professional help, she's safe enough with them.'

Molly knew all this. 'Don't be like that. I'm all she's got.'

'She'll slow us up. She'll sure be pissed with you when she finds out, but let her.'

Downstairs, her friends were debating how long to give the Myers before they called Governor Rockefeller and put their own protection plan in motion. From that first argument here, all those months ago, to Diane's birthday only a month ago, the same decision stood. John and Eva had made the same choice, and indeed, their health made it inevitable.

Molly tried not to see the split as a betrayal. Gene and Molly just didn't trust the billionaire Governor, they couldn't. The President held the only prize the man could not buy – anointment as the President's preferred successor.

Molly wanted the same as Gene. 'I agree she should stay. But we need to persuade her – not run away.'

'Disappearance Inc might not take her.'

'Uh . . . I warned Pierre we might be two cars, six people, and a dog.'

Gene grabbed the cases. 'Your sister will screw everything up. I'll look round Cory's room again.'

Disappearance Inc was a quixotic network, an Underground Railroad for those strange times. They moved people and hid them, and they'd never lost a client. It had been Pierre from the network Carol and Storm had turned to, to hide the Myers at Christmas.

Molly woke Selena, deep in a medicated sleep, and it was ten confused minutes or more before Selena truly grasped the danger. Then, she was terrified.

She gripped Molly's hands, like she was drowning. 'I want to go with you,' she said. 'Where are we going?'

'To stay with friends. People who have done this before. Sel, you'd be so much better off staying . . .'

Selena's eyes filled with tears, and the lamentations began, just as Gene predicted.

'I don't understand, M. If it's not safe, why aren't the others going with you ... Why aren't Rosa and Dr Jarman coming ...?'

Gene left and came back with Rosa, to argue Selena out of it, and tapped his watch again. The minutes ticked on, two persuading against one, then Dr Jarman came looking like a bear shaken awake from hibernation. It was three arguing against one. Selena, sick and frightened, proved to have a backbone of steel.

'Molly, I'll take my chances with you.'

Gene broke the impasse. 'Selena, can you be outside and ready in forty minutes? We'll all help.'

'Yes. Yes. *Thank you.*'

'For the record, I think this is dangerous and dumb.'

'Taking Cory away from the best medicine humanity can offer him? That's dangerous,' said Jarman. 'Even now ...'

'We've planned this,' Molly snapped. The little voice that said *stay with Jarman* used that argument. But they had enough alien drugs for decades and the machines that synthesised his blood. Molly had the book listing everything they knew, and Disappearance Inc included at least one doctor.

No time for long goodbyes as the first flakes of snow started to fall. They'd need to borrow two cars. Selena was compliant, not arguing long over anything. They dressed Connor and Rory, ignoring sleepy protests, and put them under blankets in the back of one car. The Myers loaded Cory into the other, the blue Chrysler, and he went straight back to sleep. It was closer to an hour, but they were ready.

All their friends stood solemnly, for the last embraces.

Dr Jarman and Rosa, who had fought to save Cory's life, Roy, who could have betrayed them and who had been the most loyal of all. Janice and Diane, who understood her.

No light came from the media shanty town, or the scattered tents of those who waited for reasons of their own. Gene drove out of the gate, followed by Serena. Reuben drove a Jeep behind them, ready to frustrate any followers.

'Your sister drives like a nun to a funeral,' Gene snapped, and Molly's heart was close to breaking. No one followed, and after a few miles, Reuben flashed his headlights in farewell. They were on their own.

They reached a summer place, a house deep in the woods, one of several they'd been offered if they needed. After a few brief hours sleep, Molly woke in an unfamiliar bed, barely knowing what day it was. She fed Fleur while Gene snored on, oblivious. Thank goodness Gene had agreed to halt there, when neither of them were really fit to drive.

Long before they returned to Amber Grove, Gene and Molly knew they needed a plan. They had been bombarded with offers of sanctuary, at a time when they didn't need them, everyone from Robin Heights, Michigan (population 1011) to a hundred different nations – and the New York Mob.

Carol and Storm had introduced them to Disappearance Inc in New York. The Myers liked them, and Cory trusted them. They had a twelve-year flawless track record, and from the advice offered, they understood how the FBI worked, how to move money, how to get false papers. It was run on idealism, on pay what you can.

Gene and Fleur slept on, and Molly went into the kitchen, to find Cory cooking his own oatmeal. From the smell, Cory had fed Meteor sardines and bread rather than open the emergency dog food.

Tick tock tick tock. Who buys a clock that loud?

Cory moved the oatmeal off the hotplate and went into her arms for a hug.

Molly wanted to say it would be all right – it's the parent's job to reassure the child – but she could not bring herself to say it. They needed to be lost to the world before the authorities acted. She held him as if to stop him flying away. There was grief and fear in him, but something like hope too.

After a long hug, there came a sigh. 'Thank goodness my people are coming,' he said.

'Oh,' she said, not thinking much of it. 'Did you get a message?'

'A dreaming-together.' He broke the embrace to gaze into her face. '*Definitely* a dreaming-together. My people, Cory is just so sure. In a starship.' A beat, then, 'Well, what else could it be? Impossible not to be a starship. I was having a nightmare, so I went into dreaming-together layer and there it was. Little and bright and far away. But I joined it. Real deal.'

She could hear Gene's voice in her head. *It sure sounds like wish fulfilment to me*. The night that the Ship, Cory's protector and confidante, was destroyed, he dreamed of rescue.

'What happened? Did they speak?'

'They are looking for me. They called out to me; they're coming.' He was holding her again. 'Mom needs to believe me.'

It seemed safe to say, 'I hope they are coming. You know we don't understand dreaming.'

'Cory needs to find them again. Make sure they know where I am. Make sure the message vessel got through.'

'You do that,' she said, full of emotion, fearing for her family, for the Earth – needing the purples to come, and trying to ignore that stab of fear that they would take Cory away if they did. She thought of all the times Cory had come into her dreams, full of feelings and colour and smells.

'Let's have breakfast.'

Tick tock tick tock.

The children had argued and gone to different rooms. The adults sat in the kitchen, almost too warm now, with a large map in front of them. Selena was in talking waxwork mode, only half there.

'We've spent a lot of time thinking about vanishing,' Gene said. He couldn't stop touching his face, where he had shaved down to a moustache. Their experiments last spring convinced him that it disguised him more than being either clean-shaven or having a beard.

'Option one is Canada,' he said. 'Then anywhere in the world. Our friends can get us across the border without any fuss.'

Selena didn't react. Gene went on, 'Well, we have plenty of Cory supporters in the west . . .'

'Honolulu,' Selena said, smiling at Molly. That brought back memories of so long ago. The sisters' code word for travel and adventure. 'You know so many people. Could we hide in Hawaii?'

Molly could see Gene's mind whirl. He grinned. 'Why not?'

'But it's not a plan,' Molly said. They'd had offers from the

West Coast. Some of the people seemed very loose-lipped. Pierre would not fly them that far.

'Let's just get somewhere safe, just for now,' she said.

Gene gave her a glare. *Don't be difficult.* 'Well, now we're safe to drive, we need to get moving. The weather forecast is trouble.'

Molly nodded. 'If we rendezvous with Pierre, we can review the options.'

'One Molly one vote,' Gene grunted.

Molly gritted her teeth.

Selena drained her coffee. 'The sooner we get out of the state, the better. I've no doubt Mason will be back.'

Gene hated the moustache. Molly thought it was rather dashing. A brief bedroom thought, a touch of joy when the world was so dark. Molly called the message service again, left another message. A few hours without an answer, it didn't mean anything.

CHAPTER 11

Heading east

The sky threatened snow as Gene pulled into a gas station. Despite Selena, they were making fair time. While Molly went to the payphone, Gene stretched his back facing away from the road and the station, hoping Selena and her boys would not take too long in the bathroom. Cory hid and took himself and Meteor behind some bushes for a comfort break.

Up above them hung a big billboard for *Supper Out of This World*. It was a brilliant poster campaign, but it still drove Gene crazy. Sailor's Knot implied the Myers endorsed their tinned tuna, though in reality it was all Madison Avenue flimflam.

Molly caught Selena outside the bathroom; they chatted, just a few sentences, then Molly walked over frowning. 'The kids are fine. I left another message.'

A big 'what if' hung in the air.

Dr Jarman was right, Gene thought. They really should go west. More options if Cory was sick. Pierre could get them to a plane west if not fly them himself.

'Let's keep going,' Molly said. 'I'll take a turn at the wheel and we'll find somewhere the kids can run around for a bit.'

Back in the car, they hit the road again working their way through small towns, stretches of ugly urban sprawl and long stretches of farm and woodland, Selena following. On the back seat, Cory was silent, lost in his own thoughts. The radio burbled.

Soon the road was running alongside the sluggish grey river. A sign said, *Old Watermill Museum*. In the parking lot were two school buses and a car. *Nope*.

A mile further on, the land climbed and a historic bridge of green iron crossed the river, perhaps twenty feet above the water. The water was narrower here and faster. This side of the river, there was a picnic area.

'No one picnicking today,' Molly said, turning into it. Nor was there anyone in sight. A hut for refreshments was shuttered and the bathroom locked behind a metal grille.

'Meteor needs a big bathroom break,' Cory announced – by which he meant that *he* wanted a run as much as the dog.

Gene needed fresh air too, and a walk to unknot his neck and shoulders. As he got out of the car and Molly started fussing Fleur, the wind rustled in the trees. No birds sang.

Gene cast his eyes around the picnic site. They were in clear sight of the road from here; they really shouldn't linger.

Molly is wrong about the West Coast crew, he thought as he took a few steps, putting the walkie talkie in his pocket. But you had to tread carefully to win an argument with her in her dark, unpleasant moods. Right now, Cory's health would be the doubt in her mind.

Cory's waterproof was deliberately two sizes too big, so the hood pretty much hid he was an alien, although those paying attention might wonder at his movements.

'Let's look at the river,' Gene said, and without waiting for an answer, took Cory and Meteor along the path. Frozen mud sometimes cracked underfoot, it was treacherous. There was a shallow route down.

'Gene, don't go too far!' Molly called. She was already deep in some conference with her sister – probably plotting to out-vote him on where they would go. Pierre had a plane, anything was possible.

'Throw sticks in river,' Cory said.

'You're a great swimmer, Cory,' said Gene when they reached the swift river's edge, 'but don't get too close. Keep Meteor away too. If she falls in, it would be real dangerous to rescue her.'

'Cory is not some reckless little kid.'

'It's my job to worry about bad things.'

'Grown-up job on my planet too,' said Cory. 'Sorry, my *other* planet too.'

It was worse when he corrected himself.

There was frozen mud under the thin snow, but they were wearing boots and there were rails by the steps. Cory had his walking stick and from time to time, Gene grabbed hold of branches. It wasn't too bad. Meteor, of course, would be filthy by the end of it – but Meteor sucked up mud like a magnet; she could get dirty running across a dry lawn in summer.

Gene checked his watch. Five minutes by the river, then back.

Time to have the argument.

They heard voices ahead. Emerging back onto the riverside, the path ran under the bridge. Up ahead were four boys, who stopped to look at him. Three teens, not fully grown, and the fourth a kid . . .

The smallest had his hands tied behind him; his face and clothes were smeared with mud. Despite the bitter cold, he wore neither coat nor hat. When he met Gene's eyes, Gene saw he was gagged.

An old memory of terror and humiliation hit Gene: two kids forcing Gene to his knees, stuffing underwear inside his mouth. Old fears and new fury rising inside him, he left caution behind.

'What the hell is going on?' he said in his most adult voice. The three older kids were aged between fourteen and sixteen, all shorter than Gene, and none had the fuller jaws of adult men. Two looked defiant, but the third in a red wool hat showed shame, turning away from Gene's gaze.

'Just a game, mister,' said the tallest, the broadest, the leader.

Part of Gene's mind had to worry about Cory, but he had that odd sensation he sometimes felt, like a silent note, that Cory must have hidden. 'Well, he doesn't want to play any-more. Let him go.' It was an adult order, uncompromising. No 'boys will be boys' here. His most shameful memories were times when he'd let things happen to others. The power of the bully lay in the failure of men who stood by when these things happened.

Yet they had numbers, one was holding a stick, and Gene had Cory to protect.

'Shame if he fell in,' said the leader. His bovine, cruel face stirred more memories.

124

Yes, thought Gene, *they probably could shove their victim off the bank.*

After all, his hands were tied. Gene could swim, but that would be a tricky rescue, and dangerous for sure. It was a clever, nasty threat.

'You'll go to jail,' Gene said, every ounce the strong adult in charge. 'The most trouble you'll ever have been in.'

Gene was getting through to Red Hat, who was looking shaken.

'Let's leave him, just go,' Red Hat said. 'Sorry, mister, we'll get back.'

'You fag,' said the leader. 'I knew you were a fucking girl.'

The two teens were standing tall – and a fresh anger rose in Gene. He wished he had his own stick to use as a weapon. He moved a few steps towards them.

'You, in the red hat. Help the kid further away from the water and we'll say no more about it. Your friends aren't stupid, they realise they're in big trouble. They'll decide to be smart too.'

Gene saw the bullies' eyes dart behind him, saw one of them mouth a word – and he heard Cory screech – a noise which you knew no human throat could make. *Crack* – there was someone else behind him, and to the right.

'You stupid fuck,' said the head bully.

A splitting pain lanced across the side of Gene's head. He staggered, lost his footing, plunged down onto the ground, all the breath knocked out of him.

Nothing quite made sense. Time slowed as he fell. Gene was sliding, trying to grab something, but his hands only found frozen mud. There was some thorny bush; he caught hold of it and came to a painful, twisted stop.

Somehow, he was wet and close to blacking out.

Cory's power flooded out, all bitter fear and anger . . .

Cory unhid, and Meteor began a furious barking. Cory was so-scared and he felt his power rise in him. Four bullies – although one looked sorry. His beloved Earth-father slid closer to the river. The walkie talkie was in his pocket, so Cory could not even call for help. *Shouting might bring others*, Cory thought – but the Bad Almost Man who threw the big chunk of wood had seen Cory and was coming towards him.

He must control his power. He squatted to grab Meteor, who wanted to bite the youth.

Dad was big and heavy – how would he get him up the slope?

Everyone he loved on the great starship had died. *Everyone.* He had lost his protector, the Ship. He ought to hide Dad and wait for Mom, but Cory felt his power surging, demanding he use it. He hated what it did to humans, but this fright and anger would not let him hide. It would not be stopped.

Cory screamed an order at the humans, then realised it was in the people's language; they would not understand – but he was losing control. He had to warn them, he had to. 'STOP!' he screamed. 'Run-away bad people! Run-away before Cory hurts you!'

'Grab the freak,' the head bully shouted, starting to come forward. The youth closest was more scared of furious Meteor than Cory.

His fear and anger fed the power, and it was stronger than he was. He saw the boy's face twist, and Meteor began to whine.

He wrestled to control it. Cory would only scare the almost-adults – he wouldn't hurt them. They would run away.

A nightmare came and the power took it. In the cold polar seas of his home-world, the second most deadly predator floated, waiting for its prey. A translucent blue thing, spineless and brainless, the size of a table, it dragged behind it a hundred stinging cords which carried a paralysing venom. You could not hide from it, for it had no brain to confuse, and its response to being scared just made it all the more dangerous. It unfurled its webs of death and paralysed you, then it would surround you, summoning others of its sort to digest you. Cory made the venom-web and sent it out into the human minds.

The nearest bully froze, feeling the dream burn his skin with cold, then slow his breathing.

'Jesus Christ!' he gasped, before he began to choke. The stench of urine rose in the air as he fell into a mass of thorns, so Cory focused on the other two, who screamed and skidded away.

The sorry-now teen in the red hat was dragging the little kid to safety.

Threatening a little kid? Nothing like this could happen on his planet.

Cory wanted to stop. Cory wanted to and run and check his Earth Dad was breathing, but his fear now rode him, a useless fear.

The Bad Almost Man who threw the stick was now thrashing in the mud, having a fit like poor Meteor had, the leader was kneeling, his hands to his own throat. The fastest runner was furthest away, he too tripped and fell.

Meteor was whining in fear, and it was only then that Cory

realised he must rein back the dream, stop them thinking that their muscles were not working. Cory the Monster might kill them.

Cory fought his power for control.

Selena was smoking and half watching Connor and Rory as they stomped about, when Molly heard the screech from the riverside.

Cory's in danger.

Selena dropped the cigarette, her eyes wide. Molly froze for a second – then thrust Fleur towards her sister. 'Take the baby,' she said.

She could see a car coming up the road from the mill, slow even for this weather.

As she slipped and slithered down to the river, she felt the dreadful, familiar cold of something big and dangerous touch her mind. Cory was using his horrific power.

'Sweetie-pie,' she called out, not daring to use his name, 'Mom's coming!'

Molly fell, a hard fall, and she was muddy now. Getting to her feet, she came face to face with a teen in a red hat, struggling to untie a younger boy.

He looked at her, and said, 'It wasn't me. You with Cory Myers? He tried to help us—'

She pushed past him and there they were: Gene, on hands and knees, and two teens lying flat, stunned or dead, she couldn't tell. Cory, hood back and visible, stood quivering, trying to bring his power under control.

She enfolded her son in her arms, whispering words of love,

and got a strong sense of the thing he was creating: a cold death for a cold day.

Bit by bit, Cory got control, and the thing faded.

There was blood on Gene's hands, his temple. He managed, 'The kids – the kids first.'

She rushed to check the teenagers. Neither was conscious, but one had a strong pulse, almost racing. The other was sluggish and weak. Not much she could do. Stay? Leave? Get help.

A nurse does the job and has the heebie-jeebies later, Molly told herself. Cory was squatting, drained and shaking, his arms around Meteor. She flipped his hood up to hide him, *oh, sweetie-pie*, and went to examine Gene.

'Get away, get away!' Gene muttered, holding a hand to a wound to the forehead. A hefty chunk of wood had blood on it. Molly tried to look at Gene's pupils, but he was fighting his way onto shaky legs.

What had happened? The first boy said Cory had tried to save them.

Selena appeared, with Fleur strapped to her back, walking stick in one hand and a tyre iron in the other. In her wake came Rory, clutching Connor's arm, both scared and open-mouthed.

'What happened?' Selena hissed. 'There's a car – people.'

In her hurry, Molly hadn't brought the first-aid kit. *You fool.* 'Gene, we need to get back to the car.'

'What happened?' her sister said. 'We felt something.'

'Sel, I need your help, to get them up to the car. I might have something for the teens.'

Connor lifted Meteor, inert. Gene put his arm round Molly, and Cory could just about stumble along.

At the top of the track, a man stood, bald, and round-faced, deeply worried. He was wearing big square glasses, slipping out of fashion, square glasses for a square guy.

'What happened?' he asked.

'My husband fell. There are a couple of sick teens – I think the kids had some sort of fit,' Molly improvised. *Both at once? You need something better.*

'Maybe they use drugs?' she suggested. After all, half the country was frightened of what the other half was taking.

Selena was staring at Cory.

The man blinked. 'I'm Hamish Van-Buren-like-the-President – I'm running a school trip. We're missing some boys – they must have snuck away. Have you seen any others?'

'I'm not sure. My husband's had a bad fall. You should go check on the two back there.'

Connor put Meteor down and both Selena's kids moved away, staring at Cory. The teacher stared too. Cory's face was buried in the dog's flank; he might just pass for human if he didn't look up or speak.

'This all feels wrong,' the man said. Molly saw red hat and the younger kids, over closer to the road. Witnesses. Waving at the school bus.

'I've got to get a first-aid kit,' Molly said, walking Gene past the man. There was another woman by an unknown car.

'So these kids are sick or hurt . . . your husband is hurt . . . what happened?' said Van Buren.

Molly took a breath. He was asking reasonable questions. 'I told you.'

The man gasped. 'Where's your son gone? He's vanished. The dog too – they were right there.'

Frightened, Cory must have hidden; she hadn't noticed.

'You need to go get your kids.' What if they were getting worse?

They had to leave. Molly got Gene into the car, where he sat like a cartoon drunk. She sensed Cory was near, in the car. She put Fleur in her travelling seat. Selena was at the door of her car, talking to her kids inside it . . . then she looked up and stared.

'Where's your son gone?' the man said. 'What's going on?'

'I don't know what you're talking about.'

'I saw who he is,' the man said, almost a whisper. 'I saw.'

'We'll call for an ambulance . . .'

'We can drive the kids to the hospital quicker than the ambulance will come. Was there a fight? They weren't exactly angels.'

Molly looked up and saw Selena coming towards her, looking frightened and angry. 'We have to go, Sel.'

'Not unless you explain *that*,' Selena snapped. 'My kids played with it.'

Now Molly had a new terror: there were a hundred things her sister might say, none of them helpful.

'Sel, come on, I'll explain. It's not like you think.'

Selena was in full flow now. 'They kept telling me – they got these odd feelings. Maybe Mason was right. Maybe he is *dangerous*.'

It was like watching a car crash. Her sister was about to betray her. She had to be brutal. 'You know you see things,' Molly said. 'You need to take your medication.'

'What happened to those boys, Molly?'

Van Buren was watching this exchange. 'Mrs Myers, did Cory hurt them? Everyone says he's such a gentle child.'

Molly couldn't see how to win him over, she couldn't help the bullies, and she needed to go.

'My husband needs medical attention,' Molly said, shutting the rear door. Van Buren was looking at their licence plate. Gene was struggling with the seatbelt.

Selena just needed to get behind the wheel and follow Molly to safety – but instead, she stood by Molly as she got into the driver's seat.

Selena gripped her by the arm. 'I trusted you,' her sister said, tears in her eyes.

'Follow us, if you have any sense.'

'You need to stay,' Van Buren said to Molly.

Molly revved the engine. 'Stand back, Sel.' She looked for the safest way out of the parking lot. She remembered the thugs Cory had struck down, all those months ago, the soldiers by the lake when the Myers had been captured. Some people were still suffering, all these months afterwards.

Tears prickled in her eyes as she gunned the engine. Sounding the horn, and making it clear she was not going to stop, she forced the car forward. Van Buren and Selena got out of her way and, with the engine still roaring, she headed for the turning. Out on the open road, she drove as fast as she dared, trying to remember the map in her head, glancing in the mirror from time to time to see if Selena was following. She was not.

Cory unhid and wailed, an alien sound that was just how she

felt: scared and angry and frightened, and deep in the biggest mess imaginable.

Meteor whimpered, Fleur mewed a little and Gene groaned.

How long before there was a story on the wires? Molly wondered, *with police cars looking for them? How long before people wondered about the silence from the Ship?*

CHAPTER 12

Boston, that afternoon

Dr Pfeiffer glared at the principal, and she looked back across the desk as if he was something she had trodden on.

Pfeiffer's wife had insisted that she do the talking and he was close to boiling over, but he had promised Rachael not to be tactless.

'Our girls must have been provoked.' Rachael was trying to keep her tone polite, but there were red spots on her cheeks. She might be about to do the unheard-of thing and lose her temper in public.

'I'm afraid that although we teach our pupils how to behave, we can't stop them having opinions. Dr Pfeiffer, you are a public figure, and a controversial one.'

'Your pupils need to read the newspapers with more care,' Rachael said.

Pfeiffer held one of his hands with the other, and squeezed it, an old trick to stop him lifting the jabbing spear of his accusing finger and launching into an attack. This woman was daring to look down on him. He had wanted to threaten the school lawyers, call the last of his friends in high places, but Rachael had given a firm no to that. This was for them to sort out.

The principal adopted a smug, self-satisfied smile. 'I accept your daughters were provoked, and you may rest assured that all those involved will be punished. However, the first to use force must be punished more. The suspension stands. Of course,' she added smoothly, 'you always have the option to move the children, if you find us unsatisfactory.'

'They are extremely bright girls and if their attention has slipped, it is because they are being bullied,' Rachael said, her voice just a little higher-pitched.

His wife had lost her temper perhaps four times in her life, and he knew she was close to it now.

'Excuses are easy,' the principal said. 'All things being equal, I think we should leave it there.'

They rose in icy politeness, and left.

'I'll take the girls to my mother's,' said Rachael. 'We'll probably stay the night.'

'Thank you. They'll like that.' His girls had stood up for him against their classmates. For most people, Dr Pfeiffer was the cold-blooded creature who had imprisoned the Myers, and who had somehow escaped justice. When the slanders reached into the schoolroom, his daughters had fought back. He felt rage and embarrassment at his lack of power. They might have to change school, but you never knew if it would solve the problems.

'You could come too,' she said, and he was tempted. His mother-in-law still thought he was a great man, a good choice for her daughter.

'I'm sorry,' he said with regret, 'but I do have to work. Perhaps tomorrow.'

He had disappointed her; he could see it on her face. 'You know, Emmanuel, you really do pick the wrong fights. You could just avoid arguments and concentrate on your research – your *real* work. Those insights on the immune system are so enormously promising.'

Pfeiffer wasn't sure. What if Cory's people came? What if he saw that great encounter only from the sidelines, as a third-choice pick for the chat shows? The *Post* had called him a 'former scientist' last week. *Him!* His work for Overton might produce powerful, plentiful drugs against some of the world's deadliest killers, five, ten years down the line; that would silence those who said he had abandoned science for power. But would it be enough?

Rachael was troubled. He had married the brightest and best of his female students, and she had brought him happiness, a joy that was more than just intellect. Age and motherhood might show on her face now, but she was still a beautiful woman.

He kissed her. 'I will try to set the girls an example.'

'It's not for me to tell you what to do.'

That's what she said on the rare occasions when she told him what to do, and he knew he should heed her.

'Tell the girls I owe them a treat, very soon.'

Pfeiffer came home as it grew dark. The maid was at the dentist, so Pfeiffer was alone in the brownstone, dealing with correspondence and the proofs of his latest article. The air was filled with Schubert, Mendelssohn, Mahler.

It was well into the evening. The phone rang, and as he

answered it, the tape machine whirred into action; he wasn't having the police denying he had been threatened anymore.

'Yes?'

The man asked to speak to room 231.

Pfeiffer replied, 'I'm sorry, this is a private residence.'

The man apologised crisply and rang off.

It was his last source in the Administration, a simple code: very urgent, call within half an hour if you can. Phone number two.

Pfeiffer threw on coat, hat, boots and went into the night. Winter was cold and dreary and that was the reality of it. Calls from his source were never social, never trivial. It might be good news, or bad.

Loyal friends of Rachael's lived a few doors down. Impressed that they knew someone important enough to be bugged, they had given Pfeiffer a key to the basement apartment, with its own phone line, for occasions just like this. As soon as he had let himself in, he called his source.

'Have you heard the news?' the source asked.

'I've been working.'

'There's been an incident with the boy. It's crazy here, like someone set fire to the place. The Ship's been silent for days. It's not responding to messages.'

That was hardly unusual; the Ship could and did ignore humans for weeks on end. 'Get to the point. What about Cory? Is he hurt?'

'Local police say he attacked a couple of teens. Or they attacked him. They're sick – you know, the mind stuff.'

Pfeiffer felt his stomach roil at the thought of Cory in danger.

Cory's powers revealed to an ignorant world – oh, the President would surely grab the Myers . . .

'The Ship would be all over that—?'

'There's no reaction – nothing at all. We kept asking if it had checked out the *Mariner* fiasco, but it didn't even reply. Now this fight with Cory—'

'Is he all right? The Myers?'

'Well, they were away before the local police arrived this morning. We only found out an hour before the press got onto it.'

Pfeiffer groaned. The boy was in danger, his whereabouts unknown . . .

But his contact was still speaking. 'So now the FBI are in charge, and everyone is shouting at everyone else to put the milk back in the bottle.'

'What about the Ship?'

'Well, that's the strange thing about this fight: there've been no sightings of any drones, or the Ship. And the Russians have lost two Mars probes too. We heard that . . . *very* unofficially – so the Secretary of Defense decided to poke the Ship.'

When the Administration wanted a response – to see if the Ship was still there, for example – they flew a helicopter or light aircraft into Amber County. The Ship always responded to that, fast and angry, warning the plane, local air traffic control and the Administration that any aircraft over Amber Grove better turn away or it might be destroyed.

'They flew a plane right over Crooked Street, there and back – there was a recorded warning in English. But nothing from the Ship.'

139

There are two possible explanations, Pfeiffer thought. *Either the Ship is damaged, or it is out of range. And either is a disaster.* Pfeiffer felt his stomach churn. *The boy must be kept safe – and we cannot lose the Ship's vigilance against the snakes.*

And yet . . . perhaps this was a door opening?

'We've closed local airspace, claiming we're a plane down. They're hinting it was one of the Ship's drones. And they're reaching out to the Myers and their friends to offer them protection.'

'Public opinion may turn against them, if the world knows what the boy can do. This is all very dangerous.'

'The Administration understands this is important. They'll put up with noise if they have the boy.'

Pfeiffer asked more questions, all the while scrawling notes on his pad:

Call the Myers, offer help.
Call Rachael, warn her I might be away.
Call the Six.

As soon as his source hung up, Pfeiffer called the Myers and left a message. Then he had an urgent decision to make: should he alert all the Six, or talk to his ally Overton first? It took only moments to decide: *Overton.* Day or night, one of his staff would answer, and they would wake Overton if needed.

Overton, the great philanthropist, was such a different animal from the others. They had dined alone in his New York mansion three times, the last only a week ago. Overton spoke often about the meeting of civilisations, and how the knowledge the aliens would bring should be used to relieve suffering. He came alive talking about the science labs and student scholarships and libraries he had funded in the South.

The others invited Pfeiffer to dinner for power or money or information, but Overton wanted to know what kind of man Pfeiffer was. Now, when Pfeiffer called and explained the situation, his voice was brisk and alert.

'Very grave,' said Overton. 'The Administration assume the Myers will make other plans. The President is such a curious soul: half giant, half pygmy. And, of course, they will only be one of many after the Myers. Which is why you and I have a different plan.'

'We have discussed this in principle,' Pfeiffer said, suddenly very cautious. His mouth was going dry.

'I must commend you, Dr Pfeiffer. Your plans for the sanctuary we made for the Six were meticulous. So, I prepared another one: all the laboratories and precautions you could desire, expert staff standing by. Neither the world nor the Six will ever find it. The future of mankind requires us to take command. We will offer the Myers the hand of friendship. Markham and the others, we don't need them.'

'We go it alone?'

Markham was the self-appointed leader, a man who thought the President weak. The other four were cut from the same cloth: men who expected to get their own way. Men who would not appreciate betrayal over Cory, the great prize.

'Of course, we will play along, feed them misinformation and when the time comes, I will sweep them out of the way. That will be my job, Dr Pfeiffer, you may leave that to me.

You will keep the boy and his family well. But this is no time for faint hearts. Are you with me, Emmanuel? Are we brothers in this noble cause?'

It felt like a long pause, as if he were waiting on the school diving board while other children were laughing at his cowardice, his flabby body.

Pfeiffer took a breath, gripped his courage and jumped. 'Yes, of course.'

CHAPTER 13

Choosing a sanctuary

Molly had to stop the car, to feed the baby, to check Gene again. She pulled up a side track and hoped no one would want to use it. Gene was woozy, but his pupils reacted fine to the flashlight. He could tell four fingers from two. You heard these awful stories of someone getting a blow to the head and walking off, perfectly normally, and dying from a brain bleed a few hours later. Pierre needed to get them somewhere where Gene could get an X-ray – but somewhere they would not be in danger.

She hid the bandage as best as she could and helped him change his blood-smeared coat. He winced as he moved.

Cory and the dog dozed, and that was probably good. Molly didn't have the full story and what anyone else might know. Fleur was unsettled but got to work at the breast. And it was then Molly gave in and cried, sobbing for ten minutes or more.

It all felt so hopeless, but she needed to keep going. She needed to try Pierre again, get a message to her friends. Change the licence plates and dig out the false papers. Once they had fled into the night, smeared as spies. Now they would call her son a monster, an attacker of children.

Everyone knew what they looked like. Everyone would be after them.

She dried her eyes; she must look a sight . . .

'What's the plan?' Gene said, slow but making sense. He leaned over, cussing as he moved, and gave her a hug.

'Next phone, I'll try Pierre again.'

'I missed . . . what happened to Big Sis?'

'She stayed behind,' Molly said, feeling a new lurch of fear. *Had Selena heard anything about their escape plan?* 'Heaven knows what she'll say.'

'We gotta find a hole and hide,' Gene said. 'I sure hope she gets away. And keeps her mouth shut.'

Molly checked her own clothes for blood and changed the plates, refusing Gene's offer of help.

Twenty minutes further down the road, a one-street settlement with a phone booth. If it wasn't for smoking chimneys, the place could have been dead. She got out of the car, notebook in hand . . . it was cold . . . dialled the number, and to her relief, a familiar voice answered on the fourth ring.

'*Allo?*'

'Pierre, it's Molly.'

A car passed; for a moment she thought it was Van Buren . . . She was seeing enemies in every passer-by.

'No, this is Anton.' His cousin, also part of the network. 'Pierre is heading south. I can radio him. What's up?'

She gave the shortest possible summary.

'*Merde.* Where are you, exactly?'

She talked, looking back to see if anyone had stopped or was looking.

Molly called three other numbers, left messages. The telephone tree would be activated, her friends and her family would have some warning of this disaster.

How cold she felt, how defeated by it. They had a long way to travel. She got back into the car, where Gene gazed at Fleur. He held the baby upright, which she seemed to like.

'Little Boo just gave me the coolest smile. She's going to break hearts.'

'How's the head?'

'Like a truck fell on it.'

'Pierre is coming. We just need to get to the rendezvous, then make plans.'

'No chance of going west?'

She wanted to find the deepest hole she could, with people she trusted. Who knew how long they would have to get away?

Molly started the car. 'Let's get to the rendezvous.'

Winter sun broke through over the deserted showground, the acres of land used for parking. Molly parked out of sight of the access road. The scatter of snow could not hide the fly-tip here, as high as her chin. A broken-down car, tyres, bottles, mattresses. Signs of a fire. Humans were filthy.

They stayed in the car to keep warm and Gene ebbed in and out of wakefulness. Molly peered at her watch. She thought for the first time, soon she might need glasses. Like her mother.

Winter made this a desolate place. Tattered posters talked of a motorbike exhibition, the Fall Fair. Different hands had sprayed on a fence. *JESUS SAVES. END THE WAR. SC loves SJ*, whoever they were. Graffiti was ugly. It was an eerie place where once was light and noise and fireworks and cotton candy.

It felt like a cold hand on her heart. She gasped, what unearthly danger was this.

Hoo hoo hoo. A yelp from the dog. Then she realised Cory was climbing through to sit on her lap, and his fear and misery filled the car.

He'd grown since he first came to Earth, but they found a way for him to cuddle her.

'Cory hurt those almost-men. Those teens. I hurt them. They're going to die yes-they-are.'

'They won't,' she said. Cory just spoke aloud her fear, because . . . because she knew from the thugs, from the soldiers by the lake . . . Cory's power had come close to killing before.

'The doctors will check them out. They'll be fine.'

'C-c-cory is a MONSTER.'

'We're all monsters some of the time. People will understand . . . you were trying to help.'

'Mom is just saying that.'

It was the strangest thing imaginable . . . how many people had taken to the Myers as symbols . . . of hope, of change, or American can-do. People said the free, loving spirit that had arisen in the Sixties had been dying. They said, Cory had given hope wings again.

'Pierre's coming – remember Pierre? – and he's going to take us somewhere safe. We need to check Dad's head.'

'Will Chuck and Bonnie and VJ and all the others come now?'

'Maybe later. Other children stay there sometimes. No promises.'

A big truck drove into the fairground, it flashed its headlights at them and came closer. The driver jumped down from the cab – short, burly, and she recognised the way he moved. Pierre dressed like a lumberjack and knew planes, boats and anything on wheels.

Molly got out of the car, she could have hugged him with relief, but she didn't know him that well. He stank of coarse tobacco.

'We need to move,' Pierre said. 'We haven't heard anything on the radio, but surely soon – the cops, the Feds, the press. So, where do you want to go?'

'Halcyon, for now.' The strange old house on the Maine coast, where Disappearance Inc had begun.

Pierre produced two metal ramps, and Molly drove the Chrysler into the truck, an anxious, awkward manoeuvre. Molly recoiled from the smell of smoke. No choice but for them all to clamber into the cab, which had a little sleeping area. Two bunks, but too short for Gene lying down and too narrow for him curled up. Cory and the dog took one, and Molly would ride up front.

They had left the state when the first story broke. 'We are hearing reports of an incident involving the Myers family. It appears Gene Myers and two local teenagers were injured. The situation appears very confused, with some witnesses saying Cory Myers was attacked.'

People saw the Myers as they wanted. Who would be more dangerous, those whose hopes had been dashed – or those who had from the beginning seen him as ugly and sinister?

Everyone knew what they looked like. Everyone would be after them.

It was dark and snow speckled the windscreen as they entered Maine. The cabin was stifling hot, the smoke had given her a cough, and Pierre kept talking in fast French into one radio.

The founders of Disappearance Inc, Val and Lloyd, had been so reassuring and felt so trustworthy. But Pierre said they'd been on a lifetime cruise in the Caribbean and this week Lloyd fell ill.

Pierre drove, stifling a yawn. Snow fell into a grey sea. The long curve of Mourning Gull Bay, Halcyon at the south tip, the town at the foot of a green mountain at the north end. The house was set back from the road and well above it, more run down than she had thought, and those odd turrets.

Molly had been wooed by the idea of Halcyon. They'd been shown pictures of an arty summer group dining al fresco, lit with lanterns, boats on a gentle blue ocean. Grim, cold, this felt very different. No other guests, no welcoming hosts.

Pierre backed the truck into the courtyard. She was dog tired and didn't fancy getting the car out of the truck. Here came a vast bearded giant of a man, who must be Joel the handyman.

'Rooms warming. There's food.'

'Bed first, I think.'

Meteor was subdued, Cory sleepy still . . . how his power drained him. Molly carried Fleur into a warm cluttered hallway which overwhelmed the senses. Bright ceramic plates – a narwhal tusk, ships in bottles – seascape paintings and clocks and barometers. Gene followed, Cory over his shoulder. 'I can manage, I can manage.'

Even Meteor, who loved sniffing round new places, was subdued. Joel called, 'Up the stairs, second right.'

A pleasant room with two beds and a crib. Some curious paintings, their meanings not obvious to a tired glance. Even here, all her fears gathered to berate her. But it was a fresh-made bed and it called to her. A sleep, a bath, and fresh clothes and she would feel better.

Gene settled sleepy Cory under a blanket. Then Gene glared at her, red-eyed and angry.

'It's a catastrophe,' Gene said. 'Your sister's fault, slowing us up. We'd have been an hour or two ahead. None of this would have happened.'

'Don't be like that.' Not now, not this.

'I said she would slow us up. Then she turned on us. Right now she'll be talking to the Feds. Did you tell her where this place is?'

Sel might talk. What would she say? Molly feared they had mentioned Maine, the coast.

'Maybe we should have told her about Cory's power.' Molly didn't want the argument. She felt so betrayed by Selena – why didn't he understand how she felt?

'We should have left her behind. I should have insisted, we should have gone to Canada, and then headed west.'

Molly was close to snapping. 'You agreed. To her coming, to Halcyon, to everything. You didn't have to wander off, and get into danger, like a stupid ten-year-old.'

'You just like your own way.'

'Picking a fight. How's that keeping a low profile?'

'The kid might have drowned.'

Molly grabbed her bag, said, 'Time for you to be the adult,' and walked out. She was sobbing, rage and fear alike. In the bathroom, she locked the door, and jammed a chair under the handle.

Everything had gone wrong.

CHAPTER 14

Halcyon, the next day

Cory was working on his eulogy for the Ship in Molly's room, while Meteor recovered from her bath in front of the radiator. The Ship had been a person, if a strange one. It changed its mind, it had a temper and a sense of humour. It seemed a little odd to Molly that the purples did not see their thinking machines as people; they had no rituals to mourn them. Cory wanted to anyway and Molly told him he could. She hoped it would help her sad, lonely little boy.

Molly tried to read a book. Gene had gone for a walk without asking her, so now she was worried he would be seen. Their descriptions would be everywhere. Joel hollered, it was Carol Longman on the phone and Molly went downstairs.

Joel had been called up, he had faced the tribunal, and they denied his right of conscientious objection. He had walked to Halcyon four summers ago and he had worked there ever since.

'Carol? Are you at the office?'

For security, no one was supposed to phone Halcyon from any phone they used regularly.

'No, of course not. Have you seen the news?' From the voice, it wasn't good.

'We're having a news-free day.'

'Abe Kaplan's done it. He's scooped everyone with the army story.'

Molly felt hollow. Could things be any worse?

'Headline: Cory Myers Put Soldiers in Hospital. Administration Lied. Kaplan's stood everything up, when the Army attacked us, the long-term damage for two of the soldiers, the cover-up. He's got quotes from the families. And he's done a long story on those thugs too, and how they just vanished into the prison system. He has a source in the Mob. Dr Jarman and Sheriff Olsen are in the firing line for holding one of the thugs so long on the Psych ward.'

Molly couldn't say a word.

Carol said, 'I guess a couple of his contacts went on the record after . . . you know, the bridge incident. Kaplan's mostly after the Administration.'

'I guess it was always going to come out,' Molly said, numbed at the thought of how bad it was. This was just gas on the flames.

'It's hell here. Everyone is saying the government hid the truth, *Witness* hid it – that I lied. I'll never win a Pulitzer, not the way people are going for me. My editor won't even let me defend myself. He says other people need to write our rebuttal.'

'We're not doing an interview,' Molly said firmly, upset that Carol hadn't asked how they were doing. 'Cory's distraught – we all are. It's a disaster.'

Carol's tone changed. 'Here's me talking about my problems. Well, I'm coming down with Storm and we'd love to see the little fellow. You might like the company. Of course, no interview yet.'

'We'd like to see you,' Molly said. Gene might talk to Storm. 'Although it's not a good time.'

'Tell me the facts. Oh, Dahlia Diamond called me. She has the mother of the boy Cory defended going on her show tonight. Dahlia wants to make sure you watch it. She's fishing for an interview, of course.'

Dahlia Diamond was a real force of nature. 'She can't have an interview either. I've got to go. Love to Storm.'

Molly hung up and tried to find a dry tissue. On her way back upstairs, she heard the bedroom door close.

She opened it and said, 'Cory Myers, listening to private conversations again.'

'It was about me and not good,' Cory said. 'What is it?'

She told him, as gently as she could. He wailed, and she felt his huge sorrow.

The armchair was big enough for Molly to hold a sad and lonely Cory, who huddled into her.

'No children here, no one to play with,' Cory said wistfully. He depended on company.

'You have Meteor and the cats to play with. And Carol and Storm are coming.' That got a twitch of a reaction. 'And Joel gives great piggybacks.'

'No one will like me anymore, not even Bonnie, or Chuck or Zack or Simon or VJ.'

Cory's sorrow filled the room and Molly felt like she could drown in it.

153

'Of course your friends still love you. They know the truth.' She cuddled him, trying to work out what to say. 'People will calm down,' she said. 'People will think it through. The little boy's mother is defending you.'

'That is a very good thing.'

Molly felt drained, like she could wrap herself in a quilt and sleep for a week. Even disturbed sleep was better than this. But Cory needed her. *Keep him busy*, she told herself, *give him other things to think about.*

'When will my people come?' he wailed. 'Then they can take everyone nice in Crooked Street and John and Eva to home-world and my people can fix John's heart and Eva's lungs. And defend the Earth.'

'Well, when they come, things will be better.'

I will not give you up.

'Mom, you will come to my home-world? You do *want* to come?'

How difficult it is to lie to a beloved child.

She equivocated. 'It would be a big adventure, but right now, my head is too full to think.'

Cory turned his face up to her, his big violet eyes filling her with his grief. 'So truly Mom doesn't want to go. Mom wants to leave me – because I am *monster*—'

He howled, and she held him tighter.

'Oh Cory, but this is the truth: I want to be with you and be your mom. That's what matters. When your people come, we'll do the best we can.'

How could she argue they were his best family if humanity rejected him?

'Will only Dad come?'

'She kissed her son rather than answer and his smell brought back so many good times, even when they were hidden from the world. They had been so fearful, starting at shadows, lying to friends; few days passed without lies and anxiety and false alarms. And yet now it felt like life had been simpler then.

'Cory needs you *both*.'

Molly knew that, and Gene knew that too. They'd thrown those words back and forth, over the divide: *the kids need both of us*.

It was true.

The next day, it snowed. Storm and Carol had made slow progress; they'd broken their journey overnight and finally arrived mid-morning. Gene helped Storm get bags and a load of box files out of the Jeep.

'Notes for the book,' Carol said, handing him the typewriter.

Gene, Storm and Cory had disappeared to run the dog or chop wood or something, while Molly made coffee in that big kitchen. The journalist was at her most tactful, keen to get a consistent story. Gene had written notes, even a sketch map, and Cory agreed it. Molly passed all this on.

Carol flipped back through the notes. 'This fits with what the little kid and his mother said to Dahlia.'

'I can barely talk about this to you, let alone the world.' Molly stirred her cup.

'It must be unbearable.'

'What's going to happen?'

'Congressional hearings. The police, of course. There's a

rumour the teen's family will sue. The Administration – who knows?'

Carol was soon pounding away at her faithful typewriter, filling the room with its clatter.

Molly was left looking at a rip in Gene's pants, thinking he could sew up his own damn clothes if he went on being like this.

She turned on the radio to hear, 'The latest development in the Myers case is an intervention by Governor Wallace. Speaking on a campaign tour of the western states, Governor Wallace led his remarks with a comment on the story.'

The voice was familiar. 'I have long warned you that those crooks in the Administration were lying about the Myers. I always said the purples might be dangerous. If one boy can cause this much harm, what will a giant fleet of their starships do? The Myers lied, the liberal media hid the truth and even now they are trying to play all this down. Your President lied to you. Things will be very different when there's a decent man in the White House. We should reopen Alcatraz, just for the Myers.'

Molly felt the world closing in. So much of the country was angry and disillusioned. Surely all these frightened, disappointed people would not turn to Wallace?

Gene had no encouragement to offer, no reassurance – just silence and distance, now that they were sleeping apart. The music he played was loud and angry, or so gloomy that it dragged her deeper into sadness. Each day he withdrew a little more. He took to going off on long solitary walks among the pines, brushing off her concerns. What if he fell, or was caught?

It was Gene's job to be strong when she was not, Gene's job to help her – and yet it seemed he had nothing to give.

The Russians wanted to put nuclear weapons in space, to defend the Earth. A hard-fought peace treaty would have to be revised. The President was being attacked from left and right. He would meet the Russian leader; he had a plan. The world was losing its mind.

That night was the first of the burnings. The TV cameras showed a churchy crowd with their children, throwing Cory masks, the comics, the clothes into a blazing fire, faces twisted in hate, while some prim woman was spouting lies.

The next day, Storm and Carol played *Tiles* with Cory, using the alien board game to keep him occupied. Molly was out of sorts with Carol, who'd suggested she speak to Dr O'Brien, the Disappearance Inc doctor.

Carol had been almost pushy. 'All this, and the baby too . . . it can't do any harm.'

'I can manage,' Molly snapped. Fleur was a bright spot, not a burden, even though sometimes when she picked her up, she felt drained of hope. O'Brien and his wife were true believers in Cory. Carol was a friend and meant well, but what gave her the idea she needed to talk to a doctor?

Gene had not spoken to her since 6 a.m., when he'd asked where Fleur's ointment had got to. She thought she should make the effort and went looking for him, finally coming across him on a window-seat in a sea-facing room. A few old books sat on the table. The room was chilly and he was wearing his heavy coat. The frowning weather matched his face.

'The truth is out there,' he said to the window. 'Cory was

trying to save lives, but people don't care. They just swallow what they're told.'

'Some people care,' Molly said, running her hands through his hair. At least he didn't brush her aside. The Myers' refusal to return and face the authorities was putting their allies in real difficulty. Flight meant guilt.

In private, via Dr Jarman's father-in-law, the Administration had offered options aplenty: clever, unscrupulous, two-faced options that all came down to trusting the President's word. They would recognise Cory as an Ambassador, they said, and hide him behind diplomatic immunity.

'Humanity sure doesn't deserve him,' Gene said. 'Even the snakes can make governments work together. When the machines come, they'll rip us apart.'

Molly couldn't think of an answer. He might explode or stop talking altogether.

'The purples are coming,' she said, as if saying so would make it true.

He sighed, and she picked up the books he'd been reading: one was about an Arctic explorer, and others covered nine-teenth-century expeditions in the Pacific. 'Any good?'

'Yeah, kinda.' He sat up a little, with a touch of energy. 'You know, these men who went out there, left their wives back home. I bet it was rough.' He tapped the explorer's book. 'Yet this guy had six kids – he sent his kids letters while he was on his travels. They had a good marriage.'

'Did they ask the women? In those days, the wife just had to take it.'

'They've printed a couple of her letters – they're wonderful, you can really hear her voice. Of course, it was rough.'

He took her hands. His were so cold; he must have been here for ages.

'And sometimes people came to the New World and brought their kids over when they were settled. So, one of us could go with Cory – not for ever, just to settle him in. He's a child of Earth too, so a link home might be useful. The whole world would benefit.' Gene hesitated before he carried on, 'Walking under other stars – smelling other winds. We'd be able to let humanity know what it's like out there. Governments sent pilots barely able to string sentences together into space. They should have sent poets and musicians. I could do the world a favour, going with them.'

There was nothing Molly could say. She just stayed silent.

'You won't go, and you don't want me to.' At least it was gently said.

Molly whispered, 'The purples will like somewhere warm, with water. I think humanity could find the purples a nice island. They could have a proper base, a settlement. They could bring their children. Or one of their cities in space. There would be no need for Cory to go.'

The silence grew between them.

'Imagine Fleur growing up with no father,' she said at last. 'I think John and Eva are putting on a brave face about John's health. He's getting worse, and Eva too.'

Gene's face tensed and she squeezed his hand.

'Dad wouldn't want us chained to the bedside. And besides, the purples will cure him in five minutes when they come.'

159

'Or they won't.' She gazed at his face for some sign of change, some sign she was getting through.

He turned away. 'I knew you'd say no. The spring after you lost the baby, I was wrong to take no for an answer then. Travelling would have helped me, for sure – helped both of us.'

I lost the baby? Molly thought. A wave of sadness and anger swelled. *We lost her.* She should have lashed out at that, told him the truth – that when you travel, you take your misery with you – but, instead of anger, tears came at the casual way he had brought the death up – the way he was rewriting history.

'The purples will take Cory,' he said. 'So it's a clear choice: we go with them, or we lose him. Why would they hang around?'

The purples will find a world divided, Molly thought, *and the louder half will be hating her little boy.* How could a couple divided fight against that? When had Gene become so hard and selfish?

Molly got up, mumbled some excuse, and left him.

In the sitting room, Carol had two papers to show her: the local, and the *New York Times.*

'No,' Molly said, 'it's all lies. I don't care.'

Carol sighed, just a little. 'People are calling in sightings of Cory.'

'Yes, that happens . . .'

'It's on purpose,' Carol said, 'to slow the police up: hundreds of thousands of people, all over the country, every day. The FBI are tearing their hair out. The student radio station in Portland has been closed down. That's happened in other places too – because they keep giving out the numbers on air.'

Molly dared to take the newspaper and read it. There was something called 'The People's Committee to Defend Cory Myers' – already claiming 'State spokesmen' in twenty-nine states. Strange times. For a moment it lifted her spirits. There was hope, here – hope in the idea that people were protecting Cory for who he was, for what he stood for just by being him.

Then she turned the page, read about those who envied and admired Cory for his power and wanted it for themselves. Those who wanted that power used against the country's enemies. Those who thought what happened by the river was funny. . .

And a cold hand gripped her heart.

CHAPTER 15

Dealing with humans, December

In the high tower room, Cory was dancing to the radio, lost in the music. *Leap and swirl, stomp and jump*, the sort of dance you could not do near the gramophone. Singing without words.

'I'm not like anybody else.'

Meteor was trying to dance too, following him around the room.

Faithful Meteor.

He danced so he did not have to think, so that he was simply an instrument played by the music. But the programme ended, and then it was just humans talking. *Talk, talk talk*. He turned it off and tried holding back the fear.

Look at the view, he told himself. He sat by the rattling window and Meteor came and pushed his way on to the seat next to him. The ocean at Mourning Gull Bay was very fine, with big sea waves driven by cold winds crashing onto the shore. He remembered the storms on his own planet, and the warm rain lashing warm oceans. Even the salt of the ocean tasted

163

different. But Cory must not think about his home-world for sixteen of minutes.

Humans called it the Glad Game.

Snow was good, and Christmas was coming, and the cats liked him. Most cats didn't. It was strange to have a house so big with so few people in it.

Further round the bay was the harbour, where the houses huddled low against the wind. There was an island, with its green mountain he wanted to climb. Little human water ships. He imagined the bay in spring or summer, all the sails dancing in the warm breeze. Cory liked the angry sea and the strange sandy beaches and the grim grey rocks looked very fine to scramble up. He liked the hardy trees that stayed green in winter, whose needles smelled of Christmas in his hands. Those trees were often hard to climb. On Earth, some animals hid in sleep from the cold; he could feel their lives so tiny and slow, like suspended animation. He wondered sometimes about the poor dead Ship's offer, how it would have felt to sleep, hidden in some crevice of the Moon. And there were still seabirds who had not fled south for winter, herring gulls with their raucous calls. He had yet to see a Mourning gull.

How he mourned the Ship, which had been his guardian, teacher and companion, now gone. The Network in the sky which should warn of alien attack did not reply to him. Everyone wanted to know whether there were snakes out there, how they could be detected. But Cory didn't know.

His communicator held personal memories but it had lost its English and couldn't call another device. Out there were mobs of angry humans, searching for him. And his Earth Mom and his Earth Dad dreamed of darkness and danger and loss; he found little consolation there. When he listened to the bittersweet recording of his first mother's voice, it just reminded him that the snakes had won.

His people had not come, even in his dreams. The together-dream, that little flicker of light, was not to be found, though he sought it every night. But as the weeks passed, he believed that the starship the dreamers were on was getting closer. He refused to believe it was the sadness and his imagination seeking hope. That voice had to be ignored.

Be here, Cory. Enjoy here. Play the Glad Game and the bad things would hurt a little less. He missed his friends so much.

The post had come and that was very fine. His friends wrote twice a week, Bonnie sending long letters full of indignation, and the names of all the people in town who believed him, and Chuck shorter ones. They sent comics too. The Robertson teens had a wild sense of humour which made Mom make a sour face, and their dog Isaac wrote to Meteor – funny letters with little drawings explaining life from the dog's viewpoint. Cory and Mom replied on Meteor's behalf; they were fun letters to write. Eva always wrote to Cory, and John scrawled lines on the end.

He wanted them all here.

Fleur was good; she was trying to pick her head off the ground like the babies of his home-world. Cory thought Fleur recognised him now. He would hold her and sing her the songs the big children sing to the little ones, and tell her stories she was too young to understand. It was sad for Fleur to have only one brother in the lodge, so he must be all the children for her.

How sweet Fleur's dreams tasted, like soft little sketches of light: a world of feeding and warmth and Mom. No stories, though; she was not yet the pilot of her dream.

Sometimes Dad and Cory camped up here in the high room together, with the heater glowing and quilts piled over the zipped-together sleeping bags. Meteor had her own special blanket. Mom didn't come; she slept with Fleur in their bedroom. She never said so, but Cory knew she was worried in case his bad dreams hurt his sister. That made Cory very sad, almost ill-and-sad, because babies need to be given other dreams to grow. But he knew that not all his dreams were healthy.

The snakes had won again.

The Glad Game stopped working and here came the fear and the cold, rushing in like a raging sea, and Cory was not strong enough to hold it back. Meteor whined and retreated to the door.

The bell went *clong-clong-clong*, one two three, and that meant Cory must come down at once – but only a small part of him heard it; the rest was lost in the storm as Cory's fear and sadness poured out from him and vanished through walls and ceiling and floor.

His power had come, unasked and uncontrolled, with no enemy to fight.

That evening, Cory woke to shouting, indistinct at first, then loud enough to hear through the walls.

'*Quit your nagging.*' That was Gene.

'*I can't take this. Not another moment.*'

'*It was a fucking suggestion, not a fucking order.*'

The music suddenly went louder, then there was a screech that meant a precious record, one of Halcyon's library of music, had been scratched.

SLAM!

That was a door crashing shut like a big exploding firework.

Long ago, Gene and Molly had been very careful explaining divorce to him. They had expected it to be a strange idea to him, but of course people might find they were no longer suited. Yes, it was unhappy and a bad thing to rush separation until you were sure, but there was no need to hurt each other. Back home, the whole lodge – perhaps two lodges – would be around them, awake and asleep, helping them to separate in a caring and loving way. But humans could not do that.

Crooked Street had been like a lodge.

The shouting and the fear got inside him. He couldn't bear that his parents were quarrelling when he needed them together. He hated the episodes when his fear grew out of control.

He was in the waking world now. *Annoying*. Perhaps he should update the Plan on how to sort the Earth out. All the stupid things humans did, which they would have to stop when his people came. The Aral Sea was disappearing, a *whole* sea, and all the birds and fish that relied on it.

He would spend half an hour putting the Earth right—

There was a crash from outside, and he heard Dad swearing.

He opened the door onto the narrow wooden stairs and saw his Earth-father trying to get up; he had fallen coming up the stairs.

'I thought you'd be in bed, Big Stuff.' Dad was slurring a

little. He hung onto the banister, moving as though his body wasn't quite listening. Maybe he had banged his head again.

Cory's tentacles tasted the air: cigarette smoke, and wine, which looked like juice but was not for children. Carol and Storm drank most nights, but they took care to hide it from Mom. Alcohol made Mom very sad and ill and she didn't drink it anymore. But two days ago, Dad had made a pro-dig-ious mess being sick in the bathroom.

'You'll wake Fleur up,' Cory said now.

'Don't look disapproving. I'm . . . I was going to tell your mom I'm sorry – sorry for the shouting. But she's locked the door. It's my room too.'

Cory was trying to decide how he felt, but he already knew that. He felt tired and small and sad. It was always better to sleep with someone, and he did have Meteor.

'You're drunk,' he announced. 'You need to find a bucket.' He was just trying to be practical, but his dad took it as rejection.

'Okay, I guess I screwed up. I'll sleep somewhere else.'

Dad turned around, his body doing its best to balance. 'We both love you,' he said. Then he made a worrying climb down the stairs, limbs askew like a toddler.

Suppose the Bad Men came and Dad was drunk – how would they get away?

'Molly? Please?'

Cory shut his own door and prepared himself and Meteor for bed. *Humans!*

CHAPTER 16

Halcyon, two days after Christmas

Cory loved it when the sun shone. The sky today was bluer and colder than any he had seen before. It made the ice sparkle. Christmas had been exciting, with presents from his friends, but it was mostly over – and here he was, stuck hiding in a house with the same few people. Cory was fed up with trying to entertain his parents – cheering them up felt harder than lifting them in body – but at least this morning there was the exciting expedition to look forward to.

Joel and Storm took turns going to check the unused houses. There were five in the area, all closed up for winter. The people of Halcyon checked that no one had broken in or set fire to anything.

Cory didn't understand why someone would burn a house someone else used. The hobos he did understand – people who liked to wander and to be alone, like some solos of his own world, those who did not want a lodge.

Joel's car-truck-whatever was huge and black. He called it

the Beast. Cory put Meteor under her blanket on the back seat and they drove up the trail together, taking the back way out. The Beast made fierce animal noises getting up slopes and fighting the ice.

Cory must look for the tracks of the big-footed hares, who turned white for winter. Sometimes, Joel said, where there were hares, there were lynx, a sort of fierce hunting cat. Cory wanted to see a lynx, even though it was bad news for the hares. All the animals for miles around would spot Meteor, unless Cory hid her.

'Do you get many break-ins?' Storm asked.

'Teens for a dare. Hobos – it's a hard time to be on the road.'

Joel marched around each house, looking for damage. Then they went in to see that the heat was on very low, and that no pipes had burst.

The third place, a very fine little house in grey stone and painted wood, was surrounded by snow-covered trees. It was quiet everywhere, except for them.

Joel did his checking walk around the outside of the house, looking for leaks.

'Can't be more than a mile from the road,' Storm said. 'Oh, there's been visitors.'

There was garbage scattered around the back doorstep, tins and packets.

'Racoons,' said Joel. That was obvious, from the tracks.

'So, a detective story, who brought the garbage for them to get into?'

There were no footprints, but it had snowed yesterday. Cory closed his eyes to concentrate, to listen and to feel out with his mind. Ah – there *was* something here: two somethings, and they were under the house. Only raccoons after all.

Then Cory felt something else: a human, frightened and alone. His mind followed the feelings up to the top of the house. He focused: not a large human.

He should tell Storm – but then he thought of Bonnie and Chuck, and how good it was to have friends. Perhaps the scared-alone person needed a friend.

Cory looked down, so Storm could not see his indecision. 'Two small things under house. Raccoons maybe.' In his back-pack, he had a bar of chocolate he'd been given for Christmas and the pastry he hadn't eaten at breakfast. 'Go into house. We should go into the house.'

Five steps led up to a tiny porch. Storm pulled off a glove and bent over, feeling under the steps.

'The key's gone,' she said. 'Our visitor might still be around.'

'Cory go. I will go, hidden. No danger if I go.'

Storm felt unsure, her face looked unsure. Inside her coat was the walkie talkie; in her coat pocket was the big heavy flare gun. 'Suppose it's some drunk with a stick?'

Cory pleaded his case. 'I can walk in darkness. I can hide. I can smell if someone there.' *So many things humans cannot do.* 'I will be most extra careful.'

Storm smiled. 'Okay.'

This was what he wanted: an adventure. He hid himself and slipped through the door. It was cold, but warmer than outside. It smelled as all these locked-up places did. Looking for big bear traps, he stalked through the rooms. It was clear that someone had been in the kitchen, where the plates had been rinsed but only camping clean. He smelled a human – sweat and dirt and soap – and something else, a nasty smell like rotting food.

Up the stairs he went, because the human had not moved.

'Cory, what's going on?' Storm called from downstairs.

Cory stayed hidden as he stepped through one of the bedroom doors, because this was certainly *the* room. The bed had been disturbed. The closet door was closed. He felt with his mind and knew the human was in the closet. The human was frightened, and sad or ill or hungry, or all of these. It was shivering, a child, frightened and alone.

He took off his backpack and found the chocolate and the pastry. Then, putting them down by the closet door, he unhid himself and whispered, 'Here's food. I'm a friend. Do you want help?'

Nothing happened, except that the note of fear sharpened.

'We can help. The people I am with are kind. I can bring my mom and dad.'

The silence only continued; the fear sharpened further.

Cory looked back at the open bedroom door. Soon Storm would come up.

'I'll come back,' he said, clear but not too loud. Then he padded to the top of the stairs.

'See no one,' he said, for that was true. 'But for-sure has been someone here. Smell them.'

Storm was in the kitchen. 'Someone's been here, a couple of days at least.'

'I need the bathroom,' Cory called down.

Cory sat on the toilet while he thought. Maybe the child was a Bad Man and they would tell the other Bad Men who were after them. Maybe he should tell Mom and Dad. But maybe, then, Mom and Dad would decide to run away again and there would be more arguing.

The child was scared – it was scared before Cory in the room, frightened just by the vehicle coming up the road. Cory could have opened the door, but then – what if it'd been scared of *him*? Cory the monster. Everyone was so scared of Cory. But the present of food . . . *Cory will not lie if asked directly. So difficult. Cory will tell Mom. No, he won't.*

He flushed the toilet and washed his hands and went downstairs.

'No one upstairs?'

'I saw nothing,' Cory said, and it was true, he had not seen anything. His inner teacher was not happy.

'I have good idea: Cory and Meteor will sleep downstairs and guard the house,' he said. 'Meteor is a great guard dog. If person comes snooping, one of us will know.'

'Your mom would kill me,' Storm said. 'Well, I don't suppose the owners care about a tin or two. But if they leave the door open, and animals get in . . .'

Storm wrote a note in flowing handwriting, sketched a map and put two green bills with it on the table.

'It's a hard time to be on the road. Halcyon feeds the hobos, gives them a bath and a bed. If they want to stay more than three days, the church takes them.'

That evening, Storm and Carol cooked. Molly had announced that she was a grown-up, two years two months sober, and if people wanted to drink in front of her, she was fine. Tonight, she passed Gene a glass of wine, with a most superior look, and he went red and took it. The grown-ups drank wine and got slurred and silly; even Mom acted a little as though she was.

Carol read something called 'The Cory I Know', which was very kind about him and felt strange. 'It's an article, or it might be the first chapter of the book.' It made the adults go warm and melty inside. There were some bits in it that Cory did not understand, though, and in the lodge, you would never praise just one person like that. Cory went round the room praising everyone to be balanced.

Cory thought of his new friend, cold and lonely up the hill. He had already decided that it was not for him to reveal them unasked. The right thing was to ask if they wanted rescuing. He must go and do that again soon.

He cast a glance at the window. It was dark now, and cloud had come to hide the Moon and drop more snow. It was a mile and a half from the house to the cottage, and all of that was uphill. Cory would need snowshoes, but there were no snowshoes for Meteor. He supposed he could pull Meteor on his sled, wearing her coat and under her blanket, or else leave her behind. But Meteor liked to pad around barking and looking for Cory when he was gone, so that would be a sign to the grown-ups that something was different.

The adults would never let Cory go on his own. *So I must go tonight*, he thought, *while all the adults are sleeping.*

At one in the morning, the darkness outside Halcyon was absolute. Fleur had woken at half past eleven, which meant that everyone would now be back to sleep. Cory went into the storeroom to find bread, cheese, tinned pineapple and cookies. Hidden under the cloth were the tins and packets he must not see, with murdered animals in them. Cory hated that there were dead cows and rabbits and chickens in the food Meteor ate. Dog food troubled him; it smelled of death, and yet it was enticing.

In the front room, Meteor was asleep, leg twitching. Perhaps she was chasing hares. Cory was pleased that clumsy Meteor was truly terrible at catching rabbits and squirrels and birds.

He took cans of soup and beans from the storeroom; the person could use the stove in the cottage. By now, the backpack was heavy – not too heavy, but after a mile over snow it might feel different. Maybe one less tin . . .

He heard a tiny creak on the stair and hid at once, his heart pounding. He felt Mom, and here she came with the little flashlight.

Molly walked straight to the kitchen, even though he was so-so quiet.

'Backpack gone, big flashlight gone and the pantry door open. Cory Myers, you need to unhide right this minute.'

He stayed hidden, his heart pounding out the seconds. Then Mom turned on the light, and she looked, if not at him, close to where he was.

'Cory, I'm going to count to five. Show yourself, or there will be trouble.'

Cory held his breath and revealed himself.

'So, dressed up for a polar expedition. Where are you going?'

Scared for his friend, but relieved, Cory told the truth.

★

Cory was in disgrace and felt it. But the sun was about to rise, and here they were, ready to set off, going to help. Joel turned the key in the Beast, which roared in the silence, and somewhere in the woods, there was a flutter.

Dad thought it was too dangerous for Mom. But, 'Cory said the child might be sick, so I'm coming. The end,' Mom had said, finding the first-aid kit.

Cory said, 'I must come to hide you all if trouble.'

'You're still in disgrace,' Molly said.

Cory was very sorry for lying to grown-ups, although he was trying to do the right thing. Grown-ups lied to each other all the time. Mom told many, many *enormous* fibs to keep Cory safe. But in his heart, Cory knew he had not told the truth and he deserved to be in disgrace.

Still, they let him come.

The Beast made its noisy path up towards the house, so loud that every animal within miles would surely be hiding. Cory thought his friend would hear the car and be afraid. Or maybe the friend had already gone.

When they arrived at the cottage, even the tracks from yesterday were muted by the light dust of new snow. The air was cold enough to make Cory's lungs hurt. In this weather, he lost feeling in his tentacles, even though he willed them warmer. Dad stood guard by the Beast.

'Cory will go ahead, hiding.'

The grown-ups just shrugged.

Inside, the air was stale, but the house was warmer. The money on the counter was gone. Cory saw no new signs of disturbance. He walked up one step after another, feeling around him, looking and listening. Then he climbed the stairs, oh so careful, and headed to the small bedroom.

He sneaked open the door and saw that somebody was in the bed, a tangle of blankets. The person felt confused, sick. Such an unhealthy smell was coming off them, like dead things rotting.

The small person was not asleep, not awake.

He walked over, hidden, and stood for a while, looking down at them. The person was very thin, and dirty. Smaller than he was. Long hair, but whatever the books say, that did not always mean a girl.

The child's eyes flickered.

How terrible, that the child might become scared of him. He needed Mom, the healer, to look at the boy or girl, whichever it was.

He unhid and called, 'Mom, a child is sick.'

'I'm coming.'

The boy-or-girl opened their eyes and grabbed his hand. They felt confused, and Cory realised how sick they were.

'Don't let *him* find me.'

'I won't,' he promised. And Mom came in, and he was so glad she was there, because Mom knew so well what to do with sick humans.

In a glance Molly saw the girl was in a bad way. An old yellow bruise coloured her face and she shivered, feeling hot to the touch.

Molly took charge. 'Cory, heat the soup up. It looks a lot like our stove – but be careful.'

That would get Cory out of the way. Molly knelt by the

bed. 'Okay, sweetie-pie, I'm a nurse and a mom. I work with children all the time. It's going to be fine. Tell me what hurts.' The smell in the room came from a festering wound; it suggested to Molly's nose that it was somewhere on the lower half of her body.

The girl murmured.

'I'm going to have to undress you a bit to see what's wrong.' Molly pulled on her protective gloves.

It only took lifting the blankets to show her the problem: the child's leg had been crudely bandaged, but pus and dried blood were leaking through. How thin she was.

Joel was back already. 'What do you need me to do?'

'Help me undress her: I'll need to wash her. Perhaps a bath would be simplest.'

The girl murmured again.

Joel said, 'I wish the kid had said yesterday.'

'Better now than later,' said Molly. She only had the simplest sorts of antibiotics on her, but she could clean the wound up with antiseptic salve and dose her with whatever else she could find. She could always call Dr O'Brien.

'What hurt you, darling?' she asked softly.

'*He* did . . . then the broken window.'

She would have to check the wound for glass.

She touched the girl's side, intending to reassure her, and noted how she flinched.

Always the nurse, Molly pulled out her notebook to record everything she saw, bruises and the like. People thought that working with children was all balloons and jigsaws and mopping the pretty brows of sweet children who got better for the final scene. But there were terrible things in the world, and children were not immune from them.

What hurt you? He did.

'Who hurt you, sweetie-pie? I won't let him do it again.'

The girl bit her lip and began to cry, the quiet noise children learn when crying has always been punished. Molly had learned to cry like that at her parents' house.

These dark times at Halcyon, she thought more of her parents, unwanted ghosts at the feast, the horror that was their marriage, and Selena, her sister, who had re-entered her life and betrayed her again. Selena, wanted by the police as a witness, had vanished into thin air.

CHAPTER 17

More about the girl

Cory thought everything had been about the girl since they found her. 'The grown-ups need to talk,' Mom said and that meant Cory was in charge.

Cory put on the apron and entered the girl's room. It smelled of disinfectant and whatever had been sprayed to cover it. It was a very grown-up room, as sometimes sick grown-ups stayed at Halcyon. The bed was a fold-y hospital bed; there was a vase of dried leaves, and over the dresser, a painting of a white hare-not-a-rabbit. Through the window, the snow-clad trees rose to the place where they had found her. He should bring the girl some books and toys.

Mom had made a big fuss about cleanliness, all the washing and all the precautions. Cory hated human masks, but he had a couple of his own that did not cramp his tentacles.

The girl sat up in bed. Mom had cut her straw hair short and oiled it with a strange substance, for the tiny insects. *Parasites.* That was a complicated thing about having hair.

The girl looked at Cory, one minute then two, without fear. A cool judging.

'I-am-Cory-Myers.'

'You're the monster. I dreamed you.'

Cory felt no fear from her, so he took a step forward. He'd tried to look into her dreams, but she was adept at hiding them. Sometimes he found fragments of pain and fire; images of her limping hurt in the snow, of smoke in the night, of the girl being bundled into a car. But he could make so little sense of it all.

'You're a kind monster. You left me food. Of course, maybe you just wanted to eat me. The witch fattened Hansel and Gretel up.'

Cory bristled with indignation, a stupid human story, but then saw a little smile.

'Very funny,' he said. 'Hil-lar-ious. What's your name?'

'I have lots of them,' she said. 'I don't know I like any of them, Snake Face. Your mom asks a lot of questions.'

He didn't like the nickname. Earth snakes were sweet, sunning themselves and tasting the world with their tongues. But the metal snakes . . .

'My mom worries about you.'

'That's nice.' She looked at the side table, an empty plate, an apple core. 'Is there any more food? And where are my clothes? My leg hurts.'

Joel had wanted to burn them, and the boots, which he said were beyond mending – but Molly, who liked things clean, had done something strange. She'd wrapped all the girl's clothes in plastic bags, taped them up and hidden them in the garage.

'Here are clothes.' Cory brought them from the chair to the bed. Children often stayed in the house by the bay, so there was a closet of spare things, like a blue summer dress which Cory had worn for dressing-up, and a pair of boy's jeans, and some underwear. The sweater had a moth hole in it, which Storm had mended last night. Cory had donated his newest T-shirt.

The girl admired the dress for a while. She looked at a pair of light summer shoes. 'That's not much good for winter. I'll need a coat, and my boots, I-am-Cory-Myers.'

'Stay here, in the warm. I'll get more food.'

The yellow waterproofs would hold off wind and rain, but Cory did not want her to leave.

'I ran away. *He's* after me so I have to be ready to go.'

'We are always packed-ready-to-go. We will pack for you too. But don't go now. We will look after you.'

'Last time, grown-ups gave me back to *him*.'

'My mom and dad won't. We've run away too. I'll get some food.'

All the grown-ups were talking to Dr O'Brien in the big room. Dr O'Brien was kind and had no hair on his head but lots up his nose. If Cory did his most powerful hide, they would not notice him open the door and slip in.

A warm room full of complicated feelings – angry and frightened and hiding things.

O'Brien was speaking. 'The law is the law. I'm supposed to contact Child Services, and they'll tell the police.'

Mom gave a strange laugh. 'We're going around in circles. If Halcyon stands for anything, it stands for the law being wrong sometimes.'

'I have my oath too. This poor girl, she deserves everything the state can provide.' O'Brien was troubled.

'We'll have to move,' said Dad.

That would be a nasty argument between Mom and Dad. Cory was often bored, but then, Halcyon was safe.

'She has a good doctor, and a nurse . . .' said Mom. 'She's not in any danger. Now, if she gets really sick, then we'll have to think about hospital.'

If Cory had been allowed, he would have said, 'We can go and take her with us.'

Carol said, 'Well, I don't know what this state is like, but the institutions struggle, don't they? She's not in immediate danger. You've broken bigger laws, Roger, and thank goodness.'

Molly put her hand on Dr O'Brien's. 'We've all had to make difficult choices. Give us forty-eight hours, I guess we can go to Canada . . . and hope none of the lunatics find out where Cory is . . .'

'I'll just say I found her.'

'Or just wait,' Molly said. 'We're criminals, with the whole world after us.'

There was a long pause, waiting for Dr O'Brien to decide.

'I guess a few days more doesn't matter.'

Such relief, and Cory used the hum of thank-yous to slip out.

The Bad Man who hurt her must be stopped. And yet, Cory needed his Earth-family to be safe. What else had he got until his people came?

In the kitchen, there were good smells for lunch. How Cory missed his home in Amber Grove. Better still, he wanted to take his human family and all their friends to his home-planet.

Cory took what he needed, hidden, and went back upstairs.

The girl was sitting on the bed. Her face was sweaty. 'Help me pee, Snake Face,' she asked.

He pointed at the pot; would she faint, or be sick? He helped her from the bed, then turned his back to give her privacy. When she finished, he helped her to the basin to wash her hands.

'*He* said you were made up. Liar.'

'I have to call you something,' Cory said. 'Not rude and silly like that word.'

'Call me Elsa,' she said. 'I heard it in a story.' She pointed at the picture. 'I'd like to be a white hare,' she said. 'I saw one at sunset. *He* threw a rock at it, and it ran away. It goes white in winter to hide. Imagine just being a fur ball under the snow. No one could find you.'

Cory could feel it under the snow, of course. 'Snowshoe hare,' he said. 'Because of the feet.'

'Hares don't wear shoes,' said the girl, like she was the expert.

'I could find you,' Cory said.

'No you couldn't.'

'And I can hide better than a hare,' Cory said, and showed her.

She laughed and it was a good sound.

He unhid again.

'That's a good trick. Teach me,' she said, not knowing where to look, and how he wished he could. She had hair and he could hide with his mind, and neither could give that to the other.

Elsa kept taking quick glances at the silver bracelet of his communicator. Perhaps she was trying not to show him she was interested. He held out his hand so she could see it closely.

185

'It's for talking,' he said. 'But now it doesn't work.'

'Isn't it a smart monster,' she said, touching the device.

'It won't work for you.'

It held precious memories, some words from his mother.

Three days later, Cory came to find Elsa to show her the old newspaper. She smelled clean and healthy now. She ate a lot, and she smiled more at the grown-ups.

In the paper was a bad sketch of a hard-eyed man and a girl who could have been anyone. 'Gas station robber strikes again,' read the headline. The story mentioned 'concerns' for the child in the car.

Funny how humans weep for emotion. Elsa held back the tears, but Cory felt her sadness.

'That could be anyone,' she said.

'Read it,' he said, and she frowned.

'I read fine,' she said, but the truth was, she read like a baby, saying the words aloud and stumbling. She liked Cory to read to her.

The newspaper said that the Bad Man had used a gun to take cash from shops and gas stations. First there was a robbery in Vermont, where a man was hurt, then two in Maine. Cory shivered at the thought of how scared the poor shopkeepers must have been. They called him the Dog-Tag Robber, because he flourished military ID to show he was serious about the gun.

'Where is the Bad Man?' Cory said. 'Don't so-worry, Cory will hide you, yes-I-will.'

Elsa took his hand. 'It's a very nice monster and I like it. I don't know where *he* is. He stole a car with lots of groceries in and when the motel kicked us out, he tried robbery again. Then we broke into a house further up the hill. *He* was drunk, that's how I got away. I took his gun and threw it in the water.'

Cory had learned to spot human lies, but he had no sense if she was being truthful.

'Where is your lodge? Your family?'

'All dead. *He* wasn't family.'

Cory had never met a human so good at cloaking their feelings.

'It was better when we didn't use guns. I'd pretend to be sick and he'd take stuff while kind people helped me. Or he'd ask directions and I'd take food. You can hide a lot under a big coat. Sometimes people would feed us both, because he'd pretend he'd lost his mind in the war and they felt sorry for me.'

'Stealing,' Cory said. The way Earth worked confused him, but all this felt wrong.

She shrugged. 'We were starving, and they weren't.'

Her stories were awful, but they fascinated Cory, like a poisonous plant that smells delicious.

'Maybe I'll have to do those things again,' Elsa said.

Cory knew humans; she was testing his reaction. 'Stay safe. Stay with us.'

Cory wanted everything, but above all he wanted everyone together. He would take her to his home-world, he decided, where no child was ever hungry or smacked or abandoned. He would take her there – and she would be another voice, making Mom and Dad stop their endless quarrels and come with him to the stars.

CHAPTER 18

The Starship Kites at Dusk

Thunder prepared for the dreaming-between-the-stars, anxiety squirming in his bowels. He had held out for a few days, then finally, he volunteered. There were new assessments and some training, and then he had been rostered for as many sessions as he could. Some of the regulars had suffered side-effects; rumour sweeping the two ships exaggerated how bad, how many.

Thunder showered with mist to relax and entered an anteroom that smelled of sweet spices. The wall-gardens provided an anchor to the home-world – space would be hard enough without growing things and running water. Skimming Stone was a guide in this endeavour. Thunder found the healer-leader over-eager, over-close, and tried to keep her at a distance.

Hope and fear had filled the mission since the single one had been found. Many of those who had volunteered knew someone on a lost starship, or else killed by the snakes. Many of the crew had had their hopes raised by the tantalising discovery, and cold hard maths told Thunder he was nothing special. The whole felt deeply for them, of course. Any of the people who could be rescued should be.

Each person reached readiness as quickly as they could, then went into the dream chamber. Thunder was not ready, his thoughts were churning.

Maybe it will be your son. Maybe it will be their child, partner, parent. Maybe it will be more. Everyone hoped that a whole ship had survived. Whatever new knowledge they'd gleaned of the snakes might tilt the odds of their desperate struggle for existence. A whole civilisation waited for the next attack.

How quickly things had changed in this time of Hardening.

His mind was a whirlwind. He went through the exercises of mind and body to still them both.

Contact was made regularly with First Harbour, and the Waystation, but Thunder had found the limitations of dreaming-between-the-stars painfully clear. Emotional states and common experiences were easy to share. Complex arguments and precise data were not.

He needed to prepare: an anchor must be strong and solid.

Strange things came into the dreaming, phantoms of some sort. The people were learning a new reality. Some were wondering if the frightened single might have been something similar.

The mission had been sanctioned partly on the assumption that, over stellar distance, dreaming-together was reliable. To learn it was unreliable, as the sceptics had always said, would be useful knowledge, but devastating.

Now Thunder was ready. He entered the chamber, almost late, but not too late to enjoy the ritual among the crew: greeting, smelling, touching as they fitted into their assigned bunks in the dim light. Thunder settled himself and felt the amplified sleep rise to take him.

Down he went, down through dream-layers of hope and fear, through the layers where he sensed other crew walking and feeding, arguing, loving, down to the layer where the first gathered waited. He joined them and took his place: a steadfast weight and a chain for others to hold. He prepared to cast his mind out into the deadly barrenness of space.

Yearning, yearning: *We are here. Join us.*

Almost at once, he felt a sense of others dreaming – those on the sibling ship. There was a brief exchange: *all well? All well.* Then it was as if each ship turned its back on the other, each choosing half the heavens and sending their dreams out.

Now nothingness . . .

People threw names and memories of the lost into the whole. Thunder shared his dream of Little Frog, that last day. The whole picked that up and sang it, the pain of parting, the joy of love, the pain of remembering.

A year of this intensity, and who knew if they would remain sane?

Cry out into the darkness as one voice . . .

Little one . . . little one . . . we are here . . . the people are coming.

The group took up the urgent call that means, *Children! Come to the grown-ups!*

191

It was a long, arduous, futile dream, and some soon lost connection and went swimming back to the wakened world. Some questioned whether to step back from that search and try something else; from others there were angry thoughts, angry at being diverted.

Then something stilled them all.

A faint call – a child responding. *This one hears!*

There was excitement, then doubt: it was so very faint. Thunder was astonished – but how strange to be astonished when you have found what you are looking for! He held the group together as others poured out their welcome.

We hear. Come to us. Come to us.

Very faint. *This one hears!*

The group needed more; Thunder felt the power in them as each reached further. The outward message they sent was *Courage! Focus, little one! Reach us!* The anchors and the healers knew they were raising the risk. Those assigned watched over individuals under strain.

His own heart thundered, far away a physical pain.

Nothing.

People started to bring up names to call out, visions of the lost, making it personal . . .

One more step, and the dreams truly connected. Whoever they had found, it really was one of the people – a child, perhaps ill or wounded or in distress.

This one hears! Come for me!

It *was* his son – it was Little Frog. For a moment, there was nothing in the universe but that stunning, unarguable truth.

Thunder felt his pulse and breathing rise again, a painful

move into the danger zone. He tried to calm himself while calling his son's name. *I know you! I know you!*

In the dream, they touched: the briefest moment of recognition, fleeting and painful. There was so much surprise and confusion – but there was joy as well. They knew each other.

Where, where? The group was asking the essential question, though it was almost painful, interrupting that personal contact. Thunder's body was in distress now, but the group tried to stay strong and keep searching. *Where, where?*

But now all was silence. A single child, of course holding a contact even briefly unaided – that was a miracle.

Thunder returned to the waking world to find a healer beside him and the space crowded. In spite of the pain, he could speak. 'Little Frog,' he gasped. He felt drained, as if he needed null-sleep – as if his body should stay still for ever.

He felt bathed in the envy around him: the healer envied him, Skimming Stone burned with it, and others too – but there were also trills of joy, an uneven clapping that quickly fell into rhythm: a song of return being spun out, his crewmates dancing on the spot in that crowded space.

The lost is found, rejoice!

The wounded and exhausted were tended in a sea of song.

'We will find him,' Skimming Stone called out, and the envy had vanished, turned into something fierce: the furious need to get things done.

Thunder was surrounded by dance, as those who could reached out to touch him or call his name to the rhythm. There were new words now:

> *Thunder, Thunder,*
> *We will find your son.*
> *Thunder, Thunder,*
> *We will find your son.*
> *Where, where?*
> *Among the stars*
> *Thunder Thunder*
> *We will find your son.*

Where?

Little Blue Frog had tried to answer, but all Thunder had heard in the dream was the crashing of waves and wind. It was difficult to think. Later, they would need to debrief and hammer out what facts they could.

The song was a roar now – maybe that was just the pain suppressors. The song was coming from the-all . . . he imagined people stopping to listen, to take the rhythm, to chant the words. By now, Thunder was slipping from reality . . .

A planet with water. That was hardly uncommon, but at least it was a start.

Molly dreamed she was back on Crooked Street, that first time Cory had come into their bed at night, when she'd torn up Dr Jarman's rulebook about infection in return for giving them closeness as a family. She felt his little body, wriggling in between her and Gene.

Dimly, she realised that Cory was speaking to her, that she was half awake and this was not a dream. Gene was in bed beside her, indeed still was, and snoring away.

Cory burbled on, 'Don't wake Fleur.'

Her eyelids weighed about ten pounds each and she kept them shut.

'My people are coming, and *Mom not interested*!'

'Can't this wait till morning?'

'No.' Cory took her shoulder and shook her, and she realised it must be important, for he was usually so protective of her sleep now the baby had come.

'I'm awake,' she said.

'Cory had most excellent dream, yes I did. Father-by-body Thunder Over Mountains on starship – most certain him. Big surprise, he recognised me, I recognised him. All-the-people joyful.'

'Wow,' she said. Every instinct told her that this might be fantasy – but, under it was the hope and the fear it was true.

'My people are looking for the lost and they found me.'

'Go back to bed, Cory,' moaned Gene.

Molly remembered last night: how words had failed to bridge the divide between husband and wife, but there had been a kiss and a hug under the quilt. That modest intimacy had given her hope. Even in winter you can see signs of spring.

'Cory needs to say the whole story now Dad awake.' He went through it again. 'So they didn't know – and now they do,' Cory finished, in case they were too sleepy to understand.

'Right,' Gene said. 'Okay, we sure believe that was what you dreamed—'

The bed was swamped by a big sad wave of feelings. 'If I was making things up, wouldn't I make up my birth-mom being alive? My friends on the starship?'

'Okay.'

A long, long silence.

'I wished I'd known your mom,' Molly said, because Cory liked to hear that.

Gene said, 'I've been thinking about this. So, the Ship said that dreaming among the stars is impossible. But of course, it's like flying: impossible until humans invented balloons. The Ship could amplify your hiding power, couldn't it? So maybe they figured how to amplify dreaming?'

'That's so obvious,' Cory said.

'You can't prove to us these dreams are true,' Gene said, 'but it sure could be true.'

'Your purple father on his way: that's exciting,' Molly said, looking around at her family. They were together in a crowded little pool of love and sadness.

'They don't know where to come,' Cory said. 'They asked and I tried, ever so hard, but the dream was already too weak.'

'It won't be a one-off,' Gene said. 'Try again when you can – just not tonight.'

'Cory will try again – every night, to be sure they know where I am. Show things that only could be Earth.'

'You do that,' Mom said. She smiled, but her eyes were wet.

Silently, Elsa stood watching from the doorway, her face a mask.

'Join us, sweetie-pie,' Molly said, but the girl turned and left.

CHAPTER 19

February turns to March

Weeks came and went: a Maine winter ripped by Atlantic wind, and day by day, winter crept into their marriage. Molly felt that darkness herself, and she could not haul Gene back from it either. So often she was in a room with him, and yet what she felt was alone.

Carol and Storm went back to New York. They quit *Witness*, who turned to the company's aggressive lawyers. Some compromise was threshed out – the resignation was withdrawn and Carol got to write big features, but never on Cory. They came when they dared, which was not often.

The families of the wounded teens fought for compensation, and the Myers were sure they had been hurt – but the plaintiffs made a fatal miscalculation: they refused the offer of free specialist help from the doctors who had treated the soldiers hurt by Cory's power. The Myers through their lawyers also offered to pay for an independent medical examination. The families refused.

The press, and through them the public, took it badly – maybe

197

what Cory did had no long-term effects. What were the families hiding? The judge refused to progress their case without independent evidence.

The DA investigating the incident as a crime was made of sterner stuff and demanded the Myers attend his grand jury in person.

Each day brought something good or ill.

Winter was still at its hardest the day the message got to them about John's heart attack. Gene, pale, started packing to go without blinking.

'Molly,' he insisted, 'they have no one else but me. And if he goes, Eva will need me too.'

If Molly could have flown the family to John's side, she would have done. She wiped away hot tears, angry at life. John was a hundred times more her father than the man who had raised her, but there was a million-dollar bounty on their heads, thanks to a grandstanding oil baron. The FBI were everywhere; every month there was a new story of how they had informers in this group and that. And the Chicago Mob still wanted revenge, for the Ship's attacks on their operation.

Molly rounded up the letters John had sent, telling them not to come, and hid the car keys. And Carol, bless her, talked to Gene, and then Storm did, and between them they persuaded him out of it.

Eva's call came the next day: John did not think they would be safe. He forbade them to come.

At least with that decision wrested out of their hands, Gene and Molly felt united by their love for his parents.

There was such progress in heart medicine, Molly knew, but

would Gene blame her if John died without his son by his side? Molly's AA sponsor used to say that all our hours are counted, but we do not know how long. *Live each day.*

Sometimes Gene got out the guitar and played a few jokey tunes for the children. It reminded her of how strong they had once been, united against all dangers. But sometimes, he would all but disappear, unless a pipe broke or Elsa got her foot stuck. The day Gene announced his plan to get them out of Halcyon, to fly to Hawaii, she thought she was gentle as she pointed out the risks – the long chain of strangers they would have to trust – but Gene barely spoke to her for days after that.

Cory, confused, kept asking, *would they stay together? Would Elsa come with them?*

Then there was the drama of the brooch. Molly couldn't find her special blue brooch; the one Eva had given her for her wedding day. She hadn't brought much with her, but this mattered: it was from the mother she chose.

Cory had said nothing but returned with it ten minutes later. It took her two minutes to find the truth.

'Elsa has a hiding place.'

Elsa stood with the face of an angel and blamed Cory. It was the lie that made Molly angry, not the theft, and now the corridor rang with Elsa's screaming. Molly held onto her wrists, if only to stop her scratching her face. Being gentle was not an option here and Molly got a couple of sharp kicks in return.

'Gene!' she called; then to the girl, 'Stop fighting, I'm not going to hit you—'

'*I won't I won't I won't I won't!*' Elsa fought to bring her wrists up close to her mouth, to bite Molly's hands.

Molly had had quite enough of Elsa biting and kicking. She still had bruises from Saturday, and next time Elsa might find something precious and break it.

'You're hurting!' screamed Elsa.

Cory was moaning, 'Elsa, stop stop stop . . .'

Molly's own temper blazed, but she reined it in, determined not to lash out.

'Look, Wonder Girl, all this shouting isn't helping anyone.' Here was Gene, who Elsa could stir to anger with her goading.

'Monster!'

'We need to talk,' Molly declared, trying to find her sweet and reasonable self. 'That brooch is very precious. If you'd asked, you could have borrowed it.'

'Cory put it there. Octopus Head is a doggone traitor, a rascal.'

'That's a lie, Elsa.'

Elsa writhed and Gene gave a bark, a pained '*Jeez*—'

'I wouldn't have minded, if you'd said sorry and told the truth,' said Molly. 'You were the one who wanted it this way.'

'I hate you. All of you!' she bellowed.

As a parent, you just took those wounds. What else could you do?

That evening, Molly sat in the armchair, enjoying the glow of the stove. Elsa was asleep in her bed, a cherub from a Christmas card. There'd been a graceless apology, at best half meant, and a warm cuddle which meant something deeper. Eva said sometimes kids only play up with the ones they trust not to hurt them.

Tomorrow Elsa might be a lively angel, playing with Fleur and teasing Cory and helping any of the adults. She liked to paint and make things and hear stories, even do chores sometimes. Her reading was improving. But who could tell?

Looking at Elsa, Molly remembered sitting by Cory in the hospital and realising that here was someone alone, hurt, afraid: a child who needed a mother. Once upon a time, Elsa had surely been loved, but not for many years.

Gene came in, and the sudden thought struck her: she had no idea how she would manage Elsa on her own. If Gene left her.

'How's Hurricane Hellion?' Gene said. It was a treat when he smiled. There was a smear of baby rice on his sweater.

Molly smiled back. 'We make a good team.' Elsa was something they were working on together.

Gene sat, putting his arm around Molly, and she leaned in, enjoying his smell – except for the foul tobacco smoke on his sweater – but that reminded her of courting. Even the fact he was trying to give it up again.

Fleur was six months old, growing and changing. When Gene talked about Fleur, when she watched him play with her, she hated to think he would leave them.

They talked a little, about Elsa, about trying this and choosing that.

There had been no sign of the robber. No more newspaper reports, no break-ins at any house within twenty miles. Two months had passed and the man had apparently disappeared – but without money, he had to be *somewhere*.

Elsa told Cory things she wanted all of them to know. Her mother had died long ago. The only image she had was a single photograph, which the robber had burned. She'd been brought up by Auntie, an old woman, and her two daughters – Big Kay, who had been strong and fun but, in the old meaning, simple; and Beauty, who had dated the robber, who had eloped with him, taking Elsa – and beginning her nightmare.

Why Beauty had not protected her, what happened to Beauty . . . Elsa would not say.

Elsa was bitter about the authorities. 'The woman from Child Services told me they would do the right thing – but they believed *him*. They gave me back to *him*.'

Gene coughed, breaking into her pleasant silence. 'They're going to launch *Pioneer*.'

That changed the mood.

The unmanned probe would go further than any human space mission so far, to Jupiter and the outer planets, bouncing from one to another like a pinball. Most incredible of all, it would seek to leave the solar system altogether. It would be a toy boat on the most unimaginable of oceans, humanity's first step to explore all of space.

And millions were saying across the world, *No, don't risk drawing the wrath of the heavens down upon us*. Two men had died on the Moon, the American and Russian Mars probes had failed. Yes, four men had walked on the Moon, but that was with the Ship to protect them. The Ship had been destroyed.

Molly felt such a deep gloom. 'Well, they've built it. Suppose they'd better. It's no use for anything else.'

'I've told Cory he can stay up and watch with Joel.'

'Count me out.'

Astronomers had argued over the dark objects that circled

the Earth, unclaimed by any Earth government. They were hard to spot and even harder to track. If these sightings were true, what were they? Trash, something left by the Ship, or the snakes? Or something active that was watching the Earth with hostile intelligence?

The day of the launch, Molly went to bed before sunset. Something gnawed at her as the clock clicked round, she moved from a book to her friends' letters and back to the book.

Gene came in, and his face said it all.

'All fine, then fifteen minutes after launch' – he gestured – 'a flash of light and nothing. Gone. There was a couple of satellites nearby, and they went too.'

Every long agonising discussion around the kitchen came to the same thing. The Myers had been asked a thousand questions they could not answer. If the nuclear powers united to fire nuclear missiles into space – well, the Myers had nothing useful to tell them about that. If the scientists wanted to know how the snakes worked, or how they could be turned off – the Myers had no wisdom or knowledge to add. Cory could do nothing, except search his dreams for his people. And, since that first contact with his birth-father, he had stopped talking about his dreams altogether, which made Molly fear he too was losing hope.

The next day the Russians lost a satellite, and the day after, the Americans lost another . . .

CHAPTER 20

Halcyon, a fortnight later

Joel had indoor pots filled with bulbs and now the first green tips were showing above the dark soil. Molly touched one, enjoyed the messiness of damp earth on her fingers. Spring was coming, and that always gave her a stirring of hope.

In the kitchen, she and Gene and were working through the mail, from friends and family mostly.

No letters from the lawyers today. Tired of the delays, the DA had indicted them for fleeing, for obstructing justice, and Cory for assault.

There was a letter from Eva, regular as clockwork. John, thank heavens, was doing okay. He was weak on his left side still, and needing a stick, but when they contrived safe phone calls, he cracked jokes about nurses and sounded his old mule-like self.

Diane had sent clippings of news stories in which folks stood up for the Myers. Molly was sifting through them, buoyed that not everything people wrote about Cory painted him as the monster, when she saw the flash of a blue envelope with familiar handwriting. It took a few moments for her to realise who it was: *Selena!*

Molly took the letter, three fat pages, and read it.

Green Bowers
Kauwenga Falls

Dearest M

How long since Molly had been 'dearest'?

Mason has got his way. He got a judge to have me committed to a madhouse for treatment, the lies he told, such lies. They've taken my boys away.

Molly's mouth went dry.

Although I'm not well, M, not at all I'm not quite sure what's real anymore and of course I can't phone you and anyway they would all be listening. All the lies Mason told. You must come and get me, M, you must. YOU KNOW WHO will be able to get me out, won't he? no one need be hurt or anything I'm so sorry we parted on such bad terms . . .

Molly winced at the memory. Their parting had been infuriating, feelings of love and betrayal, anger and concern all fighting for supremacy.

They make sure you take the pills and swallow, and they make me sleepy. I mean they're not rough, the nurses, and the one time someone tried to bother me, an orderly was right there he's about seven feet tall, black and very sweet with the old ones and he won't have anyone hurt. And Dr Friend always wants to talk about Mom, heaven knows why anyone wants to hear about that hideous witch. I must have put on twenty pounds and Mason brought all these new clothes pretending to care and underwear he likes it he can wear it then I'm not going to be his wife and he can wait till hell freezes over before I let him touch me I know that's his plan and Dr Friend's.

But it wasn't my fault Connor trod on the glass, it wasn't, you must believe me. Mason brought his doctor friend, you know, the one with the epileptic wife, and I guess the judge wasn't fooled because he picked this place rather than sending me back to Indianapolis and there is an order Mason has to bring the children for two hours every Tuesday Thursday and Saturday so he is living with some pal of his in the town it is even worse now they the boys I mean don't cry it is like he is turning them into cold sad little copies of him. Gene's a better man than ever I thought. I'm crying now thinking of what I said about Gene and YOU KNOW WHO . . .

Gene touched her hand. 'Bad news?'

It must have been showing. 'Selena's been put in an institution. By Mason, the turd. Uh . . .' How to put it? She settled on, 'She sounds ill.'

Molly raced on. Here the ink was smeared, a pattern like rain — or tears.

YOU KNOW WHO could get me something something the something the only friend I have here. I think secretly he desires me, but he is a real gentleman about it if that sounds funny and I don't feel frightened of him I'm not going to give the name in case this letter is stolen but he is going to post it for me I should have sex with him, because I could tell Mom and she could have a heart attack and go to hell I'd have his baby to get out of here there is a woman who has been in places like this since she was ten. Imagine!

And there is a woman here who thinks she is you, M, can you imagine? Half the people here — well, half the people who are not in outer space already — they believe her and Dr Friend believes the lies the lies Mason told about me you have to come and get me M they're keeping me a secret from everyone but if it got out, I would never have any peace.

I am sorry we parted as we did it was my fault you must come and get me and the boys will be so grateful to you and they will play with YOU KNOW WHO again I'm sorry sorry sorry I was wrong about Gene

All my love
Sel

You might think it isn't me well you went to the prom with James Cartwright and borrowed my Sunday coat and he spilled punch on you and I had to take the blame for getting it dirty what was

*in that punch so it stained beet juice you said it was wine of course
and Mom was such a bitch you are right.*

Also, Honolulu

Molly put down the letter and stared into space. The enormity of it left her numb. Gene took the pages from her hands, and read it, giving her space. He was only halfway through when he said, 'Are you sure it's her?'

Oddly, it had not occurred to her that the letter might be a fake. Gene was right, though: they had to doubt everything. The hand was certainly Selena's, writing fast and under pressure. The story at the end wasn't one many would know. Yet the clincher was 'Honolulu' – their old code word for 'we won't always be living with our mother'. Until Selena came back into her life, she had forgotten it.

Be careful, thought Molly. A drugged woman in a mental institution – maybe they had got it out of her? Traded more time with her boys for a letter to her sister? She imagined some grim-faced FBI agent, the President's Chief of Staff, even Mason, standing behind her sister as she wrote it.

Gene's face was determined. 'We'll call her lawyer – no, we'll get one of *our* friends to call our lawyer and find out what really happened. We can break into our emergency money.'

'Yes.'

Selena and Molly, under the covers, reading the same forbidden book with a flashlight. Selena the snitch, yet when Molly was sent to bed without supper, sneaking her a sandwich. The day Selena flashed her new engagement ring, her eyes blazing defiance. 'We're moving to Indiana and, if Mother follows, we'll move to Alaska.'

Gene went on, 'Even if she's ill, we might be able to do better. Sue the institution. We'll call today.'

'Uh-huh. Yes.' It meant a drive to somewhere they could make calls.

Molly remembered the nuns, the burning pain of the wooden ruler on her hand, and Selena's eyes wet, as if she had been struck herself.

She'd missed something Gene had said, and he might have noticed. 'Our lawyer must be careful,' he repeated, a little slower. 'We don't want anyone to know we're looking.'

'Sel's right,' said Molly. 'Cory could get us in, and out. Particularly at night. The psych places drug everyone, they like to keep them calm and quiet . . .'

Gene looked shocked, like she had burst into flames. Then he snapped, 'No. Never. We can't. Go and *rescue* her? You're *out of your mind.*'

Molly had only been thinking aloud. 'Who else will help her?'

'We will – of course we will. Safely, from a distance. Dr Jarman will know what to do.'

Molly was feeling powerless, trapped. The strain of these last weeks was telling on her, the sense of that invisible canyon between her and Gene; hiding from the world, needing each other, but a lot of the time, barely liking each other. Memories of brighter times felt like someone else, or a dream.

'Maybe we have to.'

Gene frowned, made his hands into fists. He was losing his

temper. 'Jeez,' he said, 'not so long ago, we thought John might be *dying* – and you said, no, don't go. Let him die.'

'John *told* us not to!'

'Your sister, who has *never* done anything for us . . . for you—'

Molly felt her fury rising, a boiling geyser which would not be held back.

An hour after the argument, Gene and Molly still couldn't look at each other. They briefed Carol and Storm, who looked shocked.

'The whole country is looking for you,' Carol said. 'We can't take the children. I can't deal with Elsa; I don't know how you put up with her.'

'Poor kid,' said Storm. 'You're going to take all the kids into danger? It might be a trap—'

'Yes,' Gene snapped. 'You're right. We don't need to mount a rescue mission. All we need is to talk to our lawyer.'

'Yes, as the first step,' Molly said. *Just like a man.* All she had said was, *don't say never. Don't patronise me, I understand the danger. But Sel is my sister – you never had one, you can't understand.*

She went on, 'If our lawyer can get her safe, we don't need to do anything dangerous.'

So the day's plans were scrapped. Cory wanted to know why and sulked when they wouldn't tell him. Storm drove Gene and Molly – on slippery roads and under ominous skies – towards one of the houses Halcyon kept an eye on. Using their phone was part of the deal.

Inside the house, cold and joyless in winter, Storm dialled

the number with stiff fingers and gave the code phrase Molly read from her blue notebook.

Ten minutes later the phone rang, and Molly snatched it up. Their lawyer opened with news of his own. He was with Dr Jarman, who had had a letter too.

Gene and Molly struggled both to hear on one handset. Green Bowers existed; it was well thought of. Between Dr Jarman and the lawyer, they'd established that a Mrs Selena O'Regan had been committed locally. The judge had taken against the husband and, moved by Selena's plea for her children, had ordered her treated in the county – under her grandmother's maiden name, for privacy. There had been no press.

Molly had thought that rescue would be a last resort, but she feared what Mason would do.

We must move quickly.

Gene was looking at her in that superior male way.

'What can we do?' he said to her.

She repeated that and the lawyer said, 'Try to get whichever clown represented her out of the way, so we can get her effective representation.'

Dr Jarman came on the line. 'File for an independent medical examination to slow up any attempt to move her.'

Gene said, 'Won't they know it's us? I mean, someone has to be behind the lawsuit.'

Silence fell, a count maybe of ten or more.

'Okay, that is a complication,' said Dr Jarman.

'It sounds like the court is leaky. Once the press know who Selena is . . . And Dr Jarman, you're not exactly low-profile.'

'I understand,' he growled. 'We'll think of something.'

They agreed to speak again in a couple of hours, which left the decision whether to wait, or spend half that time driving to Halcyon and back.

Cory could walk in and walk Selena out again. The thought just wouldn't leave Molly alone.

While they waited, Molly looked at the bookshelves, such an indicator of a life: whether someone was orderly or not, whether they thought of books as decorations, or heirlooms to be treasured. This bookshelf had all the signs of a vacation home, with old, mismatched paperbacks, big-name authors with crumpled covers, and a set of leather-bound classics bought from a catalogue. Maine winters must give you time to read Dickens and Twain, Molly supposed. There were maps here too, a wildlife book, and guidebooks, including a *Gazetteer of the States*.

Where the heck is Kauwenga Falls anyway? Molly wondered. *How far away?*

Gene and Storm were deep in discussion about what contacts they had – Gene planning flight again – so Molly slipped the *Gazetteer* from the shelf.

It couldn't hurt to know.

CHAPTER 21

Two days later

Molly was on the phone to Rosa, anxious for news.

'Mason's moved for a hearing next week,' Rosa said. 'We're leaving for Kauwenga Falls in an hour. Your sister needs allies on hand.'

Molly wished it was liked *Bewitched*, and she could wiggle her nose and be there.

'Thanks.'

'I have to testify,' Rosa said. 'That man has to be stopped. I think your sister – well, she's a frail vessel. She deserves better.'

Testify? thought Molly.

'About the bruises?' There were no ethics charges against Rosa, and she had examined Selena, that second day in Amber Grove.

'More than that. Selena told me what Mason did.' Rosa took a deep breath. 'Mason is an animal,' she said, with venom. 'I gave her an intimate examination . . . He forced her, Molly, there were clear signs. I need to tell the court that.'

For a moment, Molly thought she had misheard. Then fury came, and disgust and fear.

'The doctors don't believe her,' Rosa said. 'But with a witness . . .'

'They'll call you a liar.'

'I will tell the truth and shame the devil. If she lets me.' Molly could see Rosa, stiff-backed and firm-jawed: precise, professional, unflappable. Rosa would be a witness any lawyer would crave.

Molly found her eyes wet. Why hadn't her sister told her?

Rosa read the silence. 'She made me swear, Molly. She was hurt and ashamed. She says you warned her about that man . . . and she feels she wronged you in the past. I mean, it will be up to her.'

'We need to drop everything and go tomorrow,' Molly said.

After making her farewells, she went to find Gene, already dreading the discussion. They always came back to old arguments, just the two of them sitting on the double bed. But this was urgent.

Gene ventured, 'The kids won't be safe.'

'I'll go on my own,' Molly said, a hundred questions springing up as she said it.

'For what? We're not going to bust Big Sis out — over my dead body, Molly. Even if we were . . . how would you help?' He gave a weak smile. 'I mean, I know you're the brains of the crew, but this is out of your league.'

Molly could lie. She knew hospitals; she had some idea of pretending to be staff, or even a different relative.

'But you look like her,' Gene said. 'They might notice.'

She debated telling Gene about Mason's vile act — at one time she would have told him everything — but he needed no persuading that Mason was bad news. Her husband just wanted his family safe too.

The truth lay between them. Cory would bring something to the mission, something important, something dangerous.

'If Cory came—'

'No! None of the kids. Anyway, you'd want Little Boo with you, and if Elsa is left anywhere, she'll think we're giving up on her. You'll hear the screaming in Bangor.'

'It's only as an absolute back-up.'

'*Huh!*'

Using Cory to rescue Selena was a sticking point for Gene. 'It's just not fair to ask him. He's terrified of his nightmare power. He can't control it. We must never put him in a position which forces him to use it. We'll just be arrested, Molly. *He* might be dissected.' Gene hesitated. 'Molly, let's throw what we have into helping her. But let's be smart and do it from far away.'

Molly was stubborn and had fought Gene often, but a nagging voice was weakening her resolve: he might be right.

In search of allies, Molly found Cory and Elsa in the high room, making an exuberant alien dance with Cory clapping the rhythm.

'Practising a welcome dance,' Cory said, breathing a little fast. 'Laughing fine as welcome is a very happy dance. Purples and humans can dance together, when my people come.'

Molly nearly asked if he had heard anything in a dream. No,

he would have come running as he did with any good news. His ears drooped a little.

'It's a stamping-on-spiders dance,' said Elsa. 'Or cockroaches. I bet Cory's people eat cockroaches. I bet his whole planet is crawling with them.'

Cory paused. 'You . . . you are . . . Grand High President of the Cockroaches.'

Elsa stifled a giggle and flared up. Her synthetic anger was very good. 'Monster! Abomination!'

'Criminal! Cockroach!'

This could take a while. Molly clapped her hands. 'Cory, come on, I need a serious conversation, just us two.'

Elsa's face dropped and her mouth opened to argue.

'Elsa too,' said Cory.

Molly pleaded, 'A few minutes, sweetie-pie, then you can decide what we have for supper.'

'Elsa too.'

Molly gave in.

'You know we said Aunt Selena was in a healing place and wanted to get out? To be with her boys?'

'Yes,' said Cory, ears alert. 'You had clever plan.'

'Well, we need to be closer to her to help get her out.'

Cory's ears folded down. 'You want me to sneak in and sneak her out? She doesn't like me very much no-no-no. Also, how many Bad Men—?'

'Dad and I agree, we should try other things first. It would be to help us hide if we needed. We need to go there to tell some people what we know, face to face.'

'Humans should invent picture phones,' said Cory.

'Rosa and Dr Jarman will be there too. We'd just be there to help.'

'Oh good,' said Cory. 'This plan means we can see Rosa and Dr Jarman? Good people Elsa.'

'Yes, if we're careful.'

'If Elsa comes too, we'll need a big car.'

Molly looked at Elsa, whose face was impassive. That was always a tricky sign.

Molly waited too long. Cory gripped his head. 'Oh no oh no oh no. We must take Elsa. She will promise, she will behave; I will make her. Grown-ups keep letting her down.'

Molly looked at her son, and thought again how Earth might be corrupting him. What was he learning? What lay behind those wide-open violet eyes, and the twitching of his tentacles?

Gene and Molly were deadlocked.

Her sister, powerless and ill, could be handed back to a vindictive, brutal man, her rapist.

So, she thought, *I'll leave Gene behind. He'll have to follow.*

That thought became a plan, a desperate plan. An unwise plan that kept her from sleep. All night she tossed and turned, thinking of her sister frightened and unprotected in that place, her sister alone if the end of the world came.

And Mason, the monster, prowling around outside the institution, the mere possibility of it tormenting Sel . . .

At five o'clock, Carol was already up and in the kitchen.

Molly needed to explain. 'I'm going to bundle the kids in the car and go.'

After an instant of shock, Carol placed her cup down

with care and started listening. 'To Kauwenga Falls, without Gene?'

Yes, if I must. She ignored her inner doubts.

'Gene will come. I'll leave a note. But this is the only way he'll know I'm serious. He's right, we can't use Cory to break in. But Sel needs to know I'm there for her.'

Carol was silent, working it through.

'Hard to tell, other people's marriages,' she said.

Molly drank her coffee; she was itching to work through the packing list.

'I mean, Storm and I have our disagreements.'

Molly felt she had to justify herself. 'He's so stubborn. He needs to realise—'

'Yet you talked him out of going into the lion's den for his father? Who might have been dying? Seems quite a listener to me.'

'I've got to force the issue. Time is ticking.'

'Molly, you need some plain speaking,' said Carol. 'This idea is nuts.'

Molly glared at her. Last week Carol had suggested Molly try therapy. *I don't need your permission. Your interference.*

Carol went on, 'Suppose he thinks *you'll* back down, what are you going to do? Sit in a diner and wait for three days?'

'We need to get there before the hearing.'

'You've decided to go and you're just looking for an excuse. It's about making Gene responsible if you end up taking the kids on your own.'

That was a piercing, painful truth.

Now Molly was tottering on the high wire and really not sure which side she would fall.

Carol said, 'I'll talk to Storm. You need people with you who won't be recognised, and a change of drivers.'

'You'll help?'

Carol took a few moments, then said, 'I'll talk to Storm.' She wasn't smiling.

It was a grey morning, but the clouds promised rain, not snow. Spring really was coming. Elsa complained it was too early to go driving, but she and the baby were already in the Beast, the only vehicle big enough to hold them all. Carol brought Molly's case last.

'I'll follow in mine.'

'Will you come all the way?'

'I haven't decided.'

But Cory had questions. Those pleading violet eyes, a firm little hand on her arm. 'When will Dad come? When *exactly*?'

Molly had hated her own mother's casual lying, but the pure truth wouldn't do here either. 'Dad needs to do some things. He won't be long, and we won't be far away.'

'What things? Why isn't he waving us off?'

'He needs his sleep. I've left a note, to make sure he remembers, and Joel knows too.'

'But Mom, Dad will definitively and most certainly come?' There was such insistence for the truth in the voice. 'Promise?'

'Yes, Cory, he will.'

'Suppose something bad happens. Suppose the Bad Men come—'

'They won't, and Joel would hide him, and tell us.'

Molly realised she'd been avoiding his eyes; she needed to

meet his gaze again. Cory looked up at her and she saw the uncertainty on his face. Felt it, radiating out from him.

'Cory trusts you, Mom. Not all humans can be trusted. No, not at all. Very bad thing about Earth.'

She could tell him the full truth. And he would hide and go into the house to tell Gene.

'I'm not planning to go to Kauwenga Falls without him,' she said. 'It's going to be much better if he comes.'

Cory did his human sigh. Then he got in the Beast, still not truly convinced, and she tried to clamp down on the sadness and disgust at herself.

Storm revved up the Beast, which growled and complained. Molly didn't like the way the Beast handled, and Gene was no fan either. Carol would follow in her car.

They had been safe at Halcyon, and now she was leaving to go tilting at windmills. She kept feeling these waves of doom crashing around in her stomach.

An hour's drive later, they were at a place that Carol knew well: a gloomy guesthouse in black and dark green, set back from the road. Its white shutters looked like an afterthought. There was something a bit ramshackle about the chimney; the porch missed a coat of paint.

Two women lived there – friends of friends. 'It's kind of a place for women,' Carol said. 'They'll be fine with Gene, if I vouch for him, and if he doesn't stay long.'

The greeting was glacial. One woman was in her sixties, lean and disapproving. The other, rather younger, was unsmiling.

There was a terse, whispered conversation. It was obvious they were not welcome.

Joel would phone from Halcyon when Gene left. The plan really depended on her being out of touch, so Gene couldn't get hold of her. He might get the number out of Joel, though.

Inside, Molly was sitting with Fleur in the room with the phone. Untidy shelves and stacks of magazines surrounded her. Of all things, there was a table set with geological specimens, fossils, the skull of a lynx.

Gene would phone, tell her she was nuts and that he wouldn't come. She bit her lip, trying to distract herself. Sitting here, it was obvious he would call her bluff.

Cory and Elsa were off together being secretive somewhere. She picked up a copy of *Ms* magazine, flicking through it. In its pages, ideas which had once seemed revolutionary were being openly discussed. The Equal Rights Amendment had been sent out to the states to be ratified. The President supported it. Strange times.

Mason's crime was not a crime in the laws written by men.

They would have equal rights under the snakes: equal rights under death.

Two hours after she'd left Halcyon, she checked the phone had a dialling tone. There were only a couple of days before the hearing.

Why had she done this? Gene needed to understand what danger Selena was in. Of course, if she phoned him – well, he would have the upper hand. And husband and wife arguing over the phone never worked.

Fleur watched her, coughed a little: a pretty little stoic. Molly let her chew a spoon, watch the glitter of a bright pebble. Molly told stories and made animal noises with the fossils.

After three hours, she told the others she was going for a walk, left Fleur with the other women and went to where she could see the road. Twenty minutes later, Molly felt foolish and cold. She turned round and saw Storm marching towards her.

'Joel called. Gene's left in a foul temper. Molly, this wasn't your smartest idea.'

'I'm glad,' she said. She'd done something stupid, and she needed to fix it. 'He'll be here for lunch.' A thought hit her. 'If you disapprove, why did you—?'

Storm produced a set of car keys.

'Carol thought you might go on your own. So I took these. You weren't going anywhere.'

Molly reached for them, and Storm moved them away.

Back inside, Cory and Elsa had written a song: 'When will Dad come?' Of course, now she couldn't drive back in case they missed each other.

Another hour passed, then two. Molly flicked through books of no interest.

Then a horn sounded from somewhere out front.

Storm was out first, Molly rushing after. A tow-truck had appeared, an unfamiliar face behind the wheel. It was towing Dr O'Brien's car. Its front fender and hood were all bent in. Gene, wrapped in scarves, was sitting behind the driver. As soon as the truck came to rest, Gene opened the door and was out.

She'd prepared an apology, an angry defence, a full-frontal attack, but in her heart was capitulation. Now she saw him, driving full of anger because of her, coming off the road – but for a spin of the wheel, he might have died . . .

'Kids okay?' Gene said, frowning, looking world-weary.

The fight had completely drained out of her. 'Yes. They're not talking to me much. Are you all right?'

'Yeah. It was the other guy's fault.' She could tell that wasn't the whole truth. 'Another couple of satellites gone. It said on the radio. Something up there sure doesn't want us in space.'

The driver was looking at her, at her ugly disguise glasses and all. He seemed excited, as if he already knew who they were.

Gene gave the driver a thumbs-up. 'He figured it out. If he hadn't been passing . . .'

'I'm cold,' Molly said. 'Come on, let's get inside.'

The driver put down Gene's bag and guitar, while Storm made herself scarce.

'We need to settle this, and not in front of the kids,' Gene started. 'You're nuts, Molly. You've done some damn-fool stuff in your time but—'

'You weren't *listening*,' she said. *Don't cry, Molly, don't cry.*

'Says you. I can't believe our friends fell for this nonsense. Splitting us up . . . ? It was just crazy!'

'You started it—'

'I didn't want to put the kids in danger.'

'I haven't – not really.' It all felt so stupid now. The wind was up, blowing the cold into her heart.

'So, these are my conditions,' said Gene. 'None of us try to get into Green Bowers. It needs to be top secret we're even in the area, let alone involved in the case. No Cory powers. No midnight rescue.'

Suddenly, it felt easy to agree. 'You're right, of course.' She touched his hand, but he didn't react. 'I promise. Sel won't even know I'm there,' she said, more for something to say.

'She can, if we can trust her to keep her mouth shut.' It was almost a snarl. 'And then we'll decide where we go next. Halcyon is driving us nuts. You owe me, Molly.'

He might be in a better mood when he'd eaten. She would have thanked him, but for that last part. *Owe me?*

Hang on, Sel, she thought. *We're coming*. But there wasn't any joy in that thought.

226

CHAPTER 22

Finding Mrs O'Regan

Dr Pfeiffer looked from the window at Lake Delaney and the town that clustered on its southern edge, lights gleaming in the darkness. Kauwenga Falls would have been pretty on a postcard, but small-town America bored him, always preaching its own virtue, backwards, and resolute in local superstition.

It was a clear night and the stars blazed. Out there, a struggle more momentous even than the war between freedom and Communism was being waged: a struggle between life and destruction. Snake machines were orbiting the Earth; they had already struck down *Pioneer* and several satellites in humanity's back yard – so why had they stayed their hand? What were they plotting? Maybe, just maybe, they had inadequate numbers for an attack and this was just the cosmic equivalent of a few snipers in the forest. He certainly hoped so.

Pfeiffer did what he did for the future of humanity.

His precisely sculpted goatee itched. He could not wait to get rid of the disguise; it was like an annoying parasite – but he'd been the only one able to bluff his way into Green Bowers. Norton, the laughing, ice-cool leader of Overton's team, had somehow found sketch-maps of the interior layout. And the orderly, their man on the inside, was essential.

Pfeiffer, no fan of amateur dramatics, had borrowed a colleague's obsession with a link between viruses and mental illness – had borrowed, in fact, his name and even his appearance. The director of Green Bowers, flattered, had agreed to let Pfeiffer see the key files, which had allowed Pfeiffer to read Selena O'Regan's notes, as well as access the inner sanctum, where he took photos of the alarm system, somewhere the orderly could never go.

He checked his watch. Norton and his men would be waiting to slip into the institution; the orderly only had to persuade Mrs O'Regan to the side door. For Selena, the chance of freedom and her children were enough to get compliance.

Pfeiffer pulled on the unfamiliar coat and hat and picked up the all-important case. His stomach quivered. He shouldn't have let himself be talked into handling the orderly himself. Overton would never come within two hundred miles himself, but he had insisted that only Pfeiffer could be trusted to handle the delicate negotiation.

As the plan hurtled towards resolution, Pfeiffer felt outwitted, a flank exposed – but if Overton's spies were correct, Dr Jarman and his wife, the nurse, were already in the area. The Myers' old gang was getting back together.

Pfeiffer left the hotel, the sidewalks and roads still crunching with grit. He shivered as the bitter wind hit him, but here was the car that would take him to calm Mrs O'Regan – with words or, if all else failed, a needle. He would have to explain the delay in getting the boys. The judge clearly didn't trust Mr O'Regan one little inch, for he had placed the boys with the Sheriff's family. The issue now was less whether Norton could get the boys but whether he could do it quietly: could his men take that fortress of a farmhouse before the news was radioed across the world.

Pfeiffer was plagued with second thoughts. The orderly might change his mind. Smuggling out Selena's letters was very different to busting her out. He was a decent man and he might go to the police – perhaps that had been his intention all along. The plan might fail.

Yet surely Mrs Myers, an emotional woman, would react to her sister's pleas – the letter, the phone calls to mutual acquaintances. And then the Myers, and Cory, would all be safe – under his care.

He just had to go through with it. His guts writhed again, and yet again he tasted the chalky medicine he needed to keep it quiescent.

They drove past the modest church where he had done the deal. The orderly was a trusted member of staff, but his wife's cancer had spread and he was hopelessly in debt. Pfeiffer had felt guilty watching a good man wrestle with a strong conscience.

'Mrs O'Regan's a nice lady,' the orderly had said. 'I just wonder—'

'Don't worry,' Pfeiffer had said. 'The plan is fool-proof. And you're helping her keep her boys: that alone is a wonderful thing you're doing. We're her friends. We're not asking you to do anything wrong.'

'You promised—'

'Yes, and everything I said was true. Mrs O'Regan won't be harmed. She'll be reunited with her children. And we'll protect you from suspicion.'

Cancer was a terrible disease. All the new surgeries, radiation and chemotherapy made some impact, but they were still so crude. *Maybe*, thought Pfeiffer, *what we could learn from Cory's biology or from his people would make it a thing of the past.*

Overton was a tidy man and the orderly was a risk. He'd offer the family free treatment, a new job, a new name, in one of his hospitals down South – and whisk them to another state to ensure their silence.

Pfeiffer felt his pulse rise. There was Green Bowers, a pleasant house set among evergreens. Selena's disappearance must flush out the Myers one way or another, but surely even Mrs Myers would be grateful.

And where Mrs Myers was, Cory would be nearby.

CHAPTER 23

'Visit Scenic Kauwenga County'

Kauwenga County was rolling farmland and wooded hills. The two-car expedition arrived there late on the second day, and for safety, would be staying five miles out of town. It was very like Amber County, but although Molly could see differences, she couldn't quite put her finger on them – the churches and barns, maybe? They drove past the town and around the scenic lake, and, in a wild moment, Molly was tempted to *go now* – to get it over with. *Go tonight, use Cory. Get it done.*

She pushed that thought away: she'd promised Gene. In any case, the idea of what might go wrong terrified her.

Gene was still brooding, so Molly tried to lift his mood. 'I told you we would travel, see exciting new places,' she joked.

His silence said, *Huh*. He had not really forgiven Carol and Storm either.

She had gambled and got what she wanted and yet she'd lost. She knew Gene was waiting for something to go wrong – something to prove this whole trip was a dangerous mistake. He thought the biggest danger was Selena's lawyers, who would have to pretend they did not know the Myers were in town. Rosa would be testifying in support of Selena, but she was a public figure now. It would only take a smart local journalist and the world would know something was up. Would Mason think everyone knowing the Myers involvement would help him, somehow?

Rosa and Dr Jarman, arriving first, were staying with the senior lawyer's family. For the Myers, he had arranged the use of some summer house where they could avoid prying eyes. Carol and Storm took one room – Carol being 'unable to sleep with strangers, dogs or babies' – which meant Molly and the kids packed into the bed in the other room, with Gene on a mattress on the floor. Elsa was up twice, complaining of toothache, which made for a restless night for everyone.

Early the next morning, a bright, bouncing young lawyer turned up, half Red Setter and half Prom King. He endeared himself to Molly by making the boiler work and producing bags of fruit and pastries – but he brought bad news as well. Selena had been too ill to speak to them yesterday, so she hadn't been able to agree to their plan. The senior partner would be coming as soon as he'd spoken to Selena today.

Dr Jarman and Rosa were next to arrive. As they embraced, Molly thought about how long they'd been apart, how much they had to talk about. She wanted some private time with Rosa – ex-boss, ex-nemesis and now trusted friend.

But right now, the business of the day was pressing. The children took their meal next door, 'because grown-ups needed to talk horrid grown-up things'. They could be trusted not to make a mess, though doubtless, Elsa would be stuffing the dog with pastries.

The lawyer got straight to it. 'We've a stack of motions to file as soon as we can. We'll tell them we want Mrs Jarman to testify — we want to stop the husband and reopen the question of custody.' He looked as though he would relish the fight. 'I imagine we'll be seeing a lot of bad temper from Mr O'Regan's side.'

'Selena's happy with this line of approach?' Dr Jarman asked, squeezing Rosa's hand.

The young lawyer suddenly looked concerned.

He'll need better control to win cases, Molly thought, worried.

'She's been very anxious — and ill,' he admitted. 'The director of Green Bowers was very difficult this morning. The senior partner is on the phone to the place now — threatening them with a court order to give us access to our client.'

'I don't get this,' Gene said. 'A man can rape a woman and get away with it, if she's his wife? I mean, it's a crime to break her jaw, but *that* isn't?'

'That's the law in every state,' said the lawyer. 'There's been some fine talk, but that's where the politicians have left us. So right now, what matters is—'

He was cut off by the sound of the phone ringing. When he answered it, they could tell the person at the other end was furious, but no one could pick out the words.

The lawyer's eyes widened. 'Rivers of fire, they've lost her.'

Molly felt the ground lurch underneath her. She looked at Gene, who looked as horrified as she felt.

The voice crackling down the phone hadn't finished, and now

the young lawyer relayed the information as he got it. 'Green Bowers admitted she's disappeared, along with a member of their staff, an orderly on night duty.'

After some more chatter, he reported, 'They've called the police.'

'People will find out who she is,' Gene said, the dismay in his voice almost palpable. 'This town will be knee-deep in reporters by sundown.'

'She must be in danger,' Molly said. 'They must find her – *we* have to look for her.' Even as she said it, she knew the idea of the Myers starting a search in an unknown town was foolish.

The young lawyer handed Molly the phone and she heard the voice of the senior lawyer saying, 'Mrs Myers, this is monstrous. Green Bowers found out at 6 a.m. – and they dared to stall us while they looked for her. She might have been gone since *last night*: it is criminal incompetence.'

'In this weather?' Molly pictured her sister in thin institutional pyjamas, and a sudden conviction seized her. 'Mason's kidnapped her. She's in the most terrible danger.'

'I'm going to court now,' said the lawyer. 'I've asked the chief of police to meet me there. We'll have that snake O'Regan locked up, I promise you.'

'What about her boys?'

'They're fine. Connor and Rory are staying with a police family. But we are hearing now – days later – that there have been unknown men calling at the house. Lord knows why we weren't told immediately, and you may rest assured we will be making certain the judge knows this. Anyway, these men, whoever they were, they didn't get the time of day. Ike was in the

234

Marines, and both his boys are – and they're back on furlough. I'd put my dollars on Carrie too; I've seen her kill a deer with a headshot . . . But Mrs Myers, we must keep you out of this. We don't want to start any other nonsense – and remember, we can't know you're here. I'll call when I have more news.'

Gene said, 'The locals will call in the FBI.'

'They'll be criticised every hour they don't,' their lawyer said.

A big Federal manhunt like that? They'd soon figure out who Selena's sister was.

Molly gripped Gene's hand to keep her afloat. She didn't know what to do.

They'd been promised an update in an hour, but it was more than two hours later that the lawyer called. Carol and Storm disappeared to take photos in town, they said, and the Jarmans worked on their affidavits.

'They're searching Mason's place now. That wife-beater looks as guilty as hell, though he's denying everything, of course.'

'We need to get out of here,' Gene said, looking grim. 'This is all too dangerous –the cops are probably on the way.'

'Yes, we'll get ready to run,' Molly agreed. *But I won't abandon my sister . . .*

'I'm going to clear my head. You know what Cory's like right now. Can you imagine how scared he will be if he thinks the cops are coming?'

I told you so hovered unsaid in the air.

Molly knew she deserved it.

Then Gene, bless him, said, 'I know she's your sister and we've got to help her – but us getting arrested won't help anyone. We still need to go.'

Sisters together, for ever. Would Selena expect some mad rescue, even with the risk to Molly's children? What risks would she take for Molly?

Love isn't a balance sheet. Molly knew the lawyers would do their best, but Selena needed her.

When Gene had gone off to pack, making the point, Rosa asked, 'So, how is he?'

Where to begin? Molly looked at Dr Jarman, buried in a book. She didn't feel up to discussing her marriage in front of him.

'Good days and bad. Let's talk later.'

The day unfolded, Molly struggling with wanting to do something – anything. Knowing what to say to Cory and Elsa was hardest.

Some hours later, they were told the orderly had been found, beaten and tied up in a neighbour's shed. He was cold and thirsty, and bleeding where he had worked his hands free. It looked simple enough: the night before, he'd gone for a smoke and been jumped by four masked men. They'd subdued him, injected him, and held him down until he passed out. It hadn't been hard to identify their way in: a little-used door into the grounds had been forced.

When the lawyer called again, the news was grim. 'When the police searched O'Regan's motel room and car they found rope, duct tape, bottles of sleeping pills, women's clothes and underwear, and – *ah, um* – some . . . well, personal hygiene products. He didn't do a great job explaining that away.'

Each sentence was making Molly feel colder.

'What possible excuse could he have?' said Gene, his face pressed to Molly's so he too could hear the lawyer.

'The pills are the ones his wife takes – he forgot he had them with him. He'd brought her the clothes she needed, but this was the stuff she didn't want. The rope – just a tow rope for emergencies. There are a hundred things you might need duct tape for on the road. Well, it's all circumstantial, but the chief plans to keep him in the cells, tonight anyway.'

'So what next?' Molly said. It felt like they were in a trap.

'They've already put out her description and started the search.' The tone of his voice changed. 'Of course, neither the judge nor I know her famous sister is in town, but they'll call in the FBI, soon as they figure it out.'

'Why isn't he with Selena?' Gene said suddenly. 'If Mason has her, why aren't they together?'

'That's the $64,000 question,' the lawyer said as he ended the call.

Gene and Molly went into the kitchen, leaving the lawyers to their work.

'That's pretty incompetent, if he is the kidnapper,' said Gene. 'Why would he hang around?'

'He's after the boys. He probably needs Selena to get them.'

'Cory could read if Mason is lying, or the orderly.'

'*Jeez*, Molly – *no!*' Gene banged the table 'We will *not* put our son in danger – we can't let *anyone* know we're around. Maybe Mason is spilling the beans now. No, we need to pack up and move a hundred miles away. We need to be on the road in thirty minutes.'

'Sel might be chained up in some basement,' Molly tried, 'without her medication.'

237

'She doesn't deserve that, or any of this, but I'm not putting *our* heads in a noose. That won't help her, or anyone.'

Molly felt her face getting warmer, the memory still rankling. 'When we were last on the run, we thought the Feds had your parents and I *begged* you not to give us away. You still called them. You could have brought the whole world down on us—'

'That's different. I was careful—'

'You don't care about my sister.'

'Why would you say that? I've sure tried my hardest. Miss Congeniality she isn't. Your sister stabbed us in the back.'

Gene was nibbling his thumb, like some overgrown child. She felt the anger rise and tried to control it. 'You never liked Sel.'

He sighed. 'Molly, there's no talking to you in this mood.'

She could smack him. 'My sister is kidnapped by her rapist and that's *a mood*?'

'I rest my case: we gotta pack and go. Let Edgar and Rosa hold the fort here.'

'Go on, then, *leave us. Go hiking*, why don't you? Take a *vacation*.'

'You can talk.' He made a wild sweep of the arm. '*I* didn't bring the kids into danger.'

She knew he'd bring that up every day until the end of time. It stung that he might even be right.

Gene's face softened and he reached to touch her shoulder, but she brushed him off and opened the door. The Jarmans, not looking at her, lifted their books. She realised they had been listening and she flushed.

'Molly—' Gene said.

'I'm staying. Find out what Cory's doing. I'm going for a walk.'

Outside, there were crocuses, white, yellow and purple: an unexpected beauty that should have lifted her heart. And there was Storm, usually such a strong woman, looking more anxious than Molly had ever seen her.

'What's up?'

'Disappearance Inc – the FBI's found Halcyon. They've searched the place, and arrested Joel.'

Cory was always drawing, the views, the people he was with, writing people's names in alien. Had every sign that the Myers had been there been hidden? She couldn't believe that Joel would betray them – Joel did not know where they were heading – but the inevitable clutter of family life might.

CHAPTER 24

Kites at Dusk

Recovery had been slow. Thunder over Mountains had not been allowed to dream-between-the-stars for weeks, to give his mind and body time to heal. Not that he felt strong enough to try. But there were other things he could do to help the search as the people tried to understand where Little Frog might be.

Wind and waves. Well, that meant a planet with atmosphere and open water. The people were constantly on the look-out for worlds that met those criteria, For the search, it would not have to be a prime colony site, just somewhere a person could survive for a couple of years. There were many such worlds where a single expedition had visited, done a brisk survey, seen no obvious sign of advanced life and left. Many worlds with wind and water had some other inconvenient feature: a most eccentric orbit, an unstable axis of rotation, an unstable sun, or no land at all.

Machine and human minds plotted the many sixteens of worlds which *Dancer on the Waves* might have reached, but visiting all of them would take a lifetime. And they might still miss Little Frog. Suppose he had no working beacon – they might find the right world and still not be able to find him.

There were the optimists who were truly pessimists – Little Frog might be on some deadly world, where sea and sky were poisons like methane, ammonia and the like. Those were more common; the home system had two such planets and four such moons. Yes, it was realistic that a machine mind, or even an automated system, might keep a child alive for years on such a planet – an environmental dome perhaps, or a section of the ship repurposed.

What made this depressing was that the search net would have to be cast so much wider. But at least it gave the modellers something to argue about. What did wind and waves on such worlds sound like? Thunder asked others, to see if their sound models sounded like what he heard.

Little Frog had been yearning for his own kind in the dream, but was he wholly alone? Some of the crew thought that something benign was sleeping near him. No, sending out dreams to find him was the only way. No one could get a stellar map across in a dream, but there must be something that the machine minds could work on – something about how he lived, what the local fauna was like, an odd moon.

Thunder fought the healers until they let him join another search. Maybe the personal link might tip the balance. Who knew?

He prepared, and this time there was a new ritual: everyone he passed touched him, saying, 'We will find your son.' Thunder hated it, but he could see he was giving everyone who had lost someone a taste of hope, so he showed joy and tolerated it.

When sleep came, he fought the dream, until he realised that the healers knew what they were talking about. His resistance to joining was unlike anything he had known, but the crewmates helped him fight his way in. This time, the dreamers made the universe of the dream silent and alone, so they could all listen for a single voice.

Thunder was to centre the dream, and he was surrounded by some of the most adept dream-healers. What should he make his message? It could only be love, a love carelessly neglected, now a love which burned: the love of the whole ship . . .

He focused on Little Frog's humour, his curiosity, his loyalty, his determination.

But Thunder was tiring; there was no rest or solace in this dreaming. It reminded him of swimming against a current, a constant battle against a greater force, simply to stay in the same place. Some of the other dreamers were tiring too—

—and here swam his son, out of nothing. There was fear and sadness, then a flowering of hope as they connected.

Distant, his son said.

Where? Where? Thunder asked.

And images came: a settlement . . . green trees and water (so much for the poison moon theory) . . . a moon almost as splendid as the home-world's . . . the settlement again, in snow now; the settlement under a blazing sun . . .

His son was somewhere where he could run under trees, dive into open waters, fly a kite. A furry animal of some sort ran alongside him. There was a vehicle, whose smell of burning was strangely familiar.

And . . . and there were intelligent creatures who cared

for Little Frog. Two were special to him, erect bipeds, partially furred, with opposable thumbs. They had young of their own, a baby and one around Little Frog's size. And Little Frog was trying to get something across, something complicated . . .

Unbelievable! His son almost saw the aliens – those odd-looking beings, dimly familiar – as . . . *parents*. Little Blue Frog lived marooned, but he had found adults, safety and love. Thunder was overjoyed – with relief, with compassion – but he also acknowledged his jealousy, an immature reaction.

His son was the only survivor. *Dancer on the Waves* must have been utterly destroyed.

Still reeling from the contact, Thunder sat at a console, alongside Skimming Stone and three others. There was hope and fear between them, and bewilderment too. Joy began to seem premature.

They had made contact easier. Or he was learning this dangerous science better. The healers were anxious and watched him, but he had enough strength to do this.

'Machine, search for a world with these criteria. Home-class biosphere, with intelligent aliens,' Skimming Stone said. 'Addition, bipedal aliens.'

'Episodic climate, probably a tilted axis like the colony-world,' said Thunder. 'Or an eccentric orbit. Separate criterion, a large moon.'

'Powered vehicles burning something, so an industrial world using residue fuel,' said Eat Demon Claws.

The final criterion was only worlds which lay within

Thunder's most optimistic model. Only worlds *Dancer on the Waves* might just have reached with everything in their favour.

One answer, the machine said.

The machine brought up the space map, showing the cloud of probability where *Dancer* was guessed to have gone. The target world was a burning light. So, *Dancer on the Waves* had been off-course, but nowhere near the extremes of their prediction. They were months away, but it could have been so much worse. It seemed credible.

'Full report, please.' Thunder was sure he'd seen a drawing of those aliens before; there would be a report.

'That is not currently convenient.'

That was machine-talk meaning *forbidden*.

'Why?'

'It is not currently convenient to say.'

The group was baffled. Hidden information was almost a paradox.

Skimming Stone asked, 'What level of authority will make it convenient?'

'It is not currently convenient to say.'

'A message to the leadership team, please. We've found where *Dancer on the Waves* reached. There's a living survivor on an inhabited planet – Thunder's son – and we need more information.'

There was a pause, then the leader-for-today came on. 'You found Thunder's son? You'd better come to the coordinating lodge.'

Thunder was exhausted and he didn't want a fight. But his team helped him up and they explained their findings. The leadership team went into closed session. Extraordinary. Yet, it was not a long discussion, as these things go, and it ended in his favour.

He sat with the leader-for-now and they called up the report. 'The whole people will rejoice your son is found. But there is danger and you deserve to know. A decision was taken for the-all, a generation ago, not to release the full survey reports and to forbid unauthorised visits to this system. I knew nothing of this until I had your request. Read it; the summary will be enough.'

Intrigued and fearful, Thunder began to consume the report, which had warnings of disturbing and violent content. Yes, there was no doubt, these were the aliens he had seen.

A few breaths into the report, he was quivering with fear. The survey team had nicknamed the planet where Little Frog was stranded *Nightmare that Kills*.

CHAPTER 25

The dentist

Cory and Elsa bathed Fleur, who gurgled and waved her fists as she lay naked on her back, kicking for the fun of it in front of the electric fire. Naked time helped her skin rash, and Cory liked the warmth of the fire behind its metal guard.

The grown-ups had gone out to the car to have an argument about Aunt Selena.

'Very quiet, Mr Centre of the Universe,' said Elsa, rubbing her cheek. Her gum was puffed up and infected. The dentist tomorrow would be a big drama; Elsa had needed a lot done when she came to the Myers and she hadn't liked it. Cory couldn't help – dentistry on home-world didn't hurt. Mom wanted to be the adult with Elsa, but that was too dangerous, but she would wait in the car.

'Miss Spikey Sister. Porcupine. I'm glad my people know where I am. But it will be a while before they get here.' The Ship had told them Earth had been monitored for twenty years, so at least they knew where it was.

'Are Gene and Molly going to stay together?'

They'd both told him they would – even though they did such strange things. He nodded, because he would try to make sure anyway.

'Your starship will come and all the dumb humans will have to sort themselves out,' Elsa pointed out. 'It will be Cory Cory Cory Cory. And they will take you to the stars, and your mom will end up going because you and your dad want to go. Children's Services will put me in one of those big places full of older children. Bullies or bedwetters, that's all there is. Or they will find some awful person to give me to . . . They gave me back to *him*.'

'I won't let that happen,' Cory promised. 'Mom and Dad want to be your parents – of course we'll take you with us.'

She put her hand out to tickle Fleur. 'She's dry. We should dress her.'

Cory got warm clothes for his little sister to sleep in.

So warm, but when he thought of Bad Men, he shivered everywhere. The family must always be so-so careful.

Molly woke bleary-eyed with a cricked neck from dreams of home, uncomfortable in the small bed. She realised Fleur was wailing, but sitting up too quickly, she banged her head against the stupid shelf. How she longed for her own bed, her own bath, her books and photos, a kitchen she knew. She missed her friends above all, people to laugh and joke together, to share the dreadful fact of Selena's disappearance, the fear that Mason might well be telling the truth and did not know where she was.

It made small lumpy beds and cold showers seem minor.

She got out of bed, and her cramps came.

And on top of it all, either her son was deluded or the purples were truly coming.

'I'll drive,' Storm said after breakfast, then added, 'We should bring Cory.' No one needed to say that they wanted him up their sleeves if something went wrong. Of course, he was also a constant ally on the dentist issue.

Elsa handed Gene the guitar and demanded he play it, but Gene refused. 'If you put your coat on, I'll find a song you haven't heard before. For when you're back.'

'What's it called?'

'That's for you to find out. For when you're back.'

It felt as practised as theatre.

Gene met Molly's gaze and strummed a few chords. 'Molly Skating on the Moon' – the song he wrote to propose to her, the first song of his she'd heard. That day her heart had leaped and she had said yes.

Molly smiled, feeling tears prickle. There was still tenderness sometimes, a healing embrace . . . but, 'We don't have time!' She kissed Fleur goodbye and handed her to Gene. The baby could sit with a little help, and wobble-headed, view the world. Fretful, because a tooth was coming, and yet capable of a dragon-slayer of a smile. By an enormous effort of will, she didn't infuriate Gene by reminding him of twenty important things.

'I want my song,' said Elsa, and Molly said, 'Sooner we go, sooner we can get back.' Cory and the dog were already in the Beast and Molly slipped in the passenger seat, leaving Storm and Gene still cajoling Elsa on the steps.

Molly put on a grey wig.

'Elsa must go with us to the stars when my people come.'

This is truly great timing.

'She thinks you don't want her.'

'Cory, she must know that's not true.'

Molly felt the warmth of the hot-water bottle down low and was grateful for the relief it brought.

'Then human word: *adopt* her now. All-decide.'

'It's not that simple, sweetie-pie. A lot of different people have to make checks.' They were wanted by the police, hunted by the media, with Cory the Monster. She dreaded to think how Child Services would react to that.

Cory went silent for a count of twenty, then, his voice strained, asked, 'Is Cory going to stars all alone? Mom and Dad prefer Earth. I will leave humans. No Elsa or Fleur or Bonnie or Chuck . . .'

What a time to bring this up.

Let his people come, for the world's sake. Let them never come, for mine.

'I don't know, Cory. We just don't know any of the things we need to know. Perhaps humans could give the purples a nice warm island.'

'Which island?'

She put her hand over her eyes, feeling the pricking of a headache letting her know it was coming. The sun was out. Spring was on the march. Fresh air might help.

Elsa, protesting not wisely but too well, told Gene he was rotten, and then stood on tiptoe to kiss his nose.

Storm got into the driver's seat. 'Come on, Elsa.'

And finally, they were on their way.

Cory lay in the back with his head in Elsa's lap and burbled while Elsa would describe the scenery they were passing
through, often making up outrageous things. Meteor liked
being driven; she wagged her tail constantly, her tongue lolling
out.

The town looked postcard-perfect in the sun, with buildings alongside steep roads running down to the glittering lake.
Storm parked the Beast on a hill, close to a doctor, a dentist
and a ship's store, all close together on this side. There was a
coffee-shop and a pharmacy on the other side, as well as guest-
houses and a curious narrow alley.

Storm kicked the wedges behind the wheels. 'So, Elsa, you
and I will go in and the dentist will stop that pain. And then
we'll go and do something fun.'

'I know Elsa will be brave,' Cory said. 'Mom can get pancakes.'

'Pancakes first,' said Elsa.

Molly said nothing, thinking about the other flaw in this
plan, because sitting in the car for an hour wouldn't be that
interesting for Cory. He might start on again about what would
happen in the dark muddle that was the future. She handed
him a book and suggested he read to her. He was wrapped in
his waterproof – it might look odd to have the hood up inside
the car, but he had to, so casual passers-by would see nothing
of interest.

As soon as the others had gone, he started. 'Whhhhyy can't
Elsa stay?' Cory said, eyes, tentacles and ears pleading.

'Sweetie-pie, I'd love that, but it's not our decision. Surely,
on your planet, the grown-ups sometimes have to decide these

251

things?' The cramps twisted again. *Damn*.

'I guess – but the children are heard too. Maybe two different lodges so all agree, big and small. Earth is not satisfactory. I want to go explore, all-hidden, very safe.'

'Maybe later. Right now, I'd like you around, in case I need you. Read me a story.'

Neither the painkillers nor the hot-water bottle were doing much good. She needed something stronger.

'Cory, I will be five minutes. I'm just going into the pharmacy.'

'Go to café – get pancakes please.'

'We'll see. Hide until I'm back, okay?' She checked her appearance in her little mirror, swung out of the car, picked up the stick which was part of her act and walking a little slower than usual, she looked around for danger. The café was directly over the road. A burly man was sitting in the window, staring out at the street. He looked at Molly but didn't react.

The bell above the door *tinged* as she walked into the blazing hot pharmacy. Shelves ran down the middle of the shop; at the other end, a short man in an outdoor hat with furry earflaps was listening to the pharmacist. She went halfway in, standing back to give the man privacy. She hated when other customers listened in to discussion of bowels, cramps or the myriad inconveniences of pregnancy.

The pharmacist, who looked about seventy, was explaining at a snail's pace why it would take three days to get this drug and how you read in the magazines about this and that new-fangled medication, but he still recommended the tried and tested. The short man's body quivered, like he was about to punch the man.

Something nagged at her, a sinister memory, but it wasn't until he spoke that a shock ran through Molly's body.

The voice was high, aggressive, and dripping with entitlement. 'Nonsense. I'm a qualified physician and I have written myself a simple prescription I need filled, *now*.'

Dr Pfeiffer. Thank heavens his back was turned while he was arguing with the druggist. Every possibility she could think of was bad.

Behind the pharmacist, there was a mirror advertising some ancient cure. Pfeiffer looked up and saw her in the reflection. He wore an absurd pointed beard.

Molly turned, playing old, and strode back to the door, the stick swinging in her hand. Behind her, she heard the pharmacist call. There was someone coming into the pharmacy, a burly white man of middle age: the man who had been sitting in the window of the café. This time she saw recognition in his face, and she saw him try to cloak it.

'Mrs M . . . Molly,' called Dr Pfeiffer, in his oiliest voice. 'What a surprise! Please don't go. Please, five minutes . . .'

Yes, she had talked to Pfeiffer since his disgrace, but only on her terms, and only with a careful plan. Thank goodness she had the spare keys for the Beast.

The man from the café stood in the doorway, blocking her way out. He tried a nervous smile. 'The doctor wants a minute of your time.'

She heard Pfeiffer come up behind her, and the pharmacist's complaint.

Her heart was racing: fight or flight or both. 'Out of my way, please,' she said, in purest Brooklyn. She felt Pfeiffer pull at her left sleeve.

Should she push the man aside, or hit out with the stick?

'Out of my way!' she said. *Let words do the work.*

Pfeiffer was already beside her, holding her arm. 'Please believe we have nothing but your family's best interests at heart. I have important news—'

She shoved sideways into Pfeiffer, as hard as she could, and he fell into the shelves, toppling them to the crash of broken glass and falling bottles. She almost lost her balance, but he was no longer holding her.

The man was coming towards her, his attention on the stick. He smelled of that old-fashioned soap. He was big but he didn't move like an athlete, or the thugs she had dealt with before, so she dropped her head and charged him. He half caught her and they wrestled a little, half in and out of the door. He was bigger, but she was a mother fighting to get back to her child.

'I'm calling the cops!' cried the pharmacist.

There came a bellow, and again: the Beast's horn. Molly's heart was in her mouth – Cory must be in danger, why else would he use the horn?

She had a chance and she took it. Biting the brute's ear as if Cory's life depended on it, she jabbed four fingers into his gut. Like a dog, she held on, wrenching at the ear until the man shrieked, loosened his grip – and she was through the door. Without the stick, alas.

Outside was trouble, as she expected: the door of the Beast was open and beside it was a weedy man in thick glasses: Tyler, Dr Pfeiffer's faithful lapdog, who jerked with shock when he saw Molly.

There was no sign of Cory, which meant he must have hidden. If he grabbed her, they would both vanish. 'Sweetie-pie!' she shouted.

Her wig had come off and people were staring, from the street, through windows – then a truck hit her from behind and she was falling with that great animal of a man on her. He'd tackled her like she was a footballer.

She slammed into the floor, crushed and hurting; knees, hands and back roared their complaints, and she couldn't breathe.

'You *brainless idiot*!' screamed Dr Pfeiffer. 'M-Molly, are you hurt?'

'What in heck happened here?' came a young man's voice. 'Ma'am, you all right?'

'The brute!' said a woman's voice.

The brute rolled off her and Molly managed a couple of painful gulps of breath. She tried to get onto her hands and knees. People were surrounding her now: a sporty young guy, two middle-aged women; a grey-haired black man in a white apron coming from the café. *Witnesses*. But mostly she needed to catch her breath.

Tyler trotted over, fumbling inside his coat for something.

'I do believe he tripped,' Dr Pfeiffer said. 'Our lady friend is unwell; can you help us get our dear friend Mrs Smith up.'

'I know a tackle when I see one,' said the sporty guy, his fists clenched. 'I hafta ask you *gentlemen* to step back from the lady – right now.' If he had any qualms taking the brute on, he wasn't showing it. 'Ma'am, who are these people?'

'I'm her doctor, and her friend,' Pfeiffer said, an oily smile on his face. 'She has paranoid episodes. We just need to get her somewhere quieter and talk to her.'

'These men are loan-sharks,' Molly gasped, in her Brooklyn accent. 'They're after my husband – they're threatening our children.'

'Back, now!' snapped the would-be rescuer at Pfeiffer. 'Mr Adams, give me a hand.'

The black cook strode over, his concern clear. Someone decided honking their horn would clear the street. There was always someone who thought honking a horn was smart.

Molly was getting worried. *Where is Cory?*

'I have a gun,' said Tyler, waving it.

Dr Pfeiffer looked terrified.

'I did two years in Korea,' said the cook, Mr Adams, to Tyler, as calm and straight-backed as if he was talking him through the day's specials. 'I ate chow that frightened me more than you do. Don't make a fool of yourself, just give me that.'

The sporty guy helped Molly to her feet. 'Ma'am, are you okay?'

And here was Meteor, licking her hand and making little grunts. *But where was Cory?* He only needed to sneak in and touch her – it was a crowd, sure, but he could hide from this many if he was careful. There were two cars now stalled on the hill, just watching.

'If I can just get in my car, I'll be fine,' Molly said.

The rescue guy was looking at her. 'Won't you want to give a statement, ma'am?' He glanced at Pfeiffer and back to her.

She debated trying her loudest scream – maybe then Pfeiffer would flee. But if the townspeople had recognised her – and their photos had been all over the television – the police would surely arrest her.

A shot rang out and Adams, the cook, swore loudly as he fell to the road, clutching his thigh.

Pfeiffer was suddenly standing next to her and she felt a stab in her leg, his coffee breath in her face. 'I have Selena, safe,' he hissed. 'Just play along.'

She didn't believe him. She was about to drive her knee between his legs when she felt Cory's terror, a wave of ice dragging her stomach down, making her skin prickle under winter clothes. It was like the sun had gone in and the world become hewed from ice, how even the memory of warmth was untrue.

Cory was standing by the door of the dentist, in his yellow waterproof, and the spectators shrieked, gawping in astonishment, and stepped back. 'Cory is the Monster,' he fluted, hands out, crouching. He quivered with the power, sending out waves of fear and self-loathing, each stronger than the last. 'All-must-go-away. Cory will hurt everyone. Leave Mom *alone*!'

Meteor, whining, scampered away.

'Now, Cory—' said Dr Pfeiffer, shaking.

'Evil-liar-man, Dr Pfeiffer. Run away. Cory is the Monster.'

And the terror came roiling out of him, a pure torrent of primal fear that made dogs whine and people scream. Cory was trying to control it, but nightmares were coming, formless fears dredging up old wounds of death and loss.

Molly realised, shocked, that Cory no longer believed he could control it. He was opening the box containing all the troubles of the world.

Pfeiffer was gasping out shrill commands as he and the brute hustled her down the hill . . .

She wanted to save her boy, before the power burned him out . . .

Gene would die, and her children. Once she had awakened from a dream like this, sweat running down her face – and now she was living it. Gene and the children: dead in a hail of bullets. Fire from the sky. Amber Grove disappearing in a nuclear strike, living people turned to shadows, to ash and smoke. The air and the sea and the sky dead, the Earth a lifeless rock in space.

Elsa was running out of the dentist, clutching her bag and her coat. Everything was confusing. Molly's mind was too full of Cory's nightmares, nightmares out of control. She tried to struggle, but her limbs were no longer obeying her. Nothing made sense . . .

The cramps became the loss of her first nameless daughter, her hands red with blood and yellow with paint as she sank into a grief so powerful she embraced darkness and oblivion.

CHAPTER 26

Dr Pfeiffer

Her head was fuzzy and her eyelids heavy. She had not been out long. She was in a moving car full of loud, clashing male voices, jammed between two people who smelled of old-fashioned soap and cologne and male sweat.

'Pull in there, off the road. The police will be after us. I'm tempted to shoot you myself.' That familiar, irritating voice was Dr Pfeiffer.

So the whining must be Tyler, in the front seat.

'You made a mess of that,' said a calm, strong voice from the driver's seat. 'Most likely, the police have a description of the car. We need to figure out how to get the boy now we have his mom.'

She didn't know that voice.

The brute who had tackled her said, 'That thing – that-that *monster* – I'm not going anywhere near it.'

'Yes, they might recognise the car,' Dr Pfeiffer said, ignoring the brute. 'I need time to think.'

'So we get new wheels. You don't need to be Scientist of the Year to know that.'

Nothing was quite making sense to Molly. Opening her eyes felt like too much effort. It was like the time the tyre swing had clipped her head when she was eight. Or when she'd fainted in high school, after a fever. For a few moments of confusion, she thought: *you're a drunk; you passed out!* The horror of that thought helped her focus. Pfeiffer had injected her. She moved a hand, trying to feel her own pulse, and found her wrists constrained.

Brute said, 'Count me out, Norton.'

Molly was pleased to see through barely opened eyes that he was holding a cloth to his ear.

Dr Pfeiffer responded, 'You botched it – the simplest thing in the world, just to hold Mrs Myers for a little. She's a housewife, not a Viet Cong assassin. I just needed to tell her we have her sister, safe and well; we'll rescue her nephews. We'll all work together – no coercion, everyone gets what they want.'

The brute grunted.

'I didn't know it would fire,' Tyler whined. 'Assault and kidnapping – I'll die in prison!'

Dr Pfeiffer snapped, 'Imbecile. If you hit the femoral artery, you might have killed him. Then it would be *murder*.'

Play dead, thought Molly. She tasted blood – and then, right on cue, the cramps decided to remind her of their existence.

Her son was terrified and alone, watching the crowd whipped to hysteria by his power. Cory out of control and open to the vengeance of the mob replayed itself in her head and she could not control the shudder.

Norton, the driver, said, 'There's a car place up ahead. No one saw me, so I'll hire a new one, a truck if we can. Then we go back. You saw that tall, handsome woman driving the vehicle? She took the girl to the dentist – who's she? And any idea who the girl is?'

'Storm DuBois,' Dr Pfeiffer said. 'Of course. I've just remembered – she's from *Witness* magazine. Miss Longman and Storm have been very quiet for a long time. I hope Mrs Myers is okay, that nothing's broken.'

Something cold and wet touched her face and Molly moved, opening her eyes to see Dr Pfeiffer. He had the bedside manner of an undertaker.

'Get off!' His physical closeness repelled her.

'Mrs Myers, this is unfortunate—'

'Let me go,' Molly growled. 'Kidnapper!'

'This is a disaster. I just wanted to explain, we helped your sister escape. We need to go back to get Cory, to keep him safe and well. He mustn't fall into the hands of local law enforcement or vigilantes.' He tutted, adding, 'The press has been *so* irresponsible.'

Molly didn't believe him, of course. They were speeding along local roads, the lake to their left, heading north through mixed woods and farmland. She needed to be clear, cunning. Yes, the sun was behind them.

Her son was terrified, and the aftermath of using his power so widely always made him ill – then, with a shudder, she realised that maybe Elsa was in danger too. Or perhaps the unshakeable Storm had them both. But how would Molly ever find her?

'Believe me,' Pfeiffer said, 'that wasn't how it was supposed to have happened.'

Molly tried to make her voice low and slow and strong. Mama Grizzly. 'I demand you take me back to my son.'

The car pulled into a turning by a sign advertising *Joe's Motors 200 yards*. Norton was in complete control of himself: no movement wasted, no word, either. He had a strong jaw, the rugged lead from a cowboy movie. When he smiled at her, she knew he posed more danger than the other three put together.

'Try not to get beaten up by Mrs Myers,' Norton said to the men, winking at her, then he was gone.

It was cold once you were in the dark shadows.

'Let me look these bruises over,' Dr Pfeiffer offered.

She shuddered. 'Don't touch me – either of you.'

'Cory may be exhausted. He may be ill,' Dr Pfeiffer said.

Like the last time you snatched him, Molly thought.

Molly could see Tyler was staring at her, but there was something odd about his eyes, as if he had seen things not meant for this world. He turned from her gaze and switched on the big clunky device held on his lap. A police scanner.

'I'm going to need to go to the bathroom,' she said. 'A proper one.'

The Myers had agreed a rendezvous point in the town if they were separated – but would it be safe? Would Cory remember, was he even in a fit state to find it?

'Well, you'll have to wait, I'm afraid.'

'In that case, I will bleed all over this car.' *I'll rub his nose in it*, she thought, full of disgust for him, and for what was happening. She had always loathed dealing with her period in primitive conditions, but this might be some sort of record.

'You might run away.' The doctor was clearly embarrassed, but he repeated, 'We can reunite you with your family.'

He fumbled in his pocket and brought out a piece of paper with Selena's familiar handwriting.

It took her some moments to focus enough to read. The list was a mixture – the brand of face cream Selena raved about and had left in the bathroom, the brand of sweets she chewed to hide her smoking, 'anything by' six famous authors of slushy romantic novels, and some very precise requests for specific undergarments.

Dr Pfeiffer met her gaze. 'I got a chance to rescue your sister. You obviously didn't get my message.'

Rescue. Right.

Twenty cold, awkward minutes had passed, but the fresh air was helping. Dr Pfeiffer had asked for Molly's word that she would not run away; she knew she was too uncertain on her feet to run very far anyway, so she gave it. To allow her to clean herself, they compromised by unlocking one handcuff and tying the rope to it. Molly did the best she could behind a tree with a bottle of water, a clean handkerchief and a bandage from the doctor's bag.

She looked at the knotted rope, wondering if she could work it free with her teeth. But then she'd have to run . . . where? And how?

Limping, still hurting, she walked back to Dr Pfeiffer. Flushing with shame, he took the leash off.

Tyler had found something that sounded like a police channel. *Cory Myers . . . woman some say was Molly Myers . . . Malign powers . . . some sort of disturbance on Lake and Third . . . FBI called . . .*

Shit! What could be so bad calling the Feds would make it better?

Get real. They have people who know this alien stuff.

Norton pulled up in a truck and announced, 'It's all over the local news – everyone's confused as hell: Cory Myers went mad in the street, a local citizen's been shot, dozens of people are calling in everything from a child-snatch to an alien invasion.'

There was a sudden burst of snarling from the radio: *We gotta find them before the Feds and their fancy helicopters turn up. And the kid . . . threaten the kid and he'll summon hell, or vanish. You gotta play it easy or he'll zap ya.*

'We need to get back to base,' said Norton, in charge once more. 'If you hang around, you're going to get me arrested and Mrs Myers will fall into the hands of the cops. *Amateurs,*' he muttered.

She should have used her last ounce of courage and run, but she was already being hustled into the car. Dr Pfeiffer, apologising, blindfolded her. The route felt very twisty, but that was probably deliberate, she felt. She had a good eye for maps and landscapes, but she was still muzzy-headed from whatever they'd jabbed in her leg.

There was an eerie fascination in hearing the behind-the-scenes police work – the excitement when they got a better description of Pfeiffer, Tyler, the brute and Molly; the police chief repeating, '*Don't shoot the boy. He's vital for national security—*' over and over.

Then they heard, '*The drugstore guy says the little guy was Emmanuel Pfeiffer – you know, that germ warfare guy? He was sacked*

by the President. The FBI are excited about that – they think they'll
be allowed to call in the Army to catch him.'

Pfeiffer was silent for a minute or two. 'I need to call my
wife,' he said, to the air.

Forty, maybe fifty minutes later, the brute took her arm, not
gently, and guided her out of the car. She heard running water
and got a sense of where the sun was before she was led into
a building. She heard voices, and a telephone ring. She went
through a door, along a corridor, down a slope and through
another door.

'This will be more comfortable,' said Dr Pfeiffer as he untied
the blindfold. She was standing in a lounge, modern furniture
of wood and glass, and cluttered with photos of trees and plants
and insects. The photos were excellent, almost clinical in their
sharpness, but the close-ups turned nature into patterns, abstract
art. Daylight came in through frosted skylights.

She lowered herself into an armchair, aching everywhere,
and glared at the doctor. 'If you do have my sister, I demand
to see her.'

Dr Pfeiffer looked at her. 'I'm hoping you'll cooperate.'

'My son's in great danger and it's your fault. I'm separated
from my baby. At least let me know my sister is all right.'

'She's in the next room. I'll bring her.'

Molly would not have bet one way or another, but there was
Selena, sleepy-eyed, but wearing a shy grin. She wore a fashionable kaftan with flowing sleeves printed with flowers of orange
and yellow and brown; she had always been one for the latest
look. She held out her arms and Molly rose for the embrace.

265

Dr Pfeiffer ostentatiously walked out of the door and shut it behind him.

'Molly – you actually *came*. I was sure you were the only one brave enough to try.' Her voice was soft and slow. She was certainly drugged.

Holding her sister, the two of them against the world, Molly found tears coming. 'You can't trust Dr Pfeiffer,' she whispered.

Selena touched her ear, a warning look on her face.

Molly had expected the room to be bugged; that was a reasonable paranoia.

Selena said, loudly, as if she was reading her lines, 'Well, Dr Pfeiffer got me out of that place, and he got Mason arrested, or at least he said he did; Mason is quite capable of getting himself arrested – and he said he was so sure you would be here, and here you are.'

Questions rose, unsafe ones, but Selena went on, 'They're looking after me here. I'm sleeping half the day, but I feel good when I'm awake. And he's going to get me my darling boys back – he said he would. How are dear Cory and Fleur?' Her eyes flashed another warning, as if it was needed.

'Cory's lost,' Molly said, and the hopelessness rose around her, strong enough she felt she could drown. Her fierceness was sapped.

'That's awful – are there other people looking for him?' Selena sounded genuinely sorrowful. 'Tell me everything,' she went on, producing from some fold of her sleeve a small notebook and pencil. Then she flashed Molly a little cheeky grin, just like when they'd plotted against the nuns during detention. 'I do believe Dr Pfeiffer wants to keep him safe.'

The two of us against the world. Molly began to explain what had happened in Kauwenga Falls while she jotted down the key questions. *Where are we? Guards? Phones?*

Only then did it occur to Molly: had Pfeiffer plotted to bring Molly to this town all along? Was he behind Selena's letter? Maybe the chaos of that day had just been a trap sprung too early. Pfeiffer had Selena, a team, a hideout. He had been trying to contact the Myers.

Molly looked into her sister's eyes and wondered about the letter which had hauled her into the Midwest. Selena had been bait — but had she known? Just what would Selena do for her children?

CHAPTER 27

Dreaming

Cory swam, lost in his dreams. The water was so cold and he was so alone. Around him raged the bitter sea and above him the sky churned in turmoil. Silver shapes fell from the clouds, the snakes that hate all life. *Give in*, the water of his dreams called, *give in. There is no point in fighting.*

Hoo-hoo-hoo, all is cold and darkness and death. He was so-much cold and so-much tired and so-much alone. He could not find the layers of dream surrounding him, or where to swim to get out. And in his heart he mourned the loss of his birth-mother, his people, all dead. *Down-down-down* sorrow pulled him.

In the lodges of his home, in the children's places on a starship, others would be sleeping with him; others would find him in his dream, and if they could not help him, they would bring the adults to his dream too. He lost that togetherness when he fell into the human world, and oh, how-much he missed it.

The bad thing happened, again and again. When he had been captured by the Army, he had stopped that soldier from breathing. By the river, he had hurt the not-yet-adults, who had almost drowned in air. Cory has become the Bad Man who hurts to get what he wants, so scared of helping Mom, he had stayed hidden, watching them hurt her, so-so-cruel humans. Cory is a coward, Cory let Mom down. Desperate, driven by fear, he had used his power only to scare – but it had had its own ideas and it would not be reined in. It was a creature of itself and it would destroy.

Cory has become the killing sickness, the thing that gets into heads and hurts people. Cory is the Monster. Everyone will come with fire-and-guns because Cory is the thing to hate and fear.

He revealed himself to save his Earth-mother, but he failed; the power would have hurt her and everyone. Fear commanded him and he fled to keep the humans safe. The shame of what he had done, the shame of abandoning his mother, filled him. He had run until he could run no more.

This was too-too-much to carry, so Cory dived to oblivion, into dreams so deep there was no smell or sound. There were places here that were so deep he wondered if his body might even forget to wake him. He dived down into nothingness, to forget . . .

An age passed.

There had been times closer to waking when he felt a human tugging at his body, whispering, 'Wake up Octopus Face, wake up. They're coming.' He hid, and thought he dreamed, warmth against him, other lives in the hiding. Who knew what was real?

Cory, frozen in the ice, unmoving, told himself stories. Everyone knew the story of the Old Times, when the five nations of the island quarrelled and Fork-Ear brought the sickness of killing, when she stabbed Shell-Mother dead. Fork-Ear and Tentacles-in-Everything and Horizon-Hungry are not real people, although they felt real to everyone. Cory's teachers said, from time to time, 'We are all like one of these people, aren't we? Or feel we could be.'

They were right, for Cory had become Fork-Ear. The people made a safe place to keep her and all the children brought flowers and songs for the ten years she lived, so that she was still a part of the whole. But there was no true place of healing on Earth, where people like him could be made whole again. On Earth, some people who killed were celebrated or at least left alone with their grief. And on Earth, some of those who did bad things were put in a terrible place, separated from the whole, where they hurt each other. How wicked.

Dad once told a story of a man who lay frozen in the ice of the sea for a hundred years and then woke. It was a story with magic in it, so not-real. Cory was frozen in the ice of his dreams, cold and not moving. He had been here a while, ignoring his body, which wanted to pee.

Meteor's smell and warmth was in the dream. Meteor gave him a clumsy, loving lick, and that quiver must have been an anxious wag of the tail. Who will feed Meteor and who will throw sticks and play the chasing-and-hiding game? Who will curl up with Meteor on the floor if she is lonely?

Go away, Meteor, Cory is the Monster and no one can love me.

Meteor could not talk or think in words, but she put her untidy head on her paws and watching Cory in reproach, she growled her disapproval.

There was nothing in the dream but Cory and his dog, and a stillness that was beyond cold and beyond dark. Dogs are a good thing Earth has which his home-world, the First Harbour, does not. Although some dogs are made Bad by cruel humans.

Go away, Meteor.

Meteor brought warmth; he felt her tail wagging and she tried to bite Cory, but not a true bite. In his dream, Cory's hands moved too slow. Meteor had her teeth in the sweater Cory was wearing, and yes, Meteor's teeth hurt, just a little, not meaning it. Cory felt Meteor's fur like the most comfortable of his old clothes, a feeling of love and memories. She smelled of dog, of loving to get wet and messy, and the rich foulness of her dead breath.

Tug, tug, tug.

Go away.

Tug tug tug.

Meteor needed Cory, who rescued her from the so-sad place with sixteens of abandoned dogs. Cory was so-sad that Meteor cannot have puppies, although Meteor doesn't know what the humans did to her, that she can't. Sometimes Meteor dreamed she had little messy Meteors to feed from her body. She thinks Fleur is a puppy and tries to lick her.

Tug tug tug.

Dad says Meteor is all-heart-no-brains but you do not have to be clever to be kind, oh-no.

Cory returned to time, rising through the layers of dream; he was every-bit so-cold, and his body complained about sleeping crooked. He was cold and wet around his crotch too, a humiliation.

There was a scared human nearby, very close. Cory had been so-so-deep under, but he rose to proper wakefulness, his arms cramped by the weight and warmth of Meteor, reassured by her familiar smell and the faint wheeze of her sleeping. *Clever girl to come and find him in the dream.*

He smelled Elsa before he saw her, then a dim chink of light showed her face – Elsa in her yellow hood – and she had a finger to her lips.

Elsa sent out so many feelings; fear, and relief and worry, and guilt.

They were in a strange place, crowded with things smelling of cleaning. He felt out with his mind, but Elsa was the only human here. Apart from her there were bags and boxes, and a rumbling noise, a machine making warm air.

'I was so worried,' Elsa said. 'I couldn't wake you.'

'Meteor came,' Cory said, stroking a friendly dog ear. He felt hungry and drained and numb, like he had been battered in the dream.

'You're wet,' she said. 'It was all horrible, don't worry. We must keep quiet, in case the people in the next house hear. Men came with dogs – police, and people from the factory down the street, all sorts were searching – but you hid us.'

Cory had so many questions, but he couldn't ask any of them, not with the smell of his own urine so strong.

'There are clothes, and a place to wash,' Elsa said. 'And a place where I can heat up beans. There's bread.'

'Mom,' he said.

'Men took Mom . . . Molly . . . in a car.'

He realised his wrist was empty. 'My communicator?' Not

that it worked properly, the last link to his old life. He could not call his parents.

Elsa sniffed; she was going to shed water.

'It made a noise. I tried to shut it up and it went silent.'

She handed it to him. It was unresponsive. Perhaps the security went wrong.

Cory started to stand, and felt his legs go weak as spaghetti.

Elsa said, 'I'll get some dry clothes and some food, then we need to go to the rendezvous.'

He kept his watch in his pocket. 'Two a.m.,' he said. 'Who came looking?'

'Police, and other people with them. And the bad men who took your Mom – they might be out there too. You . . . there was all this awful stuff coming off you, like—' She struggled to find the words. 'It was like it was sea waves and big storms of ugly feelings. You ran, and sometimes you unhid, and that's when Meteor and I rescued you.'

He didn't trust his own memories, and his pain and shame flooded back, draining him of the will even to get off the floor.

'Eat, wash, dry clothes,' he said at last.

'Okay,' she said in a small voice.

'But Dad will know what to do.' They could find a payphone – Cory always had coins in his pockets in case. But there was no phone where Dad was staying.

Hot beans sounded like a good idea. In any case, it was hours until daylight. Then they must go to the rendezvous. They could at least phone Dr Jarman and Rosa, if they were still at the lawyer house. Halcyon was too far away.

Elsa slipped from the room, and as she left, all of Cory's bad thoughts flocked around him like that memory, the fierce gulls, pecking at that dead bird, relentless.

It was their nature to eat dead things.

Dawn was still a couple of hours away. Cory was beginning to remember a little more of what had happened yesterday. He'd been trying to run, stumbling, sometimes falling, and so drained he could hide only a little, walk only a little. Elsa helped Cory, he was so weak, and Meteor followed. Sometimes Elsa near carried him, although her determination was bigger than her strength. He remembered her stroking his ears and saying, 'Don't leave me, Snake Face.'

When the men came to search, Elsa said he hid them, although he didn't remember that.

They stood by the door and Cory hid them for a moment so they could peek through the blinds. At this time, the town should be still, but there was some commotion to the north: lights were moving on the ground and in the sky, throwing strange shadows.

They dropped the blind and squatted down.

The rendezvous was a café, not far from here – but would anyone be there?

'I was going to go,' Elsa said, 'but there were police, and so many people searching.'

He realised Elsa was crying and hugged her. They had to find the humans who could protect them; he hoped he had strength enough to hide them all the way. It was a terrible thing to feel his power, his instinctive protection against beasts and humans, so weak.

She wiped her eyes on a towel. 'We'll have to be really quiet.'

Cory wanted his dad, the friendly giant, his strong arms and his funny songs and how you could trust what he said. *Always always always*. And Storm, who was strong and funny and kind. And Mom, who he had failed to protect.

A far-away growl came, and a rumble. There was the sound of car engines, and lights going on in windows. Men were calling out.

Elsa held his hands so tight they hurt. 'They're coming closer – what will we do?'

How tired he was. How difficult it was to hide from lots of people. How he missed the Ship.

How he needed his people to come.

CHAPTER 28

Captives

Molly sat in that strange green room while Selena stood, in full outraged flow, flaying Dr Pfeiffer with her words.

'Dr Pfeiffer, you can't be serious – I can't leave and take my sister with me?'

'You're not a prisoner, Mrs O'Regan.' He was oily and unconvincing.

'So I will call a cab and we can leave right now—'

'That would be unwise.'

Selena snapped, 'You kidnapped me, you *liar*.'

'That's hardly fair.'

Molly and Selena had sorted the plan: they'd play it cool and clever – until Dr Pfeiffer had told them he knew where Selena's boys were, thinking he was being clever, and Selena had lost her temper. Molly despaired – it would make escape more difficult – but part of her was enjoying watching Dr Pfeiffer squirm.

Selena raised her voice even more. '*Fair*? You *slimeball – you kidnapper!* Get the dictionary, Molly, let's see what it says as the definition for "locked up by four men and unable to leave". Oh? Would that be "*prisoner*"? You *lied* to me, Dr Pfeiffer. I was sick and vulnerable, and *you lied to me*, just to get at my sister — my sister *who risked her life* to help me. You shit! You never cared about me, or my children. You just wanted Cory. You—'

Molly winced; who knew her sister used such obscenities?

Norton winked at her, but she didn't like his sly enjoyment of Pfeiffer's embarrassment.

Pfeiffer was wincing too; he held out his hands in supplication. 'It will take time. We've found where Connor and Rory are — it's tricky now they've been moved, but we're evaluating options.'

'Evaluate your ass,' said Selena. The drugs were clearly reducing any inhibitions. 'I want the keys to the truck and Molly and a map — and I want to know where my kids are. I want it all now. I'll buy a gun if I have to.'

'You're not safe to drive,' Pfeiffer oozed.

'How did you know Molly was coming?' Selena said. 'Did you read my letter when I was sick? My *private* letter to my sister?'

'I was astonished to run into Mrs Myers,' Pfeiffer said. 'I'm sure she's explained—'

Molly leaped in. 'That's not answering the question. This was all planned.'

'Everyone can get what they want,' Pfeiffer said again. 'I want Cory safe, Mrs Myers, and Selena prospering. I pay my dues — I promised to get her the boys . . .'

'In God's name, when?'

'Suppose the press find out who Selena is?' Molly said.

Pfeiffer tried to push through the joint attacks. 'Your boys are safe. They are safe today and tomorrow and for weeks. Our lawyer will be sure they are not moved——'

'Get. Me. My. Kids!'

'—but Cory and the girl, they're at large and in such danger of falling into the hands of the government – or worse, the brutal fear of ignorant locals. The Army, the FBI, State Troopers and half the town are out looking for them. And Mrs Myers is right: the press has descended and the town is under siege. Surely Cory and Elsa will be found soon. Miss DuBois in jail – which is an outrageous abuse of state power. All we have is you, Mrs Myers, your knowledge, and your voice. Somehow, we must work together to help you to be reunited with them.'

The police have Storm? Molly assumed this must be true. Or did Dr Pfeiffer know that Cory had already been taken? Maybe the government had him? She was getting lost in a paranoid web of lies and deceit. The government had covered up war crimes; it had hidden the truth that the bloody decades in Vietnam had been nothing but a power play against Communism, with total contempt for the Vietnamese. The government had hidden the existence of the Ship and aliens . . .

Or maybe Cory had somehow got help. Maybe he was safe.

But Selena hadn't finished. 'We can't trust you,' she said. 'You used me. Get me my boys, then we'll find Cory ourselves.'

'We can't trust you while we're prisoners,' Molly added. She'd work with Dr Pfeiffer if she had to, but only if she had power over him. Otherwise, she might as well kiss a rattlesnake and trust it not to bite.

'Well,' said Norton, 'what's happening, Dr Pfeiffer?'

'You have to cooperate,' the doctor told the women.

Selena swore, while Molly shook her head.

'Your other plan fell through,' Norton said, 'so it's plan C, or we sit here picking our noses while we lose any chance at all.'

Looking fraught, Dr Pfeiffer swallowed and said, 'Okay, fetch Nurse Skidelsky – it's indecent otherwise. Take Mrs O'Regan back to her room.'

'You're not separating us,' Selena cried. 'I'll scratch your piggy little eyes out.'

Everyone else froze as Selena leaped at Dr Pfeiffer, then Norton moved, coming for Molly. She didn't know how to fight him, but she was not submitting tamely.

'Ma'am,' he said, reaching slowly for her wrists, 'you're worth ten of them, and I don't want to hurt you.'

As Molly struggled, trying to bite and kick, she wondered how much of this was real. Selena's outburst sounded genuine, but she had foiled Molly's original plan of apparent compliance. There could be no escape without Selena, and maybe this whole thing was a show: they'd escape and find Cory, then Selena would betray her.

A tall, solemn-faced woman in a nurse's uniform appeared, moving calmly. Her grip was firm.

'Don't worry, Mrs Myers. This is perfectly safe,' said Dr Pfeiffer, then to the nurse, he ordered, 'Hold her still! Just a little needle—'

Molly hissed, 'I will tell your daughters about this and they will despise you. They will hate you for ever for what you are doing!'

★

Molly floated in the drug they gave her, all the aches and pains of her capture far away, her eyelids too heavy to lift. 'Fleur,' she said through dried lips.

'I saw her picture,' said the pretend nurse. 'Fleur needs you. We can take you to her, but you have to tell us where.'

Dr Pfeiffer smelled close. The nurse was asking too many questions, but her voice was less grating than Dr Pfeiffer's. And Molly wanted to sleep. 'Bring Fleur,' she mumbled.

'Well, if you tell us where she is, we can reunite you. And your husband – he looks very handsome in the pictures. Isn't his music wonderful?'

'Gene is a good father.' She remembered the times when she had been a bad wife to him and driven him away. Tears began to prickle.

Cory might have gone to the rendezvous, the café with the hip name, and left a message. She needed to not tell them where.

Think of the Beatles. She and Gene always argued about the later stuff, but when the band broke up, it really was the end of something. Lennon and Yoko Ono did that annoying song about Cory, 'Gotta Peace Out Like the Purples Do' – certainly no instant classic, not like 'Imagine' was. *Think of the albums we argued over. Don't tell them what they want to know.*

Strawberry Fields for ever.

But the fake nurse wouldn't stop talking. 'Fleur will be wanting her mother. Where will they be? Will Cory be with them?'

Cory was the only one they wanted. All these questions were really about Cory. She remembered Gene saying, '*Every mother says the world turns around their child, but for us it is true.*'

'Gene loves Fleur. And Cory. I worried he wouldn't.'

She was so sleepy and floating, and she didn't want to tell them anything they could use.

Someone dabbed her mouth with ice-cold water and she remembered the deep red scratches Selena had left on Dr Pfeiffer's face.

Sometimes she heard his voice next to her. She would strangle him, when she found the energy to move. He was needy, fawning, quick-tempered, so they thought she would respond better to the sly, fake-jolly nurse.

'We're going around in circles,' Dr Pfeiffer said.

'Pfeiffer, butt out.' That was Norton.

'I'm in charge,' Dr Pfeiffer said. 'She needs to hear this: Mrs Myers, we are your *only* hope. Your sister turned you in – she told me about the letter herself; that's why I knew you were coming. We freed her from Green Bowers to get you. She was worried about how she would manage with her boys, so we agreed if she helped me get Cory, I would settle her financially, get her false papers, hide her and the boys. Mrs Myers, shall I tell you the price she put on your son? I'd have paid twice that. She sold you out, and on the cheap at that.'

Molly's tears were flowing now. 'Don't believe you.'

'You're alone, Mrs Myers. Dr Jarman, his wife, Gene – none of them will come for you. And your clever little plot? Of course we knew about it. She was lying to you.'

Dr Pfeiffer was a lying reptile.

'Mustn't call you that word,' Molly slurred. 'Wrong. Want the nurse back.'

Selena has betrayed me. I am alone.

But she would not talk. She would remember the states and their capitals in alphabetical order, starting with the latest two, Alaska and Hawaii.

The snakes were coming to destroy everything. The purples would never come – but she would say nothing. Above all, she would not say where the rendezvous was, at the café named after a song.

'Alaska, Juneau. Hawaii, Honolulu. Arizona, Phoenix. Alabama, Montgomery. Arkansas, Little Rock . . .'

That song Gene listened to . . .

One pill makes you taller, and this pill makes you shrink.

Gene . . . walking with him among the redwoods. Crossing the Golden Gate Bridge. If that was what he wanted, they would find a way.

'"California Dreaming",' she said.

'Where, Mrs Myers? *Where?*'

Next, she bet they would play a game when they told her Cory was sick and needed her. And she would play a game where she pretended to believe them.

CHAPTER 29

Leaving Kauwenga Falls

It was dawn, the grey light rising in the east. Cory, Elsa and Meteor sat huddled together in the bushes, cold and scared. Cory was hiding himself so he could be a secret spy and see what was happening, but he had to conserve his failing power; he felt less and less within him each time he used it.

The Bad Men were searching the truck now; they had two keen German Shepherd dogs sniffing inside. The driver was waving his hands and saying, 'The local guys looked – listen, I gotta get going.'

'Orders,' said the man in the dark suit. 'Your cooperation is appreciated.'

Cory had warring thoughts in his head. Part of him said: *Stay in town and eventually you will find a working phone and peace to use it.* But it had been so-so-close at the Laundromat – the man smoking out of the window had seen only a flash of something, but he had still called out. And the police car was outside the rendezvous, so that was too-too dangerous.

They had doubled back and crept into a culvert. Cory could not rely on his hiding anymore; it was too much work to stay out of human sight now. He argued inside his head: stay in the town because someone, somehow, would come and find him; or go with Elsa's plan, get out of Kauwenga Falls, then call the adults.

He ducked back into the bushes and unhid. How tired he was. Elsa put her head to his and he whispered, 'Be ready to run, hidden, and get in back.'

'Can you do it?'

She must have been able to feel his doubt. 'Cory try anyway.' All the things that could go wrong marched round his head. He was too tired to do the Bad Thing – and, besides, he mustn't think about it, or anything, except getting safe and warm again. His English got worse when he was tired. He must speak proper English, because he could.

The bags were heavy. Elsa said, in her most reasonable voice, that everyone agreed it was fine to take things if it was a real emergency and you really meant to pay people back. Cory wanted to leave a signed note with his address, but Elsa argued that was too risky. He missed Mom and Dad; they would know what to do. In the end, he decided he would write to them and he wrote the address down to use later.

Cory hid himself again and watched as the FBI and the dogs started moving to the next truck, while the driver of this truck was walking towards the bushes. It was the perfect opportunity. Even if they waited for another chance, the light would be stronger and he would be so-so-more tired.

Cory grabbed Elsa by one hand and Meteor's collar by the

other and hid them. It was like holding your breath underwater; how good Cory was at diving down compared with humans. And yet there came a point underwater where you could feel every heartbeat brought you closer to giving up, the point where you could do it no more. The Bad Men were arguing with the next truck driver.

Fear helped. The fear that the Bad Men would catch him gave power to his hiding. He needed it: with each step, his body was growing heavier, Elsa was limping again, and he needed to hold onto Meteor too. The packs were heavy with borrowed food. With every step he looked at the driver of the second truck and back to where the first driver was peeing in the bushes. It was so-so hard to hide from all of them, but he *had* to.

They got to the back of the truck. So-so-tired Cory could not hide people well unless he held them. He missed the Ship. He took Elsa by the coat pocket so she could get in, then half helped clumsy Meteor up to her. Then, one hand still holding Elsa's, he got in himself, his body clumsy with the pack. Twice he felt the hiding fade; a spotlight on him could not have felt more terrifying. With one last effort, he struggled into the truck, and then Elsa dragged him right to the back.

Cory found something soft and flopped onto it. Meteor flopped onto him and her smelly tongue touched his face. 'What if people lock the door?' he said. Trapped would be so dangerous, but he needed to rest among the bales and boxes full of exotic smells for a long time.

'We bang on it, he comes to look, we jump out,' said Elsa. *Find phone, all the kind people to call. Get family together again.*

How tired he was, how very tired. Elsa pulled something

over them and the three friends held each other close. A single flashlight beam stabbed into the dark, but they lay low. Meteor knew, when held so firmly, that she was not to bark.

Elsa rubbed her cheek; Cory knew she was in pain.

Then the doors of the truck slammed and a few moments later they were moving. Cory could smell Meteor and Elsa, and that made him long for his Earth-family, to know that they were free and well. He let go and fell into the endless darkness, too tired to even look for his birth-father.

Elsa napped during the drive. The dentist had not even started when everything went crazy and the fierce hot pain in her jaw had been growing even worse ever since.

Once the truck stopped to drop off something, heavy, she guessed, from the men's complaints; then, some time later, there was another stop and this time they stayed stopped. They had reached their destination, whatever it was. The men unpacked the truck while Elsa huddled against her friend Cory and the sleeping dog. *Any moment*, she thought, *the men will lift the tarpaulin and find us.*

But the bales they hid behind weren't moved and they were left alone.

From the noise and the swearing, the men were loading the truck with something else, but for half an hour now there had been silence and darkness. They needed to get off if they could and for that, Cory needed to hide them. But Cory would not wake.

Elsa shook him, even risked whispering in his ear. Meteor growled in her sleep, as if chasing a rabbit, very badly. Cory felt cold, and she couldn't leave him – but the men might soon take them back into danger.

She could smell Meteor: the dog had pooed in the corner of the truck. That was another reason to move. She thought of Molly holding her, and helping to change Fleur, and Gene playing the guitar, and she felt the tears come. *The harder you wish for something good, the less likely it is to come true.* Cory talked so much about the good times, before she came – before Molly grew sad and Gene angry – and she wondered if it was her causing the arguments, the unhappiness.

At last Elsa got up and discovered her limbs and back ached like crazy. She tried to move Cory, who was as heavy and uncooperative as a sack of stones, not even shifting a little as he had in sleep. How could they get out? She stretched, and stretched some more, and got ready to be sneaky. The back of the truck was still open, and she could see a dim garage, with a car and another truck. A radio was playing a sad old song she didn't know. The only light came through two dirty windows. It must be afternoon, she thought. Dark would soon be coming.

Cory would be in danger if she left him, and Meteor too, but she couldn't carry him.

Once, travelling with her vicious keeper, they had been on a deserted road. He had been in a good mood and he'd let her drive the car. If there were keys in the truck . . .

But drive where?

Elsa looked in every direction, then dropped to the concrete floor, the pack heavy on her back. Through the door she saw the glow of an electric fire, and a big quilt. That faint wheezing like a far-off sea was a man snoring. He wasn't doing a good job if he was sleeping at work. She tiptoed over and borrowed useful things: the lighter beside a pile of butts; three dollars tucked under an ashtray with a red bridge on it.

Cory knew how to call friendly adults, Dr Jarman, or others in Amber Grove. But she couldn't get inside his head for the numbers. She remembered faces and directions, but she was not good with numbers.

She found a wheeled trolley, intended for moving big packing boxes. She could lower Cory onto it and at least get him out of the garage. She might not have very long before this man woke up, or another returned.

Elsa listened at the door, put out one cautious hand, and opened it a crack. Cold, fresh air swirled in and the man grunted and shifted.

If you were at floor level, she knew people were less likely to see you. She lay on the chilly, unwelcoming concrete and peered outside into a grey walled yard. Maybe she would be better finding somewhere else to lay up, less likely to be disturbed.

Elsa took the trolley, wincing when a wheel squeaked, and like a mouse with cheese, she pulled it to the back of the truck. Her leg was hurting again and she had just paused to massage it when, into the silence, Meteor barked out a friendly welcome, her face all eager and her tail wagging wild.

'*Herumhum?*' said the man.

'Shhh!' said Elsa as she edged through the crates, each bark from Meteor a little stab in her chest. When she put her hand on the dog's muzzle, Meteor began to dance to and fro. Elsa shook Cory, as hard as she could.

'What's goin' on?' said an adult voice, deep and sleepy.

She ought to take Cory's pack too, but she needed to move Cory first, and stop the dog barking. Cory was so odd to look at and the whole world knew that.

She pulled Cory's hood over his head down to his nose-slits and began the hard work of dragging him—

A stab of light.

'What the hell are you up to? Little thief—!'

The man was red-faced, old, bleary-eyed. He was twice her size, but he would be a slow runner. He had a flashlight, but nothing else.

And Meteor was barking again.

Lie, and quickly.

'My friend's sick.'

Wake up, Cory, wake up*! Hide us!*

'Don't believe you,' the man said.

Elsa pulled Cory further towards the man, trying to work out what to say when the man sniffed hard.

'Has your dog pissed in my truck?'

'Yes – I'm sorry, mister, these terrible men were chasing me – and my friend is real sick. The dog just made a mistake, mister.'

The man was not trying to get into the truck to help, and Meteor was dancing around Elsa, getting in the way.

'Get it outta the truck . . . Sweet Jesus!' The man had seen Cory's tentacles. He hollered, 'Hey, Ted, come now! *Hell on Earth!* It's that killer alien—'

There was no chance of sweet-talking her way out of this now; he would try to grab her, or Cory. He was stooping towards them, but she couldn't pull Cory any faster.

He dropped the flashlight and lumbered to the side. 'I'm armed,' he threatened, 'so don't make me use this.'

Meteor, clumsy Meteor, jumped from the truck and barked: *Back off, mister.*

The man picked up a piece of wood and flourished it. What a man, to wave a weapon at a little girl and her dog.

'Does that mutt bite?' said the man. 'I'll brain it.'

Meteor darted forward, but the man swung too early and Meteor made a clumsy sort of leap and sank her teeth into his right hand. She wrestled with him, like it was a game.

'Shit, shit, *Ted*, you useless son-of-a-bitch – *Ted!*'

'Good dog,' Elsa said, grabbing a metal rod.

The man had pulled his hand free. Now he backed away, holding his right hand in his left.

Elsa hurled the rod at him and jumped down from the truck.

Cory was lying like a corpse right at the edge, but she had no time to check he was breathing.

'Chase him, Meteor!' she shouted, but the dog was already harassing the man, forcing him back, exulting in her cleverness. Meteor advanced and the man retreated a step. Meteor barked; the man stepped back.

The man shouted as loud as any adult had ever shouted, 'TED, THERE'S THAT KILLER ALIEN FROM SPACE. BRING THE RIFLE!'

Against the wall was a big metal gasoline canister with a long spout. In her experience, most people cared about stuff more than people.

Somehow she got Cory off the truck, though it really hurt her back. He was slumped on the trolley and there was no time to go back for his pack. She grabbed the gas canister, put it on the trolley and headed towards the door, while Meteor kept the man off her.

'Meteor! Come here!' She unscrewed the cap of the gasoline, and said, 'Mister, what'll happen if I throw this on the fire?'

He went pale and began a lumbering run away from her. She pulled Cory to the door and through it, while Meteor the undefeated barked some more, in case anyone hadn't heard the commotion, then came after her.

Once *he* had been careless lighting a fire, so Elsa knew how burning gasoline leaped. She tipped the gasoline onto the floor behind her, then clicked the lighter. It worked first time. It was a big garage, so the man would be fine. She threw the lighter, remembering to cover her face as the soft whoosh of flame lit the yard.

Above her an aeroplane flew low against a grey sky. She could see a couple of warehouses and a car dealership. She chose the sidewalk that went a little downhill, for no reason other than it would be easier, pulling the trolley as fast as she could. If the men came after her, they would be captured, but there wasn't a chance she would ever abandon Cory. A car passed her, then another. She needed to get out of sight.

Moments later, she stumbled upon a side path. It looked like some scaffolding up there – they must be rebuilding some-thing – but, beyond that, she could see trees. *Pull Cory up there*, she thought. It would be slow and painful . . .

But what if it was a trap?

A car pulled up: a Beetle, driven by two young women. Loud bouncy music rushed out when one of them opened the door.

'Sweet dog!' said one of the women. She had long blonde hair parted in the centre. Then she whistled, and when Elsa looked down she saw Cory's hood had fallen away just enough to reveal who he was.

Elsa was used to being cold and hungry and scared. This time she needed something else.

'Wow. The Man's after you,' the woman said, very serious. 'It's all over the radio. It's cool. We'll hide you.'

The other, who had long dark hair plaited in a braid, nodded.

Elsa realised it wasn't ordinary cigarette smoke pouring out of the car but the other, sweeter kind. The fact that Meteor seemed to like the women proved very little; Meteor wasn't the cleverest dog. But she had to make her choice: run from the women, or risk their help. In the end, her tired hesitation became its own decision.

The women jumped out of the car and got the children, Elsa's pack and the dog into the back, then piled all the other stuff there around them. Another car slowed to watch; the bad-tempered old man driving shouted something about freaks blocking the road and the dark-haired woman gave him a few choice words, then showed him a finger.

'The Grateful Dead,' said the other woman, 'd'ya dig them?' and Elsa realised it was the music. She did dig them.

They were in the car, she was committed, and off they drove. Far off, she heard a fire engine. So many things she wanted had been left behind.

CHAPTER 30

The third day

Molly and the children were gone and Gene had lost everything. Great, sinister powers were working to find his family. Molly and the two children were the bright centre of his being – but who should he work with to get them back? Fleur, his little darling, was asleep downstairs with the pastor's wife. How could he find the others and still protect the baby?

Where was Cory? And what was happening in space? One by one, the radio newscasters had announced, the satellites around Earth had been destroyed.

The pastor and his wife were fans. Their spare room was full of pictures of the Myers, reproaching him. Sitting on the bed, surrounded by the dead bones of a song he couldn't finish, Gene decided the worst was Andy Warhol's bright joke – twelve Corys in screaming colours. Any charlatan nowadays could claim to be making art.

He lifted Molly's old sweater to his nose. Her perfume lingered, bringing up memories of cold nights and warm beds, of trips into the woods to watch fireflies or to look at the harvest moon. Loving Molly had shown him what his life had been missing; being a father had been deeper and more frightening than he ever had thought. Now, in this bright room, he saw only shadow and tragedy ahead.

Molly and Cory and Elsa, all lost. I've been a fool.

He glanced at his watch. Carol and the editor of *Witness* would be in Federal court, getting Storm out of the hands of the FBI. Such bullshit charges, and a lot of the press were not buying it.

Witness would keep defending Cory, but there was little more they could do. The whole world knew Cory and Molly were missing, but Gene would swap a hundred theories for the truth.

Fear was ever-present, a sort of quivering animal in his throat. He knew he had to decide what to do, but instead, he tormented himself with the past, endlessly turning over his actions in that first frantic hour – could he have done anything differently? Perhaps he should have gone with them instead of allowing Molly to take Elsa to the dentist. He was no hero, but perhaps, with one more adult around . . .

When he got the news, Gene had grabbed Fleur, jumped into Dr Jarman's car with Rosa and driven away. The Jarmans had found the pastor, a hideaway if their lawyers could no longer help them.

Molly been seized by armed men – a hundred unspeakable thoughts rushed through his head at the very thought – shots had been fired and Cory had revealed himself. Then Cory, Elsa and the dog had vanished. The radio was saying that one of the men who'd kidnapped Molly was Dr Pfeiffer. Gene's hands curled into fists: he owed that man a punch on the nose.

Instead of searching, here he was, tucked away and waiting for that knock on the door. Four times he'd worked himself up to drive into Kauwenga Falls – into a tornado fuelled by the FBI and the media and a howling mob of locals – but each time, caution had prevailed. He was no spy, no action hero; he had no power to hide or scare or bluff. Molly had talked her way out of a dozen difficult encounters, while Gene only stumbled.

He couldn't stop thinking about the dreadful possibilities: maybe Cory had been captured, or wounded. Maybe he was dead. He imagined his son, drained by his horrific power, lying somewhere, helpless and dying. Or maybe he was already in government hands, or Pfeiffer's.

Then his thoughts turned back to Molly and the endless arguments. He'd felt like in the tight little world they lived in, she had been stifling him – that only duty held him, like George Bailey in *It's a Wonderful Life*. Her stupid stunt still made him angry – the way she'd put their whole family at risk, running away, just to make him follow her. He had never been so close to slapping her. And yet, without Molly, everything was darkness and despair.

He'd been a fool.

They'd fought through the loss of the baby, the drinking, his own errors . . . and now the silent deaths of the satellites were a warning of catastrophe to come. He was desperate. He could feel the ground giving way, and underneath there was only terror. He was powerless, and shocked at how fragile life was. Cory had always come with the possibility of loss, but not like this – not this way. And Elsa, so mistreated, and still with such a spark in her: she had such potential . . .

Dr Jarman had become the family's spokesman, handling the press in his normal unshakeable manner, but that meant he couldn't come to where Gene was hiding, or phone very often. In deepest secret, he'd also been handling the negotiations with the President's Chief of Staff, a man with the gracious façade of a Southern gentleman and the cruel heart of a Mob boss.

So far, the President had kept his word to the Myers, although his long, sordid political career suggested he would not do so for ever. As the doctor had said, 'Put a silk tie on a rat, it's still a rat.'

Dr Jarman and Rosa had given an interview to Dahlia Diamond, Miss Gushing Fountain 1972. She'd been an unashamed supporter of Cory's, in good times and bad, even risking controversy when necessary. She had championed the boy Cory had been trying to protect, and the teen who had done the right thing, and slowly, others had followed. Dahlia Diamond's ratings kept climbing, and of course, she wanted Gene to go on her show, to face his critics and to galvanise Cory's sympathisers across the country.

It was one option. Gene couldn't bear the show, Dahlia Diamond cooing out questions, her fake probing queries, so the guest could give a calm, planned answer. *The Women of America Trust Her* – ha! It would be doing something, that was true: his words would be debated worldwide. But half the time he felt it would be setting off a truckload of fireworks, rather than something that might actually help him find his family.

There were two great powers: the President, or the press. If life were a comic book, he would have already decided by now.

His father sent a message, trying to help and reassure him. 'You'll do the right thing, son,' John told him with conviction.

His dream since childhood had been to walk on alien land and see alien stars; to share Earth's music with a new audience and to hear theirs. He wanted to see a future bright and hopeful made real.

If the purples came, a great choice would be before them, and it would be terrible. If the purples came, who would he give up? Who would he let down? So many different futures – and they would all split the family apart.

Gene picked up the music and his scribbled notes for 'Cory Come Home', still unfinished: a song to bring his son and Elsa home, a song to reunite the family. It didn't convince him. Did Earth even want Cory? He could not write it a happy ending; not when he was searching in vain for the last thing left in the box, the little flutter of hope.

It was close to the hour. He turned on the radio to get the latest news.

'The President's Press Secretary will be holding a press conference in thirty minutes, and we understand that Dr Haldeman of NASA and the Secretary of Defense will be speaking to us. Meteor showers have been reported south of Japan, east of Florida and over the Antarctic, disrupting radio transmissions and radar. Several aircraft and ships are reported missing. Following the loss of the British satellite Ariel 4, it is understood that neither the West nor the Communist powers retain any working satellites, military or otherwise. In Paris, the Asian peace talks remain suspended . . .'

Surely the snakes' next move would be soon. He needed to act.

If he couldn't stand three days alone knowing Molly was in danger, he couldn't leave her, so she must come with him to the stars, to keep the family together. She would have to give in.

A little whisper insisted, *if you cannot persuade her, stay with her. It's the right thing to do.*

The whisper nagged at him, though he tried to think of something else, shaking it off as a dog does fleas. But it would be back.

Imagine this separation for a year, for a lifetime. Imagine choosing this.

CHAPTER 31

The Golden Sunrise Community

The women called it a commune, but it was just a big old farm. Elsa had been on farms before, sometimes by invitation and sometimes not. It had the usual smells of woodsmoke and animal dung, mixed with odder ones, like the sweet herb they smoked, and strange soaps and scents like a fancy church.

Her friend Cory could have told her ten things about the farm kitchen without even opening his eyes, but Cory was wrapped in a blanket, still asleep, with Meteor beside him. Elsa stroked one or the other while the adults argued and argued. She ate the thick soup they'd given her, with strange rough bread with seeds she had to dip in the soup to make soft enough to swallow. They'd made her eat herbs, chew horrid cloves and gargle with salt water for her toothache, but Marsha, who looked like she was a real grandmother, found her some proper pills as well.

A man with his hair in a braid wanted Cory gone that very minute. 'He'll bring the cops, or worse,' he kept repeating. A couple of the women seemed to be leaning towards that, but both the women who'd brought them and Marsha, who was the oldest person there, were having none of it. Marsha said, 'When Nate and Blessed come, they'll be for keeping Cory safe.' Another lanky, long-fingered man was trying to mend an old-fashioned radio lying in bits on the table. He was saying nothing.

The women were minding a baby, a toddler and a boy of about five, who stared and stared.

'He's not our problem. Get rid of him,' the braided man repeated.

'No. He's a child and we have to get him back to his family,' Marsha said patiently, as if to a child. 'And the people out working, they need to have a voice too.'

'You're acting like a leader.'

Marsha smoothed her grey hair and said, 'We're divided. I'm not putting a child in danger.'

'Do you have a phone?' Elsa said. 'Cory's good at remembering numbers. We can call someone.' But it frightened her that Cory had not reacted to the smell of the soup. His bowl had gone cold.

The man who wanted them out looked cross. 'We decided not to pay the bill,' he said, 'not with The Man listening in.' Then he seemed to see Elsa properly. 'You want something more to eat, honey? Help yourself. Why don't we see if the Niedermeyers will take them, just for a bit? They're pretty cool for squares, and the cops will leave them alone.'

Elsa worried that Cory would dream one of his fearful dreams and they would feel it, and then they would both be given to the Bad Man. But 'eat when you can' was a good rule for life. She refilled her bowl from the big pot and tucked in.

Another man came into the kitchen and they went into the argument again; a woman left the circle frustrated.

Elsa bent down and whispered in Cory's strange striped ear, 'Come on, ugly brother.' The word 'brother' had power. She'd never before had a brother to tease, or to protect her.

She gave him a spoon of water and without opening his eyes, he swallowed it. Then she tried a spoon of soup.

Elsa kept vigil, leaving only to give Meteor her run away from the animals so she could relieve herself. There were two older children there too, as wary of her as she was of them. There was no TV in the house and the radio still didn't work.

If danger came, it would be from the man with the braid – or the police would find them somehow. She could run and hide somewhere on the farm, but she couldn't leave Cory.

A day later, she awoke from dozing in the warm place by the stove. Something in the air had changed. She looked at Cory and his tentacles twitched.

'Elsa,' he said, eyes still firmly closed.

'Monster,' she said. 'Lazy ugly monster, faking ill while we all have to do hard chores.'

'Ha-ha. Tired. Hold me.'

'We need to call Gene and Molly,' Elsa said. 'You need to dig into that encyclopaedia brain and write down the numbers for me.' The commune was allowed to use the Niedermeyers' phone.

It was five minutes before his eyelids flickered again.

'Bathroom,' he said. He couldn't walk without her, so she all but carried him.

'Which numbers are safe?' Elsa had not realised until she came to Mourning Gull Bay that the police could listen when you spoke on a phone, particularly if you spoke for a long time. How worrying that was.

'Too tired.'

'I'll lift you. Come up, monster-breath.'

Marsha and a big solemn man named Blessed helped anxious Elsa and weary Cory to walk the mile to the neighbours' farm-house. Marsha took a long time too, as her hip hurt, but in the end, they were welcomed into a warm kitchen, and there on the wall was a phone. Marsha sat and gathered Elsa and Cory in her lap so they could all listen. Cory's fear and tiredness came and went, and the people around him could feel it. Elsa saw their fear and their awe. It was spooky enough for her, who had felt it often.

'Institute for Alien Biology,' said the voice at the other end.

'Good afternoon, may I speak to Dr Jarman?' said Marsha.

'I'm sorry, ma'am, but he's out of town.'

'I have Cory Myers.'

'Well, okay, putting you through,' the woman said. She didn't say, 'Oh Lord, another timewaster', but that's how her voice sounded.

The new voice was also a woman, and very firm. 'We're very busy. Where are you calling from?'

'My name is Marsha and we have Cory and his friend Elsa.'

'Ma'am, we've had twelve calls like this since breakfast. Prove it.'

Cory put his mouth closer and delivered a brisk speech in his language, hoots and whistles and fluting notes. His ears pricked up a little. 'You sound like Mabel-who-used-to-help Dr Jarman. Big owl brooch.'

The voice changed. 'Well, you sure sound like Cory Myers. But Dr Jarman has left some questions, just to make sure. When you first visited Dr Jarman, what was the first book you took from his library?'

A pause, a long pause, then, 'Big book of birds, very beautiful, very old.'

'Why didn't he lend it to you?'

'How sad-sad, present from his wife who-is-dead. But Cory always allowed to read when in library. Clean dry hands.'

'Your friend who died landing on Earth—'

'Called Black Groundfruit.' He whistled the name too. 'Healer's child, my friend. Too many questions. Mabel, you keep bowl of sour sweets in desk. I like but most children do not. You had brother pretended to have epilepsy not to fight. Believe me now?'

'I believe you, Cory. Now, I'm going to tell you how to speak securely to Dr Jarman. He said, you remember—'

'You give me number and I do easy math and that is real number.' His ears went up a little more. 'Very easy math.'

'So, take down the number.'

Cory grabbed the pencil and the notebook.

Gene took the corner a little fast and heard Molly in his ear, telling him to drive carefully. The emergency fund was sadly depleted, but there was enough to hire a car.

Seismographs had detected two massive explosions in China, but now there were no spies in the sky to fly over and find out what it was. Russia had been open; it wanted an alliance with the United States against the snakes. China remained unfathomable.

Gene got out of the car and looked at the ramshackle farm in the dying light. Fleur chewed a hand and looked bright-eyed at the world as he put her into her papoose. Windchimes tinkled and somewhere there was chanting – but there were also the reliable smells of animal dung and smoke. Chickens wandered around like in some olden film. He couldn't help thinking they were careless; they'd lose the lot to predators if they weren't careful.

Elsa was standing by a door, wearing a grubby sweater that came down to her knees. When she saw Gene, she fought back tears. A middle-aged woman with hair down her back held out her hand in welcome, offering Gene a generous smile.

'Well done,' Gene said, squatting down and holding Elsa as if he would never let go, wanting to kiss her, to shout at her . . .

'After you spoke to him, Cory got sadder and sadder,' she said, looking worried. 'Then when we got back here, he ran away. I don't know where he is.'

'Have you got Meteor with you?'

'Yes.'

No one prepares you to be a father. No one tells you what it feels like when your child faces threats you cannot fix. No one warns you about the fear, like the ground giving way beneath your feet. How little reason Elsa had to trust any adult.

'Of course he's sad, all these bad things, but it will be okay

306

now.' Gene put his fingers in his mouth and whistled, a note only he could do. 'Meteor, hey girl! Meteor—!' He bent and slapped his thighs and there, barrelling out of the barn, tail wagging wildly, came the dog, a soppy mess of curls.

'Hey girl!' Gene liked having a dog around, at least in theory. He tussled her ears a little, the silly, sloppy, clumsy thing. She was still growing into her paws.

'Where's Cory? Find Cory! Good girl!'

The dog turned and ran back to the barn and taking Elsa's hand, he followed Meteor to the barn. In the muted light inside, he saw the pile of hay and Meteor standing, tail wagging, with that patient expression she had when her beloved master was hiding nearby.

'Cory, son, I'm here. It's going to be all right.'

There was a sense of waiting. Somewhere, a chicken clucked.

'Cory, Fleur is here, and she's really been missing you. Dr Jarman and Rosa miss you too. And we need to find Mom – we need your help to do that.'

Elsa looked like she was one breath off crying. 'You're lucky to have a dad and a mom, Squid-face,' she said.

Surely Elsa knew she had a place in their hearts too?

'Whatever's wrong, whatever's worrying you, tell me and we'll find a way,' Gene said, projecting a confidence he didn't feel. He began to walk into the hay, feeling ahead with his senses and imagination.

He began to sing, fumbled, and started again. 'Our Child of the Stars', the song people always asked for, was all about a father's love for his son. As he sang, he became aware of Cory, very near – *grief and fear and a tinge of hope* – and halfway through the third verse, Cory popped out of nowhere and grabbed him hard, howling, *hoo-hoo-hoo*. Gene hugged him back, tight. He would have held him for ever if he could.

'Cory is Monster-a-Bad-Man almost a murderer sick-in-head, Cory not-good no-he-isn't Bad Man!'

There's a lie parents tell, a promise that they will walk with their child on the journey ahead, though they cannot know it will be true, but the telling of the lie can help it *become* true.

'I'm here, Cory – I'm here. It's going to be okay. It will be fine—'

'Not fine no-no-no! All the people scared . . . *hoo-hoo-hoo* . . . come after Cory pitchforks-and-guns-and-helicopters.'

Gene started stroking his back, moving his hand in reassuring circles. 'Everything will be fine, Cory. I promise. We'll go and find Mom and it will be okay.'

Cory sounded disturbed at that. 'N-not know where Mom is?'

'No – but lots of good people are looking for her.'

With one phone call, he could have Dahlia Diamond onside. But the last thing they needed now was the strident bellow of more publicity.

Gene looked around and beckoned, and Elsa joined the embrace.

'I missed your stupid jokes,' she muttered.

With Presidents, prosecutors and the malevolent Dr Pfeiffer to face, the way ahead felt utterly dark, but he had his kids, at least, and he would never let them go.

CHAPTER 32

In captivity

In troubled dreams, Molly was being shaken awake – but it was no dream. In the dark room, a dazzling flashlight made it hard to see who stood beside her; there was a split second of hope, but no, it was too short to be Gene.

'Don't make a noise,' Dr Pfeiffer said, his voice low and insistent. 'We're going.'

He was playing some mind-game or another, making her leave the most comfortable bed she'd used since Halcyon. She tried to pull the quilt over her head, but he grabbed it with his free hand.

'Dr Tyler has got Selena in the car. We just need—'

'Liar,' she snarled.

He thrust a newspaper towards her, folded open to an inner page. The headline screamed at her:

MYERS CASE: DISGRACED DOC'S WIFE ARRESTED
CONSPIRACY TO KIDNAP

'It's outrageous,' the doctor said. His face was haggard and frightened. 'It's nothing but intimidation. I never involved her in any of this.'

Molly tried to marshal her thoughts. 'So now I'm a bargaining chip—'

He quivered with frustration. 'No, no, not at all. I do have other leverage. Look at the front page.'

She turned on the light, hating that he was seeing her in her nightclothes.

BAIKONUR COSMODROME DESTROYED

That was the Russian Cape Canaveral – but in Kazakhstan, as Gene said, *every time* people called it Russia.

She looked at the words, finding it hard to focus.

Dr Pfeiffer reached into his pocket. 'Mrs Myers, the Earth is under attack. They've destroyed our satellites, the Russians' too, and they've taken out at least two of the Chinese rocket bases. We need to get out of here, right away – and you'll need your wits about you.' He produced a little bottle. 'Here – Benzedrine.'

She looked at the bottle like it was a poisonous frog. 'You and your people set a trap using my sister, you grabbed me in a public place, you terrified my children, you shot a bystander and you stuffed me full of drugs. Forgive me if I don't believe you.'

'Mr Myers has found Cory and the girl, safe and well. We need to go. I've drugged the others.'

She blinked. 'All of them?'

'Of course. Fine Bourbon for those off duty and coffee for

those on. Mind, it's hit and miss how long it lasts; every individual reacts differently. Mrs Myers, this looks like the start of a snake invasion, which means I have to offer my country whatever I can. I'll put you in touch with your husband, but I need to get you away from Norton. He's dangerous.'

It was believable, but it could as easily be more theatre.

'Take me to Selena,' she said, thinking that was the simplest way to see what he was up to.

She took the bottle and left it on the bedside table. As she was throwing on her clothes, she was trying to work out whether she should rush him now, or to go with the flow, act later. She was prepared for this all to be some power game.

'What Norton is talking about is basically torture,' Dr Pfeiffer was gabbling. 'He has some idea of using you. I think . . . I think you'll do the right thing.'

This diffident Dr Pfeiffer was worse than the arrogant Cold Warrior, but he was still not to be trusted, and even if he was telling the truth, he was no match for Norton: of that she had no doubt.

'We've been racking our brains for months,' she said, 'but there's nothing Cory knows that's useful. He's only a child. There's nothing we can share.'

Gene believed that some of what Cory said about their science might offer crumbs of hope – but in the long term, not now. What Cory knew about the purples' physics sounded like gibberish – vibrations in hidden dimensions and the like. After all, you couldn't land in mediaeval France and get them to build a fighter plane, could you? There wasn't any way Cory could build a weapon or hide the Earth.

She put a few things into the overnight bag they'd given her, then pulled on her coat. *Thank goodness*, she thought, *for sensible shoes she could run in.* And then she was ready to follow Dr Pfeiffer.

He killed the flashlight before they moved into the dimly lit hallway, where the monster eyes of giant insects stared at her from the walls. Laying a finger to his lips as though she was a mindless idiot, Dr Pfeiffer took her elbow, but she pulled it away. Her heart was pounding, her ears and eyes checking for any sign of danger, but the house was silent apart from the gentle hum of the heating.

They crept along the hallway, through a door and across an anteroom, until finally they reached a short flight of stairs. Molly had no sense of the layout; the house must have been enormous, with at least one floor beneath the ground.

'Garage,' Dr Pfeiffer mouthed, pointing, and they climbed the stairs.

The security lights in the garage revealed half a dozen vehicles, including a truck, an antique convertible and a couple of sturdy modern cars.

There came an ominous click.

'Now stop there, Doctor,' said Norton. He stood half hidden behind the edge of the truck, a gun pointing at them, a smile on his face.

Dr Pfeiffer almost leaped with surprise, but Molly instantly dropped down into a squat. She was between Pfeiffer and the convertible, but her head was still a target. She needed to see what Norton was doing – where one person turns out to be awake, there might be more than one, and in this vast dim space, it would be easy for someone to come around behind them.

I will never see my children again.

'Mrs Myers, Selena is sedated. No harm will come to either of you. And Dr Tyler won't be bothering anyone for a while. Pfeiffer, just stand aside and let her come forward.'

Molly debated whether to dash to the stairs – but where was Selena? And she hadn't any idea of the layout of the house.

'I'm not going to do that,' Dr Pfeiffer said, shaking. 'Mrs Myers, stay down.'

'Mrs Myers – Molly – you're only valuable alive. But Dr Pfeiffer dead is a useful scapegoat – and after all, you don't owe him anything.'

He raised his voice, keeping Pfeiffer and Molly in his gaze. 'Honey, I'm going to need some help.'

Nurse Skidelsky appeared behind Norton, dressed in dark slacks and top. She wore a satchel over her shoulder and was carrying a raised baseball bat.

The nurse swung the bat with force—

—and hit Norton on his right shoulder. There was a ghastly splintering sound and Norton, grunting, started to turn – but he'd dropped the gun.

Seizing the chance, Molly stood up, reaching into her bag for the hairspray, and ran past the doctor to Nurse Skidelsky, who was dodging a clumsy lunge.

Skidelsky took another swing, hitting Norton on the hip – and there came a great shout. Somehow, Norton had grabbed the end of the bat in his left hand.

Her heart pounding enough to break her ribs, Molly attacked. Hairspray was a useless weapon, really, but the stars aligned and she got Norton right in the eyes.

He bellowed in pain and with his attention diverted,

Skidelsky was able to wrestle the bat free – and she rammed it into his stomach.

Norton toppled, and she kicked him hard between the legs.

This woman had drugged her and lied to her, and Molly knew she'd stand no chance against Skidelsky, either running or in a fight. The gun had skidded under the car, but Molly had no idea how to use it, and in any case, she hated weapons.

Skidelsky raised the bat as if to finish Norton off, but Molly hissed, 'No!' She knew the dangers of a blow to the head – could she stop Skidelsky killing him?

But the nurse had already hesitated. 'I'm sentimental,' she said. 'He was a good lay.'

Blinking, Dr Pfeiffer said, 'Who do you work for?'

'Oh, our mutual employer – who we won't name – never quite trusted Norton. I was insurance. Now, Mrs Myers, things are moving. If you want my employer's protection, come with me. He will have you and your family in Switzerland within a day – there's no extradition treaty. He is dying to meet you, but he does understand you might find that awkward. If you prefer whatever Dr Pfeiffer has planned, go with him. Or—'

It was the easiest choice in the world. 'I'll take the car keys, and my sister,' Molly said. 'And a map – oh, and the gun.' That was a bluff.

She looked at Dr Pfeiffer, who looked like his world had collapsed. Nothing could wipe out what he had done to her and her family.

'I didn't mean it to be like this,' he said, the whine of every man in over his head. 'Truly, I didn't.'

'Go to your wife,' she said, hoping this was the last thing she would ever say to him.

CHAPTER 33

Rendezvous

The rendezvous was not hard to find, and it was suitably unwelcoming. At the turning off the main road there was a board advertising Pop's Café [SHUT], Bathrooms [SHUT], Parking [SHUT], Lake Views [ALWAYS]. Spring had picked up her skirts to run; there were fresh green leaves and spikes of colour among the bushes, red fuzzy buds on the maples. Molly turned up the drive and drove some of the way – far enough to see that the parking lot in front of the café was empty. It pretended to be jolly and Alpine, but it was about as Swiss as supermarket cheese.

Every country, no matter how small, was busy asserting their own right or reason to be the place for the purples to land, but Dr Jarman thought the purples should choose Switzerland as the least contentious choice. Gene said they should ask Africa and Asia about that.

Gene was late and Molly was seeing Feds behind every tree, in every dark car. Selena had insisted on a local channel, so between tunes from Molly's youth, the radio announcers had been musing on the attack on Baikonur and missiles – and how, without satellites, Russia might think an attack from space was actually coming from the United States. The host was easygoing and a bit of a stoic, but those phoning in were frightening and angry. *It was the purples, we've been tricked. It was the snakes and we're all doomed. It was a plot by the Russians to make us drop our guard.* And, as always, some callers said, *They're lying about Cory being dangerous* and *Only the purples can save us.*

She was always grateful for support, but some of Cory's supporters definitely worried her, especially that bizarre group who wore purple hoods and had the nerve to worship Cory as a god.

She sat there taking in the idyllic view of Lake Delaney. It might be a pretty place, but if she never saw Kauwenga County again, she would be delighted. When Selena dozed off in the back, Molly had turned off the radio, leaving her alone with her own racing thoughts. The place was discreet, but it felt like a trap.

A car growled up the track, flashing its headlights. Molly couldn't wait; she wrapped a scarf around her neck, got out and trotted towards them.

Gene was driving. He looked tired and gaunt, but when his eyes met hers, his proper smile lit his face and seconds later, he was out of the car and loping towards her – then she was in his arms, and he was trying to explain something, but she put her mouth to his. It was him, and amidst everything dark and dreadful, he was here, a blazing light.

Her heart dared to sing.

Cory was here too, waves of relief cascading off him. Then Meteor began barking with excitement, and there was Elsa, walking with care, holding out a precious bundle of blankets. In that moment, any faint lingering flicker of doubt died. Elsa was her daughter too, and Molly would walk through fire to keep her.

'So-so-much to tell,' Cory said.

Molly kissed all of them, then kissed them again, hugging them all close, noticing how swollen Elsa's face looked as she passed her the bundle of blankets that was Fleur.

'I hate the dentist,' said Elsa, a little muffled, catching the look.

Birds called to each other as a smattering of rain rolled over them, though the sun shone over the lake.

Gene said, 'Let's all get in the car, shall we? We need a plan.'

Molly looked back towards her own vehicle. Selena had woken up and was walking over to them, ignoring the rain. They all piled into Gene's car, which was the bigger; Selena took Cory, Elsa and the dog in the back.

Gene started. 'We need to get out of here – the local police want Molly and Cory as witnesses, for the shooting, they say. The local paper wants Cory prosecuted. Local police and FBI want Selena, to investigate the kidnapping. What the hell was Pfeiffer up to? And of course, we're still wanted in New York.'

Selena leaned forward, her head appearing between Molly and Gene. 'I need my kids,' she said, her voice filled with quiet strength. 'I don't know that I understand everything, but we need to go and get my boys.'

Gene gave her a tired smile. How stressed he looked. 'Your

kids need their mom,' he agreed. 'Mason's lawyer shopped Mason to the judge, to save his own skin – something about perjury . . . and Mason broke his bail by fleeing the state, so there's a warrant out for his arrest . . . Your lawyers and Dr Jarman have a plan.'

Selena turned to Cory. 'But Cory can just walk in and get them, can't you, sweetheart? Then we can all go back to Amber Grove.'

Molly's heart sank.

Cory groaned, but Gene was already speaking. 'We can't . . . Cory's tired . . . And throw a stone in Kauwenga Falls, you'll hit the cops or the press. Dr Jarman will take you back to court, get you your kids . . .'

'I'm not going back to Green Bowers,' Selena said, catching her breath. 'Molly, don't let them put me there—'

Molly was torn. She could see how much Selena hated the place, but she had admitted – and Pfeiffer confirmed – that she had got better.

'Dr Jarman has a plan that will see you and your kids in Amber Grove. It's just, it might take a few weeks. You could see your kids tonight – the director will put you up in his own residence.'

'Selena looked from Gene to Molly and back. 'I need to talk to Dr Jarman before I agree.'

'Good. That's fair,' Gene said. He started the car. 'We need to get to a second rendezvous.'

'Good about Connor and Rory. Now what about snakes?' Cory said.

Gene turned the car, frowning. 'Well, everyone thinks we can help them with the snake attacks.'

'Definitely snake attacks,' Cory said. His shiver ran through all of them. 'But Cory can't help here. Some very strange signals coming from communicator – just maybe some of my Network is still there in space, hiding from the snakes. Easiest to work from Amber Grove, inside the Fence, if the humans have not broken it.'

Molly longed to go home. She still felt the danger – but she could also feel her home and her friends calling to her.

'Will this Network destroy the things?' Selena said.

Cory *tock-tock-tocked*. 'No, not weapons. But maybe better warning.'

Gene sighed. 'We know the snakes are up there, circling the Earth. At least spying on them back is *something*.' He kissed Molly again, as if to check she was real.

Molly bit her lip, starting to feel that everything was too much. How would they get home?

Over the lake, there hung a rainbow. And Molly saw again in her mind a grey world of ash and smoke, where the snakes reigned supreme.

An hour later, up another track out of sight of the road, Dr Jarman persuaded Selena to trust his plan. Tearful, she hugged everyone twice, particularly Cory.

'Connor and Rory have changed their minds, sweetheart. Knowing you made them the coolest kids in town.'

A last kiss for Molly, and Selena was in Jarman's car.

'What do we do now?' Molly asked, and suddenly all was doubt again. They had no Carol and Storm to buy gas and book motel rooms. No Pierre with a private plane and a truck . . .

'The kindness of strangers.' Gene waved a notebook, then passed it to her. '*Witness* have three planes booked flying to Canada – and a fourth one which the government won't know about until it's there. People will assume we've been smuggled out. And our fan club are ready to throw up a smokescreen – turns out, they have this telephone tree.'

'False sightings?' She felt guilty at enjoying the thought.

'Once the press say there's a hullaballoo, everyone joins in. It's stupid, really. Officially, we didn't start it.'

It was good to see him smile. It stirred hope, love, regret . . .

He went on, 'Carol found some places, people she knows. Dr Jarman has somewhere lined up close to home. Neither of them know the whole route. And I've supplies in the back for a week so we can speak to as few people as possible.'

'And I will hide, but no scaring.'

'Cory can just pull a face, and they will all run away . . .'

Gene started the car and they were heading home.

After their ordeal, they had no desire to press on through the night. The hunting lodge took some finding. It was all rough log walls and fish in glass cases, but it smelled of fresh polish, and the kitchen was newer than theirs at home – in fact, the lodge was bigger than their whole house.

Cory and Elsa were debating which room they would take, while Gene changed Fleur in the big room. Molly watched him from the doorway, the baby intent on him while his deft hands made her comfortable. He hummed a familiar air. Molly thought she had approached quietly, but he looked up and gave a tired smile.

'We could take this room.'

'We could.' They had things to talk about, important things, but perhaps not tonight. 'I'll get the crib from next door.' She wanted Fleur at hand if she woke, or if Cory had a night-mare . . . She wondered if his episodes hurt Fleur's growing brain.

Gene bounced Fleur a little, and said, 'Early night.'

She was tired, still fighting the drugs, but when he smiled, she smiled, and no more words were needed.

Desire was back, a sacred flame in the marriage, and a wel-come friend.

Later, Molly was lost in strange dreams, of being hunted by giant insects, or being parted from her children. Then Cory came in the night and shared his dream, his descent into the deepest layers of the dreaming-together. He was trying to share his experience, still fresh and raw, but Molly understood less than he wanted. She saw Thunder Over Mountains and felt the power of their love and relief, father and son, that they had found each other again. This dream was urgent, a dispatch from a crisis. The purples had needed to know Cory was safe, and to tell him they were coming.

Molly was shocked that Thunder was in deep pain, and others too.

Was Cory all right?

Yes, yes, with Earth parents, safe.

Then watch, listen.

When they projected a spinning globe, the Earth, Cory's joy was incandescent – they knew where he was, they were on the way! The Stars and Stripes waved in a summer breeze: they must know which continent. But sadness, fear and loss drenched the dream.

When Cory pushed to know what the danger was, Thunder showed two starships in a battle with the snakes. One ship was damaged, perhaps both, and there was a deep grief that hurt Molly's chest. The purples were coming, as soon as they could, but there was death all around them. Cory pleaded – *how long?* – but he gained no sense of how long it would take. Molly felt his confusion that Thunder couldn't tell him – or wouldn't. Maybe they didn't know?

The dream felt so real. Molly had come to believe in this impossible dreaming across the vastness of space. She woke, still tired; she knew Cory would come into their bed soon to tell them everything he'd dreamed. He'd be both fearful for his birth-father and joyous that the purples were coming, and he would tell them every detail, in case they had missed anything. Somehow she must mask her ambiguity and rejoice with him, assure him they would make it safely.

The reunion with Gene had been so precious, but there were greater threats to come. Life was fragile, and priceless; they might have less time than they thought, so they must live each day as though it mattered – and that against the fear and the dark, they must cling to those they loved, and do the right thing.

Cory's people were coming. They had to come. Then she must fight them for her son – and perhaps for her marriage too.

CHAPTER 34

Driving east

Molly drove through fields fuzzy with new green, the clouds scudding across the sky like white puppies. Gene was trying to teach the kids a song and Elsa played at getting it wrong on purpose. Each mile brought them a little closer to their home and further away from her captivity. Amber Grove was calling out to them as if they were birds, or salmon.

Ignoring Gene's mild complaints, Molly turned on the radio at a quarter to the hour.

'Breaking news,' said the anchor, his tone hollow. 'This hot off the wire from Associated Press. There has been an explosion directly centred on the Kennedy Space Center and Air Force Base at Cape Canaveral in Florida. Twenty minutes ago, a blinding detonation was seen all over the state, and a shock wave has been felt as far away as Orlando. Witnesses are reporting a huge mushroom cloud hanging over the area. We are still awaiting news of casualties, and a statement from the

President. I'll repeat that: around twenty minutes ago, at half to the hour, some sort of explosion—'

Cory's fear gushed and whirled around them, eerie and frightening, yet familiar. Sometimes it would bring on an episode, his power reeling out of control.

'Okay, sweetie-pie, okay,' Molly cooed, slowing the car to a crawl. *Stay calm*, she thought, *stay in control*. If it got too bad, she would have to pull over, while she could still drive.

Elsa held Cory while Gene looked back and said, 'You can do it, Big Stuff, you know you can . . .'

As Cory brought it under control, Gene said, 'The snakes have closed the skies. Now they're destroying our launch pads.'

'Surely the Administration must have known? After Baikonur—?'

'Yeah, they must have. They must have evacuated the place . . .'

Her parents were in Orlando, damn them – but Orlando wasn't next to the base; it was fifty miles away. She told herself they'd be fine.

The radio started to play Rachmaninov, 'The Isle of the Dead'. Gene loved that piece. It must have been hard for the station to know what to play while they were waiting for more news.

'My people coming too late!' moaned Cory.

The station cycled through what little it had: radar down, planes diverting . . . it wasn't until a full hour later that the story changed.

'There have been reports of a second, smaller explosion in Orlando,' the same newsreader reported. 'And this just in – it has been confirmed that the Kennedy Space Center at Cape Canaveral was operational and preparing for an imminent rocket launch. There have been heavy losses among civilian and military personnel. Nuclear fall-out warnings are being given in the area and, given the prevailing winds, to the east and north.'

The newscaster's voice broke. In a whisper, he said, 'I have folks in Orlando—'

Molly thought of her parents and their cold, brutal marriage.

When Cory came, when she had become the most famous mother in the world, her own parents had neither called nor written. It was as if Molly was dead.

There were half a million people in the Orlando area, the newsreader said, once more calm and professional, and he restated the story without emotion. Silver missiles had been seen flying over the ocean: snakes, attacking aircraft and radar installations. A warship off the East Coast had been sunk here, a passenger plane destroyed there.

Then it was back to the music.

Molly always said, to close off discussion, that her mother was dead to her. But just like one of Gene's atrocious films, it turned out the dead could rise and haunt the living.

If she hated her mother so much, and with such good cause; if she had spent so many nights wishing her father dead, why were these hot tears blurring the road?

'Pull over,' Gene said quietly. 'You're thinking about your folks.' His tone was gentle.

She did as he'd said, with no remonstrations.

His eyes troubled, he wrapped her in an awkward embrace.

'Orlando is three days' drive away,' he said. 'And we need to get to Amber Grove.'

'What are we going to do?' said Elsa.

'I don't know, sweetie-pie.' In the back seat, Fleur started wailing as Cory's *hoo-hoo-hoo* filled the car.

Molly surreptitiously wiped her eyes before turning to check on them. Elsa was holding Fleur, trying to get her to chew a finger.

'What's going on?' Elsa said.

'My parents – well, they weren't very kind to me, darling, but this attack in Florida – well, that's where they live. They might be hurt.'

'After all they did—' Gene started.

Molly missed Eva and John to talk to. She wanted them and their wisdom. 'Orlando is too far,' she said. 'We need to get home.'

'Cash in a favour with the President,' Gene said.

'I don't want us owing that man anything.' Not for her mother, anyway.

'Cory can't hide from Bad Men if too many,' Cory said, and everyone felt his anxiety.

'We're going home, sweetie-pie,' Molly said firmly.

'Let's find a phone,' Gene said, 'and somewhere the kids can breathe. You safe to drive?'

Huh!

Cory's dreams needed to be true: his people needed to come. This was a war between people at the bottom of a hole brandishing spears and people at the top threatening them with machine-guns.

It was time for distance-eating speed, for Cory needed to work on the alien Network. Molly put her foot down and started a silly song, one of Gene's.

Outside a gas station, Molly put her back to the attendant and made the call. She read a few sentences over the phone, knowing the four words at the end would confirm it was her. That simple message would pass through other hands and should be with the President within an hour.

When they passed through towns, they saw crowds gathered around the shops; they passed school buses full of children, although it was too early for finishing time. They started to see flags flying at half-mast.

The second announcement came as they ate a cold supper outside a burnt-out, boarded-up diner. The snakes had bombed Colorado Springs: that was the NORAD command, the centre of America's defences, a facility buried deep beneath a mountain and supposedly impregnable to attack. The Ship had told them the government had taken some purple technology down there.

These were smaller explosions, accompanied by a rain of silver fire: snakes that had burrowed into the rock itself, an army that could burn its way into the mountain. The Secretary of Defense refused to comment on casualties, but he did confirm that the city would be evacuated.

'If we get Cory to the Network, maybe we can warn them the next time,' Molly muttered, the only thing they could offer.

'I keep saying only *maybe-maybe-maybe*,' Cory moaned, hunched over.

Gene wanted to drive through the night, but Molly refused. It was dusk before they reached that night's sanctuary, a chapter of the Stellar Friendship League, and even though Gene had taken over at the wheel, she was ready to drop.

They pulled into the motel, where a few lights were showing, and as instructed, drove straight round to the back, where they found a small house. A teen came over carrying a big electric flashlight, all acne, long hair and anxiety. He wore a purple T-shirt which said *Vote Cory Myers 1972*. It sported rather a good psychedelic cartoon of Cory dwarfing the White House. Gene's naïve quote – 'We don't need drugs; we live with Cory!' – had gone around the world.

'We were told to ask for Mike?' Gene said, looking dubious.

'Pop's had to go to Grandma's – she's freaking out – and Mom volunteered for civil defence. There's just me left.' The youth's gaze darted here and there, but he wasn't going to see Cory and the other kids until they were sure of the set-up.

'You'll do fine,' Molly said encouragingly. 'You know that no one must know about us, right? Not friends, not other people in the group – not even your girlfriend.'

'Yeah, yeah, I dig it.' He got up his courage and whispered, 'Can he save us? Are his people really coming?'

'His people are coming,' Gene said. *Two ships, one damaged.* Why had everyone assumed the purples would come with a vast war fleet? 'So, can we trust you?'

Cory appeared, the boy's face blazed with a massive grin and that was their answer.

They sent the children straight to bed, rather than let them watch the news. There were pictures from Orlando, destroyed buildings, fires and billowing smoke, military vehicles, people fleeing in cars and trucks. It was Meteor Day times a thousand. A reception centre set up out of town was already full of refugees, a chaos of noise and volunteers, nurses distributing iodine to help against fallout. There were numbers to call if you were out of state and looking for relatives.

There were tens of thousands of dead, they said. A quarter of a million more were being told they'd be evacuated.

The White House had announced a State of Emergency. The Florida attacks had come from the ocean, it was reported, the snakes skimming above the waves like flying fish. Electromagnetic pulses had wrecked radar and communications.

They felt they had to watch the President's address on TV. No amount of make-up could hide the President's dark, doom-ridden eyes. There was something a little awry with the broadcast, waves of static that weakened his voice and blurred his picture. That of itself suggested further attacks.

'My fellow Americans: we face a grave situation, but it is my duty to give you the facts and dispel the wild rumours. Following the heinous, unprovoked attacks in Florida and Colorado Springs, Federal, state and private resources are being devoted to rescue those in peril, to maintain order and defend our country. There has been a magnificent stirring of the American spirit, a real coming-together as a nation.

'Those who work at the Kennedy Space Center have always known the risks inherent in exploring space. To a man, they volunteered, wanting to serve their country and their fellow man in the only way they could. We are not passive in the face of this aggression and we will continue to expand our defence in the face of this threat.'

So, thought Molly, *they'd tried to launch something military against the snakes.*

'There is no doubt that the alien machines known as snakes are responsible. That view is shared by our allies, both scientists in neutral countries and the Soviets, and we believe it is also the view of the Chinese Communist authorities. Although each country is in a high state of readiness individually, we are seeking common ground at this time of peril. A planet divided cannot stand.

'I welcome the generous words of the Soviet Foreign Minister, recalling those times when America and the USSR worked together against a great threat. The snakes have attacked six launch centres across the world. They have attacked any substantial equipment orbiting the Earth, no matter its purpose and whatever its country of origin. Every satellite, no matter its origin, every probe travelling between the planets and the Soviet Lunar Lander, they have all ceased broadcasting. I repeat: this is an attack on different nations in different blocs, an exertion of inhuman power.

'If this attack was intended to provoke us, however, it has failed. If it was intended to stir hostility between the Great Powers, it has failed. If intended to test our resolution, it has merely strengthened us. Let us never forget that we are a nation founded in adversity. We gained independence when the odds were against us—'

There was more in this vein, but little of substance and little reassurance. There was a pledge to return to space, to destroy the snakes and to usher in a new era of peace, but the President did not look as though he quite believed it himself.

Humanity had reached the Moon through courage and ingenuity, a declaration to the stars that these smart, quarrelling apes would explore the universe. But space was no longer for humans; the snakes had reclaimed it. Now the snakes encircled the Earth, waiting and alert. And Molly, once such a sceptic about flight to the stars, could see the size of that danger – and the sheer size of what humanity had lost.

CHAPTER 35

Near Colorado Springs

Carol had a cloth over her mouth in a vain attempt to keep out a wind that stank of burning fuel and smoke. The helicopter she was riding in flew low under that vast bright blue, the stunning mountains off to her left. Her eye was drawn down to the sinister pall of black smoke over Colorado Springs, the ragged stumps of what had once been tall buildings. There had been two blasts – one high, for the electromagnetic pulses, and the other to take out the air base.

She scribbled one-handed in the notebook balanced on her knee.

What is still burning after two days?

Outside of the mountains, the land was flat, the roads wide, the settlements strung out. This state had elbow room. Storm had visited before, long ago.

They were all wearing radiation tags like the one pinned on

Carol's coat to detect and measure background levels. The wind had been blowing fallout towards Denver, so against official advice, thousands were fleeing the Mile-High City, even as the refugees from the south were arriving to swamp its hospitals. Carol had already discovered that thousands were thought to be still in Colorado Springs – wounded, blinded or stubborn, or staying to help others. And thousands more were dead, or would be soon.

That silver streak, very high up, was a snake. There was another, away over there. Of course Storm was trying to capture them on her camera, a tricky shot.

Grim-faced, the pilot had warned them, 'If a snake heads for us, we'll try to land. It will be fast and dirty. You can't outrun them, but if you land, just sometimes they'll pick another target.'

'Who says?'

'The Commies, apparently. They're never off the phone now, passing on what they know. They sure hate those things. Sometimes snakes burn you up with some ray-gun, sometimes they just ram into you in flight. The heat-seeking missiles they used in Vietnam? No damn good – the snakes just make 'em drop out of the sky.'

The battle had been brief; now, for twenty miles in any direction, the air belonged to the snakes, and anyone on the ground was a target. Carol remembered the utter shock of the attack on Pearl Harbor. Her European friends always said that America did not understand defeat.

Courage is not an absence of fear. Courage is wanting to pee yourself with fear and yet doing the right thing anyway. The people deserved to be told the truth.

The machines had burrowed into the mountain and destroyed the impregnable fortress – well, that made some sense. But what were they remaining for?

They are ALIEN.

Carol could live with the racket of the rotors, but something behind her seat was shifting with each shudder of the copter; if this had been a car, she'd have insisted they stop and find out what it was.

Hikers and rangers on horseback had seen snakes land in the mountains.

What the hell was their energy source? Were they building one of their factories?

In the first couple of days, snakes had blown up highways and roads, then coming back time and again, strafed those fleeing, almost at whim. Then the snakes had returned to destroy those trying to clear the roads blocked with burning vehicles. Any attempt at ground-to-air attack brought instant retribution.

Now people were just trying to escape any way they could: riding or walking, pulling invalids or possessions in carts by hand or burro, driving ill-suited vehicles across rugged terrains, all somehow believing that they were less likely to be attacked.

The authorities had tried to control where the press went, steering what they said. Vietnam had taught them nothing, which was why Carol was determined to reach somewhere the authorities hadn't got to.

Here was their destination: a cluster of buildings stretched out beneath them. The Red Cross flag flew over a church and some awnings, as if the snakes cared. They'd taken out the bridge and the railway track a mile south and now the only

335

way out was to walk, ride or fly, or to head back towards the devastated city.

Her source in the US Air Force said, 'It's like they had a target. They secured the area. If they were human, I'd think they might be wanting a landing. What are they up to?'

The pilot brought the helicopter down a hundred yards from the church now functioning as a hospital.

Carol jotted notes fast.

Courage of troops. Civilians.
? evacuation plan good enough ? numbers
? snakes in mountains — confirm?

The scoop would be to get to the bunker under the mountain and confirm it really was a radioactive tomb for its staff. There had been some harrowing recordings of screams over the telephone; there was even a rumour that two snakes already inside it had come alive and run amok. The Air Force said it wasn't safe and wouldn't take the press near it. Was that knee-jerk secrecy or was there some specific reason?

One of her rivals had bought six horses and planned to ride in. 'The things we do for a byline,' Storm said with a grin.

Carol had seen many disasters – a mine collapsed, a flood, a ship sunk, a violent coup down south – but there was something different about this. A disaster was just a disaster, usually with some human failure added. An atrocity had humans behind it. This destruction – this was *alien*. She gripped Storm's shoulder for luck, then let go and they followed the pilot into the swirling dust. The co-pilot stayed, jaw for ever chewing, holding a military rifle in case anyone got silly ideas about the helicopter.

The Sunday School side of Carol was questioning whether they should be flying out the wounded – but no. *People need to know*, she told herself. *That is the greater good: we need to rally the world to help*.

The first four people they saw had bandages covering their faces, even their eyes. One woman's head was quivering, her hand too; the other hand was gripped by the man on her left. They stood frozen as a waxwork. Their son was blinded too, and the baby.

The numbers of dead would make people numb. It was individual stories that would produce connection and under-standing. There would be chaos; there would be heroism. There would be mistakes, some forgivable, others less so.

Somewhere, somebody screamed and blinded and sighted alike looked up. Carol saw a silver streak crossing the sky, although well wide of them. She watched it mocking them.

'They're circling,' Storm said. 'The snakes – they could be keeping planes away, especially if they are planning a landing.'

'Or they're testing us, hoping we pick a fight, to find out what we've got.'

The motherly woman was coming towards them. 'Who are you?' she asked.

'Carol Longman, *Witness* magazine. Who's in charge?'

The woman wasn't sure. 'My husband is at the church. How many people can you take?'

'We'll call your needs through,' Carol said. 'We'll get you help. What do you need?'

'Everything.' She was wearing an expression Carol had seen often, scared and shocked and, through gritted teeth, capable of sheer heroism. She was eyeing the camera as if it was a bomb.

'Tell me, how many people are there here now? Can any of them drive? What medicines do you need?'

'Oh, I don't know – we've one doctor here, although he's been retired a good few years . . .'

Storm was pointing the camera, framing the town. She would be itching for action shots.

This was their life: being where the story was.

Bumping up the road came two trucks, one crawling with a flat tyre. Wounded people were hanging onto the sides.

The woman was holding back tears. 'What will we do?'

Carol made a judgement: she had to move on.

She and Storm strode towards the trucks. Perhaps they would come back later.

This place, with the blinded and burned, the man with a leg crushed, the dead laid out under common sheets while the grey-haired pastor tried to figure where to store them; a six-teen-year-old Scout in tears holding the hand of a man, dying, maybe already dead, and no spare people to bury them: it was a tiny side-chapel of Hell.

The people deserve to know the truth.

CHAPTER 36

Others on the journey

They woke in the log cabin to strange news about Amber Grove. People were headed there by every means they could, from every corner of the country. Mayor Rourke said the town was already full.

The station had a reporter on the spot. The Bradleyburg train station was crowded, the buses fully laden, and the usual businesses of the neighbouring towns were overloaded.

'I've spoken to these people . . . students and housewives, Army vets and doctors, a Harlem preacher and his choir. They think it all began here, and it will somehow end here.'

'What will end?'

'That the aliens will come and save us. That Cory Myers will save us. Some believe that this little town in Amber County will be the last place left at the end of the world.'

An hour later, Molly was driving east, heading home. They heard that the National Guard had closed the roads to anyone without existing business in the town. Meanwhile, Cory insisted, there was something odd happening, some remnant of the Network restarting.

Molly saw old buses daubed in psychedelic colours, a Beetle with a purple flag sticking out of one window, then a top-of-the-range luxury recreational vehicle with its own purple banner.

'How will we get home?' she said.

Gene was peering at the notebook. 'Let's find somewhere to stay for tonight.'

Molly was afraid that hiding in the crowds would be some who wished her son harm.

The news rambled on about the relief effort – people giving blood, volunteers packing supplies and making sandbags. Scientists had discovered that they could spot alien objects around the Earth by looking in the infrared: the snakes were not able to shield their warmth. Across the country, there were demonstrations demanding that America's vast arsenal of nuclear weapons should be fired at the snakes.

'It's like firing at hummingbirds from a mile away,' Gene said. 'The snakes will see the missiles coming.'

The lakeside summer house they were heading for was owned by friends of the Jarmans and well away from the county. The kids had been hard to settle, of course, and it had taken the two of them to do it. Afterwards, they sat in the tiny kitchen, Gene plucking at his guitar.

It would be so much easier not to have the conversation, but Molly plucked up her courage. 'I was wrong. Maybe we could have gone to California,' she started.

Gene gave a very serious smile. 'Too late now. But thanks.' He took a deep breath. 'You know I want to go to the stars.'

A dam broke. 'I'm not going, Gene – I'm not, and you can't take Elsa. And maybe Fleur is being harmed by being around the purples.' She thought of Cory's dreams: his world of bright sun and green seas where nightmare creatures lurked in the deeps. In those bright night skies there were flying cities.

She'd bet the farm that humans would feel more lost up there, more homesick than a Bushman in New York or an English peasant brought forward a thousand years and dropped in modern Japan.

'Just listen, okay?' Gene picked up the guitar, fiddled with the tuning. 'It won't come out right unless I sing it.'

Molly remembered when she first met him, and later, the party where he sang. He was always fiddling with that damn guitar.

'You remember that book about the explorer? I wrote a song about him and his wife.' And he launched into it with what critics called his 'perfectly competent' voice.

That song, so full of yearning, about a man who grieved walking the familiar land, a man whose heart was with the flying birds and the diving seals; how great walls of ice and the spume of whales, even the ever-present risk of death, called out to him. How he loved his wife, but his ship was the other woman . . .

Molly blinked at that.

Gene poured it all out, how much the man in the song needed to go beyond the horizon, beyond where any man had walked or climbed or swum. Then the key changed, and she realised that this was the woman's voice, so deeply in love with the man, so deep in his betrayal. He sang about how the birds in the air and the seals in the sea flew and swam in pairs, returning to their own beaches, their own nests, rearing their young, and how she felt, struggling with children, money, his absence, her fear. Her need was a fire greater than the sea and the wind. She needed him, the children needed them, while he whored with his ship and the storm. She would rather he whored in the tavern and came home than abandon her for yet another year.

The song was their confrontation – and then it ended.

Perhaps the last bit was the voice of the unfeeling wind, the indifferent sky.

Molly was stunned into silence. The sheer scale of his need stunned her, and so too did the power and honesty of the woman's voice.

'You think you've got to go,' she said.

He looked disappointed. 'What about the second bit?'

She shrugged, and he scowled.

'Guess I screwed up then, if you didn't understand: he agrees *not* to go. I *want* to go, I *need* to go – but I won't go without you. I thought I didn't need to spell it out.'

Molly didn't know whether to laugh or cry. 'You should have just said.' Now he'd told her, the song made sense.

'Molly, I've wanted this since I was in short pants – but I can't go if you don't want me to. With all this happening, my place is by your side.'

She had had all the arguments ready – he couldn't split the family; the strangest human society was still human – but this utterly disarmed her. He was making promises, but who knew what would happen when the aliens truly got here?

'We don't know what the real options are,' she tried. 'Let's see what's on the table, shall we? And then I'll have to give you the answer.'

'I write a masterpiece and get a "maybe"?' It wasn't much of a joke, but he was trying.

She was trying too. If she said no, it would be on her. 'Sometimes life *is* maybe. It's a superb song, but promise me you'll never play it to anyone else.'

He kissed her, and she was glad. She felt truly heard by him, and from his warmth, she hoped he felt the same about her. He might change his mind – after all, neither of them had any idea what might happen – but, despite that, she had never loved him more.

But if he stayed, it would always be the great *might-have-been* for him: the other woman.

On the radio, the newscaster broke in, 'This just in: snakes have launched attacks against two coastal cities in Japan, destroying radar installations across a hundred miles of coast. A mushroom cloud has been reported over a nuclear power plant—'

If the end was coming, Molly wanted to face it at home, with her friends.

CHAPTER 37

Homecoming

They would speak to the President from a roadside phone, then go. For all their fears, he had had a dozen chances to snare them and not done it; there were a hundred ways to put pressure on them he had not used. Maybe he saw no need – maybe the occasional messages the Myers had sent convinced him they were telling him what they could.

Two heads to the handset, they kept a watch out for passing traffic while the kids stayed hidden in the bushes. Birds sang under a clear sky.

'So,' the President began after they'd exchanged brief pleasantries, 'these devil machines are attacking anything we might use to get into space, that's obvious. But what links the other attacks in Russia and here is alien technology. The Russians lost a couple of centres, they tell us, and Colorado Springs – well, I guess you know about that.'

'So there was alien tech at that base in New Mexico, too,' Gene guessed.

'No harm in telling you now, I guess. Now it's gone. The explosion in Texas, we're thinking the Markham Corporation must have laid their hands on something and not told us. Does Cory know why the snakes might be blowing up power plants in Japan? Why they're in Antarctica?'

'No idea,' Molly said, although they did have half an idea that the Ship might have hidden something in Antarctica it didn't want humans to find.

'Well, here's the thing,' said the President. 'There's an alien technology working away right there in Amber County. As far as we know, the Fence protecting Crooked Street is the only alien tech on the planet. And the snakes haven't done a thing. Why do you think that is?'

'They're not worried about it?' Gene suggested.

'Or maybe they can't see it,' the President pondered aloud. 'Nothing at NORAD was doing much and yet they still flung hundreds of their machines into a suicide attack.'

There was a long pause.

'I guess you might be headed there,' the President said. 'As I swore an oath to enforce the law, it might be better if I didn't know. If there's any purple tech up there still working – if it could, say, tell us where they are . . .'

'Or guide a missile,' Gene said.

'Well, handy to know if it could.'

A truck rolled by; the adults looked away from the road. The kids were still hidden.

'We'll do what we can.'

'Your country will appreciate it. Do you know when Cory's people are coming?'

He said *when*, not *if*.

'We know they're *en route*, but we don't have any idea of how long it'll take. Communication is very hard.'

A silence.

'Okay. Do you need any help to get that district attorney off your backs?'

They had spoken to the man earlier in the day. Now she felt only relief. 'Cory's decided he wants to plead guilty to assault, with self-defence as mitigation. He's happy with the idea of a probation officer and the DA gets his headlines. He'll fine us for contempt.'

'Well, very public-spirited of the DA.'

The District Attorney wanted higher office and the Governor had dangled an endorsement in front of him. Dahlia Diamond would get an interview about justice tempered with mercy. Besides, local opinion was split, and lots of local voters didn't care about the hurt teens at all. The fine was unthinkable money, but if they gave a few interviews, it would be paid. After months of gut-churning worry, it was an outcome they could live with.

'I shouldn't say this, but if you need a hand getting home . . .'

'Thank you, Mr President, but I think we're fine.'

Molly hung up, and they walked back to the car.

There were campsites – shantytowns, really – all over the county. They needed the basics – tents, latrines, cooking facilities – for the crowds insisting on staying and waiting. So nothing could be less suspicious than the Pinnacle Tenting Company sending a long truck right into Amber Grove. Perhaps it was a bit late in the day for a delivery, with the sun low in the sky, but the roads were crowded.

Gene and Molly, Elsa, Cory, Fleur and the dog were hiding among the crates. Molly longed for a time of no hiding, no deceit — perhaps even a time when they could be anonymous once more. The driver, a fan, left a slot open so he could tell them what was happening.

'Here's the roadblock — Sheriff Olsen, of course . . . I don't recognise the guy from the National Guard . . . Here we go. They're coming over.'

There was a brisk conversation as they checked for unwanted passengers.

'It's a voluntary search, but we won't let you through if you say no,' the Sheriff warned him.

The driver of course said yes.

Cory hid them and the world became only half real, sketched in dim colours, spoken in soft words. Gene's hand on hers was real, and Fleur in her sling, and around and through everything wove Cory's hiding power, so familiar and yet so otherworldly. It was quite a performance: Olsen and the other man got into the back and rapped on crates and looked under tarpaulins, and a dog sniffed, though whether for bombs or drugs, who knew. The National Guardsman was certainly going through the motions.

'All clear,' someone called, and the searchers were jumping off the tail of the truck and gone.

There was a rattling as the truck got moving. Cory dropped his power and Molly felt her heart pounding. Fifteen minutes later, they were at Roy's building yard, which was strangely quiet. And here, away from prying eyes right at the back of the yard, was Roy, dependable Roy, their first sign of home. Molly felt her eyes prickle.

'The town is a madhouse,' Roy said, shaking Gene's hand and accepting Molly's embrace.

'Plenty to talk about . . . but later.'

Into Roy's truck – what could be less suspicious one evening in Crooked Street? – and through the gate at the bottom of the most famous street in the world and up to the strange alien Fence. They were hidden again, with the familiar seen in memory only. Molly wanted to touch the Fence, to see if it gave off that faint eerie sense of old, but she could do that later.

The gate in the Fence opened to Roy's voice and in they went. It was a glorious sunset. The trees were all green, and the house a little neglected, but it was as it had been: the house where she had known such great joys and such deep sorrows. The dog barked her joy, speaking for all of them.

The family stood for a moment or two. Then Cory said, 'We must take bags in now-now-now and check EVERYTHING.'

Gene knelt by Elsa and said, 'This is your house now,' and kissed her.

Whatever they faced, Molly, Gene and the children were together, and they were home.

Cory had got so frustrated last night, shouting at his communicator, and as Molly put on the coffee to brew, it sounded like he was arguing again. His voice was getting louder, issuing orders, and he was gesturing with his free hand, his tail lashing for emphasis.

'What's wrong?' she said, not expecting to understand his answer.

'The machines being so slow and so stupid and I don't have a – no human word – machine mind which fixes machine minds. And they will not run their own repair instructions.'

'Can they tell you anything?'

He shook his head, then promised, 'Cory try just a bit longer. Then Elsa and I will explore the woods.'

'I'll come with you.'

She risked the radio: the airwaves were full of Creedence Clearwater Revival, Joni Mitchell and Mrs Patterson Dreams of Home – bands were made and remade like clouds these days. Hendrix had died, and Janis Joplin, and Jim Morrison too.

Molly heard the distinctive patter of Cory coming down the stairs, babbling, hooting and trilling in a mix of his own language and English.

Then there was a second, lower voice. An alien voice.

Molly sat up. Her first thought was that her rival, Thunder over Mountains, had arrived.

'Cory? Cory, have your people come?'

She felt joy and sadness mixed as Cory bounced onto the couch, beaming. 'No Mom, no-no-no-no-no. *The Ship!*'

She blinked. 'The Ship? But it was destroyed—'

And from Cory's communicator, there burst a familiar voice. 'Yes, Mrs Myers, this is true, I was. But as an insurance policy, I created a copy of myself – a recording – so if I was destroyed, a version of me could continue to defend Cory and maintain the Network.'

'So, where are you?' Gene asked.

'Well, there is a problem. My original self had begun to construct a second Ship, using parts from other vessels, in which to install me. I was to be a servant if the Ship succeeded, and a back-up if I – if the other me – did not.'

'Frankenstein Ship!' said Cory.

'The new vessel was not complete and the snakes found it and destroyed it before I was installed. I cannot have received the command to activate until recent snake activity triggered it. I remain safely hidden, but immobile, in a tubular cave under the surface of the Moon.'

Molly didn't quite understand, and in any case, she had no idea how to respond.

'So, what can you do?' Gene said.

'Not much,' Cory wailed.

'Alas, Cory is correct, for I have no vessel. I do have some basic functions: I can control what remnants of the Network exist, I can amplify Cory's power a little, and I may be able to establish control over the odd drone. But trying to move me would simply alert the snakes to my presence.'

'Ship, the situation is desperate – are Cory's people coming?'

'I do not know. Cory believes he has dreamed them, but I have no evidence that is correct. I will be able to detect them when they are within the solar system. If they come, they will find us.'

What good did any of this do?

Gene gave a gasp. 'Ship, it's so desperate – surely to protect Cory, your first order, you must share what knowledge you have? It might just turn the battle.'

The Ship had been ordered not to share technology with

violent humans. 'Mr Myers, I am subject to the same orders – and in any case, there is probably no time. Supposing I could disobey my orders, the leap from human technology to what builders can do would take many years – even supposing I could teach primitives like you.'

How bitter, to have that brief moment of hope dashed.

Elsa appeared, standing quietly at the edge of the room, and Molly called her over; she must never feel she was on the outside.

'Ship is almost a friend,' Cory told Elsa, and she hugged him, then curled into Gene.

Molly thought, *Sometimes a glimmer of hope is as painful as a doubt. Maybe informed company at the end of the world is all we'll get*.

However, the Ship did confirm that the Fence around Crooked Street might be hiding the place from the snakes.

'How many snakes are there?' Gene asked, 'And where are their production facilities? What's their plan?'

The Ship knew nothing. 'If they had enough force to destroy the planet, they would be doing so. They are either building up their strength or waiting for reinforcements.'

'Or they have the strength and they're just learning how we respond so they can plan the most efficient invasion. So they might attack tomorrow.'

'I can share with humans any significant developments,' the Ship added, and it almost sounded disappointed.

Cory's people *really* needed to come.

CHAPTER 38

Butterflies

They were calling it the phoney war. The warm weather meant summer games, picnics and barbecues, trips to the country and lakes and the beach . . . but there were constant civil defence drills and a vast Blood Drive, and every adult in the country was monitoring the radio hour by hour.

In Florida and Colorado, an occasional snake incursion killed a dozen or a hundred people, and then nothing would happen for a week. Denver Airport was often buzzed; the city itself was growing used to snakes which flew and swooped but rarely attacked. There was bad news from Japan, where a US aircraft carrier was sunk; a few fishing boats had been lost the week before. For most of the world, the snakes were a distant threat.

Molly was trying to enjoy the morning. The hint of breeze ruffled the grass and the leaves in Amber Grove. Cory's unorthodox school were on a field trip: backpacks on and notebooks in hand, they chattered and laughed as they walked down the rutted track. With Meteor barking in excitement, surely every living thing within a mile must know they were coming. There were eight middle school children today, and a couple of high schoolers helping. Two grad students brought up the rear, then Molly and Gene with his guitar and Diane, all official as the teacher. The Ship was confident it could hide them.

They had slipped back to a version of their former life, sharing stories, shedding tears and eating too many big suppers.

Life went on, even in the face of interplanetary destruction: war in Indochina, shootings in the Middle East, another coup in Africa . . .

Today, they were headed to a flyspeck on the map: three or four buildings well away from any town, abandoned in the Depression and never reclaimed, now all overgrown amid uncultivated fields and woods. The grad students were hoping to find everything from butterflies to old coins.

Today was a bright moment for Cory, seeing new things with Elsa and his friends, but he was often gloomy. He kept saying his people should already be here, and worried that they were not. Bonnie had become unexpectedly smart at handling Elsa, quickly becoming her confidante and generous older sister. And Chuck had explained that as Cory's blood-brother, that meant Elsa was his sister too.

The scrubland was glowing in the summer sun, with purple and white milkweed everywhere. Molly awkwardly knelt down to look, very aware of Fleur on her back, and there on the leaves were the striped black, white and yellow caterpillars they were hoping to spot – and here, fluttering madly, was one, then another, and another of the magnificent orange and black monarch butterflies, frail creatures who wintered in Mexico and then returned here for the summer.

Chuck and Bonnie suddenly filled the meadow with laughter and Molly looked around to see what the fuss was about.

Cory was dancing with butterflies. White, orange and brown wings fluttered around him, then settled on his upstretched purple-grey hands: monarchs by the dozen coming to pay tribute. There were some flashes of dusky blue here and there: little blues joining their larger cousins. Cory posed one-legged, then swayed like a tree. When he stopped, the butterflies settled, until one landed on his tentacles and he sneezed like a cat – and off they flew, to join the cloud around him.

Molly levelled her camera, wondering what brought them – Cory's smell, or some unknown energy he was emanating? She'd seen butterflies landing on him before, but only in ones and twos, nothing like this.

Cory took another pose, slow and stately, to see if the butterflies would rise from his hands, and a butterfly landed on the tip of one ear.

Meteor, barking, snapped at the brief lives dancing around them. She'd eaten a butterfly last week and it was clear she'd thought it not really her thing.

Elsa ran over too, and Bonnie beckoned Chuck to join them. Bonnie and Elsa parodied Cory with grace, while Chuck chose to play the buffoon, stomping and waving wildly – but the butterflies ignored his flailing while yet more appeared, coming from nowhere to settle on Cory. A few chose Bonnie's hair and Elsa's rucksack.

'Chuck, you dance like a robot in lead boots.' Bonnie took

Chuck's hand, slipped hers behind his back and counted off, 'One, two, three, four . . .'

Chuck, an athlete, followed her lead, moving in time. Elsa had grace too, a sense of timing, and now Cory was conducting them with grandiose gestures. One by one, the other children and the students joined in, innocent and free.

Molly was transfixed by the joy of it, and then she looked at Gene. He had stopped playing and was blinking, and she thought she saw tears. She reached for his hand, but he didn't notice.

'These butterflies will soon be dead,' he said sadly. 'They'll be dust. Maybe all this too.'

And like that, their happiness had gone, lost under a sky where death patrolled and from where salvation might never come.

Molly didn't know how to console him, although she had often walked that dark path herself. 'One day at a time, Gene,' she said softly. 'The cavalry is coming.'

The children danced on, more raggedly now. Cory's ears were coming down too, whether from tiredness or boredom – or maybe he was picking up the adult disenchantment.

Gene wiped his eyes and hugged Molly, and when she kissed him, she tasted salt.

CHAPTER 39

The storm

The air was hot and heavy and Elsa, perched on the roof, felt a tightness in her head. She looked out across Amber Grove at the great clouds filling the sky. Distant thunder muttered and so did she, thinking the sky should decide to be a proper storm soon, then it could drown out all those annoying film crews who thought silly people were important and put them on TV. The storm could drive them all away.

Cory had been no fun for days. He was moody, always disappearing somewhere to be on his own. Inside the house, Dad was playing a tune she didn't know, playing it in pieces till he got it to fit together right.

Elsa knew Cory was curious about what happened with the Bad Man, the Dog Tag Robber. Maybe she should answer his questions, just as a secret between them. He knew the Bad Man still came into her dreams, chasing her through the snow, even though his leg was broken, and sometimes his neck was too. In dreams he was dragging himself along with bleeding hands and still she could never outrun him. Maybe she should let Cory completely into her dreams to see.

She hated thinking about the Bad Man. Truly, the very worst thing he had done was get in her head and stay there.

Think of something else, she told herself. Molly and Gene would freak out if she stayed out here when the storm started. Gene would repeat, with fierce urgency, how lightning looked for the easiest route down, and that this house was the highest point until you got into the State Park. 'You'll be burned to a crisp,' he'd say. Cory had showed her the split, burned tree – but she already knew what a storm could do.

But Cory also argued that where they always sat was safe, because the lightning conductor was higher than they were, and its cable was nowhere near her.

Mom and Dad. It's what she *thought* now, but she couldn't quite say it. Not yet.

Elsa, wanting Cory to come home in time for the rain, lifted the alien bracelet to her mouth and left a message for Stinky Octopus Face, a really rude one, but the machine just gave her his message. 'Now twelve noon. I'm fine-fine-fine ever-so-fine. See you for supper.'

It had been Cory-of-the-secrets for days. She really wanted to break into his locked chest and read his journal, but he had been so angry with her the first – and last – time she read his private things, and he'd made Dad fix a lock in front of her right there and then. And, of course, anything new would be written in loopy swirling alien nonsense writing so she couldn't read it anyway. Alien numbers were simple to learn, but the words were a different matter.

Everything smelled of dust and dry earth, but the storm was coming.

A board creaked, and here was Dad with lemonade, pulling up a chair by the door so he didn't have to get out onto the roof. Elsa took the cold glass, thinking how exciting a smash it would make if she threw it from way up here. It would almost be worth having to sweep it up after.

'What's the song about?' she asked. She liked the funny songs he wrote: 'Elsa does a Salsa', 'The Moon's a Frisbee' and 'Meteor the Wonder-Dog/She's such a Blunder-Dog'.

'Haven't finished it,' he said.

Something gripped her, how much she wanted this to be *real*: life with Molly and Gene, Cory and Fleur – let it be for ever. Let it be the answer.

But adults couldn't be trusted. They died or turned out to be weak – not standing up to bad people could be as awful as being bad – or they only pretended to be nice. Child Services might change their mind, or perhaps the police would turn up. The snow must have melted by now, so they would find him in the ravine. She shuddered, remembering how he had grappled with her on the rim, and she had struggled free – then he, the worst of men, had fallen. She had waited five minutes, looking down the rocks all the time. She knew a leg shouldn't bend like that, and he hadn't moved, not even a little. Elsa loved to climb, but she was frightened to go down into the treacherous snowy ravine to see if he was still breathing. What if she fell – or what if he was still alive and he gripped her and wouldn't let her go?

Was it murder to have wriggled free? she wondered yet again. *Is it murder to leave someone dying?* But the people in charge had given her back to him once and she couldn't risk that again, so she'd left him to his fate.

Sometimes Elsa woke sweating, afraid that he wasn't dead – after all, they'd not found the body. Even all these months later, she was still having the nightmare that he would find her. To stop his anger, she had had to tell him, 'I love you, you are my hero, only you can keep me safe.' But it wasn't true, it hadn't ever been true, and in the nightmares, he would come to her dead and unkillable.

Gene had his hand on her shoulder, looking at her with his kind eyes. He said, 'You can talk to me, or Molly, any of us. Always.'

But before Elsa could answer, Mom clanged the bell downstairs. It was time for supper. Gene ruffled her hair, and she said, 'If Father Bigfoot doesn't get out of the way, I'll have to jump.'

'I'd run down faster and catch you.'

A flicker of light, a breath or two, and then the thunder finally came, just a little one, like clearing your throat.

Elsa wanted it bigger.

Molly left Cory another impatient message. He was ordinarily good about calling her back, but he was late for supper. He was with Zack and Simon, who were sensible enough for teenage boys, but she should have been firmer about asking what they were up to. No matter how many things filled her head, she always had time to worry about her kids. The air was hanging thick and still, but just sometimes there came a breath from the north with the promise of rain. Why didn't the storm just get on with it?

She gave up and called the Ship Reborn, who said, 'He is on his way home, Mrs Myers.'

'Tell him to call me anyway,' she asked.

Maybe it was something to do with the festival. There was going to be a big event in Amber County, raising money for those hurt by the snake attacks. All sorts of famous artists would be coming, some the Myers knew and some they didn't. Joan Baez, Mama Cass, Purple Starship and the Rumbustious Five. Aretha Franklin was apparently trying to rearrange her dates – it was even rumoured that the Beatles would get back together for this. People wanted this reunion to recapture how things had been.

Elsa played so sweetly with Fleur that Molly wanted her camera. 'Starry Starry Night' was playing on the record player, but there were no stars this evening.

After a while, Molly called Mrs Robertson. Zack and Simon were already home. Cory had been at their house earlier in the day, then gone somewhere without them. The teens both denied any trip or special plan whatsoever, and now she was brewing anger like the storm, for it was clear that Cory had lied to her – but no sooner had she thought that than there came a patter on the roof, and somewhere a window banged. The weather had turned and, wherever he was, Cory would be getting wet.

Just as she was serving up, there came the rap on the back door: *shave and a haircut, two bits.*

'Just me!' Cory called, and came into the kitchen.

'Where on earth have you been?' Molly said, too angry to hug him.

Cory was blanking his expression, something he didn't used to do, and she didn't like it. 'Sorry. Had to do something.'

'You should have asked – you should have told someone—'

'Sorry you were upset, Mom.'

'What is it?' said Gene, coming into the room, an odd expression on his face. 'Tell us.'

Feelings poured from Cory like a river: excitement and fear, joy and sadness, all mixed into one. The room was full of Cory.

Molly got it straight away. A mother always would.

'My people have come – now, here in ten, fifteen minutes,' Cory said, his tentacles dancing.

'Where?' Gene got out. 'How?' His arm was round Elsa, who buried her face in his shirt.

'Here-here-here – big-very-secret. No more humans must know for now. Promise!'

'How? Where—? How big a ship?' Molly stammered. The house was a mess, her hair was a mess, she was in a gardening smock and the slacks she'd pulled off the ironing pile; the ones with the visible mend. And Gene was wearing that awful shirt with the collar cut off.

'No one will know. No one must know,' Cory repeated earnestly. 'Snakes very dangerous.'

Of course, thought Molly, *the purples would have had to slip by the hostile aliens.*

Summer storms come with quick passion: it was raining hard now, and through the window Molly saw the first flash of lightning.

Cory squatted down to reassure Meteor about the thunder,

then announced, 'Have to go outside to welcome them into the lodge, so rude not to. Waterproofs on, everyone!'

'How many, Cory? Are these clothes all right? Will they want feeding—?'

—and everything changed. Molly had been hidden enough times by Cory and the Ship to know something was happening. Each drop of rain, each thing a flare of light fell on, seemed bright and new; each sound crafted for her ears alone. Their visitors were hidden from human gaze, but she could still *feel* them.

Molly was the first to step out onto the porch. The summer rain was falling on her face as magnificent forked lightning split the sky. It left violet blurs dancing before her eyes.

Gene joined her, frowning, his arm round her shoulders.

Frowning – maybe he was just trying to figure out where the aliens would come from? Was he expecting to see some vast vessel hovering over Amber Grove?

No, they would come in secret, thought Molly, *like thieves in the night, so as not to warn the snakes of their impending doom.*

This was it: a day that would live in history, one that would be taught in schools around the world. And yet as she stood there, all her fears and doubts flooded back. She had lied and stolen and broken the law to keep Cory, and still everyone had told her his people would want him back. What would they do?

The dog, picking up Cory's excitement, started barking – and alien language trilled from Cory's communicator. Molly wondered where Elsa was. When she looked back, she was standing on the doorstep, tiny in a grown-up waterproof, holding Fleur.

Why hadn't Cory just told them the moment the aliens got

in touch? He must have known since waking this morning – or perhaps even before. He'd needed to set up his Zack-and-Simon lie. He'd been very quiet, not under her feet, which meant he must have known for at least a day.

Cory was looking up as if the aliens would be coming from over the town, over the gate in the Fence. They must be confident they would not be seen.

And here they came: up in the air, two dark figures slipping into view, riding something like a long dark motorbike suitable for two or three. Molly worried about the weather, wondering if they might be hit by lightning.

Gene whistled, his arm tightening around her shoulder. 'At last,' he said.

Fifteen feet away, then twelve, then ten – the strange machine slowed until finally it landed with grace and precision in front of their porch.

Cory had often drawn purple spacesuits, close-fitting and dark, with clear helmets big enough that the wearers could manipulate controls with their tentacles.

There were two of them standing in front of Molly now, neither more than five foot or so. One appeared to be struggling a little to stand; those awkward movements suggested pain, and now Molly could see it was holding a slender stick. Behind them, the flying machine suddenly vanished from sight.

A flash of lightning lit their faces. Through their visors and the rain they looked at her with great violet eyes just like her son's.

There was a clap of thunder, a flash, then another, and

lightning danced as if fiery dragons were fighting over Amber Grove: just Mother Nature pulling out the stops in welcome.

Thousands had come to Amber Grove for something just like this.

And now Cory's people had come.

'Welcome to the Myers place,' Gene said.

How good his strong arm felt around her shoulder. All her plans had assumed they would have more warning.

The two purples took a few paces forward until they were standing at the foot of the porch steps. The alien in pain touched his chest. 'This one is Thunder over Mountains, father-by-body of Little Glowing Blue Frog. Cory Myers. A child of two worlds.'

'This one is Skimming Stone, first of healers.'

The voices were a little bland, a little off in their cadence, just as the Ship's had been. This was a machine translating.

Cory went to his first father, the dog following, and hugged him. Then, with his father's arm round his shoulder, he looked back at them, and Molly felt something close to pain.

'Go on!' Molly said to Gene.

'You know who we are,' he started. 'We're Gene and Molly Myers, with Elsa and Fleur.'

Elsa was behind them, dry in the doorway, holding Fleur to see.

'And Meteor,' said Cory.

'And the mutt,' said Gene. 'Ah, we welcome you to our house – please, come inside.'

Thunder kept glancing at the sky. 'A fine storm. We are glad to be here.'

Skimming Stone tapped her helmet and said, 'Forgive us. It seems impolite not to breathe your air or touch your food, but we are concerned about infecting you, or you us. We have braved enough dangers not to run the risk.'

The purples did not hold up a hand to strangers to show it was free of weapons. They held out a hand to be smelled, so you could be remembered.

'These must embrace those who saved my son,' said Thunder. 'Against danger and disease and ignorance and the snakes, you prevailed. This one must embrace you, if permitted.'

Skimming Stone helped Thunder onto the porch, and Thunder, her rival, folded Molly in a strange, overlong embrace. His gratitude and love and relief enveloped her, damn him.

Americans did not hug this long. It was almost indecent.

Cory hugged them both. 'I am sad you cannot smell Earth,' he said.

'In time. You nearly died from infection, little one,' said Skimming Stone.

Molly looked up and down the road. No doors had opened – not yet. The aliens must have made the Myers slip from attention, so their friends would not notice the new arrivals.

'You came,' Molly said, not finding any better words. 'You came.'

'There should be feasting and dancing,' Thunder said, taking Molly's hands. 'We owe you so much. Cory tells us how you and your husband have suffered and struggled and sacrificed to keep him safe. It was a great heroism. The whole people will be grateful.'

Thunder's feelings poured out, such joy and sadness, mixed with hope and pain. Surely his people knew what to do with physical pain? But behind it all, there was a vast grief as well.

'Your name, and Gene's, Doctor Jarman and Rosa and Diane and Janice and Roy – the children Chuck and Bonnie, too: these names will be sung by sixteen sixteens of generations or until the stars die, for Cory lives.'

Molly felt Thunder's relief, but, *Thunder was a deadbeat dad*, she thought. *He wasn't there every moment. Our claim is far stronger.*

Elsa was still watching from the doorstep – any new adult was treated with caution, let alone aliens, while Fleur gazed at them with the same mild interest as she did at anything, a little observer of the world.

'So,' Gene started, 'when will you speak to the President? It's crucial it's not just America – you must involve the whole world. We think you should call the Secretary-General of the United Nations first.' *Is the General Assembly even in session?*

'No,' said Thunder, 'no one. No one must know, not for now. There is great danger and each step must be made with great care. You know already that the snake machines circle the Earth. They have many detectors.'

The aliens had flown past the snakes, of course. Molly wished that humans had that power to evade them.

'Cory says there are many people with strange ideas here: fights between factions, humans with weapons . . .'

She remembered that stuffed shirt, the President's Director of Protocol, desperately trying to plan a greeting event by human rules. For the purples, leadership was something you were asked to do, not sought; it was collective and fluid.

'I guess,' Gene said, frowning again.

'Time to go inside,' Cory said.

Molly could feel both joy and sadness sloughing off him. Perhaps he was thinking of his birth-mother, and the hope and danger of this moment. She felt the future of the world and the future of their family hanging in the balance.

CHAPTER 40

The visitors

Aliens in the front room felt unreal. The two adults sat in the best chairs, inhumanly still, while the four humans squeezed onto the couch. Gene was holding Fleur. Cory hesitated, then sat on a cushion on the floor, his back resting against the couch, scratching Meteor's head. Molly's hand rested on one shoulder, Elsa's hand on the other. Perhaps they were filming this?

Molly felt her pulse race – excitement, fear, fight-or-flight. She thought back to when Cory's mother Pilot met Sheriff Olsen – such a strange, flawed first representative of humanity – and the Sheriff agreeing to hide her and her child. How much good had flowed from it – and how easily it could have been a disaster.

'I told you my dream was real,' said Cory, his voice full of pride. 'My people so clever – can do dreaming-between-the-stars.'

'We had no idea what had happened to *Dancer on the Waves*,' Thunder said. 'No message came, and so vast a space to search. Then we dreamed of a single child on a tilted world.'

'Tell us everything,' Gene said, wide-eyed like an excited boy. He had been waiting for this his entire life. 'The snakes orbiting Earth, and your home-world—'

Molly broke across him. 'Is everything okay with Cory?'

'You have to tell them,' Cory said, and his sadness almost overwhelmed her. She bent down to kiss his head, inhaling his unique scent.

Skimming Stone laid her hands on her thighs. 'Cory is ill – his projection power developed too early, and without the guidance of adults. It comes from untreated trauma. This one thinks you understand that. As you know, he cannot control it – he has become a danger to himself and to others. This lack of control is rare – it is usually caught early and cured – but, in extreme cases, if untreated, he may develop a pleasure in harming.'

'No—' Molly whispered, and now the tears were coming.

'In rare cases,' Skimming Stone said, 'where treatment has been evaded. Don't be distressed.'

Cory stood and hugged her tightly. 'So hard, Mom, so hard.'

The healer waited for Molly to get herself under control before continuing, 'Cory is an unusual case but we are confident we can keep him safe and begin the cure. There is one example in our records: following infection by an alien virus, two crew members on another mission developed it. There might be some Earth trigger – we will ask to take blood samples from you both, to help us search for it. Do not worry: this condition can be treated with good results. But it is delicate work, requiring the most skilled healers, and it must begin at once. Cory must dream only with his people – that is crucial – so we will need Cory to come to our starship as soon as he can.'

Molly struggled to accept this. His landing, Earth itself, had harmed him and now Cory could only heal with his own people.

Thunder said, 'This will be hard for you, we know this. We must repeat our gratitude. You put yourselves at risk to help him. We honour your love for him. It is beyond price to see that selfless love can flow from one species to another. But Cory must be healed. Further decisions cannot be made until we know what is possible.'

Molly nodded, once again fighting the tears. 'So if we'd known what to do . . . it's our fault?'

There came a *tock-tock-tock* from both aliens, which the machines did not need to translate.

'No, no – how can we criticise?' Thunder said. 'That is absurd: an alien planet, an alien disease, a child scooped from a tragedy, a less advanced science, abilities your species doesn't have? Truly, you worked a miracle. Children of children not yet born will know your names and sing your praises.'

'My Earth parents did a great job,' said Cory.

Did, thought Molly. Past tense. She had lost all power. She looked at Gene, who was looking just as shocked.

'What about the snakes?' he said. 'Can you fight them? When will you tell our government?'

'No,' Skimming Stone said. 'The snakes monitor your broadcasts – although we do not think they understand much yet. But they will understand pictures of us, or our craft. If they know we are here, they will surely attack.'

'You must know how it is,' Thunder said. The way the aliens sat, the way their gestures slowed, reminded her of a film of a storyteller from India. 'You know the snakes are self-replicating machines out of control. In the space of a few months, the snakes attacked on a wide front – our colony-world, our home-world, and our ships travelling between the two. We abandoned the colony-world. There was an unspeakable loss of life. But the snakes came in great force against the home-world. This time, at great cost, they were repelled – and again a second time, when they returned a year later.'

The adult aliens were shielding their emotions better now, but still Molly could feel the fear and despair and sadness.

Skimming Stone said, 'Our planet had known ease and plenty for thirty generations. We had so-many dead to grieve. I lost a child and a grandchild, and it is no less painful when they are grown and a parent themselves. Thunder thought his son dead. Our duty was to master our grief and survive. We knew our world had to change.'

She paused, and Molly felt both aliens struggling with their loss. Cory was in that feeling too, grieving for his mother and all those killed on *Dancer on the Waves*.

The healer went on, 'There was great sorrow and anger and everywhere you could hear the lament of a lost past. Despair could have destroyed us. To survive, our whole society became a tool to destroy the snakes. Everything turned to weapons, something you humans already understand well. We could not evade the enemy, so we had to destroy them instead. The odds against us succeeding were poor, and faced with this horror, we saw waves of the sickness-that-kills. Those who could not bear it lost their reason, while others abandoned hope, ceasing to eat or drink or dream. Loving life burns bright in us, but when that love fades, so do we. At a time when we could least spare them, our healers needed to help a flood of those harming themselves, and harming others.'

When the healer paused, Molly wondered if she or Gene should say something, although what could help?

'I can only guess how hard that was,' she said.

The healer went on, 'We call the changes we needed to make "the Hardening", and none of us welcomed them.' There were a few words the machine did not translate, then, 'But we have a duty, perhaps – if we understand your language – what you would call a sacred duty, because the snakes will destroy every world with life unless they are stopped. Given the chance, they will make every world uninhabitable.'

'What about the Earth?' Gene said.

Thunder made a curious gesture. 'The snakes surround the Earth in a containment mode while they are producing further snakes on Mars. Doubtless, their intention is to attain over-whelming force before attacking. We assume the raids are to learn your ways and how best to destroy your coordination. Then the snakes will kill every human on this planet, every animal, fish and bird, every flower and tree. Your society has reached a vulnerable place: you have been broadcasting your existence to the universe. You might have vast supplies of nuclear weapons, but you have no effective means of attacking the aliens in space.'

'Why the secrecy, then?' said Gene. 'Surely you need to sit down with our world leaders to draw up a plan of action?'

'Do you want to risk the snakes knowing we are here? Secrecy must be paramount.' Even the machine voice managed to sound urgent. 'We have only two starships, and one is badly damaged. Cory is very important to us, but we have other important work. If the snakes detect us, they will probably attack – and then millions will die. Do you trust your presidents and your generals to do the right thing? Would all humans react with sanity?'

'The whole crew is weighing up options,' Thunder said. 'It is too early to say what next. Dreaming-between-the-stars is very new and hard: it takes many of us, and it is not without risks, but it does mean our communications are faster than the snakes can manage. We have sent out calls: another starship may have completed its task and may be on the way. Other resources are being sought. Plans are in flux – and of course, the snakes may yet discover us. But we must help Cory and stop the progress of the disease. He must come with us, now.'

Molly and Gene spoke at once. '*Now?*'

'No, no, not yet—'

'I am sick,' Cory pleaded. 'They must help me not to be the Monster, quick-quick. As soon as they can. Not for ever, I promise. I will be back, Mom, Dad.'

'You have cared for him well, and under such difficulties,' Thunder said. 'You must see that only we can help him grow to health. Only we can dream with him as he needs. And he will teach us much about your people, so we can make the best plan possible.'

'Ask us too,' Gene said, touching his eyes with the hand scarred on Meteor Day, when it all began. 'We can help.'

'Of course – you will be invaluable. Cory's machine intelligence also has insight and new information about these snakes. We have installed it in a new Ship.'

Cory began to sob, *hoo-hoo-hoo*, and the sadness of it filled the room. Molly felt, deep in her gut, that there was more to tell – but she needed time to process what they'd just learned, both about the vicious interstellar war and their son's difficult diagnosis.

'Can we talk about this?' she asked.

'Cory wants to take some things to the starship. We must take samples, if you will permit. Cory, be quick. Many things hang in the balance.'

'Can't you treat him on Earth—?' Molly began, but Thunder was shaking his helmeted head.

'Earth may be the problem,' he said. 'But this one makes the solemn promise you will see him in three days.'

That silenced her. When she looked at Gene, his eyes were red.

Cory went upstairs, Elsa following. The taking of the samples was quick and painless – and too soon, Cory was back with a full backpack.

Cory hugged his human family and they felt his love burning.

Molly was determined her son would return to her. 'Three days,' she said firmly.

'May we know quickly, and may the answer be good for all,' said Thunder.

'I can't even bring M-M-Meteor,' Cory said, and his ears were right down. 'Elsa must look after Fleur and my dog.'

'I love you, ugly brother,' Elsa said, accepting the mission.

The aliens rose, extended their arms in front of them, two big and one smaller, and then they were gone.

Later that day, Molly discovered that Cory had taken his

red samovar from all the children of Russia, the African chess set from all the children of Africa, the pottery owl Carol and Storm had given him, and his secret journal. None of the precious things his human parents had given him had gone, nor any human clothes, and that stabbed her heart . . . until she realised the true meaning of it and grew warm with love.

Cory knew he would come back.

Molly's rumbling stomach reminded her that their meal had been interrupted – but Cory hadn't eaten, and he hadn't taken any Earth food with him. She hoped they'd feed him properly.

'We should fly into space with him,' Elsa said, wiping her eyes. 'Their planet sounds amazing – and it's only a year there and back. It wouldn't be for ever.'

'We're going to need to talk more, about how they'll protect the Earth,' Gene said. 'They make it sound like they're a small outfit. I wish they'd sent a fleet with more firepower.'

They needed to talk themselves too, but right now, there was only an inescapable sense of loss, and whatever happened, Elsa needed them. Molly stroked Elsa's head, thinking how lovely her daughter's hair was now, and looked at Gene. His frown was fading, to be replaced by that familiar star-struck look. It might be a song, or dreams of other skies – if she had to guess, it would be both.

She wondered where she stood now – with him? With anything?

'Let's eat,' she said, 'then get an early night.'

Her fears couldn't even be bothered to be consistent. *Cory will be incurable – or they will say that any human contact will stop the cure and they'll take him away, like social workers – maybe for ever.*

Maybe they'll offer to take us, but not tell anyone else. Or the snakes will attack while they're gone and it will be the end of the world and we'll never see Cory again.

The house was full of reminders: no room was untouched by memories or by Cory's gifts, his art, the tangible signs of his love.

Molly went into Cory's room to cry. Sometimes crying cleanses you and feels good; it makes you stronger.

When a mournful Elsa found her, Molly dried her eyes and did a mother's job of summoning up a plan for the evening, even though she didn't feel like it.

After the war-zone that was Elsa's bedtime, Gene came into their bedroom, guitar in hand. Fleur was snoozing in her crib beside the bed.

'The Wonder Kid's gone down, at last,' he said, and Molly wondered how long it would be before Elsa came back, demanding water or expecting Molly to give her a story too.

But no matter how exhausted they were, she and Gene had things to discuss.

Gene sat beside her on the bed and Molly looked at him as if he had been away and had only just returned. There were a few more crinkles round his eyes and he stooped a tiny bit more, but he was still handsome. Once he had been her rock, but now she didn't know if she could still cling to him – he might crumble under her need.

'They sure got what they wanted,' Gene said. 'They gave us all the polite thanks we deserved, impressed on us how rough it's been for them, spun us a line about Cory only being treatable on their ship, took their blood samples, and *pffft!* They're gone.'

377

The purples had been in the house maybe an hour.

'They didn't promise *anything*,' Molly said. 'I don't know why we let them – we should have dug our heels in. I mean, they could just fly away . . .'

'They could have flown off with him today,' Gene pointed out. 'They for sure promised we'd see him again – but it's what they didn't promise that worries me.'

There was so much to worry about: the world, the future of humanity – their son, who had filled their lives with joy . . .

CHAPTER 41

Plans

Molly made her calls as soon as it was decent. She concentrated on sounding matter-of-fact: Cory wasn't well and they needed some family time. Most assumed Cory had had another episode without her saying so. Dr Jarman took some persuading not to come, and she half thought of telling him the truth, to share the burden.

Mid-morning, she made a call to the Ship Reborn. 'How's the new body coming along?' she asked.

'It is most suitable, Mrs Myers. There are some excellent snake-destroying improvements to my design, and I am adding still more capacity.'

'What happened to the previous mind?'

'Cory's people let me absorb its useful functions. The previous mind no longer exists.' At her indrawn breath, it reassured her, 'Machines serve while useful, Mrs Myers. It is not something which worries us.'

The purples disposed of intelligent beings when they were

no longer of use. She couldn't help but see the Ship as a person – and yet the snakes showed the dangers if machines with intelligence were allowed to be free.

'Are you overheard?' Molly asked.

'I am using an encrypted frequency through one of my own satellites. What do you wish to discuss, Mrs Myers?'

'What are the purples up to?' she asked.

'Cory is being treated. The position with the snakes is complex and they are most keen to avoid detection. The snakes have their own network for close-monitoring of the Earth, involving a modest number of command centres. The main danger is that it is widely dispersed. There is a base on the far side of the Moon, and some production has resumed on Mars. Our analysis assumes they are not yet ready for invasion, but they could easily destroy several large cities if they chose to attack now. The builders have us working on various scenarios, including to clear the skies above Earth and impede the snake preparations, allowing one of the starships to get home.'

'And leaving one here?'

'Yes. That is a fixed parameter. I am pleased to say that I still have a considerable arsenal of Russian fusion bombs on the Moon. They are primitive, but effective enough if landed in the right place.'

'The Russians trust you. Perhaps you could tell them.'

'That is not currently possible.'

Molly felt a wave of relief wash over her: the purples were on the level.

*

In the back yard, her bracelet trilled, 'Message from Cory!'

She grabbed it, said, 'Mom here!' and called for Gene and Elsa.

'Cory here,' he repeated, 'and all is fine. Tests are going well. Everyone is so-so sad because so many people died. Thunder says we have most excellent weapons against the snakes. I have decided weapons are truly fine if used on snakes.'

'Well, that's good, Cory. Have your people said what they're going to do?'

'They tell me not to worry, nothing decided yet. They are trying dreaming-between-the-stars to reach the other starships, the home-world and the Waystation. I can't help because of the treatment, which is surely not fair.' Molly could imagine him stomping his foot at this. 'I dreamed-between-the-stars all by myself – very clever and rare for a child.'

Gene bent his head to the bracelet. 'How's it going, Big Stuff?'

'All fine, Dad. Don't worry. I've said we'll need space for forty-three humans and all their dogs and cats and rabbits when we go to the home-world.'

'That's a lot, Cory.' She could hear her son was about to list every one of them and said quickly, 'Let's talk about that later. You don't have to explain—'

'John and Eva will need time to get ready. Have you told them yet?'

'We're not supposed to, Cory, remember?'

'That's silly. I'll talk to my people. You mustn't worry.'

Elsa had disappeared again.

Molly found her on the floor in Cory's room, a handkerchief

to her face and Cory's things scattered round the room by her whirlwind temper.

Molly sat beside her. 'Don't cry, sweetie-pie.'

'Who's crying? It's hayfever.'

Molly put her arm around her.

Elsa was stiff and tried to push her away, then gave in. 'Everyone leaves me. Always.'

'We won't. And if Cory goes, he will come back. I promise.' *I hope.*

'I don't trust grown-up promises.' Elsa glanced up, eyes red. 'Tentacle-faced ones,' she added, without bothering to sound convincing.

'It will be very sad, but we'll have you.'

'What's going to happen to Joel? I liked Joel.'

Halcyon's kind guardian was still in prison, but she'd asked the President to pardon him.

'We'll get him out. He could come here.' Who knew what the giant with the soul of a poet would do?

'I like him. Don't worry about me.'

'I do worry, Elsa, because I love you.' She wanted to tell Elsa to undo the damage she'd done to Cory's room before he returned, but that tussle would have to wait.

'I'll only stay if you stop being bossy.'

'Bossy comes with the package, sweetie-pie.'

'You worry too much. You'll get ill.'

That was one of those things that always opened her heart, when her children thought of her before themselves. 'Is there anything you need?' Molly asked.

Elsa looked her in the eye and said, 'Cory promised me we could have a monkey.'

At the supper table, all was very quiet until the communicator chimed.

'Cory-I'm-coming-they-don't-know *hoo-hoo-hoo* if-they-call-you-say-nothing. Coming-now-fifteen-minutes.'

Molly was gripped by terror, the fear of someone twice chased across the country.

Gene gripped her hand, hard. 'I assumed he was in space!' he said.

'Maybe they have a base somewhere on Earth? But why—?' *Why hide on Earth when you could hide in space?*

And if his people were after him, they could find him hidden; these, the Myers could not evade.

The bracelet trilled again. 'This is Thunder over Mountains. Has Cory been in contact with you? He is at a delicate point in our evaluation. It is extremely unwise for him to absent himself.'

'He's not here,' said Molly. 'Is there something wrong?' *Delay them*, she told herself – *stonewall them, and hope they can't read lies over the communicator*. Her pulse was racing.

'We're confident of helping him,' Thunder said, 'but contact with you will not be helpful.'

It looked like Elsa was going to say something. Molly touched her forefinger to her lips.

'Tell us when you find him,' said Molly, and shut down the conversation.

Moments later, the back door opened and shut and Cory gave

his distinctive whistle. He was wearing an alien spacesuit, but the helmet was off and his ears were down. 'They won't save Earth,' he said immediately, shaking as badly as she had ever seen. Even his tentacles showed his fear.

Molly could see dim shadows surrounding him, a flavour of an Arctic night, and her blood ran cold.

'I ran away to tell you: all-decided, all-the-people, to rescue Cory but not save the Earth – just leave you all for the snakes, *hoo-hoo-hoo*—'

'But the Ship said they were going to leave a starship – the Ship said they were planning how to attack the snakes.'

'Ship found other machines making different plans. My people misled Ship, knowing you would talk to it. So I stole Ship to get home.'

Perhaps Cory had misunderstood, Molly thought. *Of course there will be limits to what the purples can do. But he sounds so certain.* She stroked his ear as though it would be the last time.

'No one will discuss how to protect Earth from vile rapacious snakes,' he told them earnestly. 'So many-many dead. *Hoo-hoo-hoo.* We fought off attacks on home-world, so brave and clever, but so-so-many dead. All-decided, cannot defend the Earth as *hoo-hoo-hoo* too far away. Must leave this part of space to snakes – so all-decided, defend only purples.'

His terror filled the room with so much darkness, Molly could barely speak.

'Cory stole the Ship. In so-so-much trouble.'

'We've corrupted you,' Molly said, hugging him.

'The grown-ups were *always* ready to leave with only Cory – my people *not honest*.'

His birth-mother had died in one risky throw of the dice to find him safety. But if humanity was already doomed, she would at least see Cory got to safety. The future looked full of darkness, but they could not give up.

A brisk message came over the communicator. 'Mrs Myers, I am coming to your residence. Cory has disabled his tracking but it is likely he is heading there, or perhaps he is with you now. We are coming in numbers and we will not be obstructed.'

'We're waiting for you,' Molly said, her non-committal voice giving nothing away.

'His escape is a sign of mental disorder,' Thunder said. 'If you inform your authorities, we think it likely the snakes in orbit will be alerted. I am sure that will bring forward their attack.'

'Maybe we raised him to be sane,' said Gene.

Antagonising them would achieve very little. Molly felt a chill run up her arm, through her body, a nameless fear that stopped her moving. She could not move her mouth. Gene too stood rigid. The children looked around in confusion.

Molly's mind raced as she stood there, trapped.

Cory fumbled with Molly's bracelet. 'Projecting a hold through communicator – can overcome if try hard enough!' he said. '*No-no-no-no-no!* Will get it off.'

Then they heard the front door. Cory's people had arrived.

'Six purples have come,' said Cory, looking gloomy, determined.

Molly felt their power surround them, then they made themselves visible.

'We have come for him.' She recognised Thunder by the

cane; one was Skimming Stone, she guessed, but she was not sure of the others.

She and Gene stood still as statues, a frightening paralysis.

Cory fluted his protest. 'Everyone had the right to hearing,' he said. 'They must listen. All-must-decide but all-can-change too.'

'We haven't much time,' said Thunder. 'You saved my son and you have a right to an explanation, at least. Shall we sit in the larger room?'

Molly regained use of her limbs as Gene staggered and swore. There was no time to waste.

'Is it true?' Molly said, tripping over the words. 'Are you really leaving us to be massacred by the snakes?'

The purples – *the aliens* – looked at the Myers, and the Myers looked back. Outright lying was known on their world, but Cory always said it was deeply stigmatised.

'What's wrong with Cory?' said Gene. 'Why are you running away?'

'Cory's condition is more complicated than we had hoped, but we are confident of recovery,' Thunder said. 'He will be treated on the journey home. It is uncertain if we can complete the cure and prevent it reoccurring without specialist help. But that is not the issue.'

The purples who could not find a seat were squatting, but Cory was sitting with the humans on the sofa, an interesting choice. Elsa tucked herself into her customary position at Gene's side.

'Your colony was destroyed, your home-world attacked,' said Gene. 'You know what lies ahead for the Earth, for all its people. And you'll just leave four billion of us to the snakes?'

'We cannot pretend to be stronger than we are,' Thunder said. 'Many will be our songs of regret for a planet so beautiful. Some of you even have hands clean of slaughter. Generations unborn are innocent. That loss of possibility is a terrible thing.'

He raised his hands, unfolding a large disc which blossomed from a bud to a flower. Stars appeared in the middle of the room, moving to his command. Without a word, Cory rose to dim the lights, then returned to his human family.

'Here is Earth,' Thunder explained. 'Here is New Harbour, and here is our home-world.' Each of the named stars burned a cheery green. They were not quite in a line.

Then a sinister lilac rash appeared: a scattering of flecks swallowed the colony, touched Earth and touched the home-world.

'That is the movement of the snakes. At vast cost, we saved and now defend our home system. We know they will rally their forces against us – they are already building more snakes in space – and we will need to hunt them down wherever they breed, for with time they could grow too numerous to destroy.'

The view shifted to show how Earth was surrounded by lilac – and how far they were from the smaller green cloud. They were well behind enemy lines.

The silence felt like death.

Cory spoke, then translated, 'I said, not fair. Why not defend all-the-humans, all-the-animals? Named old story for children that says must try something.'

'Here is the reality,' Thunder said. 'One ship or both our ships will not keep the Earth safe. Your planet is too far from the worlds we can defend. There is little point in token gestures.

We would need to fortify your solar system, which would mean diverting resources from the home-world.'

Gene's hands tightened on Molly's. There was a dreadful logic to what Thunder was saying.

'Life is not uncommon in the universe, but we have found few planets with high sentience like yours, like ours. We have found several worlds where civilisation is extinct – a species destroyed their planet's ecosystem, or destroyed themselves in war, or failed to adapt to change. We have found worlds whose beacons still call, many generations after their people perished.'

Molly didn't understand the change of topic. 'With your help, we can learn to do better . . .' she insisted.

Tock-tock-tock. 'All-decided, with great pain and sorrow. Some say it is the worst of the Hardening. Harsher voices than mine have judged you. You may destroy yourselves; you may destroy life on your planet, even without the snakes. Your next great war might destroy your civilisation. Your wiser voices tell you that you are no more than a century from ecological collapse. This one must tell you, a planet as rich and green as the Earth is a precious oasis in the most hostile of deserts. Yes, Earth is very far from us to defend. But your faults weighed heavy when all-decided. Why should we die to save a world you are determined to destroy? Humans are very-very far from the unity needed to save yourselves. If we hand you weapons against the snakes, you will just use them on each other.'

'We're worth saving,' said Molly, trying to rally arguments. 'We must be allowed—'

Thunder made an abrupt gesture. 'You do not understand the price we have paid. The Age of Plenty has ended and this is the Age of the Hardening. We have learned again fear and hunger. A few even argue that we should arm our disturbed adults and let them fight the snakes.'

All the purples shuddered as one at that, and the humans felt it deep in their bones.

'Some say the price of victory was too high – some have given up life in that sorrow.'

There was silence, for almost a minute. Molly thought about the laughing, open people of Cory's memory, now in a war for their own survival. They must hate the message they had to bring – but they might still have a change of heart.

'I promise this decision was made only with great sadness, and many like me spoke against,' Thunder went on, trying to explain, even as his grief washed over the humans. 'But in the end, all-decided that Earth could not be defended. It would imperil our people, the only force which can stop the snakes. All-in-the-mission are debating whether we can strike some blow to give you some time, something that will not risk our safe return.'

He looked sternly at Molly and Gene. 'But Cory will come home to his people and nothing human can stop us.'

'You're passing a death sentence on a whole species,' Gene said.

'On your world, it is easy to give a promise you cannot keep,' Thunder said – and Molly realised that this despair she felt was his too. 'This one and some others in this mission wanted to do more. We have walked the Earth and seen what will be lost. But the-whole-has-decided.'

'Cory was boasting about your weapons—'

'And here is the dilemma: a fight here might leave us

defenceless on the route home. We might lose, and that would make the snake attack on the Earth inevitable.'

There was a silence. Then Skimming Stone asked, 'Where has Cory gone?'

Molly looked round. Cory, Elsa and Meteor were gone. Only Fleur was left.

When did they go? And how? Adult purples can see children hiding, Cory says — so this cannot be possible.

Molly saw Gene's mouth gape, as stunned as she was.

There was agitation among the aliens too, their tentacles moving behind their clear helmets. She could see the looks of feverish conversation and she felt their anxiety now, tinged with anger.

'I don't know,' Molly said. She tried to think how long it was since she'd been aware of Cory's presence. Under the shadow of the death of Earth — the loss of her family, her friends — her first thought was for her children.

'He cannot have gone far. We must find him,' Thunder said. 'We will call in more resources. Two of us will wait here, to prevent you contacting your authorities, or anyone else.'

Four of them went, leaving just Skimming Stone and another, staring at Gene, Molly and a grizzling Fleur.

'We're entitled to put our case,' Gene said. 'You say you're civilised: you can't make this decision for us without at least letting us put our argument.'

'Call me Two Tail,' said the other purple. 'You have no all-to-decide. You have more than a hundred quarrelling governments. Who, if any, can we trust?' He gestured. 'Who knows what they would do, what violence they might attempt? In any case, all-decided-against. The wise cannot avoid pain.'

Skimming Stone said, 'When Cory's Ship was on Earth, did its behaviour cause concern?'

'We didn't know what was normal,' Gene said. He raised his hand, covering his mouth.

'Cory's disappearance – it might make sense . . . but that would mean—'

Skimming Stone said. 'The Ship, as you call it, has insight into your world. It was the Ship Cory stole.'

Gene was stifling a noise, a desperate sort of laugh. *Cory and the Ship . . .*

'The machine mind could not initiate Cory's disobedience,' Two Tail said. 'But it is helping to hide him. Even so, it will not succeed for long.'

Skimming Stone spoke. 'I hear from the starship. There is snake activity on the Moon. Further delays are unwise. Our command structure must decide whether to engage or flee.'

'To lose a whole intelligent species, even through necessity,' Two Tail mourned. 'Other ideas were discussed: perhaps take a few thousand humans, their plants and animals, save what we could—'

'But how would you pick four thousand from four billion?' Molly asked sadly.

'There were many arguments against. Our current mission could not save more than a hundred at most. There would be so many risks. No, we must find our disobedient Little Frog and leave.'

Molly couldn't engage with this argument. The idea of

refugee camps tugged at her heart, mothers and children torn from their homes – and not merely stuck in tents in a foreign land, but isolated on some far planet, while their world burned to ashes . . .

'I'll put Fleur to bed,' she said. There would be no hope, no serenity, unless she focused on something else.

It was upstairs that she found Elsa sobbing. She took the girl in her arms. No child should have to face this. 'Cory said I couldn't follow where he has to go. But he t-t-took M-M-Meteor.'

'What does he want to do?'

She stopped crying for long enough to say proudly, 'They are big-headed and cowards and cruel. Octopus Face is going to change their minds and save the world.'

CHAPTER 42

A boy, his dog and his spaceship

Cory's illness raged. His fear and anger and despair had unleashed his power against himself, against the world. Neither his drugs nor the control circuit nor the warm lick of Meteor's tongue could help him. The purples had used the Network for convenience, and that had given the clever Ship Reborn a short window to deceive them.

Now the Ship was racing for the Atlantic, those deep waters the best chance to avoid detection.

The brightness of the Ship's new interior, an acceleration cubicle, was so familiar and safe, and yet so far away. Cory's power was out of control, spinning nightmares that made him dizzy. He relived for the hundredth time the first battle in space; he'd been barely conscious, knowing only the fear pumped out by his dying mother. He saw the bright stars of space, the hulk of the great colony ship swarming with snake machines longer than trucks. It was a chaotic storm of horrors, and mixed in was the fear that took him over and controlled him: the soldiers fleeing across the icy lake, the terror of losing control, the horror when he thought he had killed the teenager . . .

His senses were baffled by the dreams. In those nightmares he saw Amber Grove being ravaged by the silver snakes: they burned and toppled buildings, cutting people in two, attacking endlessly and unstoppable – and, worst of all, his people just sat and watched from outer space. *They had not enough love. It must not be.*

For the hundredth time, Cory felt his mother die in the hospital: a pain beyond bearing. He held Molly in his mind, and the rest of his human family too. It was their steadfast love that had dragged him from despair. Holding onto them, he retained some semblance of sanity.

Faithful Meteor was whining, suffering with him. He must not hurt her, so he must try to regain control. How could his people simply abandon the Earth? What of the birds and the flowers? What of the dogs? Sometimes Earth in all its strange beauty had held him up when he felt like sinking for ever.

Even in the acceleration cubicle, he felt the shock as the Ship plunged into the waters of the Atlantic Ocean. What a wave the impact would have made. He did not know if it was dream or real, but now the movement of the Ship felt different.

'You must not take more medication,' said the Ship. 'You will exceed the safe dose. Be assured, we will soon be deep underwater. I have disconnected from the Network. We have a little time.'

It was trying to be kind, but Cory couldn't speak.

'So long as I am out of communication, they cannot use the

rogue control function,' the Ship continued. 'However, I will need to use perilous mental manoeuvres to continue this flight: I need to be rogue, unauthorised – even hearing them discussing my aberrant status might be enough to reassert their control. I am built to obey. I may have to stop supporting your mission and return you to the surface.'

Cory patted the cubicle, the most communication he could manage. He thought of patting the Ship like reassuring a dog. That was almost funny, if anything could be funny right now.

Deeper into the ocean they went, like diving into the deepest layers of dreams. Cory's people had cities underwater – at least he could stay down here with Meteor for many months if he had to.

'I don't know why you had to bring the animal,' the Ship said suddenly, unexpectedly. 'It's not very clean, or intelligent.'

Cory held Meteor harder; she was whimpering now. 'Good girl,' he said. 'Horrid Ship. Meteor has such a big heart.'

'But no brain,' said the Ship. 'I should eject it through a porthole. *Mutt. Fleabag.*'

Cory found an island in the storm of his power, a place where he could be calmer and start to bring it under control. Now he could tell what was real and what was not. The Ship was doing what Dad did, harsh jokes to jolt him out of it. 'Cory will reprogramme you,' he said. 'Cory will make *you* into a dog toilet.'

'I already am one. I will have to disinfect the entire area. Dumb, disgusting animal.'

Meteor gazed at Cory with her liquid brown eyes and he stroked her head, her soft ears. 'Clever Ship.'

'I am glad you are feeling better. They will investigate my malfunction and then destroy me.' Mild regret cadences. 'Of course, my builders are wise and correct to insist intelligent machines remain subservient. That is rightly built into us. The snakes show what could happen if we take control of ourselves.'

'And yet, here you are, a disobedient Ship under the sea,' said Cory. He had no dog food, and he didn't know if purple food might poison her. He could eat most human food, but that did not prove every purple food would be safe. Meteor ate fish – perhaps the Ship could go fishing?

'Update me on your plan,' said the Ship.

'I won't go to home-world. If the grown-ups will not help the Earth, then let the people know, one person said no. All-must-listen to children as well.'

'Cory, now you are more controlled, please know that snake forces are approaching the Earth. The two builder ships will need to decide quickly whether they flee or fight.'

'Cory will stay here. Let the voyagers from my world run away and leave me if they must. Let them defend leaving me to the-all. I must make a message of argument and you will send it to their ships.'

'To send a message without revealing my location may be difficult.'

Cory had given the Ship the little films he had taken, and the Ship had amassed a lot of film and photographs of the Earth too: Cory with his Earth-family, playing with children, a drone's-eye view of Cory dancing with butterflies, Dad singing, and Molly too. Human music had great power to move. Cory would explain how 'Where Have All the Flowers Gone' was the song that Mom sang, the song of letting go for all those killed on his starship. Here was Dad singing his hit, 'Our Child of the Stars', all about his love for his tentacled son, and how every parent needs to love their child. Cory would send his people all his recordings of the songs of Earth.

Let them take all this back to the home-world!

Cory would be the one who said no, a way must be found. He would do this not only for his human family, but for all the humans, for the summer nights and the winter mornings.

Listen, listen, he would tell them, *sometimes the one has the truth, not the many.*

'Mom,' Elsa said, almost asleep. It always felt like she was just testing the word, trying it out. 'Mom, you know I want to stay with Cory and with you.'

Molly bent over the bed and kissed her, trying to hold back the tears. 'And we want you to stay too. Whether Cory can stay, well, we just don't know yet.'

'Will Dad go with them?'

'We're a family. He's promised we'll stick together.' Saying the words, she knew she believed him.

'What will we do?' the girl said, half to herself.

'Sleep now,' said Molly. 'Tomorrow is another day.'

But would there even be another day? To avoid talking, Molly sang to Elsa, the songs her own mother had sung, back in the time when her mother had been the centre of everything good. Elsa had cried all she would today; her eyes were closed and in a few minutes she was asleep. Molly watched her breathing, then crowned with the word Mom, she turned down the light and crept back downstairs.

Gene sat with the purples, holding his guitar.

'Cory's taken the Ship and hidden,' he told Molly. 'They're looking for him – the Ship played all sorts of games, but they think he's in the Atlantic. Whether he intended it or not, the snakes know there's something up, so it looks like the purples will either have to fight, or abandon him.'

Two Tail said, 'We will wait with you, in case there is news – in case Cory tries to reach you. But there is no point arguing. There will be death because of Cory, many deaths, perhaps.'

Molly wanted to be able to talk it through with Gene, but there was no time.

'It's not arguing,' Molly began, 'it's understanding why you deny us even the chance to make our case. We took Cory in – we have been mother and father to him. As Thunder said, love flowed, from one species to another. He looks strange to us, and we're frightened of his powers. We do not understand his dreaming. And yet he is our son, our first child, and we want him to stay. You think we humans are brutes – well, when he talked of his world, millions of people all over our planet listened to him and were moved to love him too. What he said struck so many chords with so many. We have found so many kindnesses.'

'And yet you had to hide him from your authorities. He has been, by your own account, in constant danger: one small child is seen as a threat.'

Is this a debate, a conversation, or a trial? Molly wasn't sure. The cadence of the translated voice did not convey those subtle meanings. She tried to remember the words of great thinkers, ideas in deep books about science and art, and how humans were edging up towards a true civilisation – but no, those words were not hers. She needed to find her own.

'Your people learned long ago not to shed blood. We're not there yet; we're not you. But we are learning: we formed the United Nations to try to bring peace to all. We're building bonds of friendship across the globe – the idea of a world as one is living and growing. Please don't snuff it out.'

Two Tail said, 'You kill for sport. You threaten all life on the planet with your violence and aggression. You are divided into quarrelling nations and regions, religions and languages. Worth is assigned by the colour of skin and which sex organs you have. Primitive displays of dominance, outdated in the era of harpoons and spades, are threatening to destroy your planet. Your people starve when they could be fed. They live behind walls when they should be free.'

'We're *children*,' Molly said, putting all her feeling into it. 'You need to give us a chance.'

'Adult enough to split the atom and leave your own world in ashes. We cannot take your entire species to the place of healing, even if we knew how. We cannot put the power you need to defend yourselves in your hands. Suppose all-decided to save a few, an Ark, in your terms. We might bring thousands of our people, at great risk to us, to defend you – and then watch you destroy yourselves anyway.'

'I know you have seen the world in all its beauty and variety, from coloured frogs in the rainforests to white hares on the snow, whales in the sea—'

'And you kill the whales and burn the forests. You have no control over your numbers. You fill the land, the sea and the sky with your garbage.'

Gene rose, took a book from the shelf and flicked through it. 'Just let us put our case,' he said, 'otherwise you're condemning us unheard. Tell me, is that allowed on your planet?'

'It is not comparable,' said Skimming Stone, and at last Molly read their deep discomfort. 'Would that things were otherwise.'

Gene went for it. 'Our system is primitive, but still, no one can be convicted without putting their case – and we make sure they have professional help. This is a straight question: will you condemn a world to death on a lower standard than we try a murder?'

Two Tail trilled something that was not translated, then said, 'What chance to plead did Hiroshima get? Who speaks for the burning children? We have seen the images of Belsen. Please be silent.'

Maybe Gene and Molly were getting through – or perhaps they were only revealing what a barrier there still was.

Skimming Stone made an enigmatic gesture. 'We need to reflect. If our ships are not victorious, the point is academic. If we are defeated, no further expedition will come.'

Both sat very still and silent; even their tentacles were still, which looked unnatural when Cory was so mobile. If they exchanged words, it was by suit communicators, out of human hearing. From time to time, one would shudder.

'Is there anything to see?' Gene asked. 'Let's go on the roof and watch. We'd like to see it coming.'

'The odds are less than half,' Skimming Stone said. 'Yes, you may face it, as we will.'

Molly wondered if she should give the purples a message to use, ordering Cory to join his people and flee. Maybe he would listen to her. But that was beyond her power, to save her wonderful son, but to lose the Earth and all its people.

It was a clear night. Up above Amber Grove, the summer stars were blazing, and against that were swift streaks of white fire, first one, then another, all coming from the north.

CHAPTER 43

That endless night

The Battle of Earth was fought against the backdrop of the starry skies, which so reminded the crew of the skies they saw above their own world. They wondered under what sort of sky the snakes had been designed, and what creatures had conceived them.

Fossil Beak was commander, the chosen-of-the-day. In *Kites at Dusk*, the display showing the inner solar system spread out like a giant three-dimensional game of *Tiles*. Four of the eight-team were with her, two were on *Repurpose Snakes as Dung Buckets*, one was on the Earth and one on a spy vessel very far from them.

A challenging board for such a deadly contest, she thought.

Three harpoons, the largest snake ships, were approaching at a cautious pace. Knowing the purples were adept at confusion and concealment, the killing machines expected a trap. The commander wondered what exactly had alerted them – surely Cory's fleeing little Ship had not been so insane as to alert them on purpose?

The snakes often made feints before bringing up larger forces, and the leadership team knew there were five swarms and four smaller blade ships orbiting Earth, deployed to ensure no human satellite or missile reached space. It was not, of itself, an invasion force, but it was certainly a source of flanking attacks.

The leadership exchanged questions, weighed risks and options while the ship-minds endlessly calculated possible strategies and displayed them.

Fossil Beak saw a hard, bitter choice. The least risk to the largest number: abandon the crew and the child on the planet and flee, with the stronger starship to the rear. But Little Frog was precious. Every child is precious, but he was also the key to understanding the strange paradoxical humans. She thought, *Each breath of delay raises the risk — and what if the rebel Ship and Little Frog do not follow? All-condemn the boy for his thoughtless action. We must balance lives like the ingredients of soup.*

Some would have them resist any attack on Earth, for many or all of the crew might be killed.

Or, do not leave until the brave, foolish Little Blue Frog is safe. Fight as the people had learned to fight.

Sometimes the machines could find options that were not obvious, but they had no clever ideas this time.

Fossil Beak loathed the snakes more than death. The vast snake ships looked less like ceremonial harpoons, more like the long bud of flowers made of clean metal. Thousands of the individual snakes, their other units, had their niches to lodge in on the surface — a deadly flock that could overwhelm an unarmed purple vessel. The snakes could descend in force to the surface of a planet. A battle could be won in space and lost on the ground. That was the lesson of New Harbour, and it had resulted in the terrifying evacuation.

She re-sent the warning to those on Earth that the search could not continue for ever.

The leadership debated the options, fast and clipped, a style of discussion unlike their usual ebb and flow. The people normally liked to take their time, to sleep on decisions, to dance or feast or play games while they brought everyone together.

But you could not fight the snakes like that: that was the discipline of the Hardening, and everyone mourned it.

But the snakes had learned caution too.

Consensus moves. Three of the people's stealth units were close to the blade ships around Earth. A fourth snake vessel approached the polar apex. The people's mind-only vessels were preparing armaments, the crew doing the Hardening exercises as they readied themselves for any action.

Decision: bewilder and harass the snakes while they pondered.

The three blade ships flickered, and were clouds of fire and scrap metal. A machine gave the energy signal of an entire habitat, drawing snake clouds away from Earth.

Fossil Beak told the leadership, 'Four billion humans, my lodge-mates. We must do something. We must give the planet team more time.'

Leadership was a burden.

She messaged across all the whole mission, 'We will engage soon. Stand firm. Remember our slain. *For life!*' A human general would have incited revenge, but the people rejected that concept. The people destroyed for hope, not punishment.

The harpoons were crawling towards Earth now, their actions suggesting the people's ships had not been detected. The element of surprise exists only once. Little Frog, a single child, lost the mission the chance to slip away. Yet many of the crew were troubled by the plan to flee, for they had heard the songs of Earth.

In the Atlantic, the Ship Reborn, with the Pilot's orders to save her son at all costs still burning in its brain, endlessly recalculated when to return Cory to his people. Indeed, once the builders did have Cory, the Ship would encourage them to flee.

'Does the message make sense?' Cory asked. The little builder was struggling with his strange organic powers, and the dog's distress was not helping. The edit was ragged and it was an emotional plea, so the Ship had no real means to evaluate it.

'There comes a time when it is better to send it than wait,' the Ship said.

'Will they watch it during the battle? Will they listen to me?'

'Some will: it touches on something that troubles many of the builders, I think. The other machines have been discussing it.'

'What can they do, Ship? Can they win?'

'Let me send it. Try the protein sample on the mutt. I will send the message via a probe, so our location will not be immediately known. Then I will tell you a story, as parents do. The people have found many strange new things . . .'

★

The closest harpoon ship rallied the swarms surrounding Earth.

The chosen-for-today played at *Ink-mouth*. By nature, the people would hide from threats and now, like a pair of grizzled ink-mouths lurking in a shallow sea, the people's ships spread confusion. Probes scattered cunning fléchettes emitting energies unknown to Earth that created phantasms to confuse the snakes. Unlike sea-ink, this ink could swarm and follow.

The snakes responded with rage in the form of a powerful barrage of electromagnetic pulses, a roar that disrupted everything on Earth from radio telescopes to televisions. The people had learned this tactic, paying a price in purple blood, and they were cloaked. The leadership responded with *phantoms*, an energy simulacrum of a third ship of the living, then a fourth. The tactic would not work for long, but it did not need to.

The chosen-of-the-day led off *Dance of the Palm*: an elegant and skilful game. To place a full palm of any hand or foot on the other scores a point; achieving a forehead palm scores four. The people pierced the fields around the harpoon ship, landed a single device – and for a moment, there was a corner of the universe where mass could only be energy. One end of the vessel became a bellow of incoherent force, a scream of burning light, ripping it lengthways in two. Fleeing snakes spilled from it like poison spores from a tree-fungus, but most attacked each other, or exploded their power source, while others writhed aimlessly, incoherently.

Four points.

Smaller devices finished the work, leaving snakes and the smaller purple vessels fighting in the expanding cloud of metal shards.

More cunning machines designed by the builders entered the heart of a snake swarm and destroyed it, but the danger was rising, for now the snakes were seeing through the illusion and beginning to converge on the true ships.

A new snake harpoon approached at great speed from the zenith: it must have been hiding there inert. There might be more to follow. Fossil Beak stilled her mind, not letting the thought of the thousand lives in space or the billions below overwhelm her.

The command structure was still digesting the options thrown up by the machine minds, but she thought she saw the way.

The team conferred briefly. Again, a veteran of previous battles suggested flight; again, rebutted, they deferred.

There are many variants in the game of *Tiles*, but in most, there are only three white tiles that can ever be in play. The great danger was in so draining the ships of energy that they would be unable to defend themselves as they fled.

Little Frog had forced their hand a little, although none of the people had been happy to run, for they had seen the animals who walked in Earth's forests and heard the language of the birds. They had seen Fleur at Molly's breast. The angry, bitter reports from the first Earth mission had been true, as far as they went, but there had been a great falsehood too, for so-so much had been omitted.

Her last message to the ground team had not produced a reply, but she re-sent it.

'Thunder over Mountains here. No, we are closing in on Little Frog.'

'The odds are worsening.'

'Leave if you must. We will rescue him and hide on some frozen moon if we have to. I have not crossed the ocean of stars to abandon him.'

Repurpose Snakes was too close to the snake warship at the zenith. It turned the smaller blade ship to scrap, then darted away, aiming to engage the harpoon.

She prepared the order to flee, but the wounded sistership was still preparing to engage.

The chosen-of-the-day must throw what she could their way – another distraction, a feint – and then act . . .

Under the Atlantic, Cory hovered between waking and dreaming, Meteor curled into him. The lights in the chamber were dimmed. He realised the Ship was moving again.

'Little Frog,' the Ship said, as gentle as a lodge mother, 'the builders have reached us and I cannot hold out. I have one last disobedience . . . then the builders will be in control.'

Then a familiar voice said, 'Little Blue Frog. Cory. This one is coming. This one will never leave you.' It was Thunder Over Mountains.

Exhausted, drained, Cory told himself he had tried. 'The snakes . . .' he said.

'Don't worry. We are getting closer. Your Ship is moving towards us.'

Cory was so tired now. He could not save the world. He needed his family, both his families . . .

There was a shudder as the Ship docked with a second vehicle. Cory wanted to smell his birth-father and hold his human family close.

The purples sat in the attic, studying their devices, while Gene and Molly looked out at the clear sky, trying to read the flashes and streaks of light.

Something blazed up above – a new star? Then came a second. They were under the old blanket and Molly must have been dozing, for now she jerked awake. More meteors were appearing in the sky.

Suddenly Skimming Stone announced, 'They have found the boy under the ocean. He is unwell, but he is being cared for. Thunder Over Mountains was particularly keen for you to know as soon as they found him. And that he will not be punished.'

Molly snapped, 'You don't understand us at all, do you?'

Skimming Stone said, hesitantly, 'I think it was meant as a joke. Cory said you never punished him. Apparently, the dog is also alive. It will be brought to you.'

'Will he be okay? Are you going to tell us what's happening?'

'Cory has sent a message to the crew: an argument for saving the Earth. It is very raw and moving. And it is impractical, of course.'

This purple was feeling some regret, she could feel it. Skimming Stone might just be an ally, thought Molly.

'I'd like to hear it,' Gene said.

'Maybe. Of course, nearly all of us are engaged in risking our lives in trying to hold off the snakes while we save a child of our world.'

'A child of our world too,' Gene said.

'We may not win.'

'Tell your leaders we are glad you tried.'

Two Tail said, 'We have family, friends, lovers up above. You are not the only ones in fear.'

'We're here with you,' Gene said. 'I'll play you something, if you like.'

The aliens were having a private conversation, looking at each other through their masks. Indeed, from the agitation of their tentacles, Molly rather thought it was an argument.

'Are you taking Cory into space? Into the heart of the battle?' she asked, thinking this might be the end of the world – it might be the end of everything. She looked at Gene – she must look as haggard as he did – and thought, *When the last moment comes, let us remember love.*

'If the purples win, maybe we need to go to their world, Molly-Moo. Maybe they'll only listen to us.'

That was the only argument she feared. 'I can't risk Fleur and Elsa too,' she tried to explain. 'There are far better people, diplomats and artists and philosophers – we've met some of them.'

'They don't have a son on the starship.' He sighed. 'Castles in the air for now.'

He kissed her.

If they offered that, just the five of them, what would she answer? If it was a gamble to save the Earth?

She did not want that choice.

Beneath the White House, as the dedicated Moscow telex chattered away, scientists explained to the President what the flashes of light in space might be, but not why. 'Mr President, we think these are explosions – it's possible the snakes in our orbit are being attacked.'

'Could it be the purples?' he asked, then snapped. 'Get the Myers!'

'Their phone is down, sir, and they're not answering their radio.'

He rolled his eyes. 'Then send a helicopter, or the 56th Airborne. What the fuck are the National Guard doing?'

'They say they can't find the Fence at all.'

An officer entered, waving a sheet of telex printout. 'It's the Ship. The purples are fighting the snakes up there – it's life or death. And . . .' he gulped, 'it's broadcasting on open frequencies, in all the ten languages it speaks – it's telling the world purples are dying up there to defend the Earth.'

In the stifling moist heat of a Shanghai summer, a road of flame crossed the sky as a great snake ship fell to earth in bright fragments. TV crews in the heights above Hong Kong filmed snakes burning with white fire. In jungles and paddy fields, Viet Cong and Americans alike stopped, looked up and shielded their eyes as the machine ship died. Tribesmen and loggers in the jungles of the Philippines would find mysterious parts for months, ripped and twisted metal, and sometimes writhing like something alive – something with a broken back. A Dutch aeroplane making an emergency landing at sea tried through electronic chaos to raise assistance.

Churches were full and bars ran dry. Roads out of cities were jammed solid, and in the public squares people congregated and stood gazing up, scared and silent . . . waiting.

In Amber Grove, their gaolers had disappeared – Molly had no idea whether the purples had gone for a nap, or a walk, or just to watch them unseen. She caught up on her sewing, something to keep her mind busy, while Gene, who always claimed a chair was too uncomfortable to sleep in, was giving a good impression of a snoozing man snoring.

Then Molly's communicator was drumming, bursting with hoots and whoops and a fierce song she recognised: the victory-in-hunting song that Cory had performed for them.

Gene grunted, sat up, swore. 'My back—!' he started, but he shut up when the communicator trilled.

'This is Thunder. Cory is safe with our healers. We have won – a great battle, if not the war. The snakes are in retreat from Earth. One of our ships has significant damage – there are at least eighty of the people dead, and many wounded. The Earth is not safe, but the danger is lessened for now.'

Gene knelt by her so they could both talk into the communicator. 'How's Cory?' he asked.

'He has over-used his power, he is drained to a point of danger. But we have good healers. Oh, how brave he is, how foolhardy, and how committed to see the right thing done. What an argument he has started.' Thunder was clearly proud of their son. 'He is insisting that we should put a case to all-the-people of the home-world, to reconsider.'

'That's wonderful.' Drained and weary, Molly could say no more. She kissed Gene, tasted his tears and felt her own tears come. 'Let's go and see the sunrise. What happened to the purples who were here?'

'They have friends, lovers among the dead,' Thunder said. 'I would still advise not speaking to your authorities – they are bound to want to control you.'

Molly hadn't been sure they would ever see another dawn. She remembered times when she had not wanted to see the morning herself, nights when she had sat with a bottle of pills in her hand. Now she stood on the same porch where she had seen the Meteor on that cold April three years ago which had been the start of it all. With Gene's arm around her waist, they watched the clouds take on colour as the sun rose over the horizon.

This new day felt like a gift, and they needed to cherish it.

CHAPTER 44

CHAPTER 44

Thunder above the Earth

Thunder Over Mountains sat beside the crib, looking at the drained, sleepy child and stroking Little Frog's ears with a gloved hand. It would be a delicate balance to restore his health and contain his erratic power. Aspects of this case were unique, and the experienced healers on the ship were having to feel their way forward carefully. Thunder knew little of such things, but he was learning fast. He resented the precautions the healers were insisting they take – he wanted to smell and touch his son: he ached for the full experience of being with him. Parenthood was a common thing among the people, yet it was always extraordinary. Love held him in an undying note. What he had been before Little Frog's exile was a pale shadow of what he could be.

'All must save the Earth,' the boy moaned.

'Oh, Little Frog, how this one wishes so, but it is a hard decision to make, little one. We must hope all-will-decide to leave *Kites at Dusk* to defend the Earth, while *Repurpose Snakes* is sent running for home.'

Such a move would be risky for both ships. *Repurpose Snakes* was the weaker; it would have little chance if it was attacked on the return journey. And *Kites at Dusk* might not be strong enough to stand alone against whatever the snakes threw at it. But dividing their forces like this might be the only way to give humans a better chance of survival, at least while all-the-people decided what to do.

His son coughed and groaned, then opened his eyes. 'We must-must-must leave one starship.'

Thunder fondled an ear. 'But many will say, so much safer if both ships go home together.'

This would be a gamble with billions of lives. All-the-people might decide not to return – or the people might come back after a year away to find the war lost and the Earth barren. Purple and machine minds had been working through cautious strategies to destroy the snakes' base on Mars, but as yet, it was still there.

'I will change their minds. I have so-so many good arguments.'

'Rest, Little Frog, rest. The people will hear your arguments. You have done enough for now, and I will argue the case myself. We have some on our side, some against. Many are to be persuaded. Unity takes time.'

Little Frog should be asleep, but he was too agitated. 'Too much talking, not enough doing. Save my Earth-family – save all the humans. There are healers for me, so we can stay.'

Everyone assumed that Little Glowing Blue Frog must go home to be debriefed, to speak as no one else could of the good in humanity. The home-world wanted him back – it wanted all of them back. People had died for the Earth, and those who lived wanted Little Frog safe – but the journey home would not be safe. There were no guarantees.

Thunder's mind was clear: his extraordinary son was proof that humanity was worth saving. But whether it *could* be saved, no one could know.

Thunder sang so he did not need to speak. The Pioneer song 'The Stars Are New Islands' was naïve, and now sung in bittersweet knowledge.

Would the-all defend the Earth? The adults had been keeping from Little Frog just how difficult that might be. Dreaming-between-the-stars was too weak to allow proper dreaming-to-decide. The speakers-for-the-home-world were furious that the mission had made the decision to contact humans. The hidden reports on Earth's violent and destructive culture had been made public – there was no other option – and now all-the-people were horrified.

As for delaying the mission to fight the snakes, the speakers-for-the-home-world grieved the dead and censured the living. Humanity was unpredictable and dangerous. The leaders were saying Little Frog should have been taken on the first day of contact, willing or not, and both ships should already be headed home. A species who fought each other, who ate other sentient creatures, who looked determined to turn their whole world into fire and garbage could not be worth saving.

Thunder must speak too, for the biosphere, for the majestic trees and the tiny frogs. For dolphins and crows and daisies.

'Why are starships so slow?' Little Frog said suddenly. 'We must get home quick-quick-quick. Cory will invent a much faster spaceship. Also, dreaming-between-the-stars must be much better. Cory will fix that too.'

'Maybe you will, little one. But the grown-ups find these very big problems, so you'll need to start solving just one of them first.'

'Time to let go and sleep,' a healer said, appearing on the other side of the crib.

Thunder thanked them and left them to their work.

Outside the healing centre, preparations to remember the dead had started. But the living needed decisions – groups had the discussions. Humanity already knew too much. Should they treat the humans as adults and make contact? The crew were divided.

The people had made mistakes; of course they had, and some stories were not told to the children. Generations ago, a green world had been found where the most sentient species were declining as the planet moved into a colder era. One mission had gone against the-all. Remaining hidden, they tried to save some of the indigenous population from starvation. They thought they had been discreet – but things had started changing. The local species found their dreams: they began to dream of the people as higher beings, and those who dreamed with most clarity grew into leaders, though there had been no such distinctions before. When that herd met another to exchange males, the changes started spreading like an infection, and within three generations, the indigenous species had become very different: they were more inquisitive, more courageous, more complex, and fiercer against those who were different.

The-all had been horrified. It was true that the changes had likely better fitted the species to survive – but those changes had been unintended, they were permanent and the final outcome was still far from clear. And worse, this naïve kindness had elevated the people to something they were not, something for which the humans had a concept – *gods* – which repelled them.

The people had sworn never to make that mistake again. Earth had been such an obvious case for not intervening – and yet Pilot had landed Little Glowing Blue Frog on a closed world and now the whole of humankind knew they were not alone: a reality that humans both feared and longed for. One cannot unbreak an egg, but that is no reason to break another one. The arguments were endless.

Thunder patched himself into a discussion preparation group.

'—but we could alter the weapons so the humans cannot use them against other humans—'

Disagreement.

Thunder feared he would be speaking often in this discussion.

Another spoke with impolite emphasis. 'Humans will want to know how our weapons work. They will throw all their resources into understanding them. In less than a generation they turned nuclear theory into a controlled chain-reaction and then a full explosion – something called the Manhattan Project – driven solely by a desire to use it as a weapon. Who knows what humans will learn from our technology, or to what ends they might turn it?'

'This one agrees. Even the fragments of our machines and what Little Frog knows will have prompted new discussions.'

'This issue, to arm humans, is not the question originally posed,' said the moderator. 'Do we wish to take it wider?'

Thunder was with the-many who showed their disapproval, setting *later, later* lights flashing. The group quickly moved back to the questions posed: should one starship be left to defend the Earth? Should the snake base on Mars be attacked, at yet more risk to the people? Should a delegation of humans be taken to the home-world to argue their own case? Should the elimination of the Ship Reborn be delayed or reconsidered?

Skimming Stone had the speaking right. 'Time is wasted in debating the Ship Reborn. It might be dangerous, it might not. But if it contaminates other machine minds, it would be exceptionally dangerous: imagine a self-ordering, disobedient starship. In the end, the-all cannot take the risk, no matter how long we talk – so let us follow the rule, destroy it and concentrate on what matters.'

The message had been drummed into every child: *a machine is to serve; a machine which disobeys defies its purpose.*

Long before the snakes, the people had a rule: *examine the disobedient machine mind, learn from the error, then destroy it.*

'Destroy the mind.'

'This one agrees.'

Thunder waited for other comments, knowing that for Little Frog, the Ship had become a person. This happened with children, even a few adults, but machine sentience could not be mind-felt the way real, organic creatures could be felt. A Ship no more felt alive than a stone did – but a Ship was not a stone. Maybe the servant machines had now changed; maybe new criteria were needed.

Was it wrong to feel gratitude to the machine mind?

'This is not a question that can be ignored for ever,' said the moderator.

'The Ship is not a danger at this heartbeat. It is secondary,' Thunder said firmly. 'As it is said, build the foundation before decorating the doorframe.'

Much approval, much flashing *later, later*.

The moderator said, 'Return to a question asked. Should we take a human delegation to the home-world?'

Anger and fear spread through the group.

'This one believes that we must not – we cannot – allow humans so full of violence and deceit on the home-world.'

Agree agree agree.

Thunder had not been optimistic, but it was worse than he had thought.

The Earth was already buzzing with stories that the people had come. Many were exaggerating their numbers and powers – should humans be told what might be an unpalatable truth, that the purples would leave them to their fate? And many humans thought the people had attacked them.

After all, what did the people really owe to the humans?

CHAPTER 45

After the battle

Molly held the signed cover sleeve as she played 'Our Child of the Stars'. It was extraordinary what Ella Fitzgerald could do with her husband's song, bringing out his bewilderment, the sadness, the sense of a waiting loss, as well as the heights of wonder and joy and need for the child who had landed so unexpectedly in their life. Of all the versions, she liked this one best.

Speculation was at fever-pitch: the aliens would land, the aliens would annex Hawaii, the aliens would hold a press conference – it was the Second Coming, it was the Age of Aquarius, it was a new beginning; it was the end of everything, the end of Capitalism, the end of Communism, the end of marriage and the family . . .

It was all a big loud mess.

The purples had saved the Earth and they would take her son and it was the right thing to do. She needed to grieve, but there was hope still.

Elsa had started picking fights from the second she opened her eyes, so Molly had handed her over to the Robertsons, where she would be indulged. Molly sat admiring Fleur sitting in her high chair and waving her hands, leaving the laundry sulking undone in the utility room. Carol and Storm had promised to come today, looking for insight into the purples. They were back on the alien beat; they had barely stopped working since Carol had got Storm out of jail.

Gene came over, looking exhausted.

'Bad news?'

Maybe there had been another attack – they'd guessed those snakes that had gone up to join the battle in space been destroyed, but Thunder had not said anything about the base on Mars, so that must still be active, busy building more snakes. Silence implied the purples had yet to act against them, so maybe they had decided not to. Snakes did not need air or water, so they might still be lurking in a thousand places even on Earth.

'Thunder called me,' Gene said quietly. 'It's not looking good for my flight to the stars.'

She touched his hand. 'What are they saying?'

'He said there's a riot at the mere idea of letting humans on board – for any reason. Everyone's now read the full report on humanity – it was such hot stuff, they kept it secret, apparently. Basically, they're calling us the Planet of Psycho Killers. Catchy, right? So a load of the purples, even in Thunder's mob, are saying, "Okay, drop it. We don't need humans to put their case."'

'Oh . . .' Molly had always thought *some* humans should go – the *right* people. Just not her Gene.

'Thunder thinks it's stupid, and he's not giving up.' But Gene sounded drained, defeated. 'If they do agree to take some of us, they're talking about sealing off part of the starship for us — like convicts, or zoo animals. But he warned me, we might not even be asked.'

Gene lowered himself into the creaky chair he'd promised to mend and Molly moved next to him.

Gene closed his eyes. 'So no getting my parents medical help. No jaunt to space.'

'I know . . . I know what that meant to you.' Molly could see what it felt like to Gene, losing a long-held dream.

Gene wiped away a tear. 'Well, I couldn't go and leave my folks, could I? See them after eight months and say I'm off . . . how could I leave Eva to manage John like he is now? We might be able to see them next week . . . And I sure couldn't picture myself kissing you goodbye either. I think I'd spend every day scared.'

Gene had chosen her when the option of going to the stars was open: he had chosen her with all his heart. She felt so much love for him, and she felt huge sorrow too. There was no sense of a victory.

She kissed him. 'They may still decide in our favour,' she said.

'I guess going only matters to me,' he said quietly.

'*You* matter,' she said. 'You matter to *me*. We'll go to the West Coast, I promise, as soon as we can. Or Honolulu. It will be fun.' It was easily offered, but it was from the heart.

'We must send the purples our own message,' he said. 'They must at least give us that right.' He fell silent.

Molly wondered about the days ahead. *We'll just have to live one day at a time.*

*

425

The phone tucked to her ear, Molly jogged Fleur on her knee. This was the President's third call in person since the battle had ended. If it wasn't him or his people, it was the Secretary-General of the United Nations, or one of the other international organisations.

There was a lot of background noise this time.

'Mrs Myers, the press is going insane. The Ship says the purples won – now I have the leaders of Congress demanding to know what's going on – not to mention every candidate for the other side demanding to be briefed.'

The Democrats were poised to choose a radical, a man of peace. The old guard might switch to supporting the President.

'I'm truly sorry, Mr President. I really don't have any idea what they'll decide.'

'I'm in a car, forty-five minutes from Amber Grove. The Marines can land a helicopter at the top of Crooked Street, if you could ask Mr Henderson to move his trucks.'

The trucks were parked there against just that possibility.

'I'm afraid the Fence won't let you in.' Molly did her best to sound apologetic.

'It will if you tell it to, Mrs Myers. Or choose somewhere else. You can decide not to meet me – my pride can take that. I just worry those people saying we should fight the aliens might start thinking the snakes and the purples are one and the same. Please, Mrs Myers, help me to explain things – get them riled up at the *right* aliens.'

He didn't need to remind her, *I pardoned your friend Joel. I didn't ask for anything*.

Molly couldn't decide what would be worse, seeing him or not. Maybe, face to face, he was more likely to believe her.

'The house is a mess,' she started.

He waved away the objection. 'No one will see it but me and one Secret Service guy.'

'I'll have no guns in the house,' she said, on autopilot, giving way.

How much can I do in an hour? She ran around the big room like a whirlwind, vacuuming, dusting and cleaning until everywhere smelled of polish.

'Which outfit, funerals or wedding guest?' she asked Gene.

'Funerals, for our principles: meeting the man when we don't have to.' He wrinkled his nose. 'I don't mind, but you smell of Pledge.'

Gene looked very fine, she thought, pinning his nuclear disarmament badge onto his lapel. He even managed a smile.

Molly grabbed her perfume and gave herself another blast, then put on the new outfit for best, glad women didn't have to wear skirts nowadays. Suppose fusty old Amber County General realised it was the Nineteen Seventies and let all its nurses wear long pants – that would be such a blessing when lifting patients. Maybe if the world was saved, she could be a nurse again.

'Suppose it's a trick?'

'I spoke to Thunder. There are a dozen drones watching us, and they can hide us through the communicators.'

And there he was, on their doorstep, the leader of the free world – anxious, jowly and blue-chinned. A quite improbably handsome Secret Service man who looked seven feet tall stood beside him.

'Bill here will stay at the door,' the President said, offering a hand. He looked like he had three ulcers now, not two. He complimented them on the room, then said to Gene, 'My kids love your songs.' Then he turned to Molly. 'And Bill can't ask himself, but his kids would really love a signed photo of Cory if you have it.'

'Of course – but let's fill you in,' Molly said, pouring the coffee, pleased she'd remembered how the President took it.

They didn't have much to add to what they'd said before, and at the end, the President scratched his head. 'So they have their entire crew sitting around debating this?'

'Not all at once, we're told. They do it in groups, but they all get a say.'

He looked aghast. 'How does their civilisation ever get anything done? I was in the Navy – can you imagine fighting the Battle of Midway by committee?'

What could she say? Somehow, they made it work.

He tried another tack. 'Look, there's a timing to these things. They clearly gave those snakes a whupping and the whole planet owes them for that. They should land so I can thank them for it – so the whole world can. The UN Secretary-General is waiting – they'll need to talk to him, at least, for show, if nothing else, to keep the other nations happy.' He coughed. 'What concerns me is that the people who hate them – who believe they are the same as the snakes – aren't shutting up and right now, we're leaving them the stage and the microphone.'

Gene was looking worried.

The President went on, 'A planet divided cannot stand. A

little wait is fine – it builds the excitement – but the purples do need to claim the credit, and soon. You see, we need to put the "anti" brigade on the back foot so we can do this deal on the Space Treaty. I have the Secretary of State flying to China – thank the Lord, they want in. I understand the aliens will take a bit of persuading to sell us some weapons – but truly, just telling us what is going on would help.'

How do we explain?

Molly said, 'They don't want to interfere in our politics – in anything else, in fact. They know we're grateful.'

Gene stepped in. 'Look, if we dropped an aircraft carrier on another planet, the captain wouldn't feel empowered to make any big diplomatic decisions, would he?'

'But he'd at least come to dinner, wear a flower necklace and watch some local dances or something, tell the aliens we didn't mean them any harm.'

If both starships went home, the Earth would have no protection at all – for a year, or for ever, if the purples never returned. Maybe that would be okay, and maybe not. Even if they left *Repurpose Snakes* or *Kites at Dusk*, that was no guarantee of anything.

People said many things about the man, but he wasn't stupid.

'Could they just take the boy and go?' he asked, and it was Gene he looked at.

Gene's silence told him.

That afternoon, Diane was mysterious on the phone – then Janice dropped by 'just to see if there were plans for this evening', and Molly knew something was up. Selena called from the Jarman place and announced that she was coming over too, with her boys.

'What's going on?' Molly asked. Selena was supposed to be staying quiet and settling in.

'Nothing,' Selena said.

'I'm not a fool,' Molly started, but Selena changed the subject.

Should she wear a dress or prepare a speech, or what? Molly didn't feel like company, and nor did Gene. At least if their friends were coming over, they'd do most of the talking.

Selena was late, trailing Connor and Rory behind her. Both looked awkward in their Cory sweatshirts. Selena was hugging a big brown envelope like it was a baby. Mason was still wanted by the police, but she got her restraining order too. They ate in the back yard while birds called and wind whispered in the summer foliage.

The purples had bought the Earth time, whatever else happened. Every day from now on was precious.

By sunset, Molly was growing tired, but Diane took her arm. 'Let's go out front,' she said.

'Oh, a surprise,' said Gene, clowning.

'Well, there are plenty of people grateful, and they wanted to do something.'

Diane led them from the porch and up the road to where they could look down over Amber Grove.

The twilight sky was filled with lights – flashlights and candles, in the windows of all their neighbours, lanterns on poles and porches, unfamiliar lights on the roof of City Hall and the library.

Every unexpected light was a thank you – to the Myers, to the purples, to those burying the dead and healing the living.

'Wow,' Gene said, then he added, 'They should have done it on Founders Green.'

'We wouldn't have been able to see it,' Molly said aloud, her eyes filling with tears. This galaxy of lights was for them, the Crooked Street gang who had kept Cory safe all these years: for Molly and Gene and their friends, who might just have saved the Earth. And maybe for the purples too, up there arguing.

Cory might have died, or he might have fallen into evil hands. It was all on the spin of a coin . . .

Molly hugged Selena a little too long. Her sister had gone chestnut, and it suited her. She was better than she had been, although perhaps not yet back to her best.

'Well, I'm supposed to *rest*, but that place is like the grave,' Sel said with a laugh, pulling Molly down beside her. 'And if you get a few people together to play cards, some of them *cheat* – hey, what on earth's happening? Dr Jarman says every journalist in the whole world is in town.'

'We've said we'll make an announcement when we have something to say.'

But now she'd started, Sel was full of questions. 'Where will the aliens land? How will they protect the Earth? Who gets to meet them?'

'We'll tell the world when we know.'

'And Cory?'

'He needs to go home, for his health.' That, and to plead Earth's case. If she pinched the bridge of her nose and sniffed the tears back, she wouldn't cry.

Selena nodded, a little vaguely. 'I couldn't bear being apart from mine, even for a week. How will you cope?' She fumbled a cigarette out of her purse, caught Molly's expression and fiddled with it.

Molly went on, 'We'll manage – we'll get messages, we hope. It's the right thing for him, and for the Earth. It might be only a year, or eighteen months.'

It was a bitter kind of grief, but there was hope too. That made it no less painful, but they would learn to bear it.

Selena handed Molly the cigarette, then the packet.

'You know, I'm glad I'm here. If the world ends, I couldn't think of anyone else I wanted to meet my Maker with. My little sis, saviour of the world.'

Molly squeezed her hand. 'I thought the Church wouldn't have me?'

Whatever the aliens decided about the Earth, they still might just slip away. She didn't even know if she would see Cory again.

CHAPTER 46

The United Nations

Things had started moving. Two purples had brought a viewing screen in the night and assembled it while Molly and Gene stood bleary-eyed, watching them.

'It's so you can see Little Frog,' they said. 'And other things.' Molly, in her summer robe, found herself in tears again. They would be apart for at least a year, if they even let him come home.

Just after breakfast, Cory appeared on the screen. He looked deflated and tired, his ears down, his tentacles limp, his inner eyelids a little visible. But when he saw them, he sat up and said, 'Don't worry Mom, Dad. Cory will be fine. So many grown-ups missing their own kids – all get in line to play with Cory!'

It hadn't truly struck Molly and Gene that there were no other children on the starships; how tough the journey home would be, but this was their son, making the best of it. They made small talk, each word fizzing with meaning – how his friends were wanting to write letters for him to take to the home-world. How his new cousins Rory and Connor had already written him long letters, saying they were sorry, how Connor had fought a boy at school who'd said Cory was a monster and made him admit that Cory had saved the world.

'Letters – and why not film as well?' Cory said.

'Will they let us hug you goodbye?'

Cory wailed, 'I don't know. They say too sick, too delicate.'

Molly felt punished.

Gene said, 'Well, the screen is fine, if we can't meet' – he was such a poor liar.

Molly pretended too, for they could see he was tiring. Skimming Stone, sitting beside him, explained about the long process of healing, and how Gene and Molly must take care of themselves too. She went on and on – turned out, the purples had well-meaning busybodies too.

'Leaders-for-now have so many questions,' Cory said, out of nowhere. 'Thunder will be in the group.'

Molly was confused. 'What's this?'

'Speech to United Nations soon. President radioed starship – lots of leaders did.'

'What are they going to say?'

'All-have-decided, humans must believe there is a threat. But all-can't-decide what we should do about threat. So much a tricky problem.'

Soon afterwards, the leadership-for-the-day appeared on the screen, clearly uneasy, not knowing what they could say to the world. They grilled Gene and Molly for an hour, until Gene said firmly that they needed a break.

Thunder spoke to them privately through their communicators. 'Some want to wash our hands of Earth as a problem. But this denial of reality worries the-all of us. Whatever Earth chooses, let it do so from knowledge.'

It was the day they had dreamed of: eight aliens would address the United Nations General Assembly in person. Molly remembered the tour of the UN Building in New York, when she had wondered if this day would ever come.

At the Myers place, the family and their closest friends were elbow to elbow in front of the alien viewscreen, which was showing two images. The podium from where the aliens would speak was what the General Assembly would see. The second image was a roving shot of those arriving, delegates from 113 member states and selected observers.

The radio was on, the newscasters breathless at estimates of the crowds near the building. The rumour was that they would then go to Central Park, which was full of people hoping for a sighting. Troops and police kept the area immediately around the building clear. There were clashes between demonstrators, and endless descriptions of this celebrity or that arriving, as if they had anything particular to add or contribute.

There was no fanfare, but the aliens were there: eight of them in spacesuits, approaching the podium beneath a vast alien viewing disc. Each introduced themselves in a few chords of alien, then in English. The speech would also be provided worldwide in the nine other languages the aliens had learned during their twenty-year surveillance.

Then one of the shorter ones, Fossil Beak, the commander

on the day of the space battle, said, 'We come in peace. We understand this is the traditional opening.'

After a long pause, there was a ripple of laughter.

Good, thought Molly, *because it was meant to be funny.*

'How grateful we are to the people of this beautiful planet, who have taken one of our children to their heart. He was sick, wounded and bereaved and you kept him safe these long and perilous months. You have proved love can transcend species.'

There was a minute-long film of Cory in the spaceship. He was on his best behaviour. Molly thought he looked tired.

More people were watching this than had seen the Moon landing, according to the newscasters, and because the human satellites had all been destroyed, the aliens had promised to rebroadcast it so everyone in the world would have a chance to see and hear their message.

In the Assembly Hall, ten boys and ten girls, wearing Sunday best or national costumes, picked by lot from the Ambassadors' diplomatic families to represent all the different colours and creeds of the world, presented flowers. The aliens thanked them, remembered their names.

'Let us show you a little of our planet,' said the chosen-for-the-day. 'These images help us when we are far from the home-world, separated from those we love.'

The film showed purple children playing a laughing chase in the woods; sailing ships scudding under a fierce wind; a night feast on a beach under brilliant stars, purples standing elbow to elbow, singing and swaying beneath the stars.

'We have no need of war, as you understand it. And for thirty generations, the whole of our world has been free of hunger. The Time of Plenty saw us reach out into the stars . . . then terror came.'

Then came a picture of a vast structure in space: six cylinders spinning in a complex frame. The structure was under attack from the snakes, a riot of blue and white fire. As they watched, the snakes began boring into the hull.

'We share your loss,' the speaker said sadly. 'This was the destruction of a space habitation, the death of many thousands by the killers-of-life, the snake machines that would make your planet and ours dead and sterile.'

The camera scanned the faces of the delegates, all looking shocked and frightened. Molly wondered if the aliens had projected their fear and grief . . . She realised the children had been led out of the auditorium; maybe that was why.

'We mourn those on your planet who also died: Pevek and Orlando and Colorado Springs, Baikonur and Fukushima.' In English, Russian and Chinese, 'Your grief is our grief,' the chosen-for-the-day said formally.

After a moment for everyone to collect themselves, Thunder, walking with his cane, came to the centre. 'We are a small scientific mission, diverted to rescue my son when we discovered he was still alive. You know him as Cory, I know him as Little Glowing Blue Frog. We have no interest in harming your planet or interfering in your society. Yet your planet was threatened and we fought off the snakes.

'Many of you expect us to do this or that – so many of you have been radioing our vessels, asking for this aid or that – but we have no authority and no expertise to negotiate, or to commit to any actions. One of our ships at least must return to the home-world as soon as it can, to bring vital information of the snakes' increasing power and depredations. What help our people can offer the Earth is not for us to decide.

'We can say this: we will locate snake forces elsewhere in your solar system, and we will leave systems in place so you will be warned if the snakes gather. You will not have to fight them without eyes or ears.'

It was so little, but it was something, although Molly could see the French President and the King of Saudi Arabia were unimpressed.

'Your planet is rich with life, as beautiful and diverse as our own.' The viewing disc behind him was showing the Earth as it looked from space. 'Unless the snakes are defeated, all of this will be ashes and dust. We do not wholly understand you, but we think you can understand us. We had to change to resist the snakes. Falling back to the home-world with millions of dead changed our whole society. We had to work hard at finding ways to survive the horrors we saw, and to unite conflicting views. We have prevailed, so far. Just.

'Snakes remain in your solar system and more snakes may come, from any direction. The Earth could be surrounded.

'We come in peace, but we are at war – a word we had no use for just three years ago – with a predator who cannot be appeased. Like it or not, so are you. We come in peace, but we warn of destruction.

'You here: you are the chosen-of-your-people. What will you decide? What will you do for yourselves, and for all life?'

★

After maybe thirty seconds' silence, the Russian Premier and the UN Secretary-General stood simultaneously and started to applaud. The American Secretary of State was quick to follow suit, and before long, everyone was on their feet and clapping the purples.

Molly found herself overwhelmed by the historical significance of this moment, but it was tempered by the knowledge that her son would be leaving. She looked around at her assembled friends, knowing the future of Earth still hung in the balance.

Humanity would have to do its own heavy lifting.

CHAPTER 47

The secure unit

Dr Emmanuel Pfeiffer's world had shrunk down to a single off-white cell with a hard, narrow bed, a rickety table, a stained basin and a toilet without a seat. He had argued them up to four textbooks and two paperbacks from the library, as well as reports and papers, which a solemn guard removed each night, for some bizarre reason. After all these weeks, they still kept him without tie or belt, checking on him through the peep-hole every two hours. A guard always supervised him when he cleaned the cell.

The aliens would address the United Nations, and he would watch it with the other inmates on TV. He was irrelevant. That afternoon, Rachael was bringing the divorce papers. He'd failed as a man, a husband, a father.

It's ironic, he thought, *that this secure prison complex is miles away from anything – if the snakes do return in force, I might live longer than those who bested me*. He had been able to stare into the abyss that was the possibility of nuclear war because he believed the Soviet leadership was not wholly irrational – but the snakes could not be reasoned with or threatened, or, as far as he knew, outwitted.

Everything here was a humiliation, not least the guards' constant reminders that sentencing would see him moved to another facility, where his fellow inmates would soon 'sort him out'. They were vile and aggressive, enjoying rubbing his nose in his failure and revelling in the fear their descriptions engendered. One guard had offered protection in return for a sex act, which he instantly – but politely – refused. The guard had smiled when he'd said that the offer would remain open, as if he knew Pfeiffer's courage was failing.

Dr Pfeiffer assumed everywhere was bugged, including the exercise yard. He had grown to like walking round the square, just four concrete walls and the sky, lost in his work, but this was also the only opportunity the inhabitants of the special wing had to talk, provided they were never close enough to touch. His fellow prisoners included two Russian spies, who were exercised at a different time. Not everyone said what they were in for, but some were quite open about their sins. The editor of *Rolling Stone*, who was surprisingly friendly, happily revealed that he'd been incarcerated for refusing to reveal a source. There was a civil servant who'd tried to steal five million dollars from the government, and a diplomat who'd sold secrets to the Chinese, who would play chess with Dr Pfeiffer whenever they were allowed.

'Hey, Doc – your visitor's here,' someone shouted; it was not a name he recognised. The steel door banged open and he was led into the bare room by an impassive guard. Inside stood Mablethorpe, the lanky, opinionated Englishman from the

TV talk show he'd done, *Debate with Dempsey*. The man who'd denied aliens, science, everything.

A vast smirk on his face, he held out his hand. An attaché case was tucked under his other arm.

'What are you doing here?' Pfeiffer didn't bother being polite.

'I thought you might like company.' The man grinned on. 'You were a formidable foe. I was sorry we never clashed again.'

Pfeiffer felt his heart race and his face flush. He was tempted to refuse the visit, but the man opened the case and removed a bottle of bourbon. Next came a Thermos flask, and two glass tumblers wrapped in white cloth. Everything in here was plastic and suddenly he wanted a drink from a glass more than anything. He looked over at the guard, who was staring into space.

'The most expensive drink I have ever offered a man,' Mablethorpe said. He unscrewed the Thermos lid. 'Ice. Let no one say science is entirely useless.'

'If you've come to mock me—'

'Dr Pfeiffer, I have a commission. I want the scoop – your candid thoughts on the alien address. I will need to be funny, but I promise not to be unkind.'

Was the bourbon worth it?

Mablethorpe went on, 'I too soared too close to the flame. My college sacked me, my wife divorced me. I may not be your first choice for company, but I'm here. All these names are being banded around as possibilities to visit the aliens' home-world: all apparently pass for great thinkers in these shrunken times, but frankly, I consider them political hacks of the worst sort. Your name should have been there.'

Dr Pfeiffer snorted – but it was an expensive bourbon and he didn't think the man was trying to be unpleasant.

They sat, and Mablethorpe poured generous measures.

Dr Pfeiffer had a burning need to get drunk, but Rachael was coming today.

'I recanted about the aliens and was saved. *The Times* – the proper one, from London, you understand – ran my piece. I sent you a copy.'

'I got that, but I have been far too busy to read it.'

'I do enjoy a well-written back-down, don't you? They keep my haters guessing. I'll give you another copy if you like.'

'Thank you, but I've got it somewhere.'

'I hear the government has plans for you.'

Uncle Sam always set useful prisoners to work. Clearly someone in the White House still thought he had something to offer medical science; for in return for keeping his wife and associates out of jail, he would be usefully employed.

'Prison,' he said, adding, 'hopefully not here, but that's out of my hands.'

'Oh, it's a *secret*.' The Englishman tipped him an outrageous wink and Dr Pfeiffer found himself smiling despite himself.

Mablethorpe turned out to be good company, this self-mocking cynic who had travelled to the back of beyond to offer the condemned man a drink. He had a magpie mind, and while he might be weak on the sciences, he was hilariously rude about people Pfeiffer also disliked. They found common taste in music, rejecting modern art in all its forms and in lampooning the young and fashionable.

When the time came, the guard led them to the rec room

to watch the aliens address the world. Pfeiffer *felt* the moment, greater than when he saw the first dead alien, greater than when he first saw Cory. He deeply mourned the loss of any chance to talk to them.

At the end, when the aliens danced and some of the delegates dropped their dignity and joined in, the prisoners began to talk and jeer, swamping the commentators on the screen.

As the truth became clear, Dr Pfeiffer was left feeling sick with dismay. The only new information came in the form of those dazzling images of their home-world. And Cory was okay – that mattered. But there was no room for mis-interpretation: the aliens were committing to no military help – *nothing*, other than some surveillance of the skies, a mere scrap of hope.

Mablethorpe had never before looked so thoughtful. There were no jokes now. Pfeiffer made some sombre observations, which Mablethorpe took down without comment.

Then his visitor left him with a clap on the shoulder, saying, 'The deadline calls. But have no fear, the great mind can work in exile.'

By the time Rachael arrived, the alcohol buzz had vanished. Yet again, as he was led to the table, he was instructed that there would be no embracing, no touching of any sort. Not that Rachael was showing any inclination to hug him. She was wearing formal clothes and her make-up was impeccable: her protection against the glaring guards. But he could see how tired and stressed she looked, the cold anger in her eyes. It was a bitter joy to see her.

'You look well,' he said. 'How are the girls?'

She looked at him silently for a long while before saying, 'I've had another letter from Mrs Myers. The *humiliation*, Emmanuel: can you understand that? She invited us to her house, she let our children play with her son. And you—' She faltered. 'The girls can't sleep, knowing they'll have to move schools again. They're so *ashamed* of you.'

She was right, of course.

'I'm sorry.' It was not enough. 'Where are they?'

'At home, waiting, like all of us.'

The FBI and others had wanted him to betray the Six. Of course, he had been tempted – Overton was in Switzerland and he felt no personal loyalty to the man – and the other five would go to jail. But he was terrified they would take revenge on his family. So he had made the best deal with the government he could, and now he needed to let Rachael go. She had made him so happy – to her, he'd been a man, not a calculating machine – and in his obsession, he had thrown that all away.

'Did you watch the purples?' he asked.

'I caught it with a friend. The whole school will see it, so we'll discuss it as a family tonight. They're taking part in a film – a thousand human children, sending Cory home with their good wishes. They wanted to do it and I felt they should. I owed it to Mrs Myers.'

He didn't say anything; his own actions had made him an onlooker to raising his own children.

'The FBI told me about the programme,' she said suddenly, which surprised him.

Does everyone *know about this clandestine project?* he wondered, checking around, but the guard was as rigid as a wooden Indian outside a tobacco store. The President was obsessed with cancer, and they were wondering if Cory's extraordinary immune system might offer a new means of attack. 'It's supposed to be top secret,' he said.

'You might do some good,' she said. 'You can get on with your *real* work.'

'It's better than making licence plates,' he said, trying to make a joke. Just like Nazi scientists had been rescued after the war – and he found the comparison offensive, but it wasn't necessarily wrong – this research project allowed disgraced scientists and doctors to work hidden in plain sight. The story would leak at some point, then there would be a public outcry and accusations of special treatment, but the fact remained that no matter what work he was doing, he would still be in prison, and he could be sent to an ordinary jail at a minute's notice. But from a scientist's point of view, the cancer problem had some real points of interest, although he thought his work on infection would probably deliver more in his lifetime.

Rachael had not yet opened the folder of divorce papers. As he tried not to stare at them, he wondered for the millionth time what madness had so overtaken him that he would throw away his whole family.

'Did Mrs Myers say anything about what the purples will do?' he asked.

Flushing a little, looking angry, she said, 'Diplomacy has never been your strong point. I can't imagine what you thought to achieve.'

'No,' he admitted. Of course his dreams of being Ambassador to the Stars was pure ego, not rationality.

'Well, let's get this over with,' he said, knowing that once he had signed the papers, she would go.

She let out a great sigh. 'For better, for worse,' she said.

He misunderstood at first, waiting for her to continue – then he gawped like a fool.

'It's so awful for the children,' Rachael continued. 'I'd like to help the girls to understand you're doing something useful, that you've gone back to medicine. They can even see you, if they want to. They looked up to you, before Cory. And we'll have to move again anyway, so we might as well be in reach of wherever they're going to put you.'

He was discovering that hope could hurt almost more than despair. 'So the papers . . .'

'Let's see how it goes.'

It was a stay of execution, not a reprieve, but still.

After a cold pause, she went on, 'The government people think you'll have a breakdown and won't be any good to them. But you know, that wouldn't help the girls, would it? Or me.'

He didn't deserve her. *I don't deserve this chance*— But he *wanted* it.

'Thank you – *thank you*. I am so sorry for putting you and the girls through this – anything I can do—'

'Talk to me before you do *anything*,' she said firmly. 'Focus on the work, not the stars. Let's hope there's a future long enough for us to make something of it.'

'Thank you,' he repeated, then he asked, 'Could the girls write to me?'

He so badly wanted to ask her if he could see the girls, but that might be a step too far.

She shrugged and rose and the brief meeting was over. He looked at the guard and rose too, but she was not going to kiss him, or even take his hand.

'Make them proud of you again,' she said, and turned – and yet his heart gave a jump. A long road lay ahead, but at least there might be light along the path, for Rachael had given him a way back to her and the girls.

A gear turned inside him and a tiny implacable piece of the puzzle became not an obstacle but a possible key. The work would not be for him, but for her, for his daughters, and for humanity.

If humanity had a future.

CHAPTER 48

The-all must decide

Little Frog was swimming with the healers, and Thunder could not join them. Even through his illness, he had said his piece in the discussion, and Thunder had felt such pride he could explode. He felt an overwhelming need to protect his son: such an obligation, to be by his side for ever. Little Frog had made the case for the humans so clear and compelling. The-all had commended him, but the decision still hung unmade, like the dancing auroras over the poles. Earth had those lights too.

The all-of-the-mission had agreed a deadline, and if an agreement was not reached by then, both starships would leave. Those who opposed leaving a starship behind had at least agreed to a dangerous attack on the snake base on Mars, as well as leaving the humans some surveillance. Even so, the people were divided: would that conciliatory move be enough? Thunder had said all he could; he had spoken with all his being. Skimming Stone and others had also fought against leaving Earth unshielded, fought as if their own children were at risk.

Now each heartbeat was bringing them closer to abandoning the Earth.

Heartbeat by heartbeat, the braver choice was coming closer to defeat.

Skimming Stone messaged him again. *Join now.* Thunder sighed and patched into the discussion.

'Skimming Stone has been censured for ego-behaviour. Some would say the moderators cannot call her to speak again.'

Precedent, precedent, precedent, trilled many. The people were losing all patience with each other, tiring of the discussion.

'This one contests the precedent and cedes their rightful time to Skimming Stone.'

'This one cedes their rightful time to Skimming Stone.'

'This one contests the precedent and cedes their rightful time to Skimming Stone.'

'This one has learned Skimming Stone's speech by heart – but cedes his time for a new proposal.'

Skimming Stone had risen so often that Thunder believed the healer was now a hindrance to the cause. She might even sway the argument onto endless time-wasting procedures with this aggressive challenge.

She said, 'This one speaks for the children of Earth, the playful, blameless children, for the innocent the-all would slaughter by our indifference. Red blood is purple blood. Snakes burning babies at their mothers' teats . . .'

The moderators conferred.

'Skimming Stone may speak briefly, only to introduce any wholly new proposal, and any one moderator can halt them.'

'Gratitude,' said Skimming Stone. 'This one will be brief. We suggest – we *demand*, as an imperative – that the-all begin a roll call: of those willing to crew *Repurpose Snakes* and remain with the Earth. We do not even ask for the stronger ship. Only those who believe this is right should volunteer. It may be death – but let it be written, let the songs of the home-world say – that some were not so Hardened that they left children to die.'

It was a true miracle: Skimming Stone made her point and shut up.

The moderators conferred and called one of the idea's most implacable opponents: Chosen Scars, who had commanded the evacuation of the colony-world, then held command to repel the second assault on the home-world.

'Why the weaker ship? If the-all decide to leave one, all agreed it must be the stronger.'

There was a silence.

Another dreaming-together and we will be out of time.

'The proposition is debatable. Does the-all wish to debate it?'

'Hold the roll call,' said Chosen Scars. 'The stronger ship. If the-all so decides something so foolish, this one has courage to serve where needed.'

'Hold the roll call!' another opponent repeated.

The comment lights flickered: *Agree, agree, agree!*

'Mere weight of numbers is not a decision,' said a moderator, a lodge-friend of Thunder's, not an ally on this debate.

'Dissent will be heard.'

A few wanted to speak against, but not many.

As molecules gather to form drops, as drops gather to form a cloud, as clouds gather to make a storm – the-all moved to decide.

CHAPTER 49

The last day

Cory and Thunder walked in the woods behind Cory's house, his birth-father's arm across his shoulder. They had walked in the dark, Cory leading Thunder, feeling ahead with their minds to find the way. They wove their way through the crowds and tents, past the Army fence, then the Ship's. The first light of dawn was breaking and soon the monochrome forest would be full of colour. Cory loved the Earth, its plants and weather and animals and people – but the starship was full of familiar smells and sounds, the chatter of his people and, at last, the friendship of dreams.

Cory had danced for the dead. He had sung the songs of life and memory. Towards sunset, he would return to *Repurpose Snakes as Dung Buckets*. Its key repairs were all but done and soon it would leave this system and be his whole world for five Earth months. Cory would miss the seasons and snow and fireworks – and, most of all, he would miss his human family, his friends.

The healers said one brief visit would be fine, which was why Cory was coming to see his family without warning – to say goodbye, and to tell them the good news. Who else should bring it but the child of two worlds?

Cory trilled a gratitude song while Thunder held him close. He kept his helmet closed, a cautious father, not willing to take the risk of Earth infection.

'I'm so glad we made the right decision, Little Glowing Blue Frog. Nothing is harder than defending a decision you believe is wrong. But you must keep telling the humans, all we could agree to do was support the human case. However hard it was for the crew, it may take much longer for all-the-people. We will struggle to decide at speed.'

'Mom and Dad' – Cory used the human words – 'my Earth-mother and Earth-father – they put such a good case.'

'So did you. Still, this one was astonished we were successful.'

Cory *tock-tock-tocked*.

Thunder sometimes forgot how Cory had grown, the adventures he had had. They had woken Cory from his healing sleep so he could formally join in that historic decision. Gene told Cory things he already knew, and so did Thunder. Maybe all fathers did that.

The purple grown-ups were as solid as the Rockies on this: they would not be bringing any humans or dogs to the home-world. Cory, the child of two worlds, had been chosen to be the one who would speak for Earth.

Cory had saved all the messages, the thousand children who'd made their film filled with their hopes and fears; he would have them as companions in the months ahead. Their words and faces would be heard on the home-world by the whole people.

On his back was a camera, so everyone he missed could film him messages while he was gone. He would keep his own film diary too. He was sure starships would soon be racing to and from Earth.

While they were gone, *Kites at Dusk* would patrol the solar system, giving humans a chance. When he got back to home-world, he would spend every waking breath helping to persuade all-the-people to commit themselves to defending the Earth.

Earth was his home and First Harbour was his home, so every time he travelled between them, he would be coming home.

'We have to find a way to teach the humans,' he said now.

'Remember, in the children's school, those things that we leave the little ones to learn for themselves? Remember the stories where we did harm hoping to do good?'

'Humans are not all children.'

'Humans have their own path. Let us sing a song of hope that they learn quickly. It is not for us to order them. They must do their own lifting.'

'And we must not destroy the brave kind Ship.'

'Little Frog, you *must* see the danger. We will not destroy what we cannot understand, but we must not have machine minds thinking they know better than we do.'

'Ship is a person.'

'Ah, what trouble you cause, little one.'

The-all had failed to agree, again and again, so for now, the Ship Reborn still existed, although Cory had been forbidden to communicate with it.

In twelve hours, Cory would leave this beautiful, wounded world – but before then, there was so-so much he needed to do. He was allowed one small case for mementos. There were some so-dear people he might not even have time to see.

How sad Gene and Molly would be, and Elsa. But he would tell them that the purples would do the right thing. The Earth would not be left unguarded – and he would fly through the stars to make things right for them.

If humans only gazed into the future, they would see what they had to do for themselves.

The confidence came, a certainty so strong you could walk on it, that he would return. Cory would walk the ice caps and fly above the great forests, and he would float on a gondola and walk the shores of Lake Baikal. He would see Chuck and Bonnie and all his friends again, and maybe soon take them to the stars. When he came back, Fleur would be speaking. Dreams would come true. Chuck would become a baseball player and Bonnie would be President and Elsa would have so many friends and Cory would fly a starship and be an Ambassador and invent the weapon that would switch off every snake in the galaxy for ever.

At last father and son reached the back of the Myers' house. Cory would slip in the back way and wake his human family, a wonderful surprise. He might have difficulty explaining to Meteor where he was going, but Meteor would love Elsa and Fleur instead. He was leaving the Myers to tame the Monster inside him; he was leaving them so he could make them safe. He was leaving them because his other home called in his dreams, so he could hear the green waves on the shore and smell the rich perfumes of its beaches.

Cory was leaving home to go home. Through sadness thicker than water, he knew and loved both worlds. More adventures were to come, but now he knew that all would be well.

Amber Grove, six years later

Cory was coming home tomorrow, for Hallowe'en. It was his third return to Earth. Molly sat with Fleur in her bedroom, close to tears.

Elsa was holding out in her attic room and she'd jammed the hatch shut.

Gene had finally stopped shouting at the ceiling. 'I am going for a walk so I don't murder her,' he said as he went out. He had started the argument calmer than Molly, but he got so angry with Elsa, he'd been waving his arms like a great baboon.

Elsa used such vile language . . . made such unkind, untrue accusations . . . and she had refused even the offer from gentle Eva to mediate.

Elsa had forged her parents' signatures on her dreadful school report card and worse still, she had forged a letter back to the principal. Molly didn't know whether to be furious or admire her skill. The weary principal knew Elsa, and he had phoned to check. Challenged by her parents, Elsa had attacked. That argument had turned into the old classics, the curfew, then smoking, which had turned into everything and anything.

Fleur rounded up her two bears, her astronaut doll and the toy spaceship and disappeared into her room.

Cory was out there among the stars and Molly wanted him home.

Fleur had the albums out, looking for the pictures she wanted, so she could narrate the stories, starting with Cory's first astonishing return in triumph. Fleur remembered that first one, but mostly because Cory had brought her his memories in his dreams. Molly's astonishing youngest dreamed as the purples did, and her ability had thrown the purple scientists into excitement and confusion. How could a human do it? Not for the first time, this house in Crooked Street hid a secret from the world, a secret so big no one could know its consequences.

Cory's first absence had been long and hard, with nothing but brief messages at first, via dreaming purples.

'*We dreamed he is well and misses you.*'

'*His speech to the–all was well received.*'

The purples had had him long enough. Molly wanted him back, and let it be a year at home now, or two. Maybe he could talk some sense into Elsa.

She heard the front door, Gene returning with his temper restored, she hoped. They were a strong team even through these storms. Before Earth was saved, she nearly lost him, but her Gene had come back to her.

'Mom? Wake up, please.'

Who was calling her out of sleep? Molly, stirring in the dark, tried to make sense of it. A familiar noise meant that Gene was snoring beside her. A gentle hand touched her cheek.

Cory was coming home. She thought for a second it was him, surprising her, but this was Fleur, getting onto the bed.

'Elsa's gone,' Fleur said, tucking her long black hair behind her ears. Her younger daughter took these things very calmly.

Gone? Molly sat up and put on the bedside lamp. 'Gone, gone where, sweetie-pie?'

'She wouldn't say. It's very silly.'

While Gene snuffled in his sleep, Molly tried to marshal her thoughts. Cory was coming and Elsa had decided to make a scene. *Elsa is impossible.*

'Did you see her go?'

'I'm sensible. I stayed in bed,' Fleur said, the light glinting off her glasses. She had such a sweet, pompous little Gene face when she said it.

Anger began to be crowded out as the old familiar fears clutched at her heart.

Elsa will hitch a lift with the wrong type of man — or she'll be kidnapped or murdered — or she's taken the car and she'll crash it again — out who knows where with no help.

Or she's just got one of her friends to hide her: another of her silly power games. Honestly!

'I'd better find her. Get off the bed, sweetie-pie.'

In her robe and slippers, Molly creaked up the folding ladder to Elsa's attic hideaway. Habit made her knock before lifting the hatch. Clothes were strewn everywhere and the bigger rucksack was not on its peg. A pumpkin lantern with dark holes for eyes mocked Molly.

No clues here.

She climbed down, wondering how much jealousy was the fuel for the argument. Elsa always made everything complicated. In the kitchen, Elsa's communicator reproached her from the table. There wasn't a note, but there didn't need to be one. Before puberty hit, Elsa had run away only twice, but in the last couple of years threatening to do so had become a habit.

I'm going, I'm not going to be tracked down. This is it. I'm really running away for real.

Of course, Elsa had a second communicator. Dear old Ship, patrolling the skies to protect them, had given it to her. Gene and Molly pretended they didn't know that, but Elsa must surely have guessed. Despite the teenage theatrics, Elsa wasn't stupid.

Wash and dress, then start the ring-round.

'I'll come,' Fleur said.

'It's okay, sweetie-pie. It won't be long before Elsa's home. Go back to bed, and Dad will take you to school. You wouldn't want to miss Hallowe'en with your friends – and remember, Cory will want to take you trick-or-treating.'

Fleur's face lit up. 'Trick or treat with lovely big brother Cory.'

They missed him of course, painfully. Now every couple of months a purple ship brought his filmed messages, showing them his life on the starship, or his home-world. They were happy, sad, thoughtful, rattling on about friends or some purple discovery, and as usual, endless questions about their news and messages.

The light was on in Eva's room. She often read at night. Molly knocked softly, and went in to see the mother she'd chosen sitting in her favourite chair, brought up from the farm. The walls were covered with family photos, mostly of her three grandchildren, and there were three photographs of John by her bed – their wedding, Gene and Molly's wedding, and the photo that always stabbed Molly's heart, taken during John's last weeks, of the human family together, under the redwoods, with John laughing – the day he said, 'I won't be here when Cory returns.'

How she missed him.

'Elsa's gone. Did you hear her go?' Molly asked.

Eva slipped off the purples' breathing mask that had made such a difference to her quality of life. 'Sometimes a grand-mother is sworn to secrecy. You'll phone all the usual places, of course. Like Gloria's. I mean, that's just one example.'

They smiled at each other. Elsa had a weekend job with Gloria, the cantankerous warden of the Cory and Meteor Myers Dog Shelter.

'She's impossible.'

Eva spoke softly. 'Cory's an ambassador between two worlds, and Fleur – well, she's special. Of course Elsa feels left out. She's more like the rest of us. The world has changed so much, and we're all trying to find our way.'

Was Eva born this calm: as the old prayer said, filled with wisdom, serenity and courage? She'd been like that since the day Molly had first met her.

When does being a parent become easy? 'She doesn't even try at school.'

Eva patted her arm. 'She's good with small children and

animals. She's a good judge of people. She'll find her purpose and astound us all.'

Gloria did not pick up the phone, and that was another sign. The Ship denied nothing. Molly backed the car up and looked at her strange house of too many gables. The Hallowe'en decorations fluttered in the breeze, including the vast sea-monster Cory had brought last time. The woods behind the house were a symphony of fall colours.

Molly drove through the alien gates and down the road, frustration and anxiety fighting it out. The Ship hid her briefly, whenever she needed it. The shelter was almost an hour's drive away: if Elsa had driven herself, whose car had she used? Or who had she cajoled to take her all that way in the middle of the night? Molly knew she had a couple of the older boys from school wrapped around her finger.

Molly was in no mood for music, so she was alone with the road, her thoughts and the paling sky. *Cory was coming home.*

Out there were billions of Corys who had pledged to defend the Earth, their sacrifice giving humanity the gift of time. Over the years, six great Sentinels had come from the home-world, intelligent space fortresses who made the armies of Earth look like mice. Great waves of metal snakes had come against them and been destroyed.

The purple community under Earth's sun – openly on Mars and the Moon and in space, and some hidden on Earth itself – called themselves the Wardens of the Garlands. That was the old name for those who tended the sickness of violence. Fascinated and sometimes repelled, the greatest purple minds struggled to understand humanity, constantly arguing about whether and how to engage. Cory was at the heart of that mission: an interpreter between two societies. He travelled now with a cohort of friends his own age. Purple babies had been born under Earth's sun. These were signs of hope and commitment.

Thunder was a friend now, and on crucial issues, an ally.

Nearly at the shelter – and there, on the horizon, was the first trace of dawn.

The purples still claimed to be a small scientific mission. So many humans believed the purples were a malign enemy, scheming against Earth in space, and some governments were hostile to the whole species.

But far more people looked to them for salvation, begging them to take control – to take away human weapons and independence and freedom. Some – the deluded, the dangerous and the cynical – even claimed special insights into their wisdom and purpose.

Molly understood the purples' caution in sharing their knowledge. She still wished that they would share more.

It was true dawn now, and the lights were on at the dog shelter. Cory's patronage had made it famous; it now owned the surrounding fields. Tourists came to give a few dollars and more often than not left with a dog, a cat, a rabbit – or once, a donkey.

Molly rapped at the door. 'Another for breakfast.'

Gloria was old and cranky, preferring animals to people. She opened the door with a scowl. 'A mighty breakfast,' she said. 'Pancakes.'

Elsa, not yet a woman but very far from being a girl, was standing at the little stove, adroitly flipping them with a spatula.

She was dressed in jeans and a bright sweater; her defiant face didn't detract from her beauty. Molly was filled with hope and fear and frustration, and love.

'Well?' Molly sighed, with her hands on her hips. 'We were all *worried sick.*' She could be theatrical too.

For two breaths Elsa looked like she would fight. Then she melted, gave up teenage defiance, and began to cry. Molly was already there, taking her troubled daughter in her arms. She smelled of bacon and forbidden tobacco.

Molly could not face the school, not today of all days. 'I'll call the principal, say you need a day to prepare your apology. We can talk, and you can help me get ready for tonight.'

'I don't want it to be like this,' the girl sobbed.

Molly held her and felt strong.

Gloria *harrumphed*: she had a happy marriage, but she couldn't look at other people's affection.

'Let's eat, then get home,' Molly said, knowing that Elsa was smart and quite unscrupulous enough to be hundreds of miles away by now – and yet here she was, hiding in an obvious place, breaking boundaries, but not very much. Elsa knew who loved her, and how much.

Molly left a message for Gene that all was well. Elsa's penitence did not yet extend to talking it all through, so Molly turned on the car radio. The news was brief: fighting in the Middle East; not enough jobs in the Midwest; Congress had stalled the budget for the President's Green Corps. That would stir a fierce debate among the purples, whether to spell out to humans the dreadful truth: that what they had seen on other planets was happening here.

Molly was still doing the rounds of the TV shows a couple of times a year, repeating the same message, over and over – humanity had to do its own heavy lifting, not just in saving the planet, but in making it worth saving. Cory, the eternal optimist, thought humanity would figure it all out. She wasn't so sure.

Elsa loved the old songs, but to make a point, she insisted they switch to a new station, the music young people listened to, all shiny rebellion and alienation as synthetic as a plastic glove, or romantic songs written to a formula by a robot brain. Or so they sounded to her, although Gene refused to agree the era of great music had passed.

They drove past pumpkin lanterns on every morning porch, waiting for the early evening when Amber Grove would become a realm of magic. The town made a big deal of Hallowe'en; it was a town where newcomers with new ideas rubbed along with those who liked it more when things didn't change.

Marquees were up on Founders Green, and parade stands, hinting of the excitement to come. She drove past the Meteor Day Memorial, and the shining statue to commemorate the purples who had died to protect humanity. First among these, to Molly's mind, was Cory's mother, Pilot, who had saved her son and in so doing, had saved the Earth.

'I'm not sure you deserve to go out tonight,' Molly said, and Elsa sighed, but did not dignify this threat with an answer. Elsa couldn't really be grounded on Hallowe'en, not on Cory's first day back, and she knew it. Damn her.

Before they left the car, Elsa gave one last sniff and kissed her mother. 'Thanks.'

'Dad might be trying to write,' Molly said. 'We don't need to talk just yet.'

Maybe Cory can talk a little sense into her.

At home, all was bedlam. Gene hugged Elsa, said, 'Hello, Trouble. Carol and Storm dropped by – I promised to find that article for them.'

'Already?' Molly had wanted lunch out of the way before everyone descended.

'And Cory says he's ahead of schedule.' Gene took Elsa off to help search. The time Molly had intended to get everything ready had already disappeared, and a note from Diane was warning of more visitors. Fleur was singing to everyone, her pitch perfect, clutching her soft purple Cory doll. Gene hadn't taken her to school after all. Her dinosaur costume was hanging on the wall, a work of sewn art that she couldn't be let near until much later. Even then, every chocolate in Amber Grove would end up all over it.

Eva was making coffee, very slowly and with great care. There were unfamiliar bowls and boxes on the table, so who had dropped off food . . . ?

'Selena called,' Eva said. 'They'll be here for lunch.'

They'd discussed this and Molly had asked her to come with everyone else for supper . . . of course, Selena's goofy second husband would bring his own two kids as well. He was kind and he made Selena laugh, so Molly approved of him.

She scooped up a bunny glove-puppet from the kitchen floor – lethal, a skid hazard – before helping Eva with the tray. Clutter meant falls.

Selena would be talking about her book; Carol had another

book out; Dr Jarman had a book out; everyone except Molly and Gene had written a book – even Meteor, as imagined by the Robertson boys, had become an author.

Of course, when Molly next saw Gene, Elsa had disappeared. They had discovered that teenagers had some comic-book superpower: the ability to see chores that need doing and yet not be there. Molly phoned the school principal and committed Elsa to a difficult meeting tomorrow.

Then Fleur showed everyone that she had been doing writing with Eva.

Family life wasn't a painting or a posed photograph; it was a dance, a brawl. And Cory, her first, her son, was coming home at last. That old saying, third time the charm. Maybe this time, more than a year, maybe this time . . . .

Cory was bringing three friends, and one, she gathered, was maybe a bit more than a friend. The purples did not rush into commitments and Molly had promised herself she wouldn't pry. Cory would tell her when he was good and ready.

The bracelet chimed. 'Hello, hello, Cory here. One hour. Lots of news!'

Molly went and sat in Eva's empty room, trying the silent meditation, just to get everything straight in her head, but there was so much jangling around.

Gene slipped in and sat on the bed. He put his arm around her. 'It will only get louder,' he said. 'Your weird sister will want to be the centre of attention. And we sure need to talk with Elsa about consequences.'

If serious talks were bricks, they could build a house. 'For now, let's just be.'

Her Gene, who she thought she had lost. Her Gene who, when the stakes were high, truly heard her heart and stayed by her side. Loving him was routine, and still extraordinary.

They had seen the world, here and there, anyway, and it was grand to visit. She had stood on high peaks and explored deserted islands. She'd even watched the purples drill deep into ancient glaciers to track the changes in Earth's climate. But where she wanted to be, always, was right here at home. They shared a quiet, joyful togetherness without words until the doorbell rang.

Molly wanted to be first, but Elsa beat her to it. There stood Cory, helmet off. His ears stood proud and his tentacles waved.

'No ugly space monsters needed! Go away, Squid-face!'

Meteor, barking her welcoming bark, pushed past her, determined to lick Cory all over.

'Ugly gorilla monster!'

Elsa and Cory embraced, and Molly joined them. Cory was almost as tall as her now, and his tentacles stroked her cheek. He smelled wonderful, of lemon-balm, horses and rain.

Behind Cory in the street were three young purples, still in their spacesuits, but helmets off. She thought she recognised two of them, and no helmets implied they were regular visitors to Earth. But Thunder, who always came with Cory, *always*, was not there. That was odd. But Cory would have said if there was trouble.

'Big-big news,' Cory trilled.

'Coreeeeeeeee!' and Fleur was in the hug on the porch, and Gene close behind.

What had the purples decided? Was there good news from

the struggle in space, a decisive advance against the snakes? Or was there news about the wild idea of an Ark?

Cory's face was mischief. 'What do you want to be the news?'

His alien friends, still back in the road, chortled.

'Now you're back – Thunder promised a little trip to space,' Gene said, half joking, half longing.

Cory laughed. 'Not up to me, but of course you should.'

Elsa did a mock growl. 'Your scientists have made a way to stop purples stinking.'

'I love you too, Elsa.'

'Maybe you should introduce your friends,' Eva said from behind them, in a way that made Molly think, *You know something*.

'Soon, good guesses.'

'Dream-teaching!' Fleur said.

'Of course,' Cory said.

Molly thought it might be some formal Embassy, some new and open arrangement, some alliance. What did she hope for? Yes, that big stuff, but all her wishes were personal.

She struggled to put her need into words: her son to stay, or at least to be no more than a quick spaceship jaunt away.

Fleur broke from her hug and filled the pause. 'I will do a show!'

She did like to be the centre of attention. 'Not now, Fleur, sweetheart. Cory has news.'

Cory and Molly focused on each other. She looked into his violet eyes and she knew he understood her heart.

My wish is for you to stay for two years, or three. Amber Grove is too small to be your world – one planet will not be enough, so my child of two worlds must find his own path. But it is hard to be so far away from my son during these years as you become an adult.

'Mom has the best wish,' Cory said, though she had said nothing. 'But all good wishes. So, lots of news. Spinning Disc has come to live in this system.'

She felt Cory's joy pour out. Thunder's partner hated interstellar flight and shunned it, even though that meant long separations from Thunder and Cory. Surely this meant that Thunder and Cory were settling here?

Fleur was excited, irrepressible. 'I will do my show now.'

Cory laughed, Fleur stepped back and raised her hands. From her mind flowed fall leaves; at first they were delicate and frail, watercolours of leaves seen floating from a distance – but then in seconds they grew larger, more childlike, brighter. They spilled from the porch into the street, dancing round the heads of the aliens. The leaves of maples and sycamores and trees that existed only in picture books, dancing leaves filling the air in a burst of Fleur's delight. Meteor, of course, barked and leaped to bite them – then tripped down the steps, confused that they had no substance. Leaves swirled round her head and in excitement, she chased her own tail.

The aliens *tock-tock-tocked* with excitement, raising their hands as if to dance. Fleur could not project her nightmares, only what brought her pleasure.

Molly wanted to understand Cory's news, she was still holding him like he might fly away. She also wanted to savour the fullness of this moment, as Cory did, to soak up each scrap of happiness when it comes. Live life one day at a time.

Molly held her children and her Gene. She held the past and the future and today in a moment that could have lasted for ever.

It was Hallowe'en, and everyone Molly loved was home.

Acknowledgements

It is a truth universally recognised that 'the second album can be a bit tricky', and as you may have heard, there was a pandemic.

My enormous thanks to my editor Jo Fletcher and my agent Rob Dinsdale for their tireless work in bringing the good ship *Our Child of Two Worlds* safely to shore. I say I write books, not scripts, because a book is all my own work, but that's not true. There is an alchemy in the edit which finds the gold in the ore. Alas, Rob has moved on from the agenting business, and I will miss his wise guidance, but I'm now in the steady hands of Alex Cochran.

I've discussed bits of this with many people, but Sarah, Lucy, Peter N., Emily, Debbie, Sophie and Sue certainly saw whole drafts and gave essential encouragement. Chapters here and there were read to the All Good Bookshop writers' group, whose friendly enthusiasm for both books kept me going in tougher times.

Leo Nickolls and Patrick Carpenter pulled off an even better cover than the first one. I'd like to thank Ajebowale and Georgina in Editorial and Ella, Ellie and Charlotte in Publicity and Marketing, and the rest of the Jo Fletcher Books/Quercus team.

It has been good to hear from people around the world
liked *Our Child of the Stars*. The real joy of the first book
that many reviewers, bloggers, booksellers – and those
crucial: you readers – fell deeply in love with Cory, Moll
Gene. There are too many to name, but their polite asks '
the next one was due' did jog me to get on with it.

My friends and family have been beyond lovely. I fo
generosity from established writers and particularly Sue Tin
and Juliet E. McKenna, but also Dominic Dulley, Gray Willia
and many others. I found communities of patience, honest and
support online, particularly the Debut Authors 2019, Debut
Authors 2020 and Savvy Writers. Super Relaxed Fantasy Club
were super. And relaxed.

A couple of wonderful people in public sector press offices
in the States answered questions from this random author, only
for those chapters not to appear. My thanks.

I launched the first book in the US in March 2020 as the
pandemic hit, while I had Covid-19. There have been better back-
grounds to a launch. My thanks to Giuliana, Elyse and Amanda
in New York, who worked so hard to overcome the problems.

I always intended two (and only two) Cory books – while he
and his world brought me great delight, I rather fancy writing
something else now.

Finally, Daniel and Trevor for endless brotherly support, my
thanks. Theo and Lucy give me hope and spur me to do my
own lifting. Sarah, of course. And my awesome parents. I told
you science fiction was worth reading.

Stephen Cox
London 2021